SUMMER
VEIL

SEASON'S WAR: BOOK FOUR

OLENA NIKITIN

VIPER DAWN PRESS

CONTENT WARNING

Dear Reader,

We appreciate that everyone has a different level of sensitivity and may be triggered by different topics. It is up to your discretion whether you can handle the content in our books.

The book is intended for a mature audience of particular interests and contains a certain amount of coarse language, graphic sex scenes as well as sexual innuendo. You can also find scenes of death, and physical violence that are expected with similar historical settings.

It is a work of fiction set in a world with different racial, cultural and social norms. Any resemblance to actual persons, living or dead, events or localities is entirely coincidental, and the names, characters and incidents portrayed in it are the work of the author's imagination.

CONTENTS

SEASON'S WAR SERIES

***

AUTUMN CHAOS

WINTER DRAGON

SPRING BLIGHT

SUMMER VEIL

***

A free prequel (short story) available upon subscription to the newsletter:

A Little Accident

Other books, series page, snippets and more: www.olenanikitin.uk

For free books, ARCs, giveaways and more, sign up to : NEWSLETTER

Don't want to commit - follow us on Amazon to get updates about new

releases.

SEASON'S WAR SYNOPSIS

Autumn Chaos

Lady Inanuan of Thorn, Ina to her friends, is a former royal mage exiled from the court ten years ago and has been living a peaceful, if slightly unorthodox, life in the mystical Black Forest because of her sharp tongue and uncensored opinion. Still, she grows to love the magical forest until, one day, the local villagers deposit a half-dead warrior on her doorstep. With no other means to heal his mortal injuries, she resorts to performing her variation of a forbidden spell called the Sacrifice, linking his life energy to her's in the process.

After awakening in a strange woman's bed, her patient reacts with an unchivalrous lack of gratitude. To make matters worse, Ina's property is overrun by a gaggle of nobles accusing her of killing Marcach of Liath, Captain of the King's Guards. With the supposedly dead captain standing alive and well beside her broken door, an officious judicial mage decides to take our hapless mage into custody, suspecting her of being a person of interest in a slew of recent monster attacks. The same monsters that Marcach—or Mar, as we learn he is referred to—has come to investigate.

On the way to the capital, Ina is forced to heal the captain's best friend, Sa'Ren, an exotic Yanwo man and skilled swordsman whose troubles bring him to the Kingdom of Cornovii. The spell she performs now connects her with him as well, awakening dark desires and creating an intense rivalry between the brothers-in-arms. After an intense confrontation with the Magical Council, Ina is allowed to go free. However, her conscience is weighed down by the possibility that the mutagen she developed during her university years is now being used to turn ordinary citizens of all races into flesh-eating monsters.

Mar can't stop thinking about Ina and sends Ren to investigate and guard her secretly, finding, as time goes on, that not only does he think she isn't involved, but that he's drawn to her passionate soul. Despite their differences and fighting their mutual attraction, Mar and Ina team up to investigate the citizen's disappearances and find the mastermind behind the attacks.

Trying to reacclimatise to city living, Ina drags her friend to their old haunt, the *Drunken Wizard*, a dive of a pub run by a loveable, suspicious troll called Gruff, but this attempt at a normal life signals an increase in monster attacks and Ina herself is attacked in her new home by a giant spider-like creature. Once Ina and a frustrated Mar defeat the creature, the warrior realises his feelings for this fiery spitfire have grown.

Ina realises she needs help and asks her long-time friend, tavern owner Gruff, to find her a gem able to store significant amounts of magical energy, only to be unknowingly given one of the chaos regalia. Forced to crawl through the sewers of Osterad to find answers, Mar has to fight for his life, and the witch finds out her chaos magic is not as useless as she was taught. Ina soon learns she has some fighting skills, and much to her displeasure, she realises she cares for the brute who the fates have partnered her with. Their progress is disrupted by the king's death, which comes conveniently during Ina's convalescence, as the two men supposed to guard the king fight for her attention.

The grand coronation ball reveals the identity of our villains, but not their plans. While Mar makes headway with the investigation, Ina explores a different path, resulting in her capture by her former boyfriend, a mind mage called Liander. She learns an extra dimension to her magic, saving herself from Liander as Ren comes to her rescue, killing several mercenaries in a hypnotic dance of death. However, her moment of triumph is disturbed by the ominous sound of bells ringing in the city. The battle of Osterad had begun.

The battlefield reveals the true and terrifying potential of her chaos magic and the destruction it can bring. Unable to hold herself back, seeing her friends hurt and the mindless slaughter of innocent victims, she resorts to the ultimate measure and calls to the very thread of reality, dismantling the transformed monsters. Her command, "Bring them back to what they truly are," has unexpected consequences. The golden spark she'd discovered during Mar's healing is the long-buried secret of Liath, which responds to her command and transforms him into his true self—a beautiful, terrifying dragon.

Even though the battle is won, Ina feels she lost the war. She learns that whilst the king's older sister, her former friend, had orchestrated the attacks, seducing Mar's lieutenant Senad to carry out her plans, the young king knew about it and did nothing to prevent the carnage. Instead, he used his sister's greed for power and gambled on Ina's magic to secure the full support of his subjects. Rejecting the position of the court mage once more, Ina prepares to search for Mar in the Grey Mountains, the last known location of dragons in Cornovii.

Winter Dragon

Ina and Ren travel to Liath in their search for Mar, encountering a blizzard on the way. Ina uses her magic to create a protective dome, saving herself and the dwarves they meet during the storm, receiving a promise of help in exchange. Still, the amount of magic used makes her ill, and together with Ren, she is forced to rest in a nearby village.

Meanwhile, Mar flies away from Osterad to prevent further bloodshed after the battle, heading to Liath thanks to a memory of his grandmother's stories, but as he gets injured by a ballista, he is forced to seek refuge in the ruins of a temple. The next day, while recovering, he meets Ayni, who teaches him to speak in dragon form and feeds him, revealing her true form.

Under the mountains, Tar'eth, a drow prince, has enslaved a local kobold tribe, searching their mines for the tomb of the last drow empress, Sowenna, the World Breaker, to retrieve a piece of her magical regalia. Already possessing the ring, given to him by a necromancer, he craves to gather a full set of regalia. After encountering Ina in Osterad, he knows she has the necklace. Now, Tar'eth wants both Ina's magic and the gem she carries.

Unaware of his plans, while recovering, Ina trains with Ren in swordsmanship, letting him teach her his Jian-kata style. In the meantime, with no other choice, Mar heals in the dragon temple while Ayni teaches him about being a dragon. They begin forming an emotional bond thanks to the strange situation. Unfortunately, the dragoness mistakes his friendly curiosity for romantic affection. The next day, Ayni takes him flying. Unaware of the custom, Mar unwittingly begins the mating dance with her.

After defending the village of Stary Brod from bandits, Ina and Ren arrive at the castle, receiving a frosty reception from Mar's parents. Her story leads to the revelation of the hidden dragon heritage of Liath. The next day, two dragons arrive, and an overjoyed witch runs to welcome Mar, but to her shock, Ayni separates them, claiming that Mar is her husband after they'd completed the mating dance.

The feeling of betrayal makes her reject any voice of reason despite Mar vehemently denying being married. She later announces her plans to leave Liath, but during a tense supper, Alleron uses her new court position and forces Ina to investigate some unusual kobold attacks. Mar is so focused about Ina that he's oblivious to Ayni's flirting with him, which causes further discord between him and the witch, encouraging Ren, who loved her from the moment she healed him, to act on his feelings.

After retreating to her room, Ina is visited by Ren, and the chaos mage confesses she knows how the warrior feels about her and, still feeling hurt, embraces him. Despite her determination and his desire, Ina cannot move past her love for Mar, and Ren accepts they will always be close but only as friends.

It takes more than a few bruises to clear the misunderstanding between the men. Still, it allows Mar to explain what happened with Ayni and convince Ina how he feels. Ina reflects on the conversation with Mar while his father takes her on a journey. On the road, they meet a strange man that Ina insists on helping, and in exchange, she receives a blessing from the mountain in the shape of a horse-like mountain spirit called an orein.

After some planning, Ina, Mar, Ren and Ayni head further into the mountains to investigate the attacks. During the night, they are attacked, Ina is forced to use her chaos magic, and the situation gets out of hand.

The soldiers they capture inform them that the drow prince is preparing to attack Liath. After a short debate, they split, Ren and Ayni heading back to Liath to prepare for the war with the drow while Mar and Ina continue the expedition.

Arriving at a beautiful protected glade, Ina makes an important choice and reconciles fully with Mar, renewing their relationship before, at the sign of pursuit, they head into a cave to hide, becoming trapped when the ceiling collapses.

With the entrance blocked, Mar and Ina have no choice but to continue further underground, with Ina feeling a strange pull towards something in the direction they are travelling. They find a peculiar cavern filled with crystals and gemstones. While they're resting, an old man appears, and Ina recognises him as the guardian of the mountains. He offers to take her to Sowenna's crypt.

On arriving, Ina discovers what is causing the alluring attraction, Sowenna's diadem—the remaining piece of the legendary chaos regalia, which the guardian offers to the witch. Ina refuses to take the circlet, afraid of its power, which seems to amuse the powerful god.

After leaving the cave, they decide to fly to Liath, but Ina discovers a fear of flying, and they are forced to land. While recovering from her shock, she meets Tar'eth, who finds her thanks to his ring's connection to the witch's necklace. Tar'eth uses his affiliation with mind magic to take control of Ina's chaos and fight Mar with her power. Mar is forced to retreat to Liath. Kidnapped by the drow, Ina fights to regain control over her magic, and Mar has to stay and prepare Liath's defences.

During the attack, Tar'eth tries using Ina's chaos to break Liath's wall, only to learn she has regained control. They fight and, fuelled by the immense wave of chaos, Ina kills him. Feeling overwhelmed by the sheer amount of raw magic, she notices the drow mages performing blood sacrifices to help their forces.

Shocked by the sheer atrocity of it and feeling her control will slip any moment, Ina sacrifices herself, opening a chasm that kills the drow mages. She falls into the abyss with them, unaware that Mar witnessed this and transformed into a dragon, diving in to save her. Later in the battle, Ina uses a vast amount of chaos magic to force both armies to their knees, creating a spell with a single word. She gives them a choice: surrender or die.

During the peace negotiations, Ina persuades the kobolds to become a part of Cornovii, gives the shifters citizenship rights, forces the capitulation of the drow, and returns, triumphant, to Osterad.

Spring Blight

Ina and Mar are trying to enjoy the peaceful family life in Osterad. They both keep themselves busy as Mar is tasked with organising a new army of Cornovii while Ina becomes one of the king's advisors and the head of Magical University. Arun asks her to teach students about chaos magic.

Their family life doesn't last long as, by order of the king, Ina goes south to investigate recent unrest and brewing rebellion. While she is looking for an excuse to travel there under the guise of family issues, the missive is sent to the king, calling her back to Castle Thorn under the threat of Nerissa's imprisonment.

Acting impulsively, Ina drops everything, storming off the Council meeting and heading to Thorn, but her escape is accosted by Velka, who is clearly in a bad mood and insists on going with her. After resisting this offer, Ina has no choice but to take her travel companion for a trip, despite how dangerous it is.

While they head south, encountering bandits and the cult of Marzanna, Mar and Ren dispute the military issues with the help of alcohol until aa desperate Daro storms in, complaining Velka is missing and that it must be Ina's fault.

When Mar learns it wasn't Ina's plan but a threat to Nerissa that prompted her journey, he drops everything and, taking the enraged orc with him, follows his woman to aid her on her mission.

The events in the village turn hostile, and both women are forced to run away through the escape tunnel that ends up in the forest's heart. That's where they encounter a mamuna, and the swamp demon's obsession with Velka reveals the nature mage is pregnant and her husband knows nothing about her state.

Injured after a fight with the mamuna, Ina struggles while they travel to Thorn, only to face a magical battle when her grandfather tries to destroy her mind in his hatred toward chaos magic and her origin. Ina learns he not only forced Nerissa to make her infertile but also placed a geas on her, which is responsible for all her relationship failures and inability to trust people.

After a magic duel that incapacitates her grandfather, Ina is healed by her aunt Mirena and begins investigating family affairs, finding a connection with the southern rebellion. In the meantime, Mar travels through the province, learns that Verdante—the southern kingdom that has always wanted these lands—supports the insurgency and actively recruits their soldiers here.

Mar and Ina reunite in Castle Thorn, only to be shocked when her grandfather dies from poison. They both suspect there must be an assassin in the House of Thorn, and while Mar investigates servants and mages, Ina discovers that both poison and the flames that consumed the body have origins in the northern region. She also finds the letters that incriminate Kaian's clan.

During the family dinner, Daro learns he is to become a father by Ina's slip of the tongue, and all hell breaks loose. Ina uses this opportunity to tell Mar she loves him, but he is free to leave, as she won't be able to continue his bloodline. Her dragon has none of it and discloses that he has already renounced his claim to Liath because of his potential immortality and the fact he loves her and won't be able to live without her. The couple reaffirms their commitment when Ina lets Mar leave a claiming mark on her body.

During the family meeting, Ina decides to divide and conquer to tackle all the southern issues. She also dreamwalks to Ren, asking for the king's arrival for the spring equinox. Mar and Daro are sent to Alsia, the city that has become the centre of rebellion, while Velka stays behind to work on the cause and cure for the blight.

Mar and Daro find out a large army has gathered in Alsia together with Verdante's support, while Ina learns about an ancient curse that tied the goddess of winter Marzanna to this land, causing the blight.

Rewan arrives at Castle Thorn, and the entire company prepares for the ultimate battle. Before the battle, Ina celebrates with the soldiers, kissing a few and gaining the respect of many for her upfront manner. The war ends in success and the capture of the leader of the rebellion, Wawrzyniec.

After the battle and using her chaos magic, Ina arrives back at Castle Thorn, where Velka and her new ally, Rurik, devise a solution for the blight. Ina is grateful, but none of them know Rurik has secretly instigated the problems in the south and is the one to blame for the curse in the first place.

While Velka and Rurik reverse the curse, Ina battles Marzanna herself, temporarily losing herself to the madness of chaos when she notices her bonds have been broken and she can no longer count on the support of Mar or Ren. With Velka's friendship and the help of the goddess of spring, Lada, Ina wins the battle, but the biggest surprise is waiting to crush her when the dust settles after the fight.

With a broken bond and only Velka to support her, Ina learns her most vital ally, her aunt Mirena, was the one to betray her, and intends to sell Ina to the Iron Empire. While Daro fights for their freedom, Rurik takes the two unconscious females, Ina and Velka, to spare them captivity.

CHAPTER ONE

The carriage raced down the road at breakneck speed, the two unconscious women rolling across its floor with no control or protection.
Ina was the first to be woken when her forehead connected with the
wooden chassis.

'What the f— Why are we—?' Ina struggled to concentrate, her surroundings fading in and out of focus as her body bounced around, but
one thought was at the forefront of her mind: *Is Velka all right?*

She rolled to the side, trying to sit upright, nausea roiling inside her
stomach, unwilling to give in till she checked on her friend. Ina fought with
the jerking movements of the carriage, bracing herself against the floor and
sides before looking around, grabbing the unconscious mage as soon as she
saw her, checking for signs of life.

It took Ina a moment to realise the golden light surrounding her friend
wasn't a side effect of hitting her head, but the Zmij, protecting Velka and
the baby. Its coils and wings wrapped around the pregnant mage, preventing her from being hurt by the violent jouncing. The winged serpent
raised its head, meeting Ina's gaze, and she thanked Lada for her thoughtful
gift. The strange mark on the witch's arm had become a spirit that now
protected the woman she cherished as a sister.

Ina relaxed slightly, nodding to the creature. 'Thank you for looking
after her,' she said, shuffling closer, watching the beast slowly fading into

a golden tattoo wrapped around Velka's forearm. Ina pulled the other woman close, placing her friend's head on her lap.

'Wake up, Flower. I can't do anything with you like this, my sleeping beauty.' She gently patted the nature mage's cheek, but the only response was a few muttered words before Velka drifted off again.

I need to keep her safe till she wakes, Ina thought, unsure of their situation. The carriage was jerking wildly over the road, driven by a madman, while she tried to recall what happened and why she was in it, going to gods knew where. The last thing the witch remembered was fighting Marzanna and the wave of spring rolling over the land with Lada's blessing.

'Then we rested... somewhere... in the camp?' she whispered, willing her memory to return. Anxiety awakened her magic, and chaos wrapped around the witch's body like a needy cat demanding caresses. Ina looked at her hands coated in the red mist with a confused frown. She'd been exhausted after the fight, her magic gone. That part she remembered clearly. But looking at her necklace and ring, both pieces of the chaos regalia were pulsing brightly, synchronised with her heartbeat as if she'd been resting for days, not straight from battling the goddess of winter.

'How much time has passed?' she asked, reaching for the bond out of habit. The void in her heart brought all the memories back. Her connection with Mar and Ren was broken, leaving her alone and unable to use her magic confidently. The reality of what had happened and Mirena's betrayal stung worse than her aching body. *Be yourself and let the chaos reign.* Her aunt's words echoed in her mind. All this time, she'd trusted Mirena, seeing her as one of the few decent members of the Thorn family, and Ina had been led like a lamb to the slaughter. *Why would she do this? And more importantly, how? Did she know that destroying the curse would break the bond, or was she the reason the bond was broken?*

Chaos still pulsed like a second heartbeat, its red tendrils dancing around her fingertips as she moved, but the fear of losing control prevented her from trying something more. *Well, we're back to being the useless Baba Yaga in the hut. Filled with a power I'm too afraid to use,* she thought and looked around. Whoever had put them in this carriage hadn't removed Ina's sword or dragon-skin armour. The sword's presence was the most reassuring. Having something to defend herself with gave the worried witch confidence, as she could not use the chaos regalia.

'Open your eyes, Flower. It is time to escape.' She shook the sleepy mage, grinding her teeth when her efforts had no effect. With an incapacitated friend, all she could do now was search for answers. Ina placed her hand on the side panels and carefully sank her magic into the wood. Dust and debris fell to the floor, and eventually, a small gap appeared, just big enough to see the passing countryside.

Ina looked through it, hoping the mercenaries weren't surrounding them or that no one noticed her minor act of vandalism. It took some twisting and uncomfortable poses, but finally, she could see trees and the mist-shrouded grey mountains through an occasional gap in the foliage. No soldiers, attendants, or people of any kind were to be seen, and with a vicious grin that would put the real Baba Yaga to shame, she shouted at the top of her lungs.

'Stop this bloody wreck of a crate, or I'll destroy it beneath your feet!'

The carriage careened to a halt, and Ina gripped her sword, bracing herself for a fight, when the door suddenly opened, revealing a tired, dusty face streaked with bloody tears.

'You are awake, thank the gods. One more day, and I thought I'd have to find a healer. Is Velka awake as well?'

The voice was Rurik's, and Ina was surprised when the necromancer fell backwards, only to realise her fist was in the place his face had been mere moments ago.

The mage sitting on the dusty road was barely recognisable as the proud necromancer she knew, and while she remembered him trying to defend them, Ina didn't trust him an inch.

'Stay where you are and tell me what in the Veles's pit is going on here and where *here* actually is?'

'I'm not your enemy, Ina. I never was, so you can lower your sword. We are close to the northern province, and I'm taking you to the only safe place I know. Your aunt Mirena.... I'm not sure what you remember, but things didn't go well after the temple. I know you've lost control over chaos, and I thought I should take you somewhere quiet for now.'

Ina rolled her eyes upon hearing this explanation but relaxed her hand, putting her sword back in the scabbard. 'Somewhere safe would be Thorn or Liath. Even Osterad would be reasonable, especially with Kaian's and Gruff's forces combing every part of the city, looking for spies. Instead, we're in the middle of nowhere and all by ourselves. Even if I trusted you enough to give you the benefit of the doubt, it would disappear when presented with this.'

'Yes, well, we were being chased, you were unconscious, and I was running out of options. I might not have made the best decision, but it was all I could think of, especially if you'd woken up in a city and used your magic. Gods know how many might have been hurt.'

Ina felt her cheeks warm, his argument echoing her fears, so she nodded and let go of her magic, finally relaxing.

'I can... accept this, for now, until I have a better idea,' she said, and for a moment, Ina looked at Rurik, wanting to question him more, but her pragmatism won over distrust. She would still have to deal with her aunt's betrayal, but first, she needed to take care of the basics. The witch was hungry, thirsty, and had a pregnant woman to protect. The grimace she forced through her tightened lips was the closest thing to a smile she could muster.

'Just slow down and drive more carefully. I have bruises on my bruises from bouncing around like a sack of turnips. Make sure to stop at the next communications post. I have to send a letter to Mar—'

When Rurik raised a hand to protest, Ina held a finger to her lips. 'No matter what you think is best, if Mar believes I'm hurt or in danger, everyone will end up regretting it if he loses his temper, especially the man spiriting away the woman he loves. Speaking of which, what happened to the orc that was with us?' she asked, realising there were only two people in the carriage.

The necromancer looked down for a moment before replying. 'I don't know. He was still fighting when we escaped, but, well, it wasn't long before we were pursued, so....'

Ina cursed under her breath. Daro might not have been a close friend, but Velka loved him dearly, and it would devastate her to learn her husband might be dead. *Or rather, I'm too much of a coward to tell her right now*, Ina thought, looking at Rurik.

'That will be our little secret for now. I don't want Velka upset till I know whether she's all right. As far as we know, he could be licking his wounds in Thorn or chasing after us.'

A silent nod was all she received from the prostrate man. As Rurik climbed to his feet, Ina looked around at the lush growth surrounding them. It felt as if spring had bloomed into summer with miraculous speed, and the witch felt lost, having only just left winter's icy embrace, once more reaching out for her dragon. *I wish I could tell you I'm all right. You must be worried sick about me disappearing like this... again. I only hope Ren can stop you from doing something reckless.*

The memory that came to mind, of Mar professing his love, saying he would burn down the world to be with her, was strangely reassuring, and Ina tried feeling guilty for the thought, but the little smile that blossomed on her lips wasn't going away. *I'm alive, free, and able to look after myself. I will get my bond back or die trying. As for Mirena.... I will find you, Aunty, I will drag you in front of the king, and I will watch how justice is served to you with a smile on my face, you treacherous bitch.* It was a darker thought than she was used to, but the witch ignored the brief twinge of conscience and turned back to help her friend.

'Take us to your safe house or the nearest village, and remember, not a word to Velka.'

'Not a word about what? Where's Daro?' The tussled blonde head of the sleepy mage moved upwards as Velka tried to get up, wincing so hard it reminded the witch about her own headache pounding behind her eyes, and a moment later, Ina was by her side, supporting her head.

'That I must avoid other people until I restore my bond, but Rurik will take you to Osterad as soon as he makes sure the road is safe. As for Daro, Mar needed him, so he stayed behind.' Her words seemed to calm her friend down, and Velka let Ina fuss and help get her seated.

With a final check on the nature mage, Ina looked at Rurik. 'Come on then, let's go. And slower this time, Rurik; I don't need any more bruises.'

CHAPTER TWO

I t wasn't long before they were moving again, this time at a reasonable pace, and rather than guess where they were going, Ina created a few more holes to make seeing outside easier.

'Ina, where are we? What happened? And please don't lie to me this time.' Velka hissed the words into Ina's ear in an effort to be secretive, but so loudly that if anyone had been listening, they would have heard everything. The witch could hear the worry in her voice, and guilt flooded her eyes with tears.

Ina sat next to the mage, covering her with cloaks and propping up her head with makeshift cushions till her friend caught the witch's hands, stilling them.

'It's not good, is it? Just tell me. The longer you avoid the answer, the more unsettled I am.'

The witch nodded and sat heavily on the bench. 'I don't know the full extent of the problem, but after our confrontation with Marzanna, my aunt gave us some potion. You fell asleep almost straight away. I tried to fight but couldn't. I remember little of how we ended up in the carriage, but my intuition tells me we would be in chains now if not for Rurik. I'm sorry, I didn't mean to get you into so much trouble.' Ina lowered her eyes, and her gaze settled on Velka's rounded stomach. 'I will get you back to Osterad as soon as possible,' she said, her words subdued.

'What about you?'

Ina winced at her friend's concern and shrugged. 'For now? I'll stay at Rurik's safe house. I suspect Mirena or Marzanna did something to me. My bond with Mar and Ren is no longer there. With two chaos regalia and nothing to anchor me, it's best to stay away from people and places I love.'

'For how long?'

'I don't know. I must restore the connection or learn to use chaos without their support. I feel a bit lost, and maybe, for the time being, it would be best to collect my thoughts in a place where I won't cause any damage.'

'You know that's not going to happen. I bet Mar's already a roaring terror in the skies over Cornovii, not to mention Ren, and I doubt Daro is sitting around waiting for me to waltz in with a pretty smile on my face. We will have to prepare to meet them and explain, so if you're worried and want to do that away from civilisation, then fine, we'll do that together, as family. Now, could you please stop avoiding the subject and tell me what happened to my husband?'

Ina looked at Velka, sitting there calmly, hands wrapped around her belly while she enquired about her man's whereabouts. The words were quiet, but the tone was firm, despite the obvious worry. Ina chewed her lip, wondering how she could break the news to her friend.

'I'm not avoiding the subject. I simply don't know. Daro was fighting with Mirena's men when Rurik dragged our unconscious bodies into the carriage. I'm sorry, Flower. That's all he told me. I don't know the answer, but I know he'd not stop trying to get to you.'

Velka closed her eyes, and when the silence became awkward, Ina worried her friend had drawn her own conclusion, but after a moment, Velka looked at her and reached for the witch's hand.

'I know he is alive. It is hard to kill a Steppe orc—a chieftain's son, at that. Some of the stories he's told me of growing up on the Steppe, the trials, and battles. No, a few brigands won't be the death of my husband. That's why I'll stay with you for now and help you stabilise your magic. If I could stop you from going berserk in the temple, there's a good chance I can help you control your magic again, and before you argue, I also have my best interests in mind. I don't want to deliver my son in the middle of nowhere, surrounded by strangers. Besides, I trust you'll find a way out of this situation. You always do.'

'Oh Flower, when did you become so grown up and levelheaded? It is very scary.' Ina chuckled slightly in relief as Velka's steadfast belief in her husband's battle prowess helped ease her anxiety, and the witch smiled, looking through the makeshift window.

'There is a village ahead. Let's stop to get some food and information,' she said, tapping on the front of the carriage. The chance to gather intelligence and sustenance was worth the risk of exposure to their pursuers.

It didn't take long for the small carriage to arrive in front of a slightly crooked inn with a wind-battered sign, and Ina was the first to set her feet on the ground, looking around for potential danger. The village was small and built around a square, as in many settlements. The stench of cattle manure mixed with spring flowers and the voices of playing kids saturated the air, whilst most adults, especially the females, were outside busy with work, silently observing the strangers.

After their time in the South, the faces that looked at her appeared almost unhealthy in their paleness, their features uncannily similar, and Ina wondered how far off the beaten track they were for such uniformity to be commonplace.

She helped Velka out of the carriage, leaving Rurik to tend to the horses as they headed inside. The inn, as expected, was the same as inns the world over, only a little more weathered than one from a bigger, more populated town. It was clearly well cared for, but suffering from the state of its patrons, the smell of pigs and sweat causing Ina to wince as they entered. The unwelcoming stares of the usual derelicts brought a reminiscent smile to her face.

'What do you want?' A hostile voice from behind the counter made both women turn their heads. The innkeeper showed the same prejudices as his clientele, and Ina reconsidered her need for food and water, but Velka moved closer to the man, giving him a friendly smile.

'Can we have bread and something warm to eat, with dark ale, if you have any? We're passing through and are willing to pay well.' A small silver coin rolled on the counter, instantly improving the man's attitude.

'Of course, your grace. We have freshly cooked stew. We don't have ale, but my brother-in-law has an excellent rotgut, good for the bairn and no lie. I hope your excellency won't mind such humble offers.'

Ina pursed her lips to hold her laughter at the innkeeper's words. She suspected that was the most money the owner had seen in his life, but the way he mixed the titles and bowed, barely avoiding hitting his forehead on the edge of the counter, helped her relax for the first time that day.

'Are you sure you want to eat here, Flower?' Ina asked quietly, noticing Rurik walk into the inn.

'Hungry people can't be fussy,' she said, pointing to a table in the corner. 'Let's sit there. Then we can ask if anyone has news. I don't feel comfortable with so little information.'

The witch worried at her bottom lip with her teeth. 'Me neither, with what happened at the temple, then Mirena betraying us like that.'

Velka looked at Ina, confused, before saying. 'That's the second time you've mentioned Mirena. What happened? Wasn't she helping?' With a sidelong glance at the innkeeper, who pretended not to eavesdrop on their conversation, Ina explained what she knew, watching as her friend's eyes got bigger and bigger till the witch had to stop to hold in a laugh at the nature mage's expression.

'Bring the food and drink to the table, kind sir.' Velka's sudden outburst surprised Ina till she looked in the direction of her friend's gaze, noticing Rurik in the doorway and waving him over.

Although well made, the table had seen better days and was sticky from spilt drinks, so, lips tight in disgust, Ina muttered an old witch's cantrip, and the table's surface expelled the dirt and shined with a hint of its former glory.

'That wasn't wise. The barman will surely remember the domestic goddess who cleaned his table so well you can actually eat of it.' Rurik's quiet voice rebuked the witch as he joined them at the table.

'If that's the only reason he remembers three well-dressed, softly spoken rich people, then it's easily remedied. There's enough filth on the floor to dirty five tables and still have plenty left over. The real question is, why does him remembering us pose a problem?'

Rurik frowned, and Ina saw how unsettled he was. His long fingers tapped the table's surface as if he were gathering his thoughts. When the necromancer raised his head and looked at her, she saw something unexpected in his eyes—regret and desperation—but before she could ask why, the innkeeper came back with bowls filled with stew, a loaf of bread, and a bottle of cloudy fluid that must be his famous rotgut. He looked at the table before his gaze drifted towards their faces.

The deep crease on his forehead deepened even further when, with a huff, he placed the bowls in front of them. 'Milady mage, don't go north. It is not a good place to be, not since the king executed the old lord of Elaran.'

Ina had wondered if the king had already dealt with the ducal house of the Water Horse, and this news confirmed the swiftness with which he'd addressed the traitorous duke's dealings. It seemed a good idea to ask what else was happening with such a warning from their unfriendly host. 'Tell me what is going on there, good sir. I need to visit my family, but if it's too dangerous....' Her voice hung in the air, and another silver coin rolled on the table. The innkeeper caught it like a hawk, but much to Ina's surprise, he turned around and walked to the inn's door, bolting it shut before he returned to the table.

'I don't know much, lady mage, and I want no trouble. We rarely see strangers here, but those who pass our village tell us of fear and plans. Dancik is recruiting the free companies and fighters. They say the Iron Empire is coming, and there is no one to protect us, not since the Duke of Water Horse was killed, and his only son is a mattress in the king's bedroom. They said the Iron Empire has alchemists who can shoot fire, and they don't get tired like our mages and that the man itself, the emperor, collects the skins of those he defeats to make a carpet for his court.'

Ina's eyebrow shot up while Velka gasped at hearing such revelations. Even though most of it sounded like exaggerated gossip designed to scare the gullible, sieving through it, Ina had to admit that mercenary recruitment, especially in Dancik and the disarray in Water Horse dukedom, sounded plausible. 'Thank you, we won't cause you any trouble, and we will leave after the meal. From where can I send a letter? Do any couriers pass through your village?'

The man scratched his head, pondering the question. 'No, lady mage, but they pass through the village closer to Kion, and I sometimes send my lad down the road to deliver to them.'

'If I write the letter, will you send your lad to deliver it to Kion? I will pay well, but I will also place a sigil on the letter to stop the messenger from taking the money and discarding the message,' Ina bluffed, hoping the innkeeper didn't know the limitations of magic. When he returned with a few sheets of crumpled paper and the quill, Ina passed one to Velka.

'Write to Daro. He must be worried sick about you,' she said with a smile while preparing her letters.

'It is not wise, Ina. They will trace the letters and find you.' Rurik seemed distressed by the prospect. Ina placed her hand on his, letting chaos's tendrils tickle his skin.

'I don't care if they do. I may have lost my bond, but I haven't lost my magic, and if they come to take my life, I will unleash a hell that will consume their souls. Mirena will be the last person who tricks me into dancing to her melody. Now it's my turn.' Rurik withdrew his hand, rubbing it to dispel the prickling burn of pure chaos.

'I saw your face when the innkeeper mentioned the Iron Empire. Do you intend to fight them if they come? You are not ready, and how can you do it without holding the complete chaos regalia?'

'No, the Iron Empire is not ready to meet me, and I don't need more gems. All I need is an anchor to keep me grounded in the maelstrom of the chaos madness. I need the bond with Mar and Ren back. If this threat is real, I need it back as soon as possible. Otherwise, I'm just a useless alchemist with the potential to destroy the world.'

Velka looked at her as if seeing her for the first time, and Ina hesitantly smiled. 'I'm still me, Flower, but I've come to accept there's a darkness inside me that revels in the destructive power in chaos, and the bond is the only way to control it. If I hadn't been manipulated into fighting time after time, I would happily live a quiet life, bouncing your bairn on my knee without a care in the world, but now? Whoever did this will pay for what they've done to the people of Cornovii and me, and I won't shed a tear for their deaths.'

Velka nodded and averted her eyes, avoiding looking at Ina's face, and the witch bent over the parchment. The first letter was simple. A few words to Ren came with a smile.

Prepare the army. Rumours abound of a northern invasion. Don't let Mar worry too much or do something reckless. I trust your judgment, my Moonlight Guardian.

Bi chamd khairtai

Ina

Ina learned those Yanwo words after Ren used them to express his love. Each time she attempted to say them, she brought a smile to his face and knew utilising the phrase and the moniker she used for him would convince her careful friend to trust the letter. The second parchment was for Mar. Ina struggled to find a reason solid enough for him to stay away, knowing her dragon would start searching for her as soon as he realised she had disappeared. Finally, she wrote.

Soon your heartbeat will lull me to sleep again. Trust your stubborn witch, lord marshal. Listen to Ren, please. This kingdom and Rewan need your help, and I will join you when I'm ready. Don't be an oaf.

Ina

The innkeeper promised to deliver their messages to Kion in the upcoming days, and Ina addressed them to Jorge, knowing the judicial mage would know what to do with them. They finished the meal before Ina looked at Rurik.

'Let's go. The sooner we get to your place, the sooner I can find out what's wrong with me and fix it. I can't let my enemies wait for too long.'

CHAPTER THREE

Their brief stop at the tavern left them feeling unsettled, and everyone gave the surroundings a much closer scrutiny as they travelled
northwest. The road to the village had been reasonably wide and well-trav-
elled, but the further north it took them, the more it dwindled and fell into
disrepair until there were hardly any traces to follow. The threat whispered
by the innkeeper soon drifted into the back of Ina's mind, and she dozed,
lulled by the creaking sway of the slow-moving carriage.

Just as the sun kissed the tops of the few salt-stained trees behind them,
Rurik turned to them and pointed slightly to the left. 'We're almost there.
It's not the most comfortable house, but it's mine, and no one will disturb
you here.'

Both women leaned over to stare, and Ina found herself smiling. Rurik's
home, it appeared, was an old manor house, covered in ivy and surrounded
by an undulating expanse of pink and mauve Cornovii heath, interrupted
here and there by the shaggy sheep common to the area.

'It is beautiful, Rurik. I didn't realise you lived all the way out here.'
The lack of light in the windows and faded paintwork prompted Ina's next
question. 'You live alone, with no family or servants for such a large home?'

'It belonged to my mother's family before they went bankrupt, then the
moneylenders sold it from under their feet. It stood empty for years, as no
one was interested in a place in the middle of nowhere. I learned of it when

researching my past, and I bought it as a surprise for my mother, but, well…
I never had a chance to tell her before….' Rurik lapsed into silence as he
looked at the old building.

'So they just left it to rot?' Velka was surprised at such waste, but Rurik
just shrugged.

'They said it was cursed, especially after what happened to the daughter
and her family. It suited me; the price was low, and it was my birthright, so
I bought it. At least now we have a place to stay no one knows about.'

'So no one lives here? Who maintains the grounds?' Ina kept asking,
grinning as her persistence earned an eye roll from Rurik.

'No, I have revenants to do some minor tasks. It works well once you
give them simple instructions, and I don't have to care about servants.' His
explanation made Ina laugh, and Velka looked at them, horrified.

'Don't tell me you'd eat something cooked by revenants. That is just
wrong!'

'Yes, but I can appreciate how resourceful our new friend could be,' she
said, jumping out of the carriage as it slowed to a stop. Standing in front of
the mansion, Ina felt a shiver of foreboding, possibly the previous owner's
ghost breathing down her neck. Still, it didn't stop her from entering and
looking around curiously.

'Well, I've lived in worse places,' she said to herself as she looked over the
shabby wallcoverings and thick dust over every surface.

As the necromancer walked through the door, he turned to the side and
sketched a complicated glyph on an ebony glass plate, then shouted, 'Rise!
Your master is here.'

Ina turned to see the heaps on the floor she mistook for rags rise, uncovering the preserved bodies of Rurik's revenants, Nawia's eerie light shining
in their empty eye sockets.

After marking two rooms for their quarters, both women retreated to the garden while Rurik and his freshly raised servants prepared the house. Velka was strangely quiet, busying herself, coaxing wild strawberries to ripeness with her magic.

'I know you're worried about Daro. Have rest for a day or two, and I will ask Rurik to take you to Osterad.'

'No, Ina. Please, please don't send me away. I'm....' Velka looked into her friend's eyes, one hand sliding over her stomach to enfold the life inside. 'I'm scared. When Lada blessed my child, I knew the gods turned their eyes on him, and then this damn thing'—waving her other tattooed arm in the witch's face—'was stuck to me. What if they want to take my boy away?'

Velka's eyes were wide as panic overtook her, and Ina grabbed her friend and cuddled her close, murmuring softly in Velka's ear. 'Hush, Flower, hush. You're safe, the baby's safe. Lada will never come near your baby, even if I have to burn the Zmij off your arm and beat her to death with it.'

Velka hiccuped, nearly laughing and slightly panicky at the image Ina painted with her bloodthirsty words, but they managed to stop the nature mage, and she slipped her arms around Ina gratefully. 'I'm sorry, Striga, I know I'm being silly. Lada is the purest of love and would never be like that. With Daro....' The hitch in Velka's voice tripped over the word she was about to say. 'With everything that's happened, I want you by my side when the baby comes. I promise, no more silly panicking, but I know the birth will go well with you to help. And Ina? I love that you'd fight a god for me, but this time, I just need my caring, wonderful friend to be by my side.' While slightly teary, the mischievous smile Velka gave her melted the witch's heart, and Ina squeezed her friend a little tighter, huffing as she pretended to be annoyed.

'I should kick your pregnant arse for putting yourself in harm's way. Didn't I already say I could end up losing control?'

Velka just snorted and pinched the witch's side. 'You'd never hurt a child or a friend, you big fluff.'

'Your rooms are as ready as I could make them.' Rurik approached them slowly, visibly tired from spellcasting, and Ina, in a gesture of goodwill, stood up from the grass and reached her hand to him.

'Thank you,' she said, biting her lip as an idea came to mind. Seeing his exhaustion, with careful manipulation, Ina sent a pulse of power through her hand. Rurik gasped, but the dark circles under his eyes faded, and his posture straightened up, revitalised by the energy of her magic. When he sent her a questioning look, Ina smirked.

'I'm a living power gem, remember? I'm sorry to use you for my experiment, but after we collaborated in the temple, I thought it might be possible to bolster your strength. I couldn't try it on Velka first with her baby, and you looked like you needed the help.'

Rurik huffed when Velka sniggered, then turned to leave. 'Just go to your rooms. There is nothing to eat here today, but I will see what I can arrange for tomorrow.'

Ina nodded, helping Velka up from the grass. 'Come. We need to rest, you in particular. Go to the room, and I will set up some warning spells. Our host seems friendly, but my life taught me to take every precaution.'

After Velka's departure, Ina walked around the grounds, anchoring her detection spell. It came to her so effortlessly now, compared to the first time she'd used it in Osterad. *My home, I miss it so much. Boruta, my love, I wish you were here*, she thought, feeling guilty for leaving the cat alone for so long. He might have been half forest spirit, but Ina couldn't help missing the one companion that kept her sane during her exile all those lonely years in the Black Forest. 'He's not alone; he has Marika to give him company,' Ina muttered to herself between the spells, but something in her chest felt heavy and homesick. She would have given anything to put her head on Mar's lap, with Boruta, as usual, sat on her chest, purring like crazy to Ren's flute as they relaxed in front of the fire.

At the thought of the men in her life, Ina looked inwards, searching for their connections, but the bonds were still missing, nothing but emptiness where they used to be. The witch thought about the moment she'd gifted Rurik her power and the bond she'd formed with the two mages during the battle against Marzanna's curse. Had that connection cut her off from the two men? She had channelled a terrifying amount of power, so maybe that caused this emptiness in her soul. Ina wrapped her hands around a nearby tree, cuddling her face to the rough bark.

'Leshy.... Elder.' The witch shook her head, still uncomfortable at being related, however distantly, to a god. 'Leshy, I don't know what to do anymore,' she whispered. The forest god was the only one who never failed to help her see the right path, even if that path caused her pain. A warm breeze brought the scent of damp moss, and the bark warmed beneath her cheek, as welcoming as hugging a beloved parent. Tranquillity followed, making Ina sigh, and her tumultuous thoughts stilled. Suddenly, she gasped as something grasped her ankle. When Ina looked down, a vine wrapped around her calf, growing and moving until it smacked her bottom, making the witch laugh.

'What was that for? Never mind. I miss you so much.' Ina affectionately stroked the trembling leaves that had slowly withdrawn to their previous position. For some time, she'd known the Leshy would come to her when she asked, but not once had he resorted to disciplining his unruly child.

'You could have sent Boruta. His disdain would keep my self-pity at bay for longer. No need to smack my rear like a toddler,' she said.

Not only had her giant forest cat been a gift from Leshy, but since she moved to Osterad, Ina believed Boruta was the Leshy himself, or at least an avatar of the god who'd helped her so much in the past.

Calm and reassured, Ina passed a few revenants en route to her room. The corpses ignored her presence, mindlessly sweeping the floor, and Ina pursed her lips, trying not to laugh, thinking about how Rurik had gone from terrifying death master to domestic goddess with his army of slightly smelly helpers. It took some gymnastics to avoid the swinging brooms, but she returned to her room undisturbed, as the other mages were already resting for the night.

The chamber she had chosen had been cleaned to a reasonable standard, but the furniture was too rickety for her liking, marred by time and neglect, so she quickly arranged a makeshift bed on the pristine floor with a few blankets.

Despite the closed windows, the sound of owls and other night predators pierced the silence. Sitting on the floor, hands in her lap, Ina inhaled deeply. The natural sounds of the night reinforced the sense of tranquillity inside her mind as the witch meditated, concentrating on the core of magic in her soul, calling to the men she loved. Her thoughts drifted towards the dragon, imagining his warmth, and strong, rough hands embracing her, his golden eyes shining with the steadfast love that broke the geas in her mind. *Mar? Please hear me, my ferocious dragon. I promise I didn't run away this time.* Imagining the plea winging its way to his heart along the bond she could no longer feel, Ina added a silent prayer to the forest god.

The witch couldn't help thinking about her stubborn, wonderful dragon and the miracle of his love. How it had survived the trials of this last year was a mystery, but despite the adversities they'd faced, affection had blossomed and grown. *Gods, he must be going insane right now.* Hopefully, Ren could help him control his fury, or her dragon would hurt too many searching for her.

As if thinking his name brought him to life, Ina's thoughts turned to the quiet warrior. It was selfish, she knew, but their relationship meant the world to her, his touch filling her with an inner peace that felt like the heart of the forest, and somehow this quiet, loyal man became a part of her soul. After the first night, when he guarded her sleep, playing his flute in the moonlight, the endearment she used perfectly captured their relationship.

Still, no matter how long she sat there calling them in darkness, the threads of their connection were gone, erased from her core like the sacrifice spell had never happened. With it, her sense of safety and love faded, and the loneliness that had accompanied Ina most of her life crept back into her heart.

Her magic responded, filling that void, and looking at the crimson blaze crawling on her skin, the witch wanted to scream her anger and frustration. Chaos devoured her anguish, building into a pressure that awakened the dark side of her soul. The dull throbbing pain in her heart reminded her how close she was to becoming a monster.

Her control of chaos, always sensitive to her emotions, fractured, and the raw magic swirled around her, disintegrating the blankets. Ina sighed in annoyance, focusing on it. Red strands obediently retracted into her body, blazing over her skin before fading slowly into nothingness.

'The magic seems intact, if not stronger, after my confrontation with Marzanna, so why is the bond gone? They both were tied to me by chaos. What could break an unbreakable bond? Unless it's not broken... but then what the hell happened? For fuck's sake, why can't I feel them anymore?!'

Ina screamed the last words, destroying a piece of furniture with a blast of magic, before trying to recall the last time she'd felt the two other souls. Reliving past events, slowly going back over her memories, the witch stumbled over the scene of Mirena, giving her a 'strengthening potion.' And that was the last time she remembered feeling her men.

'Bloody bitch!' Ina rushed to the window aiming into the sky, as this time, the torrent of magic exploding from her felt too strong for the building to contain. The stars darkened as a sudden formation of clouds obscured their light, and torrential rain poured down, interrupted by thunder and lightning. The weather's sudden change made Ina look at her fingertips in shock.

'That was unexpected. Since when can I affect the weather?' she muttered, clenching her shaking hand into a fist. Fuelled by the chaos regalia, the power she wielded became strange even for her. Ina took a deep breath and returned to her ravaged bed. *Can I find the antidote or reverse it if it was a potion? She may be a great healer, but I'm a master alchemist*, she thought, closing her eyes.

Her chaos was too unstable to rely on, especially after this latest incident, but she still had her knowledge and, if needed, fighting skills. Ina thought of what her chaotic life had taught her, and a smirk appeared on her lips. *Everything has a purpose, and you, dear Aunty, might force me to bend, but I'm not broken, and I will show you the strength of a chaos mage with a grudge*, Ina thought, falling asleep, but at the back of her mind was still one question that needed to be answered. Why had Mirena done all this, and what had Rurik's role been?

The morning sun and the distant sound of cursing awoke Ina, and she welcomed the very ordinary sounds and smells of the countryside with a smile. The vivid greenery had benefitted from her magical outburst the previous night, but when a loud clattering and another round of cursing interrupted the witch's musings, she realised it was time to go to the kitchen before Velka broke something or someone in her frustration.

'What do you want me to do with this...? It's alive!' her friend shouted, pointing at the wiggling hare in the revenant's hand while Rurik stood there in complete confusion.

'What do you mean? Just cook it. Women normally know how to make a rabbit stew,' he said, and Ina rushed forward, snatching the pan from

Velka's hand before it came in contact with Rurik's head. *Master of death? He's just another man with a death wish*, Ina thought, turning to her friend as she stood beside the fireplace.

'I will take care of it. I would be grateful if you could help me with some vegetables,' Ina said with a smile before she addressed Rurik. 'Tell your corpse to pass me the rabbit... and stop courting death while I deal with food shortage.'

Ina took the rabbit outside. 'I'm sorry, little one,' she said while her magic brushed against the soft fur, stopping the racing heart for a quick and painless death. The spark of chaos that appeared lingered on her skin, but the witch refused to take it. Instead, she placed her hand on the ground, feeding it to the earth.

With the rabbit problem solved, the company made a quick meal of fresh meat and the remains of their supplies.

'I will go to the village to buy some food,' said Rurik, trying to rise from the seat, but Ina raised her hand, stopping him.

'That can wait, because I want some answers. What do you know about the rumours of the Iron Empire invading? And no prevaricating; something tells me you know more than you let on,' she said, and the way Rurik averted his eyes showed her instincts were right.

'We need food more than we need stories,' he said, but Ina's raised eyebrow and the crackling sparks of chaos appearing on her hands changed his mind.

'I'm not asking, I am demanding an answer. Don't let the relaxed atmosphere of us eating breakfast together fool you into thinking I won't hurt you. I lost more than you can imagine at that temple, and my magic is unstable. So stop avoiding my question, as my self-control is all that's stopping me from destroying this house and killing us all. So please, sit down and tell me what you know about the Iron Empire and how much of a threat they pose.' Ina's voice was calm, but the overwhelming pressure of magic didn't match her serene pose.

Rurik and Velka looked at her like she'd grown a second head.

'Are you all right, Ina?' asked the nature mage, concern plastered on her face. Her expression made Ina send her an apologetic smile.

'All right, I will tell you all I know, but there is not much of it.' Rurik approached Ina, raising his hands in a gesture of surrender as though trying to tame a venomous viper. Their reaction made Ina clench her fists before she exhaled slowly. Last night's events and the lack of sleep had left her on edge, but she should know better than to lash out at her companions. Still, the craving to release the chaos was there, and its presence worried the witch more than anything else.

'I'm sorry, but please, tell me all you know. The sooner I get some answers, the better. I don't even know much about Mirena's origin. Do you know anything that could shed some light on her actions? I will take anything; stories, gossip—anything.' It never occurred to her to ask about her aunt's earlier life, and now she was paying for this, only knowing that her aunt had been married into the Thorn family against her will and no one talked about it. Since the couple seemed to learn to respect each other, she hadn't felt the need to enquire about the past until now.

The necromancer looked down, avoiding Ina's gaze as he began. 'She came from the North, a minor noble's daughter from the Water Horse clan, sent to court to serve the queen. Then there was a massive scandal that died down suspiciously quickly despite court gossip, and she was hastily wed into the Thorn family. Someone powerful removed her from the palace when it was discovered she was expecting. That's all I know. It was a long time ago, Ina, and not a word of it was recorded in the court chronicles.' Rurik stumbled over his words, giving her the impression he knew more than he was saying, but in a gesture of goodwill, Ina left the subject alone.

'That connects her to the North, but nothing else. Is there any connection between her and the Iron Empire, or is it pure coincidence? Give me your best guess if you don't know.'

'She wanted to deliver you to the emperor. That was clear from our brief conversation after she drugged you.' Rurik's words made her rub her temple.

'But why? What would they want from Cornovii? They are not merchants or mages, and brute force won't encourage trading where diplomacy will,' Ina mused, and Rurik's quiet sigh followed her thoughts.

'Again, I don't know much, but I was in Dancik, the only city they trade with, and what I learnt there is worrying. You know they are military zealots ruled by a man who thinks of himself as a god, believing in survival of the fittest. He eliminates every threat, taking what he wants from the lands he conquers, and Cornovii has become an easy target in recent years.'

Rurik shrugged while Ina and Velka looked at each other before the nature mage asked, 'What does this have to do with Ina? Her legendary disobedience to any orders makes a military career difficult.'

'I don't know, but I don't think a military career is on offer. The emperor seemed to be fascinated by chaos, or so I heard. When I was at the university, there was gossip he'd sent his son to find such a mage and bring them to their island. That must be it, as the Iron Empire sees women in only three roles: servant, bedmate, or mother.'

'Choices, choices.... What path should I choose?'

Ina's mocking tone made Rurik frown, and after a moment, he added, 'It's a rumour, but some say the Iron Emperor likes to gather female mages with rare talents. He calls it his personal collection, but I don't know how true this is.'

'Well, that sounds better than being a servant or a whore.'

'Ina!' Velka looked at the witch with disbelief, shocked by such a dismissive tone. The bitter smirk on Ina's lip made her frown even more.

'He has to catch me first, Flower, and I'm not so easy to handle, especially right now. But enough of this and the Iron Emperor's perversions. Rurik, do you have an alchemy workshop here? I need to confirm something; basic equipment will do.'

'I saw something in the matron's quarters, but I'm not sure how good it will be after all these years.' The necromancer hesitated, but Ina had turned to leave.

'That will do. I'm sorry for earlier. Please look after the supplies, and I will do what I can to find out what disrupted the bond. I suspect my dear aunty gave me a potion of sorts.' Before Ina could finish, Velka stood up and followed the witch with a determined expression.

'I will go too. Leaving you to your own devices could leave us sitting in rubble, and I prefer a roof over my head.'

CHAPTER FOUR

Mar spent precious minutes searching for Ina, but either through magical interference or his incompetence, he couldn't find any traces of the witch. Returning to Ren and Daro, it took several moments to recover his human shape, to put aside the desire to fly after his woman, despite not knowing which way to go. The quiet warrior had finished bandaging the orc and looked down at their friend, deeply concerned.

'How is he still alive?' Ren's quiet question made Mar raise his head.

'He's an orc from the Steppe. Life is harsh there. Besides, what else do you expect from the chieftain's son?' Mar looked at Daro, concerned about the ashen hue of his skin, the shallow, laboured breathing, and the red-tinged foam on his lips. 'He won't live much longer if we dawdle there. We need to get him to a healer.'

'Fly. That's the only way you'll get there in time,' Ren said and spread his cloak on the ground. Together, they swaddled the unconscious orc until he was safely secured, and Mar promptly transformed, grabbing his burden.

'Ren, scout the area. Look for any hint of what happened here. If Mirena really is involved, I.... It's hard to believe, but... see what you can find, and be careful; if they defeated Daro, they will be dangerous. Please, my friend, find something for me, and I will be back as soon as possible.'

Ren approached him and placed a hand on the dragon's shoulder. 'Go, trust me. If there is anything to find, I will find it. When I discover Ina's trail, I will go after her and leave you clues. If not, I will take Ina's orein. I'll meet you at the camp if the mare lets me ride her. We must warn the king and the head of mages of what happened here. Besides, we need to take this dimwit back....' Ren looked around, searching for Wawrzyniec, but the young noble was nowhere to be seen. 'We lost our prisoner.'

'Fuck him. He won't last a day out here with the wolves so hungry. I shouldn't have let her go without me. She broke the curse, but was it worth it? Ina said if she loses the bond and her magic becomes unhinged, she would prefer to be dead than turn into a nightmare. What if that is why we can't feel her anymore?'

Mar's words hung in the air, and man and dragon stared at each other, worrying. 'No, not Ina.' Ren was the first to speak up. 'I refuse to believe it. Daro said Rurik took them. Whoever this man is, if we find him, we will find her. Mar, Ina is alive. I refuse to believe otherwise.'

Mar nodded and spread his wings, ready to take off, but suddenly paused. 'Ren, I can't lose her to chaos. I have never been so afraid of something as I am of this. If you find her first, do what needs doing to get the bond back. I can live with it, but I can't live without her. Please help me keep her safe.'

Ren slowly shook his head. 'That is your desperation talking, not you. Besides, I don't think it is that simple or that Ina would allow this. She finds comfort in our friendship, and while it is a close relationship, she has never desired intimacy. We will help Ina when we find her, both of us. She won't have to face this alone because of our failure.'

Mar nodded, his giant wings already beating the air despite the ache of strained muscles. Daro seemed heavier than usual, more like a dead body, adding to the dragon's worries. He felt responsible for the orc who trusted him. He'd practically raised Daro after the clueless teen appeared at the guard's garrison doors, carrying a scroll detailing an ancient pact between the Steppe and Cornovii, a pact no one had heard of, so despite the objections of his superiors, the newly appointed captain had enrolled him in the guards, taking him under his wing.

Mar never regretted accepting Daro. As a warrior, he was outstanding, despite being hotheaded and a womaniser. It hadn't hurt that he'd captured Velka's heart, and when the nature mage was happy, Ina was happy, so Mar could forgive his volatile temper.

Mar forced himself to greater effort, flying as fast as his exhausted body could manage, hoping he would arrive in time. Even as he strained to reach the camp, his thoughts were on Ina, worrying over her safety and the state of her mind, and it took immense self-restraint not to turn around and search for her.

What if Ren is wrong? What if the bond is broken because she's dead? Mar roared in anguish as his thoughts spiralled. *I should have performed the joining ritual, and I will, even if I have to drag her kicking and screaming from Veles's hands.* Resolved to keep Ina safe, no matter the cost, the dragon focused on the task at hand and forced his body beyond its limits to save Daro.

The roar that shook the camp made all the soldiers raise their heads and grab their weapons, frightened, as the dragon's body blocked out the sun.

'Healer! Now!'

Onlookers scattered as he landed, calling for the healer. Soon, several mages in green robes ran towards the frightening spectacle. Mar lowered Daro gently, placing him on the stretcher two men were carrying.

'Take the captain to the tent. Make sure he survives,' Mar said before pointing to the healer. 'You, come here and ease the pain in my wings. I need to go back, and I can barely feel my arms.'

Ayni interrupted before the healer could start. 'She can't. Human magic does not affect dragons in the same way. Only a chaos mage can help you.

Where are Ina and Ren?' The dragoness stopped by his head and now looked at him with concern in her azure eyes.

'I don't know where she is, and Ren is looking for clues on the temple grounds. I don't know where my woman is, and I can't even fly to search for her.' His bottled-up fury exploded, and grinding his teeth, Mar transformed, grabbing one of the passing soldiers. 'Saddle my horse! Now!'

'But my lord, Woron is still with the king.'

'Than any horse big enough to carry me.' Mar looked around, seeing many faces staring at him, startled by his anger.

'Mar, come with me. You need to eat and rest. Please. You would ride the poor animal to death and still wouldn't get far. Your wings will carry you further and faster, but only if you recuperate.' Ayni's gentle touch made him look down at a much smaller woman. When she grabbed his elbow, guiding him to the tent, he didn't resist, exhausted by the previous events. Ayni said something to a passing soldier, and as soon as they sat down, trays of food and drinks were carried to the tent.

'Thank you for your kindness. I shouldn't lose my temper,' Mar said, tearing the meat apart. In a motherly gesture, the dragoness smoothed stray hair behind his ear.

'You're afraid you've lost your mate. On top of this, you're also hungry and exhausted. I would say you handled it better than most dragons.'

'I didn't lose Ina, she's simply missing for now. What do you mean *handled it better?*'

'When I lost a man I thought was my mate, I tore the old dragon temple in Liath apart with my claws, then spent millennia buried in its ruins. Deep in your heart, you know Ina is alive; otherwise, your dragon would drive you insane. The part of us that lives in the Other is always connected to our mate, even after death.'

'You never mentioned this before. Is that why you are so relaxed with Ina and Ren? Ayni, does Ren know...? Do you still miss him, that man?' Mar knew he shouldn't ask, this was a deeply personal affair, but the dragoness only smiled sadly.

'No, you are the only one I've told. I should have mentioned it earlier, but I doubt whether you'd choose a different mate, anyway. To answer your other question, yes, I missed him every day until I met Ren. He makes me happier than Olve ever could. That man was passionate but arrogant, and that arrogance was the reason he died.' Ayni quickly wiped away the tears that suddenly filled her eyes, and Mar gathered her into his arms, comforting the dragoness as she bared her soul. With a sigh and a slight sniffle, Ayni rested her head on his chest, then pushed away before continuing.

'With Ren.... I love him. I thought Olve was the one, but I was mistaken. He is my rider, and the fact I can love again is a miracle. I hope one day he will be ready to enter the mating bond. Even if not, it's fine. When the dragon meets his mate, nothing else matters. We are made that way. That is my secret and the reason I will fight to keep Ren safe. Before I make a bigger fool of myself, care to tell me why you left him alone in an area an orc was nearly killed?' Ayni was snarling by the last word, and Mar couldn't help but smile.

'Ayni, I think he's ready, and I'm honoured you shared your past with me. I want you to know I'm your friend, and there's no foolishness in opening your heart to someone who shares the same woes. As for Ren, his nickname is Ghost for a reason, and anyone encountering him when he's this angry will learn exactly what it means. So please, try not to worry; if he doesn't find Ina's trail, he'll return to the camp, or we can fly to the temple and go from there.'

Ayni planted a soft kiss on his cheek and stood up to let him rest, but before she left, the dragoness turned around. 'Thank you. It felt good to talk about it. Once you find her, do whatever it takes to join your life force with hers. Your arrival and Ren's love saved me from becoming a pile of bones like many of our kind, so cry, beg, threaten her, but never let her go behind the veil without you.'

Once the dragoness left, Mar kneaded his tired muscles. The food and wine had done an excellent job, making it possible to think again, which was a good sign, especially since his soul pushed him to fly back even now with nightfall upon them. By sheer strength of will, he forced himself to relax, remembering his favourite memory of Ina, their morning cuddles, waking up entangled together, and breathing in the warm, welcoming scent of her hair. *I will find you, my love. And if someone hurts you, I will avenge your pain until they pray for death's merciful embrace. My fiery spitfire, please wait a little longer... without breaking too many things.* His last thought made him smile. Whoever had taken his woman didn't know the trouble they'd earned if they thought she'd go down without a fight.

A cough from outside disturbed his thoughts, and Mar raised his head, looking at the officers at the entrance.

'Lord marshal, during your absence, some letters arrived from the king,' a lieutenant mumbled, passing him the sealed envelopes.

Mar took it and sent the men away as he opened the king's correspondence. The first letter confirmed the agreement made before Mar left; an alliance that would be ratified by the marriage of King Rewan and Princess Łyna with all the pomp and circumstance that entailed, each party agreeing to help mitigate the shortages caused by the late spring. With that, the power balance changed, and now the southern march alliance were more than willing to cede their claim to the southern province of Cornovii.

The following letter was more of a report from the soldier in charge of logistics, detailing the release of the peasant army, with a side note about the appearance of several women and the ensuing scuffles as they dragged errant sons and husbands home by the ears. It seemed planting season trumped rebelling against the helpful king in their eyes.

The report also held details of the southern nobles. After pledging to the king, they had been sent home with a small contingent of Rewan's men to distribute aid and news of the failed rebellion, with extra orders to monitor the situation for the next six months. Mar snorted at that, knowing just how bad a tour that would be and was determined to make sure the men were well supported.

'Tricky, but if we assign some of our newest mages from the training camp, I think that will help make life easier, perhaps even help them integrate more,' he said, thinking out loud. The mages, arrogant to a fault, were still struggling to accept that soldiers were just as useful outside of a battlefield, but with them seeing the relationship between the healers and his men, things were slowly improving.

The last letter was for his eyes only. Rewan asked Mar what happened to Ina, and if, judging by his sudden reaction, it was as bad as he suspected. That he unequivocally permitted Mar to do what he needed to find her was a tremendous relief.

I know you are connected on a deeper level than I could hope to understand. I saw how your expression changed when the wave of spring almost knocked us off our feet. If something happened to our Ina, find her and bring her home. I give you free rein on how you manage it, but please keep it secret. Ina has become a symbol to the ordinary citizens of Cornovii as someone who will stand up for them and protect their right to live free. That is bigger than her magic, that hope in the hearts of the people that has allowed this country to

withstand storm after storm, and they need it now more than ever. I hope you
will find her. May at least one of us be happy.

Rewan.

The letter's tone was bitter, and Mar felt pity for the new king. Even with
the hideous title of Royal Dragon, he was free to choose his bride when
Rewan was forced to sell his love for peace. He knew Kaian would accept
it. The master assassin was down-to-earth and knew the world's ways, but
what would the future queen do with this unconventional arrangement?

Mar called his squire and sent him to summon the officers in charge
of the army. When they arrived, he detailed the king's plans, gave a few
suggestions, and asked them to organise the camp for His Majesty's return.
Finally, he wrote a letter to Ren, detailing his plans, in case he missed his
friend's return. Slowly exhaling, Mar stretched out on the narrow bed. He
would need to check on Daro soon, but his experience with Nerissa told
him not to disturb the healers whilst they worked, not if he wanted to
escape intact at least.

He whispered a quiet prayer to Perun, asking the capricious god to save
Daro. The gods had been an abstract concept before he'd met Ina. He'd
firmly believed every man could forge their own fate, but his striga had
changed his outlook. Maybe not his beliefs, but his outlook on the deities
and how they saw the mortal world. So he prayed for Daro because the
wounded orc could use any help he could get.

Mar closed his eyes and let his thoughts drift towards Liath and the
stormy sky over the mountains. As soon as Ina was safe in his arms, he
would take her back home to visit his parents, but more importantly,
return to the valley where they had finally accepted each other. There,
he would make love to her and fuse their souls with the dragon spark.
Instinctively, he searched for the bond between them, hoping for the soft

caress of her love, but the void in his soul was a stark reminder of his failure to protect her.

It took a conscious effort to relax and not grind his teeth in frustration, but Mar took a deep breath and tried to sleep. Tomorrow would be arduous if Ren didn't show up in the morning. He'd have to fly back to the temple, find whatever clues there were to Ina's whereabouts and then kill all who thought to hurt her. The thoughts of revenge calmed and comforted him, letting Mar finally fall asleep, knowing the dragon's rage wouldn't be satiated with anything less.

Mar awoke before the sun rose, and stretched. His muscles were still stiff, but at least he could properly spread his arms. He didn't bother to dress in anything but his dragon armour, suspecting he would spend more time airborne than on the ground, then set off to check on his friend. After promising the healers he wouldn't stay long, they allowed him inside to see Daro.

The orc was pale and listless, his skin more ashen grey than its usual warm brown.

'Will he live?' Mar asked the healer, but a very irritated Daro answered before the woman could speak.

'Yes, *he* will. Where is my wife, Mar? Tell me you brought them back?' The desperation in Daro's voice was difficult to bear, especially when the man attempted to sit up, and one of his bandages turned red.

'No, I didn't bring them back, but I will find them, I promise. But first, I need to know what happened there. Can you tell me what you remember?' Something inside the dragon screamed for him to grab Daro and shake the answers out of him, but Mar knew better than to hurt his friend. After all, the orc had done all he could to protect the women, even risking his own life.

'I have no fucking idea. Everything went as planned, or at least I thought it did. Velka, Ina, and that necromancer, Rurik, went to the heart of the temple ruins. They must have done something because the next thing, the ground shook, plants grew everywhere, and the villagers looked like someone had slapped them awake. We gathered them up, trying to contain the situation. The mages looked exhausted, so I hunted for food. After all, the curse was broken, and in my stupidity, I didn't expect any trouble.'

Daro looked at his hands as they curled into fists, shaking with a fury he struggled to contain. As a small trickle of blood began seeping between his fingers, the captain looked up at Mar and, in a frighteningly calm voice, recounted the events that followed. 'When I came back, Velka was on the ground, unconscious or sleeping. Ina... was trying to fight, but she was swaying like a drunkard with several brigands surrounding her, commanded by Mirena. I heard something about the Iron Empire, but couldn't make out the rest, so I drew my weapon and attacked. After that, it got a little hazy. All I can remember is the necromancer dragging them to a carriage; that's it.'

Mar sat next to him, placing his hand on the orc. 'You did well. Rest now. I will find your wife and mine, but I need you fit enough to fight. So listen to the healers, and I will return as soon as possible.'

Daro looked at Mar like he'd suddenly sprouted horns and pulled his hands away with a smirk. 'Yes, mother. Just promise me you'll leave Mirena to me. I deserve to taste that bitch's blood.'

Mar shook his head, standing up from the bed. 'For this, my friend, stand up in line. There are several others unhappy with her deceit.'

CHAPTER FIVE

Despite searching the camp and the temple, Ren couldn't find any trace of Ina. There were plenty of signs of a struggle, including the bodies of Castle Thorn's guards, but nothing else, and the warrior doubted Daro hadn't sent some of their assailants to Nawia. The settlement was eerie; the inhabitants slumped over in small groups surrounding a fire, all dead except for two frightened peasants he found huddled in a small hut. After a bit of encouragement and reassurance, they told him about a middle-aged woman who offered everyone a healing draught, smiling as the villagers fell unconscious and died.

'Why didn't you take the draught?' Ren asked out of curiosity, and the man smirked.

'I don't trust mages. I came to ask the goddess for my wife's return. Instead, I found a man who took my free will with his lies and tied me to this place. No, I won't be taking any magical drinks again.'

'The mages who brought back the spring, do you know what happened to them?'

'No, and I don't want to know. The crimson witch unchained the goddess of winter, but I saw the hunger in her eyes, so we hid till the mages left.'

Ren's lips tightened as the same caution that saved this man's life hindered his investigation. Before he left, he passed a golden coin to the man. 'Tend to the dead per your customs.'

There was nothing more he could do for these people. When he returned to the small camp, Zjawa kept pushing him with her head, and Ren patted the unsettled orein. The road was empty, with no markings of carriage or horses, only the footprints of Wawrzyniec, who'd run towards the forest. It was as if the area had been wiped clean by magic. *Was it you, my lady, or the one who took you away?* Ren wondered, thinking of chasing the escaped prince but dismissing the idea immediately. Wawrzyniec was not the leader of the southern rebellion. He was simply a puppet used for his birthright and stupidity to instigate the unrest. *Wolves have to eat, too.* Ren smirked at his thoughts and turned towards Zjawa.

'I need to get a mage here, but I must return to the army to get one. Will you carry me? Please?' he said, pleading with the spirit. Zjawa nodded and stood patiently as Ren settled himself on her back. As soon as he gave her a gentle nudge, the mountain spirit set off at a blistering pace, galloping through the fields.

Ren was swaying in the saddle when they arrived at the military camp. No normal horse would sustain such a strenuous pace, but Zjawa was not your average horse, and the orein loved Ina. Still, her sides were foaming, and she didn't protest when the stableboy took the reins, leading the mare to the stables.

Ren stretched his cramped muscles and marched towards the commander's tent, greeted by some passing soldiers. He'd expected this, but it still troubled him that Mar wasn't there. However, the person who greeted him was most welcome, and he opened his arms as Ayni rushed to him.

'Mar flew to the temple grounds. I couldn't restrain him any longer. Any trace of Ina?' she said, embracing him.

Ren bent down, nuzzling her neck and inhaling his dragon's warm, spicy scent, before gently cupping her face and claiming a kiss.

'I'm not surprised he couldn't wait. And no, I found nothing. We'll need a mage to check the area. All traces have been removed, as if Ina was never there. How is Daro? Did he survive?' he asked, and Ayni placed her hand over his heart.

'He is alive and kicking, trying to leave the healing tent to find his wife. He's not making many friends with this attitude, but how do you feel? The bond... it's still missing?'

'Like someone tore out a piece of my heart, and it's still bleeding. I need to find Ina and restore the connection. I thought I could live without it, but I can't. Her absence is unbearable. I'm sorry, mi'khairtai.'

The dragoness shook her head, giving him a beautiful smile and pressing something into his hands. 'I accepted I would have to share your love with her when we were in Liath, and you will never have to apologise for how you feel. Ina is... different from how I expected. Here is the letter Mar left for you. Read it, please. I will call for food and search for a mage good at tracking,' Ayni said, trying to leave, but Ren pulled her to the chair and, despite her weak protests, sat her on his lap.

'I need your presence, my lady, more than food or rest. I would never lie to you or hide my feelings, but let me repeat it. You are my world and the woman I want to spend my life with.' With each word, Ren's lips touched Ayni's skin, starting at her wrist and working his way upwards until he captured her lips in a passionate, consuming kiss that left her sighing. It was several moments before Ren could stop and read the letter. As expected, Mar had left as soon as he knew Daro would survive, but the marshal had outlined the plans for the army in case circumstances overtook their desire to search for Ina.

Ren stroked Ayni's head and closed his eyes. The painful emptiness was still there, and being unable to sense the witch left the warrior feeling empty. *Mar... this must be like torture to him.* For the first time, Ren was grateful Ina had put some distance between them, trying to weaken the bond. He never wanted it gone, but at least he could think straight instead of thrashing in desperation like his friend. Exhaustion began dragging his eyes closed, but just as he rested his head against Ayni, the sound of trumpets jolted him awake.

Rewan shouted to someone outside before pushing into the tent. 'You there, bring some food, drinks, and a healer.'

Ren looked at the king, who approached them with an apologetic expression. 'I'm sorry, Sa'Ren. I know you're tired, but the situation is urgent, and we need to talk.'

Ayni elegantly stood up from the chair and gave the kings a small curtsy. 'Should I leave, Your Majesty?' she asked while Ren stood up, but Rewan shook his head.

'No, I'm sure Sa'Ren will tell you whatever's said, anyway.' He paused for a moment, waiting, and soon the master assassin, Kaian, joined the company with a tray of food and drinks.

'I'm sorry for the delay. It looks like your orders were fulfilled, as the camp is clearly packing,' he said, pouring the wine for everyone. 'I made sure no one will disturb us as well.'

Rewan looked at his lover, and for a moment, Ren saw a flash of pain in the king's eyes before he gestured for everyone to sit down.

'Do you know where Marcach is and what happened to my witch?'

Ren was taken aback by such an unorthodox question and flashed the king a tight smile. 'I'm not sure, but if I can guess, Mar is on his way to the temple grounds, trying to find a trace of Ina. We're still unsure of what happened except that her aunt is involved.'

Ren noticed Kaian's hand squeeze Rewan's shoulder before he spoke. 'Families can blindside us with their misdeeds. I haven't thanked you and Ina for not judging me by my house's actions.'

Ren knew precisely what the assassin meant. It must have been hard for Kaian to despatch his elder, but he'd acted without hesitation for his lover's sake. Now even this would be tainted, as the king had to sacrifice their relationship for the promise of peace. Ren nodded before turning his attention to Rewan.

'Is that all, Your Majesty?'

'No, Sa'Ren, that is just the beginning. Kaian received a message from a member of his house still loyal to the crown. I don't know how true the news is, but the Iron Empire is on the move. Bastards must have sensed blood in the water. They've always coveted Dancik as a gateway to Cornovii. The army, being so far south, has created the perfect opening.'

'Mar already issued your orders. The army is on the move. They will march for Osterad tomorrow. I will inspect the temple grounds again, this time with the mage and follow Ina's trail—' Ren stopped, seeing the king raise his hand.

'No, my friend. I can't lose two military commanders now, not even for Ina. Marcach will chase her to the end of time, and no force in this world can stop him, but for the sake of Cornovii, I must ask you to abandon this quest.'

Ren ground his teeth, rising from the chair before Ayni's hand on his shoulder stopped him, but even his lover's touch didn't cool his anger. 'You will leave my lady to her fate despite all she did for you, for this country?' Ren asked quietly, and the menace in his voice made Kaian step in front of the king, but Rewan dismissed him.

'No, that is why I'm not trying to stop Marcach or condemn his actions. No matter how much I love Ina and how grateful I am, I have more people to protect, so I ask you to take command of the army until the lord marshal returns. We must incorporate two squadrons of southern cavalry and a detachment of elven archers as part of the peace treaty. I wrote to the Duke of Liath. He will ask the Stone Halls for a unit of dwarven axemen. I need a skilled man who can oversee this all.'

'You know Ina is and always will be my priority,' Ren said, pinning the monarch with his stare, but before Rewan could answer, Ayni interjected.

'What would Ina want you to do?' Her words shocked Ren, and he looked at the dragoness with a hint of betrayal before his shoulders dropped, and he answered the king.

'I will coordinate the army's march. Kaian, pick some shifters to secure His Majesty's return. It will be faster that way, and we will follow as soon as we are ready.'

Rewan nodded and smiled at the dragoness. 'I would like to invite you to the court, my lady. Your ability to take an overall view may be useful to the crown.'

When Ayni curtseyed, Rewan looked at Ren, this time with a more relaxed expression. 'One more thing, Sa'Ren. I received a personal missive from Lord Alleron mentioning the issues he's had determining Marcach's replacement as heir and has asked for special dispensation to appoint you as scion of House Liath. In his words, you are as close to Mar as any brother and should be afforded the rights to that position. If you and Marcach approve, I will issue the decree on my return to Osterad. I had already planned on offering you a title in thanks for your contribution, and the future Duke of Liath sounds very fitting.'

Ren looked at Ayni, whose expression had suddenly brightened. Despite loving the bustling Osterad, he knew his dragoness missed her mountains. The quiet warrior thought of the proud castle and the people who followed him when he was simply a friend of the scion of Liath. Ren looked at the king, who waited patiently for his answer. Bowing slightly, he placed a hand on his chest.

'Only if Mar and Ina agree.' The idea of having a domain after he renounced his claim to Yanwo was strange but, in many ways, appealing. *Sa'Ren of Thorn doesn't sound too bad.* Ren's lips quirked slightly at this thought, and his gesture didn't go unnoticed by the king.

'I'm sure they will be thrilled with your happiness. I will leave you to prepare the army, and if you feel anything from Ina, please inform me immediately.' Rewan placed a hand on Kaian's chest, quietly adding, 'I envy your bond so much. To always feel the one you love, even if you parted ways....'

Ren refrained from commenting and bowed as Rewan and Kaian left the tent before turning to Ayni, who wrapped her arms around his body.

'It was the right choice, my love. I'm sure Mar will find her, and Ina would want you to keep the country safe,' she said, but Ren didn't answer, stroking her long, raven hair. He knew Ayni was right, but that didn't make it any easier. *Mi'khairtai, forgive me*, he thought, feeling the bitter taste of his choice choking him.

CHAPTER SIX

W arm air lifted Mar high above the landscape as he flew towards the temple. With Daro recovering and the king's orders set in motion, he could focus on finding Ina with a clear conscience. He tried not to think of her alone with no one to rely on and a magic too volatile to use. *She's not alone.* He held onto that thought as panic raced through his heart. She has Velka, bless the nature mage. If nothing else, their friendship would help them endure any difficulties. That thought calmed him down enough to land in the small clearing. Ren was nowhere to be seen, and neither was Ina's mount, Zjawa. That could mean one of two things: his friend had returned to the army, or he'd followed the trail to find Ina.

Mar searched the settlement again, but no matter where he looked, there were no clues except the small camp on the outskirts of the village. There were no bodies in the settlement, but it didn't take long to discover where some kind soul had gathered and cremated their remains. With a whispered prayer for safe passage to Wyraj for the departed souls, Mar turned to the broken remains of Marzanna's statue.

'It looks like you had the last laugh, Winter's Death, but I won't let you take my Ina,' he said before looking at the road north. It was strange. There was no sign of horses or carriage wheels in the dirt. The few footsteps he saw could belong to Ren and Wawrzyniec, but even using his enhanced senses, Mar couldn't find a trace of Ina's scent. It had been the same with the other roads, so whoever had covered their tracks had done so well. Still, what one mage could mask, another could uncover.

Mar looked at his hand, realising how right Ayni had been. Claws and translucent scales distorted his humanity, giving it an otherworldly appearance. His dragon half was becoming unsettled and wild, whilst the rage inside his soul, which had helped him through so many battles in the past, was threatening to unleash itself upon the world.

It took longer than Mar expected to relax and take control enough to plan his next steps. Osterad would be the best place to go. If he met with Jorge, the order mage, with his talent for predicting the future, he could point Mar in the right direction, even if the uptight manipulator claimed chaos disrupted his pattern spells. Without a second thought, Mar transformed, launching himself upwards. It would be a long flight, and to distract himself, Mar reminisced about their home in the city, the cosy townhouse with its modest yard, Ina's enormous cat competing for her attention, and the strange one-armed housekeeper who gave him bruised knuckles each time he forgot to take his shoes off.

He would bring Ina home and never leave her side again. Mar sighed, catching a thermal and resting his weary muscles. With the sun warming his back, his eyes closed as he relaxed in the moment, then suddenly, for a split second, he thought he felt Ina. Desperately grasping for the elusive gold thread of their connection, his body transformed midair, and he plummeted towards the earth.

As fast as the sensation had appeared, it disappeared, but even as he screamed his frustration, Mar transformed, beating his wings with renewed vigour. Ina was alive, and nothing would keep him from finding her now.

He landed in the palace garden grounds, frightening courtiers and guards alike, and rushed towards the Court offices. Anybody who tried to stop him or ask a question soon fell back from his unblinking, golden gaze.

Mar didn't bother listening to the servant's objections as he pushed his way into Jorge's office.

'Sit down.' The mage didn't even bother to take his eyes off the diagram on the table.

'She's alive, if that's what you've come to ask. Her chaos is still there, disrupting my equations,' Jorge said begrudgingly, trying to adjust the pattern.

'I know she is alive, but where is she?' Mar growled, his patience wearing thin.

'I don't know, why don't you check your bond? It should lead you right there. I thought you learned that long ago, so why must I tell you such simple things? Go now, there is something wrong with the North, and I need to look at it closer. Your presence is distracting.'

Jorge didn't even look at Mar until the dragon slammed his hand on the desk. 'If I had the bond, I wouldn't come here asking for your help. I don't care about the North unless Ina is there, so I will ask you kindly to pull the stick out of your arse and tell me where I can find her, or I swear to god this kingdom will never hear your predictions again.'

Mar knew he shouldn't have threatened the mage, but the tension building in his body over the last few days was ready to explode. However, when Jorge ran his trembling hand through his hair, his words weren't to scorn the rude dragon.

'What do you mean you lost the bond? What about Sa'Ren?'

'As far as I know, Ren can't feel her either. We both tried.'

'Gods have mercy on us. What happened? I saw that the southern region settled, and the magical flow through the matrix was restored. I thought...

but then the North flared up, and I didn't have time to look at Ina's pattern. What do you mean you lost the bond? Gods, this is a catastrophe! Why didn't I foresee this? Bloody chaos!'

'I mean, I can't feel her, but why is it a catastrophe to you? It is not like you're the one who lost part of your soul.'

'You foolish dragon, you know nothing of magic.'

'Then fucking enlighten me! What's so terrible?' Mar was at wit's end, and the order mage's distress didn't help. Jorge sat down, pouring himself a good measure of wine and drinking it in one gulp.

'Ina bonded with two chaos regalia, and although she denies it, she is already a chaos archmage. Her bond with you both protected her when she used her magic like a lightning rod, protecting a building from the ferocity of the lightning in a storm. Now she is defenceless against a power that can even wipe the gods from existence. It's not just her life at stake, but us all. She is a resilient woman, but when facing the eternal power of raw chaos...?'

Mar shook his head, rejecting Jorge's words. The mage looked so old and fragile, like he'd aged a hundred years in the last few minutes. 'When Sa'Ren returned with his dragon, I thought it would disturb the balance, but somehow Ina managed, but now.... You must find her, connect with her again, and ensure Sa'Ren does, too. The stakes are too high to allow social norms or personal feelings to get in the way.' Mar tried to free his hand when Jorge grabbed his forearm.

'I'm trying to. So stop falling apart and tell me where she is.'

The mage clumsily swept his desk clear and drew a new diagram, the complex equations meaning nothing to Mar as he stood there, afraid to breathe in case he spoiled intricate work. When Jorge filled it with magic and threads of magic shone in the air over the map of Cornovii, Mar leaned closer.

'Where was she last seen?' asked Jorge, and Mar pointed to the southern region. Jorge carefully drew a small red character there, and for a moment, nothing happened. Mar was about to turn away when the lines lit up, moving and changing shape. More light glowed in the North, and Jorge kept manipulating the threads. Suddenly, the red character pulsated with unsettling colours, but when Jorge tried to alter its magic, the entire map exploded into crimson light, knocking both men to the floor.

'I can't help you. Ina resists all manipulation. All I can say is there will be trouble in the North, and where there's trouble, Ina will surely be in the thick of it. The question is, will she be the solution or the cause this time?'

Mar felt the need to break something or someone to stop them from treating Ina and her magic as the cause of Armageddon, but he had a direction now. Unfortunately, the North was vast and covered with forests and swamps, and Kaian's treacherous clan controlled it.

'Even if we had a tracking spell, her magic would distort it. I'm sorry, Marcach.'

'Tar'eth tracked us in Liath. Do you think a mind mage could help?' Mar asked, then remembered something. Ina had told him about a spell Skarbnik taught her to block mind attacks whilst in Sowenna's crypt. If the gods could help.... Mar gasped, cursing his stupidity. He should have remembered this from the start. When they had been hiding in the mines, Ina had been drawn towards the tomb, and the old god had told Ina that the chaos regalia wanted to unite. Tar'eth hadn't tracked them through the mind link; he'd been led by his ring, like a dog on a leash.

Mar didn't know where his woman was, but knew exactly where he could find the last chaos artefact.

'Thank you, Jorge. That was very helpful. Tell Ren and the king I will return with Ina or die trying,' he said, walking out and leaving the mage confused and worried.

As soon as he found enough space to spread his wings, Mar transformed, oblivious to the screams and curses of the citizens, and launched himself into the heavens. He was a fair distance from Liath but, with a clear plan in his head, it was time to find out if the gods really favoured his beautiful spitfire.

CHAPTER SEVEN

The house was larger than Ina realised, and after following the path cleared for them by the helpful revenants, both women walked into parts unknown, searching for the alchemic workshop. As the stairs creaked ominously halfway up, Velka sighed in irritation.

'I hope they don't break. Everything is so neglected, but there is a beauty to it still.' Velka turned, an evil glint in her eye, stroking her stomach. 'You know who Daro will blame if I hurt myself here?'

Ina snorted and slapped her friend's rear. 'Best hurry then, or your orc will be facing a dragon's wrath, and the baby will pop out to watch. With the size of that tummy, I doubt it'll be long before he says hello, anyway,' Ina said, then, taking pity on her friend, reached out to help. 'How are you, Flower? Did you sleep well? I—'

'Have mercy, woman. You just told me I'm huge, and I forgive you this transgression in the name of our friendship, but if you fuss over me like some bleeding heart healer, I will push you down those stairs.' Velka's exasperated tone made Ina laugh.

'I was going to offer you a back massage, or maybe a block and tackle, to help you carry your lovely burden, but I'll be quiet now. You are the mighty mage with only slightly swollen ankles.' Ina bowed extravagantly, and her antics made both women laugh before they started exploring the next floor.

Most of the rooms were derelict, and the witch was losing hope of finding anything useful, but just as they were ready to concede defeat, their luck changed. As Ina lost the last of her patience, she kicked a loose piece of plaster, causing an entire section of the wall to crash to the ground, covering the two women in dust and debris.

After much coughing and spluttering, Velka gasped, seeing the door revealed by the witch's vandalism. With a smug grin, Ina grasped the rusty handle and forced her way into the room, only to stop and gape at the veritable cornucopia of alchemic equipment before her.

'Veles's tits! Pinch me, I must be dreaming. Just look at this. It's perfect. Dirty, but perfect.' Giddy with joy, the witch danced around the book-shelves, worktables and apparatuses, the dust of years billowing up as her skirt disturbed it. Suddenly she stopped, her eyes meeting the gaze that haunted her dreams. Ina had been so absorbed by her discovery she hadn't noticed Velka moving in her direction.

'Are you done wrecking the room?' she asked between sneezes, but Ina stood quietly, gesturing for her to come closer. When her friend approached, the witch grabbed her hand and pointed at the old portrait on the wall.

'I think I'm seeing things.... Tell me, do you know who she is?' The tension in her friend's voice made Velka frown, and, using her sleeve to wipe away the dust, the nature mage studied the face in the painting but could not understand what caused Ina's anxiety.

'What am I supposed to be seeing?'

The witch pointed at the female in the picture. It was a young woman with an open, honest face, shy smile and bright eyes, but Ina couldn't tear her eyes from the image.

'It's Mirena. I know the girl here is young, but I swear, that is Mirena.'

Velka once again looked at the portrait and shrugged. 'There is some resemblance, but how can you be certain? Faces change over the years, and it would be a pretty big coincidence.'

Ina just stood there, her whole body shaking with anger. 'If it is Mirena, it means I'm in the workshop of the woman who broke my bonds. How the fuck did we end up here? And... oh!' she mumbled, her exclamation startling Velka. In a sudden frenzy of activity, Ina dived to the floor, gathering books and parchment to her chest.

'Striga, what are you doing? Ina... Ina, stop it!' The edge of panic in Velka's voice barely penetrated through her haze, but as soon as Ina raised her head, Velka gasped and moved back. The witch's eyes, just like her namesake striga, were blood red and swirling with chaos. Velka swallowed hard, then reached out, laying her trembling hand on Ina's shoulder.

'Whatever you're looking for, we will find it, but now come back to me. Please, let the chaos rest,' she said as the wisps of destructive magic coiled around the witch's body.

Ina blinked, taking a shuddering breath. Something in Velka's touch eased the rage at being in Mirena's house, and the red mist slowly dissipated. As she looked around at the mess she'd made, the witch blushed, releasing the creased parchment before standing up.

'My anger... I'm so sorry. Why can't things be normal? I want Mar and Ren and the peace of relaxing by the fireplace with Boruta on my lap, not this blind fury that steals away my soul. Just last night, I caused a bloody storm. A storm. How is that even possible? I must fix the bond before chaos destroys more than a few books.' Ina rubbed her face to erase the tears making tracks over her cheeks. 'Somewhere in this room is the answer to my problem; it has to be. If I know what caused the problem, I can fix it. I must fix it.'

The sob that escaped brought tears to Velka's eyes, and she gathered Ina into her warm embrace. 'We will find the answer, and soon you'll have control and your bond back. Until then, remember I am here for you and will never let you go.'

It took most of the day to catalogue all the manuscripts, with both women crawling around to gather them from the floor. Ina insisted on looking at each parchment herself, and soon Velka left her to concentrate on cleaning and organising the equipment. By the time they finished, the sun was setting, but the workshop was pristine, with all paperwork and books organised in neat stacks. Unfortunately, Ina had found no reference to bonds or the sacrifice spell.

'I think my aunt wanted to become the next Nerissa. There's nothing but recipes for healing ointments, prescriptions, and herbal notes. Nothing about bonds, poisons, basilisk venom, or necromancer's flame.' Ina sat on the chair and looked at the paper cuts on her fingers.

'Few are born naturally evil. Maybe something forced your aunt to be that way. You said her marriage with Cyrus was arranged.' Velka looked tired and was half lying on the only available sofa.

'Maybe. My grandfather could push anyone to murder, but why me? I didn't wrong her; even my blood ties with that bastard shouldn't make me a target,' Ina said, squeezing another droplet from her fingertip. Suddenly, the witch's back snapped straight.

'It still may be in my blood,' she said, approaching the table and opening the vein with a quick cut to her forearm.

'Ina, what now?!' Velka shouted, shocked how her unfazed friend gathered her blood into the alembic.

'I'm only guessing, Flower, but if Mirena used poison on grandfather, maybe she used the poison on me. I drank a fair share of her *strengthening* mixtures without a second thought. The venom may still be in my blood.'

Excitement from her idea brightened Ina's expression. When the alembic was half full and the witch's face a few shades whiter, Ina let Velka close the wound with the simple healing spell.

'Let's see what I remember from our university classes. It can't be harder than distilling moonshine,' she said with a smile, making the other woman sigh.

'It is not a moonshine, Striga. You will be performing blood magic. That is dangerous.'

'Not more dangerous than living with chaos and no anchor,' Ina said without looking at Velka as she weaved intricate patterns around the vessel. The witch's magic lit the room with a golden glow, fading into a dark crimson when her chaos altered the spell. The blood in the alembic bubbled and started separating.

Velka moved to the far corner of the room, observing Ina as she manipulated the pattern's threads while her blood stratified under the irresistible demands of her spell. The nature mage gasped when a thin green and oily layer appeared on the top of the liquid, and Ina reached for a glass pipette to gather it. This sudden noise broke the witch's focus, and her magic danced angrily in response.

'Velka, go downstairs.' The commanding tone of Ina's voice brooked no argument, and Velka quietly slipped from the room. Once the door was closed, the witch leaned over the alembic and transferred the foreign substance into a smaller vessel, biting her lip as she worried. *I know it's an impressive lab, but this would be much easier with fresh ingredients or a knowledgeable assistant.*

The thought of maintaining the spell as she worked left Ina sweating, making it difficult to read the labels on the jars, but she persevered, wiping her forehead with a dirty sleeve and pouring her strength into the enchantment. The green substance shivered as a wave of chaos nearly broke her concentration, making the witch curse as she tied off the spell and collapsed onto the nearest chair.

Despite finishing her experiment, Ina forgot to control her chaos, and the backlash shattered the alembic, spraying congealed blood and debris everywhere, but the witch didn't care. Her focus was on the liquid in the vial clasped in her hand, its colour now a shifting iridescence that defied description. *My bond with Ren might have faded, but not the one with Mar, and it disappeared before the confrontation with Marzanna, not forgetting the strange way my aunt encouraged me. It's too big a coincidence. This must be the cause. Mirena, what were you trying to do? If I'd lost control, you would be dead now.* Her thoughts were racing when she heard a soft knock at the door.

'Ina, are you alive?' Velka's voice made her smirk. It looked like the nature mage had little trust in her alchemic abilities.

'Yes, still alive and kicking, and I have something I can work with now. The room is safe, just a little messier.' When the door opened, Ina saw Velka frown, and her shoulders slumped as she entered the room.

'You're covered in blood and... whatever that sludge is in your hair.' Ina's friend sighed, looking around. 'This takes me back, but at least the room is mostly in one piece. Anyway, come downstairs. Rurik returned with supplies, locked himself in his room, and won't answer my questions.'

'I don't have the patience to deal with a male's tantrum. You used to bed the man, can't you deal with him?' Ina tried to offload the problem onto Velka to allow time to investigate her discovery, but her friend was persistent.

'No, trust me, something's very wrong. Have a little faith in my instincts for once.'

'Fine. I need to ask him about Mirena, anyway. Please sit down, your ankles already look like sausages. I will sort it out.' It took a moment to convince the nature mage to rest, but after gentle persuasion and some light blackmail, Velka went to her room.

When Ina went downstairs, she had to give it to Velka. Something was indeed very wrong. The revenants were frozen in place, creating an eerie tension as she walked past. When she stood in front of his room, the witch could hear smashing glass and cursing so explicit it would embarrass a sailor. Whatever had caused his anger must be significant, so taking a deep breath, Ina knocked.

'Rurik, we need to talk,' she said, not surprised as silence fell on the other side. 'Rurik, open the door, please, because if I open them, you will have a pleasant breeze in your room till the end of your stay here.'

She waited a moment, but soon the shuffling of feet and the sound of a turning key told her the necromancer was coming.

'What do you want?' he asked through a slit in the doorway.

Without another word, she pushed in, moving past the surprised man. Empty bottles of wine were everywhere, and looking back at him, she had to admit Rurik seemed as drunk as a log, barely able to stand up straight. Something in his trip to the nearest village had triggered this, and the witch was determined to find out what it was.

'Clean yourself up, or I'll drag you to the river by your ear. We need to talk,' she said, but the man roared with laughter.

'Like you're any better. I can smell the blood on you. Did you kill someone?' He returned to the chair and grabbed the nearest bottle, emptying its remains in one go.

'Rurik, what the hell happened? Why are you trying to drown yourself in liquor?' she asked, coming closer and moving the next bottle out of his reach.

'My life, my useless life, the things I did, all for nothing. I hoped I would make things better, make them even. With you, we had a chance. Now all is lost.' His muttered words made no sense, and she barely understood the last passage when sobs overtook his body, and he covered his face with his hands.

Rurik looked like a man who'd lost everything, and Ina was the worst person to try consoling him, so instead, she decided to distract him. The witch took his hands, uncovering his face and exposing the raw grief he tried to hide.

'Why did you bring us north, Rurik?' Ina took a chance, using her intuition. 'Why are we in Mirena's house? Who is she to you?'

Rurik stared at her for a long time, visibly debating with himself until she raised an eyebrow. 'Yes, you're right. You deserve to know. It won't change anything, and Veles will punish me for my actions. Mirena is my mother, you are in our ancestral home, and I brought you here because I had nowhere else to go.'

'Your mother?' Ina's shocked face made him laugh.

'Oh, you must have heard the gossip of the scandalous debutante who fell pregnant to some rake who died protesting his paramour's wedding to Cyrus Thorn. When everyone knew Roda took a fancy to her and ruined the girl's life. Not the first lady-in-waiting to be treated that way, and likely not the last.'

'I didn't know Mirena suffered through that. I knew her marriage had a rough start, with no children for years, but I never knew this. You were given away?' Ina gently touched his face, lost at what to say at such a tragedy, but Rurik pushed her away and stood up unsteadily.

'Given away? That sounds so civilised compared to reality. Mirena's house couldn't have a king's bastard in the family. What a threat to the kingdom. I was ripped from my mother's bosom and sold into slavery in the North. I don't remember much from childhood except the pain, orders, and whips that often marked my back. That's why I wanted to change it, so no one else would suffer,' he said, yanking his shirt off while Ina scrambled to stand up.

The witch gasped when his scars were revealed, the barbaric marks where slaver's whips had torn the skin covered his back. She tried to blink away the tears, but the history of pain written on his skin was overwhelming.

'I'm sorry. For what it's worth, I'm sorry. I will talk to Rewan. He will outlaw it, I'm sure of it.' At Ina's words, Rurik's head snapped up, and he rushed forward, grabbing the front of her dress.

'Rewan?! Rewan...? No! Ina, you should be our salvation. You and your chaos can stop it all. I did this for you, to ascend above the throne as the chaos archmage, wielding the power of the regalia. I did this so you can change the world, but you just threw it away for Rewan and that dragon.'

The zeal burning in the necromancer's eyes, whilst disturbing, didn't frighten Ina, but the words shocked her to the core. *Was he behind events in the South?* Crimson wisps filled the air with the sweet scent of decay, but Ina didn't try to control them this time.

'Tell me what you did, or even Veles will pale at what's left of your soul. Now remove your hands from my dress or lose them, death master.' Her voice, cold and menacing, broke through Rurik's fervour, his fingers loosening their hold as he collapsed, sobbing once more.

'Death master? Puppet master, you mean. From the Black Forest and Osterad to Liath, I arranged it all. That was supposed to be the crowning moment—*pfft*, literally—but no, you solved that masterstroke without even trying, so then I turned to the South and piled the problems so high I knew you'd take the circlet. What a fool I was. Why didn't you take the chaos regalia in Liath? Why, Ina? You could have controlled them all, overseeing peace throughout Warenga with kings bowing at your feet.' He grabbed another bottle, lost in his hubris, whilst Ina stood there, her body shaking as rage burned throughout her body.

'You helped Sophia and brought Tar'eth to Liath to make me into some all-powerful saviour? Like Empress Sowenna, breaker of the world?' The punch that followed sent the necromancer stumbling backwards. Ina flexed her hand as a vortex of magic raged around her. 'So many dead, tortured, mutilated.... Gods help me, but I want to kill you so much right now.'

The witch struggled to control herself, her magic nipping and biting as it lifted Rurik off the ground. The voices whispering of dark revenge, of painful, righteous justice, clamoured for her attention. She could tear his soul apart for his crimes with no remorse, but as she lifted her hand, the view of his scars made her hesitate. The moment passed so quickly that Ina dismissed the feeling, readying to exact her revenge, when the doors behind her suddenly crashed open.

'Inanuan Zoria Thornsen, what the hell is going on here?!' Velka stood at the threshold, the coils of Lada's Zmij wrapped around her, protecting the nature mage from the maelstrom of chaos. Ina felt the urge to reach for that beautiful creature and take its magic along with the woman he defended. The smile that flashed on Ina's face made Velka gasp, but instead of flinching, her friend stepped into the room.

As if approaching a dangerous predator, Velka walked closer till she faced Ina. When she reached out to touch the witch's chest, Ina saw how much Velka's hand was shaking.

'Striga, come back to me, please. Whatever he said, you are right to be angry, but you are not a murderer. Please let him down. You are the strongest person I know. Don't give in to the anger.' The plea, filled with tears, touched something inside the witch, and Ina pressed Velka's hand to her chest, feeling the darkness subside until she could finally reason again.

'You shouldn't have come here. If you see me like this, run as fast and far away as possible. Never risk your life for me,' she said, looking to the side, lowering ashen-faced Rurik to the ground. The chaos dissipated, and Ina closed her eyes as Velka stroked her hair affectionately.

'I will do what I feel is right, so don't bother. I know your heart. You would never hurt me. I doubt many things in life, but I've never doubted you, so please tell me what got you so distressed that you almost lost killed Rurik?'

Ina looked at the necromancer as he regained consciousness and shook her head. 'He admitted orchestrating the palace coup, the winter war and unrest in the South... in order to make me into a second Sowenna. All this time, I thought it was me, my magic, that caused all the atrocities, but no, it was him. Oh, Velka, I'm so tired of fighting, of trying to hold back the chaos. I want my bonds, my dragon, my moonlight warrior, and my sweet, sweet Boruta. Everything in me is so volatile, Flower. I'm sorry for being such a mess. I shouldn't place this on your shoulders.'

'He did what?' Velka looked at Ina, outrage clear on her face, before approaching Rurik and ruthlessly kicking him. 'Daro almost died because of that, you arsehole, and Ina... and Mar was changed into a dragon. What is wrong with you?' She burst into tears while the necromancer spat bloody saliva on the floor.

Ina rushed to her friend, hugging her close. 'Shh... please let me do this. I'm calm now and promise to find the truth without too much blood, but I don't want you to see what happens, so go to the garden and relax.'

'But your chaos?' Velka tried to oppose, but Ina placed her hand on Velka's tummy.

'I'm calm and much less angry. Everything will be fine, but I must find out what Rurik knows to plan our next move. Please trust me.'

Reluctantly, Velka left the room, and as soon as the doors closed behind her, Ina turned to Rurik, who had already crawled back on the chair and poured himself more wine.

'I will tell you everything, so there's no need for torture. I lost, and I'm ready to pay for my crimes. I knew I would die for what I'd done, but I thought justice and protection for those unable to defend themselves were worth it. Now I'm nothing more than a villain in my own story, ready for judgment.'

Ina dragged the remaining chair over and sat opposite him. 'Well, I'm here now, your fabled archmage. Tell me your illustrious plan for making me the second Sowenna and how this would help anyone.'

As Rurik related his story, Ina squirmed, uncomfortable with the abuse he'd suffered. Rurik had been a child slave forced to labour on the docks of Dancik until the fateful day when his magic awakened, raising his dead friend and killing his master. After looking through their ledgers, he'd found his way to Mirena, and despite her initial awkwardness and hostility, she soon warmed up to her newly returned son and even sent him to the Magical University, where he'd met Velka and Ina. Through them, he found acceptance, and when the witch had her "little accident" with the frog, his outlook on life changed entirely. Rurik found his saviour, the mage who could reshape the world to make it a better place. Ina was shocked to realise she admired his goals and that, instead of seeking petty revenge, he'd used his torment to try, however misguided, to help others.

It took a second bottle of wine, but he described sharing his ideas with Mirena, her initial scepticism, and how, after he mentioned removing Roda from the throne, she changed her mind and actively helped. Unfortunately for them, Ina had shown her claws in court and was banished to the Black Forest.

'Well, I'm sorry I spoiled your plans.' The witch's voice dripped with sarcasm, but Rurik just smiled.

'Spoiled, no—merely delayed, and maybe for the better, as the Iron Empire envoy noticed your presence. His interest was... intense and disturbing. So I took your absence as an opportunity to better prepare everything. Cornovii's court, Verdante, the southern march, and the drows all rubbed their hands together in glee at my plans. Only the elven court didn't fall under my influence. All it took was money, and greed did the rest.'

'And where did you get the money from?' She pointed at the state of their surroundings. The amount needed to open the doors of the royal courts must have been immense.

'My mother supplied them. And no, before you ask, I don't know where they came from. I was so blinded by my cause and the many plans I controlled that I never asked... I preferred not to ask. I was such a fool.' Rurik was getting drunker and drunker, but while he continued, Ina didn't mind.

Ina had to admit Rurik's manipulations were nothing short of brilliant. Supporting Sophia's coup to remove Roda, using Ina's formula to end her exile, then supplying her peridot to Gruff for it to find its way into the witch's hands. He hadn't even waited to see the outcome of that scheme before whispering in Tar'eth's ear about the chaos regalia, helping him to claim the ring and find whispers of the circlet hidden beneath the Grey Mountains, knowing chaos-tainted drow couldn't resist the temptation.

The necromancer looked at Ina. 'After the battle of Liath, I knew you were ready. Lady of the Crimson Veil is such a perfect name for you. You fought with a frightening ruthlessness, then ended the conflict with such mercy and generosity that you created two new alliances and a hesitant peace with the drows. The king followed your advice, and I almost stopped there, but something—someone pushed me south to finish our work. I should have known all mother cared about was revenge, but I was blind to her plans.'

'Let me guess, while you were creating havoc in Liath, Mirena made sure the South would rebel, and to achieve this, she incapacitated my grandfather, turning him into a raving maniac. Not that he was a nice man to begin with, but he was never a stupid one.' Ina reached for the bottle. It all felt overwhelming, and she wasn't sure she could face more revelations sober.

'I had my doubts, and once I understood she wanted to destroy Cornovii, I tried to help you. Verdante didn't abandon their ally just because the king showed up with the dragons,' he said. In drunken despair, Rurik kneeled before her. 'Forgive me. I didn't know she would bring the Iron Empire here. I'm not asking for my life as I deserve to die, but I didn't know that she would sell us all—sell her son to see Cornovii destroyed.'

The witch gasped when he embraced her legs, begging for redemption, but she couldn't give him this mercy. She pushed him away, averting her gaze to not see the depth of despair in his dark eyes and the scars on his back.

'I can't forgive you, Rurik. It is not in my power or my heart to forgive your crimes; the deaths of Liander's victims, of Sophia's coup, or the kobolds and soldiers who suffered and died because of Tar'eth's madness. I cannot absolve your guilt for those starved in the South, and the poor souls sacrificed to bind Marzanna. My mercy means nothing to those you have wronged. Perhaps you can find absolution when you stand before Veles, but never from me.' Ina stood up. She had heard enough. She was a judicial mage, and now it was her decision if he lived or died for his crimes, but the rage burning in her soul prevented her from making an impartial judgement. *The monster that created you is outside my reach, and I can't blame your intentions, just your deeds*, she thought, turning to leave, but Rurik's voice stopped her.

'The Iron Empire has taken Dancik. The vanguard army arrived to destroy all I hoped to preserve, and more will follow. People say the Iron

Emperor himself is leading the invasion. All is lost, Ina, and I am the reason for this.'

The witch looked at him sitting on the floor and shook her head. 'I'm still alive, and there is more to Cornovii than one crimson witch. Sober up because tomorrow we will work on stabilising my magic and returning to Osterad. Perhaps then you'll be allowed to repair some of the damage you have created.'

CHAPTER EIGHT

She let him live. No one was more surprised than Ina, and the beautiful blue sky seemed to mock the foul mood her choice had created. Yesterday, she'd almost killed the necromancer, but even though he deserved to die for the suffering he'd caused, the witch wasn't sure she could make a rational decision when it came to Rurik.

Her night terrors were back, and the visions of a desolate desert with bleached bones lying under a crimson sun robbed her of sleep. Add to that her guilt at not dragging Rurik to Osterad and the even more disturbing desire to tear the magic from his soul meant Ina was closer to breaking than she'd ever felt before.

The possibility of becoming a world breaker worried her the most. Without Mar and Ren to help, something inside her soul was eroding, and she lost her temper more and more. First, she'd caused the storm, and then her hold on chaos had slipped in the alchemy workshop. If not for Velka's intervention, Rurik would be a sad, wet mess splattered across the room.

The quest to restore her bond was no longer about the ability to control her magic, but about survival itself. *You never know how much you rely on something until it's gone*, she thought, rubbing her chest. The safety of the bond and the power of two stones made her reckless—arrogant, even. Now, she was worse off than before that hairy oaf was dumped on her doorstep. At least then, she'd had a modicum of control over her emotions.

Thankfully, the situation wasn't a complete loss. With Rurik's confession, his plotting, at least its core, was laid bare, and without his interference, Liath and the South were as safe as they could be. The threat of invasion by the Iron Empire had terrified the necromancer enough to lock himself away and seek the oblivion of intoxication. That left Ina with a dilemma: did she travel to Osterad and warn the king of this latest threat, or try to repair her bonds so she could help defend the country from invasion?

'Right, let's try to fix my magic first. There's no point in warning Rewan of an invasion if I lose my mind and kill everyone,' she said, before turning from her inspection of the ceiling and sitting up. Ina looked at her clothes. Ayni's armour and the simple dress she used to cover it were all she had, but for the alchemy workshop, she needed clothes that were easily replaced after any of her usual accidents. Her gaze fell on the storage chest next to the bed, and determined to find some work clothes, Ina opened the trunk to find a violet dress with lots of frills and puffy sleeves, which had been fashionable before she was born. The witch looked at the monstrosity, grinning at finding perfection for her messy experiments.

It took her a moment to push her bosom into the dress, but Velka's horrified gasp was well worth it when she saw her at the top of the stairs.

'Do you like it?' Ina asked, twirling extravagantly before Velka grasped her shoulders.

'So it finally happened. The last thread of sanity abandoned your wretched soul, and now you think you're the Empress Sowenna. Ina, what happened yesterday? Could I have saved you from this if I'd stayed?' she asked, shaking her friend frantically.

'Don't be silly, Velka. I just found some old clothes I can ruin without worrying. I'm sorry for scaring you last night, but I promise I'm calm enough to focus on repairing my bonds now.'

Understanding brightened Velka's eyes. During their university days, Ina had always returned from alchemy class with stained, ripped, or burnt clothes; sometimes all three. 'Damm it, Striga, you should have told me. I thought you'd lost your marbles after yesterday's discussion with Rurik.' Velka relaxed her grip, laughing with relief.

'So you can face me down when I'm about to destroy the world, but one look at me in a dress, and you're terrified?' Ina enjoyed the absurdity of the moment before sobering. 'I will be in the workshop. If you see Rurik, send him up. I'll need his help to find out what poison Mirena poured into me.' Ina turned to leave, but Velka grabbed her wrist.

'Why do you ask for him? He's the source of all our problems. I stopped you from killing him, but I didn't intend for you to trust him. I can help you identify the herbs—'

'In any other circumstances, I would gladly accept, but you are with child, and my experiments usually end badly. I can spoil this dress and won't shed a tear for Rurik's sudden demise, but I wouldn't forgive myself if something happened to you,' Ina said, gently prying herself from her friend's grip, pretending not to see Velka's sullen expression.

As soon as she stepped over the workshop threshold, Ina rushed towards the vial of toxic essence she had extracted yesterday. The sample looked so small, and the witch sighed quietly, knowing she'd have to bleed herself more before finding the answer. Still, it was a good place to start. Ina put a few drops on a piece of fabric, burning it over a small flame, observing the reaction. The flame was bright with some strange golden hue, and the scent accompanying it was like tree sap.

The witch found some paper and noted her observations before setting up several vials, adding a different herbal and magical reagent to each, only stopping to mumble something at a knock on the door before noticing Rurik slip into the room.

'Good. Tell me what your mother's favourite poisons were, and if you know what she used to dissolve my bond, tell me now and spare me all this trouble.' After last night, she still felt hostile and didn't intend to hide it. Rurik nodded and approached the table, looking at the vials.

'I don't know what she used. I didn't even know she was planning to do something like this. You are right to doubt me. I did terrible things that cannot be forgiven, but I never meant to harm you. This is Mirena's doing, and Ina I... I may have been careless in the town yesterday. It's only a matter of time before she or the emperor comes for you with a small army.'

Ina stopped working for a moment before extending her forearm to him.

'Well, then we don't have time to spare. Draw more blood,' she said, pulling up her sleeve. 'Why didn't she simply kill me? It would have been easy when I arrived dying from swamp fever or again after I broke the curse. Why target the bond?'

'Because destroying Cornovii is her only goal,' Rurik said, and Ina looked at him sharply. 'Don't look at me like that, Ina. I didn't know it till it was too late. I wanted to unite the continent under the chaos archmage. Weakening them before you could step in was a well-calculated move meant to minimise deaths as you rose to power. My mother, though, had different plans. Did you tell her what the bond meant to your magic?'

Ina groaned as she realised she had done precisely that. After snapping out a quick curse, she explained. 'I told Aunt Mirena everything; she was of great comfort during my stay, helping me with my problems.'

'Now you know why she jeopardised your magic and brought the Iron Empire here. She used us both, but at least you have a valid excuse.'

'You, of all people, have no right to complain, and she hasn't used me yet,' Ina said, observing the drop of her blood fizzing sluggishly when it came into contact with the essence of hawthorn seeds. The reaction was less effervescent than she had expected, but all ingredients in this room were ancient, and the witch was happy it had worked at all.

'So she used oleander oil. I'm lucky to be alive. Let's see what other poisons the old hag used on me.'

Rurik cast a troubled glance in her direction when she passed him a vial of black fluid and asked to rotate it slowly while she poured the extracted poison into it.

'I haven't seen this potion before. What exactly are you attempting?'

'I'm trying to nullify the magic used on this potion in order to extract the components, using a simple mixture of aqua regia, antimony and a touch of chaos, so don't drop it unless you want that conversation with Veles sooner rather than later.' Ina smirked, seeing Rurik's hands tremble.

'Do you want to kill us all?' he whispered, hypnotised by the fluid in the glass.

'No, but it looks like you do. Steady your hand and rotate it slowly before you cause an explosion,' she said, watching the ingredients as they separated. Ina brought over a rack of vials and poured each element into a different container, smirking to herself at the unfortunate necromancer's efforts to keep his hand steady. 'You can stop now. I have all I need.'

When he sighed with relief, Ina passed him some chalk and a piece of paper with alchemical symbols transcribed into a sigil. 'Draw it on the floor—and do it as neatly as possible, please.' The necromancer nodded and began drawing the symbols expertly, slowly constructing the sigil while Ina observed him, biting her lip. The idea for this sigil, one able to detect the type of spell Mirena had used on the mixture, had come to her yesterday. She combined a stabilising net with an advanced detection spell usually employed to find mages, hoping it would follow the trace of Mirena's magic. Now she only needed to saturate it with chaos and her blood to see if it worked.

'How long will this process take? Until you can restore your connection?' Rurik asked, rising from the floor, efficiently completing his task.

'Why? You have somewhere to be?' Ina's sarcastic tone made him lower his head, and the witch sighed. 'I don't know. I have to find a way of countering the potion, then if that doesn't restore the bond, find a spell that can. Why are you asking?'

'We are on borrowed time here. Those savages won't stop at Dancik. Soon, this place will be overrun by them or my mother's people. In these circumstances, would you consider taking the last piece of regalia?'

'You still won't give up on making me your magical overlord? The answer is still no, now more than ever. You underestimate Cornovii and Rewan. He is an excellent strategist, and he has Mar as his lord marshal. Without the bond, uniting the chaos regalia could turn me into the bane of this world, and the Iron Empire would be the last of your worries when I lay waste to everything.'

'You can't be sure. Maybe it would help you contain the chaos,' Rurik said quietly, but his words made Ina laugh.

'Maybe, but do you really want to test this theory now when I can barely hold myself together, trying not to kill my dearest friend every time I stub my toe?' Ina approached the necromancer with strands of chaos dancing around her, looking up to meet his eyes, her gaze devoid of anger, holding only sadness and resignation.

'I'm sorry. I thought I could change the world, but I made everything worse. Pride comes before the fall, and I fell to the depths of Nawia, but please let me help you because the Iron Empire respects nothing but brutal strength, and I know their ways. You can kill me later.'

'What is with this death wish of yours? I will do it my way. No sacrificial victims or chaos regalia needed.' Ina snapped and turned towards the sigil.

'Guard the door from the other side. I don't want anybody here when I start the spell.'

Ina studied Rurik, who nodded and exited, locking the door from the other side. After undressing from her hideous frock, she stood in the centre of the sigil and, with a long precise stroke, sliced open the vein on her forearm, letting it saturate the chalk markings before she compressed the cut with a strip of fabric.

She could feel the chaos magic in her blood, and, closing her eyes, the witch chanted the spell quietly. The sigil hissed as crimson flames burned through the blood, energising the enchantment, and the witch gasped when her bonds appeared, connected to her midriff, fading into the void behind the sigil's borders. *They're still there!* Her rushing thoughts radiated joy when she tried to touch them, but as much as the bonds were visible under her spell, she felt nothing as her fingers passed through the glittering tethers, her senses blunted.

The witch muttered to herself, letting her magic dissipate in the air. She burned the remains of her blood off the floor to not leave any anchors for someone to use against her, and redressing, she sat next to the workshop table.

Six vials with mysterious substances stood there mocking her when the witch, frowning, sniffed each one. 'She poisoned me with oleander, and two of the vials smell like nightshade and henbane. She must have numbed my senses with something, but which is the oleander?' Ina knew one of them must contain the sap, and lighting a piece of paper, she moved it over them; the toxic fumes quickly identified it, and that vial was isolated. The rest of the day was a blur as the witch tested and probed the remaining three vials to reveal their contents.

By the end of the day, her eyes were red and sore from the fumes. Half blind from it, Ina tripped over a sleeping Rurik as she prepared to leave. His overworked mind had been resting after their labours, and as he fell to the floor, the necromancer woke, cursing in confusion, making Ina chuckle.

'You took this task more seriously than I expected. Please inform Velka I will be downstairs shortly. I just need to change.' She pointed to the wet and charred remains of her dress before leaving the room.

When they gathered in the drawing room, Ina looked at Velka's pouting expression and pulled her braid.

'Stop it, Flower. I've looked worse, and you know it. You couldn't be in the room with all those poisons, but thankfully that is done with now, so I will happily accept your help.'

'Help you how? Did you figure out what happened with your bonds?' Velka's mood instantly changed from surly to vivid interest, and Ina chuckled slightly.

'The bond is still there, but Mirena somehow suppressed my ability to access it. I know how to reverse the damage, but I need your help. I need mugwort and amanitarii mortis to create the antidote, everything else I found in the workshop.'

Velka looked at her and shook her head. 'I can grow mugwort, but amanitarii? Ina, why do you need *The Quick Death*?' Velka used the assassin's term for the fungus. Ina gave her an apologetic smile, knowing her friend wouldn't take her following words calmly.

'I need to get as close to death as possible to unravel Mirena's spell while the mugwort and aqua vitae cleanse my body.'

'You are out of your fucking mind if you think I will let you kill yourself for this! You have been such an ass the last few days. Here I am, beside myself with worry for Daro, and now you want me to help you with this? I will not do it. Besides, amanitarii is hard to find and grows only in the swamps.'

'I can send the revenants to retrieve your herbs, but is this a good idea?' Rurik said, ducking as Velka's fist almost hit his face.

'Shut your mouth and do not make the situation worse.' Velka was in berserk mode, and Ina approached her friend.

'Without the bond, I'm as good as dead. No, you're as good as dead, and I can't have that on my conscience. Mirena and the Iron Empire are coming after me, according to Rurik. Eventually, I'll be forced to use chaos, or something else will tip me over the edge, and I'll grab it with both hands. Then everything I love will be destroyed. It will be up to Mar to kill me because, somehow, our connection made him resistant to my magic. How can I burden him with this? I may die using this poison, but I won't go down without a fight, so Flower... Velka, please help me.'

Velka looked at her with a deep frown until she snapped. 'Fine, I will grow your mugwort, and dimwit here can send his minions for amanitarii. But if you die on me, Striga, I will force Rurik to bring you back, and I will make your corpse wear that bloody violet frivolity for eternity. You are worried about your bond, but what about our bond? Mar can't watch you die, but I can? You've been my friend longer than you've known that overgrown handbag.'

Ina gently squeezed Velka's hand and nodded to Rurik. 'Send the revenants, please. The sooner, the better, and find me when it is done. There are a few details we need to discuss.' When Rurik left the room, Ina turned towards her friend, noticing how she barely held back her tears.

'Come, let's cook ourselves a nice meal. We've had nothing special since we left Thorn. Maybe we can even find some wine left from Rurik's supplies. That would be the perfect solution for all our sorrows. I promise from the depths of my rotten heart not to die on you.' Ina smiled, trying to cheer her friend, but Velka shook her head.

'No, I will go to the garden. Mugwort takes a lot of time to mature, even with magic, but give me two days, and I will grow some suitable for your needs.' Velka turned to leave, but before disappearing, she shook her head, and Ina heard her muttering. 'I don't like it. As if I'm not worrying myself grey over Daro, she wants help poisoning herself. Bloody reckless striga, never stops to think.'

Alone in the room, Ina sat in the armchair and pulled her knees up. Velka's words stung, but she wasn't reckless this time; simply determined to hold on to her sanity. The dreams she endured weren't just unconscious fears, but an actual threat to everything Ina held dear. No, there was no other way. Maybe with time and a better workshop, she could find a less dangerous solution, but the witch lacked both time and resources, and the clues she'd found in Mirena's journals pointed to this solution.

Ina looked up when Rurik walked into the room. He was still the same tall, handsome man, his beard sprinkled with grey flecks. Still, in the last few days, his shoulders had slumped. The once proud necromancer had been replaced by a lost and defeated soul, desperate to find redemption for the futile schemes. *There are stupid ideas, and then there's Rurik, trying to end suffering using a flawed mage with dangerous magic. It would have made a good joke if his vision hadn't cost countless lives*, Ina thought, observing him when he approached her.

Maybe it was his charm or belief in the possibility of a better world, but she didn't want to kill him. She knew she should, but knowing him better and learning the motivation behind his idiotic campaign, she struggled to hate the man despite his deeds.

'Sit down, please. We need to talk.' Ina waited till he found a chair and looked at her. 'I want you to take Velka to Osterad as soon as I have all the ingredients. If the situation is as bad as you say, I need to get her to safety, and I don't want her here when it's time to use the antidote.'

'You shouldn't be alone when you take it. Velka was right about the dangers,' Rurik said, and she heard the hesitation in his voice.

'That's another reason to take her to Osterad. If my magic slips from my control, best everyone I love to be far away from here,' Ina said with a smile, and when he nodded, she continued. 'When you arrive in Osterad, you will hand yourself over to the judicial mages. I know you saved my life, but you must face the consequences of your actions. I can promise you one thing. Once I regain control over chaos, I will do my best to stop the Iron Empire. Now give me your hand. I don't trust you enough to care for Velka without ensuring her safety.'

'I would not betray either of you, Ina. How often must I tell you I did all this for you and a better future? I will do what you request, but if you spare my life, I can help. My knowledge of the North, the Iron Empire, and research of chaos magic would be invaluable,' Rurik said, and didn't flinch when Ina cut their forearms, mixing their blood while he repeated the oath promising to care for Velka and protect her from all danger. Magic filled the room, awakened by his words, sealing the minor wounds as the echoes of the covenant faded.

'It's not up to me to punish or absolve you. I'm in the centre of this shitstorm, which makes me biased, but Jorge is fair, and he will know what to do. Make sure you deliver Velka safely to her husband. As for the rest, we will wait and see.' Ina looked through the window, giving herself a moment to admire the green meadows and blue sky. All seemed so peaceful, like the world around them was not at war. 'I'm sorry for your past. For what it's worth, once things settle, if I'm still alive, I will make sure Dancik adheres to the laws of Cornovii,' she said, and the necromancer stood up, smiling sadly.

'That is the spirit that inspired me all those years ago. I will do my best to protect Velka,' he said, leaving Ina alone with her thoughts.

CHAPTER NINE

After a brief stop in Osterad, Mar lost track of the hours he spent airborne. Now, his wings trembled with every beat, the formerly powerful movements weak and slow. It didn't matter, though, as each time he thought of Ina's predicament, he felt a surge of rage-driven strength that soon brought him to the foothills of the Grey Mountains.

Mar briefly considered stopping at the castle to rest, but he could not allow himself the luxury now that he finally had a way to find his missing witch. Once he'd flown deep into the mountain range, it didn't take long to find the small valley they'd spent a brief respite, reaffirming their feelings, and as he descended, it made him smile, seeing it was as beautiful as he'd expected, before his weary body ploughed a rough furrow in the field of wildflowers.

'Ouch. Fine, I admit it; I need a rest.' Mar closed his eyes, too exhausted to find a better position, promptly falling asleep. Despite the warmth of summer, it was still high in the mountains, and as the sun set, the chill air woke the dragon, so he dragged his sore body to the hot spring, transforming as he fell forward into the welcome heat, sighing as it eased the pain of his overworked muscles.

'How do I call Skarbnik to me, my spitfire?' he asked, as if the stars could answer him. He knew what Ina would do, smiling at the thought. *She would stand here shouting and cursing to Nawia till the god answered or blast the hole in the solid rock to get his attention*. Mar looked at the granite walls, almost invisible beneath the veil of darkness, and his lips quirked. That was precisely what he'd do when the sun rose over the horizon. He would shout Skarbnik's name till the old god took notice. As the hot water from the mountains' heart slowly relaxed him, Mar fell into a long dreamless sleep.

If Mar thought the air was cold last evening, it was nothing to the temperature after a cloudless night, and while his body was warm, there was an embarrassing icicle hanging from his beard as he woke to greet the day. Breaking off the cold protuberance, the dragon stood and exited the pool, shivering as he clad himself in the armour of his kind. Strolling to the granite cliff, the warrior remembered there had been a tunnel entrance here, leading directly to Empress Sowenna's tomb, and now Mar was going to try his luck. He hammered the wall with his fist, making a dent in the rock.

'Lord of the Mountain, Marcach, son of Liath, requests an audience!' he shouted, unsure what to say, and waited for an answer, but the wall ignored his plea with the indifference of aeons. He hadn't expected an answer immediately, but had to admit he felt disheartened by the silence. Mar repeated his call, using every name Skarbnik was known by, but no matter how he begged, demanded, or cursed, the mountain remained unresponsive.

Hours later, Mar looked at the mountain as tears began tracking dusty trails over his cheeks. His hands were bleeding, and frustrated anger was building to a crescendo, fuelled by the sense of impotence. The gods were happy to use Ina, but no one answered when she needed help.

'You pig-headed whoreson, why won't you listen to me? Ina needs your help, you ignorant bastard. How long must I stand here like a desperate beggar while the woman I love is isolated and in danger?!' Mar shouted towards the wall, stepping back as the mist of the other swept across its surface, but before he could reach for his dragon half, the murk faded away, revealing a robust old man glaring back at him.

'What do you think you're doing, hatchling? Look what you've done to my mountain, impatient wretch.' The disgruntled god reached out, slapped the dragon on the side of the head, and turned to walk back into the cliff face, a tunnel opening as he stepped forward. Mar rushed towards him, anxious Skarbnik would close the entrance to spite him, but the old god just gave him a scornful glare when Mar almost ran into his back.

'Forgive me, my lord. Ina, the mage you gifted with the orein, is missing. I came here to ask for the last piece of Sowenna's regalia, as this is my only hope of finding her,' Mar said, lowering his head, ready to beg and weep if this gave him the circlet.

'No, I told her the diadem will be here if she wants it. For her, not you, hatchling,' the mountain god said and turned to leave, but Mar stepped forward, blocking his way.

'What does it matter who takes it? I need it to find her. You said the circlet belongs to her, so why don't you allow me to remove it? The bond is broken, and if Ina loses control of her magic, the consequences for the world will be catastrophic. Name your price; I will do whatever you ask.' With desperation in his voice, the dragon nearly fell to his knees to beg as he tried to convince the old god to agree.

'Even if I take you to the crypt, you won't be able to take it. The chaos regalia only obey a chaos archmage. If you try to pry it from the rightful owner's body without chaos in your blood, you'll be lucky if death finds you quickly. The autumn child was right to leave the circlet behind, and whilst you have good intentions, I can't let you touch it.' Skarbnik looked at Mar's body coiled in fury. 'I feel pity for you, dragon. So I will give you some answers. She is not in Liath. I would sense her if she were. Leave the mountains and search for her as other mortals would.'

His last statement was greeted with the explosion of the dragon's rage. Mar partially transformed as he grabbed the god's tunic. 'I make my own choices, treasurer. Lead me to the circlet, and if it kills me, so be it. I will leave Liath with the means to find Ina or as a spirit to Nawia. Either way, you never have to hear from me again.'

'How could I deny such a polite child when he asks to die?' Skarbnik's body grew, pushing Mar back and breaking his hold, the mountain god's voice filled with amusement. 'So hotheaded and ready to risk it all. Are you ready to challenge the gods for her? I'm unsure if I should commend your bravery or laugh at your stupidity, but I will grant you your wish. If it doesn't kill you, you can take the circlet, but your lady won't thank you. The crimson fury inside her grows daily, and she took a hard path to contain it. You should let nature take its course.'

Mar staggered forward and bowed deeply, apologetically. 'No, my lord, I'm afraid I can't let that happen, not if there's the slightest chance I can help her. Ina is my world. Please, show me to Sowenna's tomb so that I may find her.'

'If only it were that simple, hatchling. Follow me, and do not think to complain when Ina curses your name for interfering. I tried to warn you.' Skarbnik turned and opened the passage in the solid wall, just like before. Mar followed him, trying to keep pace with the ancient being, nearly missing Skarbnik's following words.

'I hope it ends better this time. The autumn child is strong, but they all fall for the elusive lure of chaos.'

'How did Sowenna come to be buried in your mountains? The drow kingdoms are so far west, yet her burial crypt is in the heart of your realm,' Mar asked, unable to contain his curiosity.

'Her son brought her here after ending her life. She begged him to stop her, tearing the ring from her finger to accomplish it. When he used its power to tear the necklace from her throat, killing her, the princeling brought her body here to protect it from the raging mob. I hope you have the strength to love Ina as much if she loses her battle with chaos.'

Mar stared at Skarbnik, horrified. 'Why do you think I'm here? I will stand with Ina before the gates of Nawia and offer her my last breath to hold back chaos. My spitfire is not Sowenna to bow to madness or gods who toy with her life.' Mar clenched his fists, not liking where this discussion was heading, especially when Skarbnik's derisive laughter mocked his statement.

'Isn't she? I haven't seen a chaos mage who could resist the seduction of rebirth. Destruction is only one side of chaos, but from death comes life, and in the end, they all lose themselves in the power of creation. Do you think Sowenna reshaped the world because she enjoyed gardening?'

Skarbnik marched forward purposefully, forcing Mar to jog in order to keep up. 'Ina is different. She also has Ren; the bond we share will protect her,' he said, breaking into a run that came to an abrupt halt when they entered Sowenna's crypt, still glowing with its strange green light.

'Ah, the bond, the famous sacrifice spell the Leshy's child performed to bind your heart and soul for eternity. Do you think it will protect you now? The relic stones Sowenna harnessed to make the regalia are older than even the dragons, each one still connected to the mother stone in the source of life, and you think you can tame it because of your bond. I will lay your bones next to Sowenna's as a warning to all those who reach for a power they were not meant to have.'

Mar looked at the god, inscrutable as the mountain they walked beneath, and snarled his disdain. 'Whatever you say, it won't deter me. Do you think she would turn away if my life were in danger? Because right now, she is

in danger, not just from those who wish to harm her, but from the magic
that is part of her soul. So if you've finished demeaning the people who
care about the world you're supposed to protect, I'd like to complete my
mission.'

Skarbnik bowed, mockery clear in every movement, and Mar slowly
approached the sarcophagus. He could feel the enormous power contained
within the crystal casket, feeling it blister his soul as it pulsed like the
heartbeat of the mountain. Despite his earlier declaration, he felt hesitation
rising in his heart. He hadn't looked closely at the empress during their last
expedition. Now he could see green lines of power beneath her skin, giving
Sowenna's body the illusion of life. Ina had wanted to avoid touching the
last piece, asking him to hold her when the stone's power tried to force her
mind into compliance. Mar cursed under his breath, stopping beside the
carved stone and looking at the face of the last chaos archmage.

The ethereal, beautiful face, untouched by decay, lay in serene repose,
and Mar wondered why she looked so peaceful after the destruction
wrought by the magic she contained, which even now drew the dragon
forward with its deadly allure.

'There would be no shame in giving up,' taunted the voice behind him,
and Mar closed his eyes, fighting the urge to retaliate.

'Forgive me, my lady,' he said, reaching for the diadem in the most
respectful way he could.

Mar didn't know what to expect. Ina's peridot necklace, a permanent
fixture on her body, felt as warm and inviting as her beautiful soul. He
could feel its power whenever his fingers brushed against the gently pulsing
stone, but not once did it feel like a dangerous weapon.

However, as his fingers brushed against the stone in the circlet, Mar's
muscles locked as a torrent of power tore through his body, flinging him,
twitching and shaking to the floor. His dragon half tried to protect him by

forcing the transformation, but Mar resisted, scales appearing and disappearing as he fought to remain conscious.

'Just let go, and the pain will stop.' The voice, devoid of emotion, came from nowhere and everywhere, crushing his mind in an agonising vise, but it focused his mind, and Mar looked down at his hand. All he needed for this torment to stop was to relax his finger and let the golden diadem fall to the ground. This thought was so appealing that the dragon's fingers twitched, trying to comply. *Was this how Ina felt healing me? And Ren?* Mar thought, remembering her torn face when he forced her to perform the sacrifice spell for Ren. Shame and regret filled his thoughts, firming his courage and determination. If his woman could withstand it, twice, then why was he, a warrior and dragon, even considering surrendering? Forcing his hand to move, Mar drew the circlet closer to his face.

'Stop trying to burn my insides to a crisp. All I want is to bring you to your rightful owner so you can be with your brothers again. Search inside me instead of causing so much pain, and you'll know I'm telling the truth,' he ground out through gritted teeth, gasping out his relief as the pain was replaced by the strangest feeling of curiosity. Mar climbed unsteadily to his feet, noticing from the corner of his eye Skarbnik was leaning over the crystal sarcophagus. When Mar turned his gaze to the object of the mountain god's attention, he saw the body of the drow empress, untouched by decay for millennia, finally succumb to the ravages of time and crumble into dust.

'It seems our autumn child isn't the only entertaining one. I'm impressed. It appears your bond with Inanuan is deeper than any of us predicted, but now that you have the circlet, you won't have much time. Do you have the courage to betray the woman you love in order to save her life?'

'Betray Ina? What have you bastards done to her now?' Mar's outraged expression brought a sad smile to Skarbnik's lips.

'Done, hatchling? We have done nothing to the harbinger, but the spinner of destiny is cruel and has sealed her fate. Take your bauble and find Ina. I just hope you don't live to regret your choices. Go on, get out, boy. Let those older and wiser grieve their poor decisions.' Skarbnik's words staggered Mar with the weight of sadness and longing they carried, and with a lone tear escaping his eyes, the warrior left the god to his contemplation of the past.

Fresh air never tasted so sweet as Mar gulped down a lungful when he emerged from the darkness, spinning around as the mountainside crashed down behind him, sealing the tunnel at his heels. The mountain meadow looked as serene as when he'd left, only darker as the sun disappeared behind the tall peak. Skarbnik's prediction had left a foul taste in his mouth, worse than even Jorge's convoluted explanations of his auguries, their seeming finality more worrying than their sad undertones. Turning slowly from the closed passage, Mar was distracted from his thoughts as the diadem in his hands suddenly warmed up, nearly scorching his fingers.

Lifting the bejewelled headdress to frown at it, Mar cursed. 'Look, you overpriced hairband, stop trying to hurt me and help. Ina told me you wanted to unite, so I need you to show me the way.' He didn't know what to expect, and after a moment of waiting with absolutely nothing happening, Mar turned to sit on a rock to ponder over the situation. As soon as he twisted his body, he felt it; a gentle tug at his hand, pulling towards the northeast.

The gleam that appeared in Mar's eye was well known to his men. If they'd been there to see it, each one would be sharpening their blades as their commander tracked his quarry, a predator hunting his prey, with no mercy given, and for the first time since he learned about Ina's disappearance, the lord marshal smiled.

'You may not be happy with my method, Spitfire, but you can't say I didn't move a mountain to find you,' he said to the wind, the relief at discovering a solution so immense that Mar leaned on a tree, trying to calm his racing heart, resting his cheek against the rough bark. It was a gesture he'd seen Ina make whenever she had something on her mind, but the dragon was still surprised when the angry face of the Forest Lord appeared in his mind's eye.

The Leshy had accosted his dreams several times in the past, mostly to pass on his disapproval or enigmatic messages that always ended with a mouthful of cat fur, but this was the first time Ina's ancestor communicated whilst Mar was awake. The Forest God, antlered head towering above the warrior, stared down belligerently as spirits from his realm danced around them with frenzied gyrations that invited madness if you stared, but when he attempted to bow, the Leshy raised his hand.

'We have no time for this, Ophidian. Stop wasting time with Skarbnik and find Ina before it's too late. The daughter of my heart will not die due to your failure.'

'Die?' Mar's bellow echoed over the small valley, but as soon as he broke contact with the tree, the Leshy was gone, leaving him confused and terrified for the witch. All thoughts of resting fled his mind, and the warrior leapt forward, arms flung out and already changing.

The transformation was almost instantaneous, and the dragon quickly gained height with powerful beats of his wings, his golden burden gripped in his teeth, held out towards its magical draw. Before the last stars disappeared behind burgeoning clouds, Mar confirmed he was heading north and redoubled his efforts, straining to fly as fast as his strength could carry him, fighting the rising gusts of wind.

A sudden flash of lightning blinded him, and his wings folded instinctively, losing precious altitude. When thunder followed, it became painfully obvious he flew directly into a summer storm. The only good thing that came from this was the shape of the land below, briefly appearing when the lightning struck, helping him identify the river with its scattered settlements below.

After the thunder and lightning came a torrent of rain, battering his wings, slowing his progress, but when he tried to fly above the relentless assault, the deluge turned to ice, freezing the supple membranes, leaving him no choice but to travel in the middle of the storm.

He knew he should have landed, but Skarbnik's dire prediction and the Leshy's words terrified him beyond reason. Disregarding the electrified air, the dragon fought the storm, following the signals from the circlet.

Suddenly, the searing pain tore through his back, and the stench of burnt flesh ripped an agonised roar from his throat, sending him spiralling downwards. Mar desperately fought to remain airborne, but his body refused to respond to commands, and the ground rushed to meet his helpless form with alarming speed. Stripped of choices, Mar curled his body around the circlet, which had miraculously caught on his teeth, before hitting the earth, ploughing through dirt and rock until his head struck a cairn, and the void swallowed his thoughts.

CHAPTER TEN

R ewan couldn't stop staring at the letter in front of him. Since returning to Osterad with the army, he could not shake a strange feeling of dread. With Ina missing, his lord marshal gods knew where, looking for her, and now this. He crushed the message in his fist, throwing it across the room in frustration.

'Just one day without worrying the country will fall apart, is that too much to ask?' he said, reaching for the carafe of wine on his desk before his hand stopped mid-gesture, and the young king grimaced. At this rate, he'd end up a drunkard like his father; constantly drunk and sleeping with anything that moved. Instead, he clenched his fist, stretching on the chair to analyse the situation.

Ina was his best asset, the witch who'd defeated two armies, faced Winter's Death and defeated an ancient curse, a deterrent that should be enough to frighten any potential enemies. Now she was missing, and he had no control over the situation, worrying about her as a friend and the king who had to consider the possibility this weapon could be turned against him.

He still remembered his coronation ball and how she'd subverted Sophia's plan to humiliate her during the sash and dagger dance, the spectacular magical display, ending with a pledge of loyalty so sincere he'd won over half the court that night.

My honest, foulmouthed Ina, I hope you are safe, wherever you are. The thought brought a sad smile to his lips. Although many complained about the witch's lack of respect for the king and his authority, Rewan had to admit he liked it. Her straightforward manner made him feel more like a person and less like a puppet performing for the masses.

'I won't give up on you, my friend, but I may not have a choice,' he said, looking at the parchment on the floor. A soft knock interrupted his musing. Rewan raised his head to see Kaian enter the room and approach him. A deep frown on the assassin's face didn't promise good news, and Rewan pointed to the chair next to him.

'Just tell me, my love,' he said, and the resignation in his voice brought sadness to Kaian's eyes.

'Dancik was taken. We just received the news. The vanguard of the Iron Empire landed on our northern shores a week ago, and the citizens of the so-called free city welcomed them with the keys to the city gates carried on a velvet cushion.'

'They chose survival rather than perish before an implacable enemy; can you blame them? They have been drifting from our rule ever since the debaucheries of my father wiped that northern family from existence. Why would they die for the country they don't feel they truly belong in?' The bitterness in the king's voice drew Kaian to his side, and the master assassin knelt at his lover's side, stroking Rewan's hair.

'I'm sorry. For what it's worth, I'm sorry for my family, the North, and my failure that left us in this position. I should have known better, but I was blinded by my elders. Today I learned some of them also conspired with the enemy—'

'Conspired?' Rewan frowned, looking down, his hand stilling on Kaian's hair before he moved it to tilt his chin. 'What don't I know?'

'Mirena, the mage who disappeared with Ina, was seen in Dancik and, apparently, was the driving force behind their capitulation.'

'Cyrus's wife? What does she have to do with you or your family?'

'That northern clan you mentioned earlier? Apparently, Mirena was the girl at the centre of the scandal. She was sent to court to meet her betrothed when your father... did what he did. My family covered it up, finding some poor mage to be the scapegoat, making a very public display of his death and disposing of any evidence of the actual crime.'

Rewan moaned softly, covering his eyes with his hands. 'How long, Kaian? How long will my father's shadow cast a pall over my reign? Do we know how she ended up marrying into the Thorn family?'

'Who knows? As a favour to King Roda? We've seen how manipulative Ina's grandfather was and surely gained much from such a favour. Unfortunately, we now have two problems. There could be another heir to the throne somewhere, and Mirena, possibly with Ina held prisoner, in a city controlled by our enemies.'

'Daro's report makes more sense now, at least. Ina's aunt must have headed north to meet with her allies, hoping to use our royal witch to conquer Cornovii. Still, it seems what I thought was the country's death knell might actually be a lifeline.' Rewan walked over to the crumpled message, tossing it to Kaian and nodding. 'Go ahead, read it.'

'*As a gesture of goodwill, we will cease further incursions into Cornovii soil under certain conditions. First, the city of Dancik will be ceded to the Iron Empire, and all its citizens, together with surrounding lands, will belong to the emperor from this day forth. Second, Lady Inanuan of Thorn will be surrendered to His glorious Majesty as a guarantee of peace to unite and seal the agreement between our two nations. Failure to comply with these conditions shall be treated as an act of war and shall be met with the full might of the Iron Empire.... Blah, blah, etc..*'

Kaian's frown grew deeper as he read the letter, full of insults and insinuations. Finally, he pushed the letter towards Rewan.

'Do they take us for idiots? They invade, take control of our main trading port but promise not to go any further, only as long as we give them our strongest weapon?' The master assassin seethed as he paced, thinking over the implications.

The king shook his head, smiling sadly. 'I'm not sacrificing a good friend nor giving my enemy the most powerful mage on the continent. We have enough trouble as it is, but before I respond to the letter, I need to know what Ina thinks about it.' He didn't miss Kaian's mischievous smile. 'What is so funny?'

'Well, if they don't have her, and we don't know where she is, that means our little Striga is free, hiding somewhere, ready to reveal herself when *she* is ready.' Kaian's statement was met with the king's absentminded nod and a soft sigh.

'I certainly hope that's the case because, if she doesn't return, I doubt Marcach will give up searching for her to help fight our battles. In the meantime, we'll keep our fingers crossed and prepare the country for war. Summon Sa'Ren and Jorge to my chambers so that we may begin.' Rewan took Kain's hand, kissing his palm tenderly, trying to keep the worry from his face as he considered the situation.

'I will talk to Gruff as well. If anyone can ferret out information on our striga, it's him and his information guild.'

'His what?' Rewan's head snapped up. He knew Gruff was the unofficial head of the seedier side of Osterad, but a guild of spies was completely different.

'Yes, I was quite surprised myself when I found out. I considered quietly removing him at one point, but it seems, thanks to Ina, the innkeeper decided to place his talents at our disposal.'

'Fine, call him in. Talk to Arun as well. That way, we'll have enough knowledgeable people to form a war council without the endless politics. If we present the nobles at court with a plan, we may avoid my arse going to sleep as they argue over how to respond to the threat.' Rewan reached for the wine as he finished, lost in thought as Kaian departed; both men fighting to hide their concerns as they made endless plans to protect each other from this new danger.

The sun was threatening to set by the time Kaian had gathered most of the people for the meeting, and the grim looks on each face left the king with little optimism.

'Where is Sa'Ren?' he asked.

'Still with the army. Since our return to the capital, he's been driving the soldiers hard, training night and day, with little rest. I hear the men consider the lord marshal to be a cuddly puppy in comparison. However, he assured me of his presence at the meeting.' Kaian gave him a reassuring smile, and Rewan nodded, spreading the map of Cornovii on the table. Sharing the details of the situation, the king stuttered under the hostile scrutiny of Gruff, the troll making no effort to hide his feelings.

'I told Kaian, and I will repeat it to everyone here. I am not sacrificing Ina in order to placate the empire. Unfortunately, that means a war on an unprecedented scale for which we are woefully unprepared. Jorge, what do your predictive schemata say?'

The mage removed a scroll from his satchel, rolling it out on the table. 'I have few answers, much of it disrupted by the presence of the Lady Inanuan itself, a reassuring factor. One thing, however, is clear. We cannot cede Dancik to the empire. This city is the gateway to the northern seas; our major export route, that is—*was*, fully dependent on Cornovii's produce. If the Iron Empire cut us off from this trade route, the results would be devastating for the economy, leaving us with more than just a few disgruntled merchants to deal with.'

The king's lips quirked in a bitter grimace. 'Tell me something I don't know. Do we have any chance against them, with our budding army freshly raised from the ashes of my father and sister's greed?'

'That's where prediction becomes complicated. My schemata become heavily disrupted by Lady Inanuan's presence, making any auguries wildly inaccurate, except those where she doesn't survive whatever trials she's currently undertaking.'

Jorge's words forced Gruff from his seat, the troll placing his large hand on the judicial mage's scroll as he snapped out a question. 'Where is Ina?' His concern for his friend was evident as he towered over Jorge, happy to take out his frustration on the mage.

'In the North, that's all I know, and as this region is the centre of an invasion, you shouldn't be surprised at her location,' Jorge said, looking Gruff in the eye.

Rewan appeared calm as he interrupted, but tightly squeezed fists revealed the king's emotions. 'So why did you say if she survives her current trials? Are you saying the empire already holds her captive?'

'As much as it pains me to admit, I don't know, but on some schemata, Ina and that dragon disappear completely,' Jorge said, alluding to but refusing to say what that meant.

'And Cornovii?' Arun's quiet voice broke the silence that followed Jorge's words.

'Without them both, there will be no Cornovii. The Iron Empire will rule everything from the northern seas to Verdante.'

Shock silenced everyone as they considered their potential fates until Gruff shook off the feeling and, walking to the map on the wall, pointed to an empty region near the captured city of Dancik. 'Several tribes from the old races call this region home. If I alert my network, we can contact their leaders and use their skills to monitor the area and keep an eye on the enemy.'

'We may need more than this, Gruff. Will they be willing to fight with us?' Rewan asked, looking at him hopefully, but the troll smirked.

'For you and Cornovii? Probably not, but if the child of the Leshy asks the forest, it will answer.'

The confused look on Arun's face was soon eclipsed by disbelief as his mind made some unknown connection. 'No... you don't mean?' Turning to Jorge, his look changed again when he noticed the lack of surprise. 'You knew? All this time, you knew, and you didn't think it appropriate to share that information with me? Just what do you hope to gain from all these schemes?'

'The kingdom's preservation. I do not serve the university or even the king. I am the judicial mage of Cornovii, Arun, bound by my oath to preserve the balance. If that information benefitted the kingdom, it would be distributed to those involved. Otherwise, I'd never share the secrets of my apprentice.'

Before the university dean could express his displeasure further, Rewan intervened. 'It only adds to our need to find Ina as soon as possible, especially if she is in danger.'

'What danger?' The words, iced steel laced through with the threat of imminent violence, captured everyone's attention as Sa'Ren Gerel, still clad in full armour, entered the room.

'Master Sa'Ren, welcome. As for the danger, general, we don't know the details, which creates problems in planning a strategy for the future. We believe the Iron Empire doesn't have Ina, as they kindly demand we hand her over in the name of peace. Do you know how she is? Your bond—'

'Is broken. I can't feel her anymore, but Ina sent me a letter from some scruffy inn in the North, asking me not to search for her, saying that she will return when she is ready.' Ren was still standing in the doorway, the tension in his body growing with each passing moment.

'What? How could this...? What do you mean, your bond is broken?' Arun, now ashen-faced and visibly trembling, exchanged glances with Jorge before slamming his fist on the table. 'You knew about that too? What else are you hiding from me, Jorge?'

'Sometime between travelling to the temple and her disappearance, our bond disappeared. That is why Mar abandoned everything and flew to find her,' Ren said, observing the mages who seemed more interested in his news than the impending war. 'I must say, I'm curious how the judicial mage seems to know what happened.'

'Mar came to me a few days ago and demanded I find Ina. When informed that I could not locate her, he rushed outside and flew away, frightening local merchants.' Jorge's monotone voice silenced the room until the king spoke.

'That is terrible news. I was hoping you could still communicate with her, Ren, but if that's impossible, I must ask you to prepare for war. In the absence of the lord marshal, you are to stand as his proxy, so please make sure we have a chance of defending this country.' Rewan turned to the troll, who studied him with an unreadable expression.

'Master Gruff, I would ask you to ask your network to locate the royal witch, supply whatever aid she requires, and contact your friends in the North to see if they are open to talking with us. Kaian, please inform the Lord Chamberlain that we expect an influx of refugees and to make preparations to receive them.'

'Your Majesty?' the former battle mage interrupted, looking uncomfortable, refusing to meet the king's eyes.

'Yes, Master Arun?'

'I'm sorry to bring this up, but as much as I respect her, an unrestrained chaos mage, especially with Sowenna's legendary regalia, is potentially a bigger threat than the Iron Empire, one that we should be prepared to face if she uses her magic on us.'

The sharp sound of a drawn sword cut through the conversation, the crackling of a fireball bursting into life its reply, and Ren confronted the university dean in silent fury.

'Stand down, Sa'Ren, Arun. You will behave in my presence or be forcibly removed. As for preparing to fight the Lady Inanuan? I refuse to betray a friend as steadfast as her. Ina has my trust, so I suggest you focus on aiding the general rather than trying to find a way to defeat an ally.'

Ren relaxed his grip on the sword's hilt, slowly putting it back in its sheath. 'As you command, my lord. My loyalty lies with Cornovii for as long as your loyalty lies with Ina. Your army will be ready for whatever comes. I also came here to inform you that a squadron of Verdante cavalry arrived in accordance with the peace treaty. We must expand the military camp's stables and add further pasture to accommodate them.'

'Do whatever is needed, Sa'Ren. Talk to the Lord Chamberlain if you require supplies.' Rewan sat back, cracking his knuckles, and Kaian walked over, placing a hand on his shoulder.

'I will go with Gruff. We need more information, especially since we know Ina is also in the North. We will need to position someone in Dancik. I don't trust this letter and want to know their next move. It would be quite an achievement to assassinate the emperor, but his security will likely be extensive.'

'Sa'Ren, despatch what you can now to the northern cities still under our control. I want the empire to bleed each time they attempt to reach further, but will this be enough?' Rewan smiled bitterly and nodded to his advisors. 'The meeting is adjourned for today. We cannot agree on more unless Ina arrives or the Iron Empire makes a move. Tomorrow I will decree county-wide recruitment of both soldiers and mages. Please prepare your peers for this. I don't want any disagreement on either side. Master Gruff, non-humans are also citizens of Cornovii. I heard what you said about the blood of Leshy, but I plea to you as their representative to help me keep this country safe for all.'

'We will look, and I will talk to the tribe elders, but that is all I can promise,' Gruff said, bowing slightly. With the feeling of foreboding hanging in the air, the gathered men left, bowing low to the king as they went.

'Sa'Ren, stay for a moment, please.' The tiredness in Rewan's words stopped the quiet warrior's steps, forcing him to face the weary monarch, who waited until the office door closed before speaking. 'If there is anything you think I should know that wasn't suitable to share in front of the mages, please tell me now. I won't do anything that will hurt her. You can trust me.'

Ren sighed softly, shaking his head. 'No, sire. I wish I knew more. I wish I were in Mar's place, free to search for her, but all I have is a single letter and the feeling she is alive and will return to me.'

Rewan nodded, reaching for the vine. 'I hope you are right, as I need her now more than ever. Have you heard about the Iron Empire, Sa'Ren?'

'I have military intel, Your Majesty. The rest is just folk tales.'

'You know why they are called the Iron Empire? It isn't from an abundance of the metal ore or the material of their weapons. No, it's from the reputation of the first emperor, a despot who cut a bloody swathe through his enemies, shackling the royal families of the conquered countries, sending the men into his mines and the women to his harem; a practice his successors have gleefully upheld, though lately, those defeated have been siblings and cousins. The entire society is built around the military. They were not as blessed with magic as Cornovii, and the few mages they have are collected like precious gems to be displayed as trophies. I don't blame Dancik for surrendering. They were unprepared, and the emperor would slaughter them all at the hint of opposition. That is his strategy, to kill his opposition and enslave those remaining. Even without Jorge's predictions, I cannot allow them a foothold on Cornovii soil.'

'And how do you know all of this, Your Majesty?'

'Several years ago, a small group of them came asking for my sister Sophia's hand in marriage in an attempt to make an alliance. I met one of them, an envoy, right before Ina offended my father. He was obsessed with her. I thought all empire men were taken by magic, but maybe it was about her? Especially since now the emperor wants Ina, the crowning gem to his collection. My father considered the suit, but after an investigation, Roda was so frightened he cut off all trade and diplomatic connections and tried to marry her off to Verdante. For months afterwards, Sophia couldn't stop talking about her dreams of being just like the emperor with his ability to frighten the great King Roda.'

Ren frowned slightly before pointing out the issues with the king's story. 'Sire, the only thing we are certain of now is that the warriors are well-trained and taught the art of war from childhood. We must assume they will come in large numbers, especially with a deep sea port at their disposal now.' Ren paced, his frown deepening. 'If they truly have a lack of magic users, that is a weakness we could exploit. I need your permission to recruit not just mages, but also all the old races of Warenga, including the drow of Arknay. The result won't be pretty, but the advantages would offset our lack of warriors.'

Rewan smiled and waved him off. ' I have confidence in you, Sa'Ren. I only hope our lord marshal returns before he misses the war.'

'He won't unless he finds Ina.'

'I know, Ren, and this is both good and bad. Go now. I wish to be alone. Whatever you decide to do with the army, I will support it. Just win this bloody war for me.'

CHAPTER ELEVEN

Ina cursed as her latest attempt at an antidote for Mirena's poison turned into a dull brown sludge in the crucible. The witch wondered why she'd thought using ingredients older than the king would be successful, even with the countless hours spent poring over her aunt's notes and textbooks. With all that reading, though, Ina had gained a new respect for Mirena's genius. Her insightful observations into the Water Horse clan's poisons opened the witch's eyes to a new world of toxins and antidotes that fascinated and surprised her; it was just a shame it had been used on her.

The delay in creating an antidote wasn't the only issue. The mugwort Velka was coaxing into maturity was refusing to grow, almost as if it sensed the nature mage's reluctance and was in cahoots with her to stop Ina from performing the dangerous procedure, but the witch kept smiling, holding onto her temper and the magic that seemed determined to escape her control.

To make matters worse, the revenants Rurik sent to the swamps returned with many strange mushrooms but very little amanitarii, and there was barely enough of the killing fungus for one dose.

After the latest failure, Ina spent her days gathering ingredients from the surrounding area, keeping her fingers crossed anything from the workshop she couldn't find fresh wouldn't disrupt the potion's effectiveness. Once the witch had done that, she went back to her experiments, unfortunately discovering that to compensate for the older ingredients, she needed to increase the dosage, making the antidote more dangerous than the original poison.

Now with the added worry that she would prove Velka right and end up killing herself, it became harder to control her magic, the guilt of keeping it a secret from her friend adding to the internal conflict as wisps of chaos escaped, affecting her surroundings often without her knowledge.

Finally, one evening, as the witch finished creating her latest concoction, Velka came to the workshop, distracting Ina just as her magic brushed over the potion. The nature mage carried what the witch could only describe as the angriest-looking plant she'd ever seen before placing the monstrosity on the counter with a loud thud.

'Here, this should be potent enough for your needs, I....' Velka spun away mid-sentence, heading for the door, biting her hand to stop a sob escaping, only to stop, her shoulders shaking. Without a moment's hesitation, Ina rushed over, gathering her friend up into a fierce hug, tears in her eyes as she felt Velka sobbing in her arms.

'Please don't do it, Ina. What if the potion doesn't work, or the dosage is wrong? Do you know how dangerous amanitarii is? We weren't even allowed to touch it without gloves and healers in the room. Just this once, could you not be so stubborn? If we return to Osterad, Nerissa or Jorge will repair your bonds. Or you can repeat the sacrifice spell. You can even do it with me right now. I don't care if it hurts. I just don't want to risk your life if there is any other way. Please—'

'I can't. Mirena did too good a job. She used her magic to combine several poisons that, somehow, didn't hurt me physically, but instead affected my magic in a way I still don't fully comprehend, and whether it's connected or just a natural reaction, my anger is causing me to lose control. Each day is worse than the last, with nightmares of desolation robbing me of sleep, and when I wake up, my magic surrounds me, changing everything I touch. This had to have been my aunt's goal, to strip me of my sanity till I destroy everything I love. Everything feels so... amplified.' The witch didn't try to hide the fear in her words. Velka turned around and embraced her, crushing fiercely as they both released their pent-up fear.

'We should still try it, especially now when I have Lada's pet for protection. We are closer than sisters, and if the sacrifice spell is needed to help you, just do it. I'd rather try that than risk your life with unproven magic.'

'Will you endanger the little one's life for this?' The witch placed her hand on Velka's round tummy. 'The bond I made with Mar and Ren... we nearly died, Flower. It wasn't until I nearly perished that my magic forged the bond, creating a conduit for me to take on their injuries and heal myself. There's no guarantee it will even work with me poisoned like this. What if we try, and I cannot heal you? No, I will risk my own life, no one else's.'

When Ina saw the guilt flash across Velka's expression, she tried to lighten the mood. 'Besides, I can't let you feel what I feel. It would complicate our love lives immensely.'

'I don't want to lose you, Striga. Not when you've only just returned.' Velka squeezed her fists, but Ina reached for her hands and pressed them to her chest.

'You won't lose me, trust me. I'm a master alchemist and have a lot to live for. I wouldn't miss all those years of annoying your husband, corrupting your son, and making sure Ren doesn't get gobbled up by that decrepit dragon he lives with. Anyway, I can't die. Mar already threatened to beat up Veles if I take one step in Nawia, so I have to save the venerable old god from having to fight at his age. All you need to do is smile for me, Velka, and tweak Lada's nose for a little added luck if you feel like it.'

Ina smiled, wincing as her friend squeezed her tight once more, muttering something under her breath as she let go and left the room, leaving the witch to extract the heart of the mugwort, attacking it furiously to get herself back under control. Once she finished, she added it to the latest attempt of the antidote.

Ina was grateful no one could see her concerned look at the remains of the various ingredients. It would likely be the last chance to make a working potion, but after last night's dreams and waking to the sad remains of her room, it was clear she had run out of time, anyway.

As the potion bubbled away happily in the crucible, Ina prepared another. She crushed lavender and chamomile into a paste, adding a little honey before setting the mixture on an intricate pattern and muttering the trigger words. She knew Velka would never leave her to face this trial alone, but if the situation ended badly, the blonde valkyrie would never forgive herself, and Ina could not allow that.

'You and I will have a lovely cup of tea tonight,' Ina said, breathing in the delicate aroma. If anything, Mirena taught her that no one suspected a drink from a friendly hand, and now, here she was, putting sleeping herbs in her friend's tea. She waited until the antidote was ready and poured the transparent fluid into the small bottle. One way or another, this would solve her problems. Ina's lips quirked with a bitter smile as she headed downstairs carrying the two potions.

Velka was in her room, but Rurik was in the kitchen and was the person she needed to enact her plan.

'Prepare the coach for a long journey after sunset. You and Velka are leaving for Osterad. Make sure you remember your oath,' she said and noticed the necromancer's surprise.

'Did Velka agree with this? She was very determined to stay when we last talked.'

'I didn't ask her. Just make sure the carriage is comfortable enough to sleep in, and I will handle the rest,' the witch said, lighting the fire to boil water.

'Yes, my lady.' He bowed, but not without a sardonic smile that twisted his lips as he left her to her task.

Ina gathered two mugs and went upstairs, finding Velka staring at the beautiful landscape as the sun faded into the horizon. With a sad smile, the witch placed a cup next to her friend, and when Velka reached for it, Ina took a brush from the bedside table and gently freed Velka's braids.

'Let me help you with this. Lately, you've been looking less like a royal mage and more like Lady Midday,' she said, loosening the strands and coaxing the brush through the thick, golden hair.

'Pot calling the kettle black, Striga? You could easily pass as your name-sake as you are now,' Velka said with a soft chuckle, without taking her eyes off the beautiful, summery panorama. Slowly, the tea, gentle caresses, and spell entwined with the lullaby Ina hummed, and Velka's head lolled to the side. Ina guided her to the bed, sitting on its edge and touching her friend's cheek.

'I'm sorry, Flower. Some things I have to do alone.'

Ina didn't have long to wait before Rurik returned, a light cloak thrown over his shoulder to ward off the chill of the night. His bemused stare at seeing her cradling Velka's head made the witch smile.

The necromancer's expression shifted to one of concern as he asked, 'Are you sure you want to be alone for this?'

Without meeting his eyes, Ina nodded. 'I don't know what will happen when I take the potion. If my magic reacts unfavourably when I reach death's door... You are a wicked man, Rurik, but I believed your confession that you didn't want to hurt us. Look after her and make sure she knows whatever happens to me is not her fault because I'm sure she will blame herself for not stopping me.'

'Well, if things go wrong, I could always reanimate your body so she can kill you herself?' The necromancer's smirk made her frown until she realised he was trying to ease the tension.

'Just look after her. As for my body, return it to the forest, where the Leshy's legacy belongs.'

'Ina, Velka would never allow you to talk like this if she were awake, so please, for her, don't treat your life so carelessly.' Rurik picked up the sleeping mage as Ina brushed her friend's hair back into place.

'You're right about Velka, but don't misunderstand me. I will fight with everything to stay in this world, but I am more afraid of becoming a monster than crossing the veil,' she said, following him to the carriage, kissing Velka's cheek in a silent goodbye.

Once the dust settled after her friend's departure, the undead servants slowly slumped to the floor, the animating magic disappearing with their master, and Ina rolled her eyes as she felt her curiosity poke her to examine the bodies before forcing herself to ignore the feeling and walk to the library.

Ina stripped back the carpet from the floor, leaving it next to the bookshelf. The witch drew a containment sigil, climbing the travelling ladder to examine her handiwork, confirming it would restrain any chaos unleashed while she flirted with Veles's domain.

The witch looked out into the darkness of the night after making sure the preparations were complete and, in a moment of intuition, decided to wait till the morning to use the dawn of a new day to encourage life to fill the magic circle.

After spending what felt like hours trying to relax enough to sleep, the dawn came too quickly. As she thought about performing the spell, Ina dressed in a simple summer dress, deciding that any uncontrolled chaos might damage her dragon-skin armour. Her fingers trailed over the soft scales as thoughts of Ayni came to mind, making her smile. At least Ren would have someone who loved him and, with that support, could help Mar if things went awry. It took her some time to do her hair in a fancy crown braid before she realised she was stalling for time, trying to delay the inevitable.

Unsure how long it would take, Ina placed a few pillows in the sigil's centre and sat cross-legged, looking at the bottle in her hand. The fluid didn't look threatening in her shaking fingers, but fear built up, speeding her heart rate.

'Oh, for fuck's sake! Bottoms up, girl,' she said, popping the cork. The liquid was utterly tasteless and didn't even linger on her tongue, making Ina's lips quirk in a half smile. 'Well, it is my first time making something that doesn't taste like a goat's arse. Whether that's a good or bad sign, I guess I'll find out soon,' she said, seeking comfort in the sound of her own voice.

Initially, nothing happened, and after several minutes of sitting there, waiting for any sign of the antidote working, Ina lost her patience and stood up, staggering when a dizzy spell overwhelmed her, forcing her back to the floor. While fighting nausea, her body tried to expel the poison, the pain forcing Ina to close her eyes. When the witch opened them again, the room had lost all its colour, her surroundings now varying shades of grey. Ina looked around, holding back panic by sheer force of will. She noticed two vibrant lines attached to her chest, one silver and delicate, the other golden and robust.

A strange sensation washed over her as she reached down to the tethers. Something about the view seemed wrong, but the witch dismissed it when her fingers stopped short of their destination. A glassy substance coated them, preventing any attempt at grasping the vivid strands. The curse that passed Ina's lips was silent, but the witch didn't fail to notice that as her hand moved, so did the coating, its hard surface dissolving as she watched. Grinning, Ina screamed with joy as she felt shock and relief radiate from her bonds, still muted, but gaining strength as the patina thinned. Her insane plan was working, and while Mirena had tied her spell to the witch's life force, it seemed she hadn't expected Ina to go to tempt death to remove it.

Ina waited as the antidote cleansed her spirit of the lingering effects of the spell, making sure it removed everything. Raw, untamed chaos began swirling around her body, its power perfectly balanced by the restored connections to her men, and smiling, the witch ignored the slightly muted feeling, blaming the spell for the phenomenon. She began waking her body from its dormancy, feeling the call of the veil growing stronger with each passing moment. Her brow wrinkled when nothing happened as she tried to fill her lungs with air.

She fought for her breath, but something was wrong as Ina's lungs failed to rise no matter how hard she tried. The mist of the veil continued to thicken as it surrounded her body, panic overtaking her mind when the omnipresent beat of her heart stuttered and stopped. Chaos magic burned brighter as the gentle eddy gained in power till her body rose from the floor, at the centre of its terrifying vortex, and the witch swore as her view became obscured by the mists of death before everything shifted.

'Fuck, now I've done it.' Ina stood there, strangely calm after the staggering fear. Even her annoyance at failing felt lacklustre and pointless, but Ina didn't care as she looked at the changing panorama before her.

The quiet, slightly decrepit library had disappeared, to be replaced by the landscape from Ina's nightmares, desolation as far as the eye could see, bleached bones partially obscured by the red dust that scoured the terrain.

'Oh no, you don't. I refuse to be tormented by a disaster I didn't cause!' she shouted to no one in particular and marched off in search of her persecutor. The red dust blew past her even though Ina couldn't feel any wind causing the phenomenon, so she stopped, looking around in frustration. *This is worse than a nightmare. At least I can wake up from a bad dream or use my talent to change it.* The thought gave her a pause. She took a moment to centre her mind. *I am the harbinger of chaos, destined to bring change to the world, so let's change it.* The budding smile turned into a grin as the witch imposed her will on the surrounding landscape, and crimson flames appeared, wrapping themselves around her body. The power in this realm was intoxicating, unlimited, and apparently hers to command.

With a single thought, Ina commanded the dust to move, directing its movement like a ballet. She recalled a place brimming with happy memories.

'Change...' she whispered to eternity, closing her eyes and channelling her memory into the magic, feeling it shift and transform, snapping her eyes open at the sound of someone clapping their hands slowly.

'Well, well, well, that was unexpected. Few who come to Nawia arrive with such calm control. You are full of surprises, autumn child, but I'm disappointed. Your nightmare should have held you until your memories faded.'

Ina looked around. She stood in the middle of a small mountain glade, a hot spring in its centre and pine trees sheltering the meadow flowers from the wind. The place where, for the first time, the witch accepted her love for Mar, but the man before her was not her dragon. This male was tall, with a slim build, raven black hair, and a matching pale complexion. He looked at her with burning eyes and oddly familiar features, but Ina could not pinpoint where she'd seen him.

'So who might you be?' she asked, raising her eyebrow.

'The master of the ravens and the lord of this place. I was curious about you, little godling, especially after you maimed my mamuna, so I decided to welcome you personally to Nawia.' He smiled, moving closer, and Ina couldn't help but try looking at his rear after cursing it so many times when she was alive.

The man followed her sight, and his lips quirked. 'Like what you see, Inanuan?' he asked, and the witch shrugged.

'I just wanted to see if my cursing your arse had any effect, Lord Veles. Now, if you'd be so kind as to send me back? I have some unfinished business and a dragon to deal with.'

The guardian of Nawia, Veles, god of the dead and father of dragons, laughed with childlike joy as Ina stood before him, impatiently tapping her foot. He differed from how she'd imagined, expecting a dour-faced old man. Instead, she got him and didn't know how to deal with such a vibrant, attractive male.

'My dear harbinger, your confidence is exhilarating, but there is no returning from these lands unless someone offers their soul in exchange. Come, forget the life you leave behind and allow me to accompany you on this journey. It had been an age since I met someone who could look me in the eye without fear.' The youthful god approached her, his hypnotic stare dancing with mischief, freezing Ina in place. When his fingers touched her cheeks, her willingness to fight melted away till a sharp, painful tug at her chest woke her from his spell.

'My lord, your offer is tempting, I'm sure, but would it be an imposition if I declined?' Veles blinked, shocked at Ina's resistance, removed his hand from her cheek, and curled his fingers into a fist in frustration.

'Decline? Oh dear, you would beard the dragon in his own realm? You have spent too long with that hatchling if you think I'm giving you a choice. Why do you want to return, anyway? Here, you are free from the burden of your magic, madness, constant wars, and fools relying on you to save them from their mistakes. Why do you cling to a life full of suffering and pain?' By the end of his tirade, the god's voice was little more than a whisper, the anger nearly eclipsed by confusion.

Losing hope of persuading him, Ina pleaded her case. 'I don't expect you to understand, Lord Veles, but while my life may not be perfect, it is worth fighting for. I have a love so strong it broke a magical geas, a friendship I would walk through fire to keep, and a sister of my heart who shares my joys and sorrows. This power I was given, whether curse or blessing, has saved the lives of so many and given my life a purpose bigger than I deserve, so if you need a reason I fight, pick one that answers your question. I will be yours eventually, but I will not surrender hope until I fulfil my purpose.' In desperation, Ina reached out, grabbing the god's hand, tightening her grip when he tried to pull away.

'You are the Lord of Nawia, brother to Svarog. What use do you have of me here? I am nothing but trouble, but I did free your daughter from her cursed chains. Can you not grant me this boon? Please send me back.' Ina's bargaining seemed to disgust the god, and he pulled his hand free, stepping back to distance himself.

'You would bargain with me? Nawia's law is immutable, not something you can trick or pay off. A soul for a soul, so accept your death or sacrifice the soul of a loved one. Can you make that choice?'

Ina bit her lip. 'How about I make a promise? I have many enemies I would gladly send beyond the veil to free mine.'

Veles shook his head as he answered. 'It doesn't work like that, child. It would release chaos throughout the realms if it were possible, destroying all existence. Besides, why would I give you up? Your fierce soul has left me feeling more than I have in aeons. However, I offered you a choice, a sacrifice for your life, someone your heart would mourn, who would scar your soul to lose, or acceptance of your fate. Tell me your decision.'

Veles reached out when Ina lowered her head, clenching her fists in defeat. 'I thought so. So predictable and yet so sweet. Come, autumn child. I promise you will find happiness with me, and if the burden of remembering is too great, I will help you forget.'

Forget Mar, Ren, Velka? Our antics in the Drunken Wizard *and the Leshy's affection? Lose everything that made me the woman I am today?* A single tear fell to the ground as she pictured those memories before she looked up at Veles. 'No, my lord. I choose the pain of remembering those I love and lost from your blissful oblivion. You wanted to feel? Oh, I will make you feel. I will turn this place into a nightmare. Your nightmare, and you will regret keeping me when I begged you for mercy,' Ina said, and Veles approached her, grasping her neck and lifting her spirit off the ground.

'As you wish, Inanuan. I will enjoy fighting you. You can't win against a god, not even with this little drop of divinity from the Leshy. It will only make your struggles more amusing and my victory much sweeter,' he said, ignoring her struggle to escape. The force that ripped Ina from his grip surprised them both. The contours of her body blurred into crimson light, and the witch shook as an intense pressure forced a scream from her lips.

'Impossible...'

Veles's shocked expression revealed this wasn't his doing, but as Ina tried to focus through the pain, looking for the cause, a golden light burst from her chest, burning through the mists that now surrounded her, a feeling of love and desperation overwhelming her senses. When she stumbled forwards, following the light's pull, Veles grabbed her wrist.

'No, you are mine! Even bearing the chaos regalia will not be enough to free you from death!' he shouted in her face, but Ina didn't listen, looking down at the searing golden light burning in her chest. Veles followed her gaze, and his face twisted in rage as he tried to pull her closer.

'Hands off my woman!'

The words, filled with anger, boomed out, and Ina rolled her eyes. That beautiful idiot of a dragon had crossed the veil to fulfil his oath and fight Veles for her soul.

CHAPTER TWELVE

(the day of Velka's departure)

Consciousness returned to Mar in fits and starts. The first thing he noticed was the intensity of the light on the other side of his closed eyelids, followed closely by the pain of prising them open. That slight discomfort must have triggered something in his brain as, at that moment, he realised his whole body hurt—no, not hurt, screamed in agony, and with it, the memory of why flashed before his eyes: Perun's hammer.

Mar couldn't help the groan as he turned his head to inspect the damage. Blackened scales trailed back from his wings down to the right side of his tail, leaving the dragon to curse his luck and the deity who'd struck him down.

After deciding that with this much pain, he must be alive, Mar looked around, trying to regain his bearings, losing the last of his temper as the endless fields of golden wheat left him with no clues to his whereabouts.

'Fucking asshole gods and their pointless games,' he snapped, then stopped, remembering why he'd been flying in the first place. Panic washed over the dragon as he scrambled, searching for his precious burden, collapsing in relief as Sowenna's diadem rolled to the side, seemingly undamaged from his little mishap.

Lifting the powerful artefact with a talon, Mar closed his eyes, concentrating on the circlet, allowing himself a small smile as he felt it still drawing him onwards, and with a laugh, Mar leapt up, beating his wings, nearly passing out as his body reminded him of his injury.

'Not my best idea,' the dragon muttered as he shook his head, trying to ignore the dizziness before climbing back to his feet and setting off towards the diadem's pull. Whether it was real or his imagination, there seemed to be an urgency transmitting from the artefact the further he walked, and Mar hastened his steps until, hours later, the urgency strengthened into fear and, praying to the gods he'd been cursing throughout the day, the dragon spread his wings, roaring a challenge to the pain and launched himself into the heavens.

Mar couldn't recall how he'd gained so much height, but being able to glide meant his quivering muscles could rest. Even so, it wasn't long before he needed to land and rest. In the morning, Sowenna's circlet was burning hot and, overtaken by desperate need, Mar battled exhaustion, taking to the skies, pushing beyond the limits of his endurance to get to Ina's side, almost missing the first, stuttering awakening of his bond, but when the sensation intensified, Mar roared joyfully to the heavens. *I knew you'd find a way, my spitfire*, he thought, sending his love to her, gasping when the bond disappeared, leaving him bereft.

Since they'd started living together, Ina had never ignored him. She'd shouted, insulted, kissed and teased, but never once ignored him, even going so far as stimulating their bond to express her feelings. Now, however, there was nothing. Even the quality of the silence differed from before, and Mar realised the bond hadn't been gone, just muted. This time, though, it felt like it wasn't just the bond that was gone, but Ina, too.

Something within Mar's chest exploded outwards, and power burnt through his body, eclipsing the pain of his injury as instinct pushed him on towards his mate.

Moments later, a building appeared in the empty countryside directly in his flight path. Knowing it was his destination, Mar dived, ploughing into the ground gracelessly in his haste and transforming without conscious thought, crashing through the door heedless of the damage he caused.

The desiccated corpses crushed beneath his feet fed the dread burning in place of his bond. He broke through another door, a sword appearing in his hand as a violent wind ripped the remnants of the door away, only to disappear when Mar was confronted with the sight of chaos magic cocooning Ina within its roiling centre, her body as pale and still as a marble statue, serenity softening her unmoving features.

Anguish and grief tore the breath from Mar's lungs as he stumbled forward, erasing parts of the sigil on the floor, repeating one word over and over. 'No, no, no, no.' He fell through the vortex, its magic tearing at his flesh as his arms encircled the woman he loved.

Unable to stop himself, he kissed her, needing to feel her lips, desperate to bring her back from wherever she was, unwilling to believe their love couldn't conquer all.

'Please, my love. Wake up. You can slap me, kick my ass to Osterad and back, just come back to me. I can't live without you,' he begged, but Ina remained motionless despite the searing kiss and desperate plea. Mar ripped her shirt and pressed his hand to her chest but couldn't feel a heartbeat, and the roar of a grief-stricken dragon shook the house to its foundations.

'Fine, if you refuse to listen, I'll just have to follow you. Not even death can take you away from me.' The dragon punctuated his words with the transformation of his hand, reaching for his own throat with the sharp talons, but before Mar tore open his flesh, he glimpsed Ina's necklace, the peridot pulsing with fading green light. *Pulsing. Damn it, she must still be there.* The circlet he dropped during his mad rush inside was still on the floor, and Mar reached for it, looking at its corresponding peridot with reckless hope.

With his hand lifting the final piece of Sowenna's regalia, Mar hesitated. Ina had refused to claim this artefact, despite being confronted by overwhelming odds time and again. She had rejected its power to live the life she'd chosen for herself, but here he stood, ready to ignore that decision in order to rip her from death's embrace. Mouth curling in bitterness, he acted, lifting the diadem. If Ina rejected him for this, then so be it. As long as his love survived, he would face whatever punishment she deemed fit.

'I'm sorry, my love. We need you... No, fuck that, I need you. Please come back to me,' he said, knowing she could hate him for his actions.

Mar moved forward with determination, placing the circlet on Ina's brow, and startled as the world around him froze. The crimson maelstrom was silent and unmoving, his own body rooted in place, the moment stretching into infinity, until, with deafening force, the world exploded, launching him across the room, smashing his body into the wall in a shower of plaster and stone.

Blinking away the dusty remains, Mar looked at Ina, blinding crimson light shining from her eyes as she floated in place before him, the magic giving her body the semblance of life, even as her chest remained still and unbreathing. *If only we'd united our life forces, then this wouldn't be happening.* Mar cursed the thought, even as it spawned a desperate idea.

The idea turned into action as Mar sank his talons deep into his chest. Ayni had described the coupling ritual, telling him that if his partner refused his life energy, he would die, but he'd never dared share that with Ina, knowing what her reaction would be. Recalling the dragoness's instructions, he concentrated, seeking the golden light in his heart. Ayni called it the dragon spark. Once Mar found it, it took intense focus to force it through his body to the wound he'd created. Then, grasping its elusive energy, the dragon tore it in two. Now Ina needed to accept it. In the past, the recipient cut their own chest to mark their commitment, but that was impossible in her present state.

The little Ina knew about sharing his life force had prompted her refusal. Knowing her death would cause his demise prevented the witch from accepting its benefits, but at this moment, he didn't care if she rejected him. He would die happy, knowing they would be together in Nawia. Returning to his lover's side, Mar made the incision over her heart, pushing the light inside, concern bubbling to the surface as the spark flickered and the dark mists of the veil washed over him, blinding him to the world.

Mar looked down, sighing as he noticed a shining strand exiting his chest, a broken laugh escaping as he remembered Ina's description of their bond, its weak glow disappearing into the swirling clouds surrounding him. More importantly, he felt his striga's emotions, anger, worry, and love. The feral grin on his lips hardly faded as he stepped forward, the feeling of his mortal body falling to the floor at Ina's feet ignored in his desire to find the woman he loved.

As the mists parted, revealing the mountain glade they'd reconciled in, Mar felt hope bloom, only for fury to overwhelm his happiness at the sight of Ina struggling to escape the grasp of a dark-haired male, her body surrounded by snapping tendrils of chaos. All the frustration built up since he'd lost the bond fuelled his rage as he leapt forward, roaring.

'Get your hands off my woman!'

The dark god turned from Ina, surprise flickering across his features, before sending Mar, with a flick of his wrist, tumbling across the meadow to be met by shackles of mist that secured the warrior's wrists and ankles. Mar fought with all his strength, forcing his way forward, inch by inch, the amorphous fetters tearing at his flesh.

'You have a stubborn man, autumn child. He performed the unthinkable, binding you together after death, but if he thinks making you his mate will bring you back, he is sorely mistaken. I will not be challenged in my domain.' His visage darkening, Veles lifted his hand, pausing as Ina stopped struggling and looked into her tormentor's eyes.

'No, please. You wanted me, not him. Let him go, and I will comply. Love makes people do stupid things. He is not challenging you. You want your jester, fine. I will perform on your command. But let him go, please.' Ina didn't even look at Mar as his struggles brought him to her side, maintaining eye contact with the cunning god.

'Do not touch my woman. She doesn't belong to you.' Voice hoarse as he resisted transforming into a dragon, Mar reached out, attempting to grab his mate.

'You seem very sure of that, hatchling, but Inanuan made her choice. Her latest *little accident* stopped her heart, and she stepped beyond the veil. I did not take your mate or anything else you want to accuse me of doing. The veil is older than time and more powerful than any god, and it will always claim its soul, but please, keep trying. I do so love to hear your helpless mewling.' The amusement in Veles's voice irked Mar immensely, and he bared his fangs, challenging the master of Nawia.

'You're twisting the truth for your own gain, Veles. Ina may have crossed the veil, but she isn't dead. The magic in the regalia still glows, and now, with the circlet bonded to her, she has the power to leave this place.' Mar pressed a hand to his chest and smirked at the fury on the old god's face. 'Now you see it, don't you? With a dragon's life force to sustain her, you have no dominion over her soul.'

The fear on Ina's shocked face wiped the smile from the dragon's lips, but he didn't back down, even as she stroked his cheek and asked.

'Mar... why?'

Before he could answer, Veles slashed his hand through the air, strengthening the shackles that held Mar and forcing him to his knees. 'Do you think anchoring her soul to her body will prevent me from taking this little morsel? Did the Leshy put you up to this to save his misbegotten scion?' The ferocity in Veles's voice transformed into a wave of power, eradicating the beautiful glade and leaving behind a desolate wasteland as the elder god stalked forward to the pinioned warrior, seizing him by the throat.

'Neither; I was simply willing to sacrifice everything to save her. I don't expect someone surrounded by death and despair to understand the depth of my love for Ina.' Mar gasped as an inferno of magic tore into his body through his bond, the pain forcing him to look at the magnificent sight of Ina embracing the full extent of her power as she faced the god of the underworld.

'RELEASE MY DRAGON!'

Mar couldn't help staring. Ina was floating in the air, her body terrible and glorious, glowing like a crimson sun as power pulsed out, forcing the men backwards with its strength.

Silence washed over the realm as the witch released her magic, her voice suddenly quiet as her rage condensed into icy fury. 'Let him go!'

As she finished, the ground shook, staggering the elder god as her will overrode his, reshaping their surroundings into the mountain meadow once more.

Veles turned to Ina, his playful smile replaced with disdain. 'And if I don't, autumn child? You think to command me in my realm? You've grown arrogant, little witch, and I think it's time to put you in your place.' Mar felt the pressure crushing him to the ground disappear as the elder god turned his attention towards Ina. Using the opportunity, he transformed, wrapping his body around the witch to protect her.

'Put me in my place? What makes you think you even know what that is? Still, it matters little what you think. Now tell me what you really want, and stop playing these parlour games with our souls.'

'Ina, why is it always so difficult to rescue you?' Mar muttered as the witch sighed, sending her love through their bond, but they both sobered as Veles grew, transforming before their eyes.

'Oh, Inanuan, it's not about what I want. There is nothing I desire that does not die and join me eventually, and I am a patient god.' As Veles uttered the last word, his transformation ended, and before them stood a massive dragon, his scales so black they absorbed the light. Spreading his wings, the elder god enunciated his words, engraving themselves on Ina's soul. 'There is a price, autumn child, for the actions of you and your dragon this day. For defying the veil and joining with this hatchling, you shall pay with tears and sadness, and Marcach will be there to witness your grief, knowing he is the reason for it.'

Mar surged up, confronting the massive dragon. 'Leave her be, Dark One. If you want a price, then take me. I—' Ina punched him in the snout before he could finish, the pain of her fist surprising him less than the fact she'd stopped him from trying to help her, again. Mar tried to explain, but the witch refused to listen.

'Fucking knights, wanting to save the damsel in distress. When will you finally understand I don't want to live without you? Do you think you're the only one who loves so deeply? And if you stay here and I go back, what do you think will happen in my grief with the completed regalia at my command? I would destroy the world and devastate Ren as he tried to calm the tempest burning in my soul.' Ina placed a hand on her hip, glaring at him, and Mar ducked his head like a scolded child.

'I... I hoped you loved me that much. Since the bond disappeared, I've been too frantic to think—'

'Gods save me from hopeless romantics. I love you, my overgrown lizard, but you can't jeopardise the rest of the world just to save me,' she said, turning at the sound of Veles's vicious laughter.

'Oh, and let's not forget the almighty guardian of Nawia. Why did you pout and make a fuss when you knew the dragon's spark anchored me to life? Was the upstart witch not docile or obsequious enough for you that you tried to keep her here out of spite? Well, here, just for you, oh great god of the underworld, I bow to your greatness and could never hope to challenge your power. Happy? Does it make your cock look bigger? The mighty Veles, defeating the Leshy's misbegotten offspring, and for what? What have I done that I must be punished for wanting to live?'

The chaos surrounding Ina took on a life of its own as she spoke, pulsing with each question until, with her last word, it blasted outward, forcing the god to take a step back, dispersing his magic. Mar didn't hesitate and used the distraction to snatch away the witch and leap into the sky, grimacing as his bruised body protested the continued abuse. The power of Veles pursued them, and the mists of Nawia thickened, miraculously held off by Ina's chaos magic as the dragon pushed past the limits of his endurance to escape, but even as they barely held off the threats, it felt more of a pretence than a genuine effort to keep them in.

With the mist finally thinning, presaging their departure, a furious voice thundered its final warning.

'I wasn't trying to punish you, ungrateful child, merely protect you from the pain of your choices. A loved one will answer the call of the veil for you. Live well and long, autumn child, but know that you will be the reason for their demise.'

Mar felt Ina's magic disappear as if it had never been, and looked down into her horrified eyes.

'Mar, I don't know what to do. Let me go. If he's telling even part of the truth, I can't sacrifice another for my life.' The desperate plea in her eyes broke Mar's heart as he tightened his grip and surged forward.

'You aren't sacrificing someone, I am. Blame me for whatever happens next,' he said as they burst out of the underworld.

Reality warped as they broke through the veil, their spirits crashing into their bodies, and pain tore through them as hearts and lungs restarted, leaving them both helpless on the floor. Mar forced himself towards Ina, determined to ensure she survived even as the maelstrom of her magic continued to rage around them. As the last of his strength failed, the exhausted warrior cradled Ina in his arms, willing his lover to open her eyes, but despite her heart beating, the witch remained pallid and unresponsive.

With the possibility of failure staring him in the face, Mar felt grief and rage when he kissed Ina with bruising force, tears falling from his eyes. As he pulled back, ready to admit defeat, crimson lightning blazed through the violent vortex, crashing into the witch, filling her body with power as the swirling chaos dissipated, forcing her to take a life-giving breath. Mar threw out all thoughts of being the stoic warrior and crushed Ina to his heart, words falling from his lips as he held her.

'I'm going to take you home, chain you to our bed, and never let you out again. No more bloody wars, meddling gods, or saving the country from destruction. Rewan has the army I trained and doesn't need your help. Oh, Ina, why do you keep endangering yourself? It tore my heart out to see you there. I thought I'd lost you, that I failed you, again.' Mar broke off, unable to continue, burying his face in her hair, breathing deeply, losing himself in his lover's scent. How could he tell her that no matter how used to death on the battlefield he was, losing her terrified him, and he would follow her back to Nawia if she returned to the afterlife? Even as those thoughts tumbled through his mind, Ina reached up, gently stroking his cheek to comfort him.

'I died, didn't I?' she whispered, feeling Mar's muscles tense at the statement, a kaleidoscope of emotion flashing across her features at his reaction. 'I hoped it was just one of those fever dreams you get when close to death. Mar, we must fly to Osterad. Ren... what if Veles was right?'

'I can't fly right now, love. I'm as weak as a kitten after sharing my life force and travelling through the veil, but I will take you there as soon as I can spread my wings. In this state, though, it will be an arduous journey. Are you sure you can manage?'

'I still have Ayni's outfit. I can't abandon my friends. What if he meant Ren or Velka and the child? I have to get there. I need to stop it.'

Mar sighed slowly, stroking the small of her back. 'Give me a few hours, and I will take you there. You'll help no one if we crash because my wings gave out.'

Ina nodded, rubbing the bridge of her nose when her fingers brushed over the last piece of Sowenna's regalia, and the witch gasped.

'Fuck, I forgot about that.'

CHAPTER THIRTEEN

Ina woke from her nap feeling guilty for being so comfortable. She felt a completeness that had been missing since the battle with Marzanna, her heart overflowing with love. So much so, in fact, that she had to resist the urge to shout her happiness to the heavens. The only shadow on her heart was her worry over Velka's safety, which burned with the intensity of Swarozyc's fire. Ina turned, throwing a leg over Mar's hips and sat up, stroking his chest hair before grabbing a handful and pulling it to wake him. The poor man looked exhausted, whilst she felt invigorated by the dragon spark within her chest.

'How long were you searching for me?' she asked, looking at his sunken face. 'Have you eaten? No, I guess you didn't,' she muttered, answering her own question, and Mar flashed her one of his disarming smiles.

'Since I lost the bond, and no, I didn't think about food,' he said, gently rubbing her thigh. He hadn't stopped touching her since they emerged from the mist, as if worried she would disappear again. Her stubborn oafish dragon, whose love had saved her from the veil. If she only could make him feel this loved.

'Marry me,' her words surprised her, but Mar's shocked face told her that was the last thing he'd expected from her.

'Ina, I— You never wanted this before,' he said, sitting up. Ina felt her face flash various shades of crimson. *Can't he just say yes?* she thought, turning away.

'Nothing, you are right. I never wanted this.'

'Ina?'

'Just show me your back. I saw you wincing every time you moved.'

'Ina, please...' He looked lost, but she felt lost too, realising the prospect of marrying him was more appealing than she wanted to admit. It didn't help that, like an idiot, she'd proposed while Veles's threat hung over them, and after so many times explicitly telling him she didn't want any commitments.

'I don't want to talk about it now. Please, let me help you first.' She smiled, standing up and extending her hand to help him.

When Mar sat forward, Ina kissed his cheek to distract him, then slipped off his lap to look at his back, gasping as she saw the charred flesh of his wound. She tenderly trailed her fingers next to the damage, pouring her meagre healing talent into repairing what she could, tenderly kissing whatever her ability failed to improve.

'That's the best I can do for now, but I could try again later. Is it hurting a lot? Why were you flying in the storm in the first place? I should beat your scaly arse for such recklessness,' she said, chastising him to mask her concern as his muscled body shook with laughter.

'Ina, you just died, and you're trying to tell me off for being reckless? It's fine, my love. I will be ready to fly in a few hours, but chasing you all over the Cornovii, fighting with Veles and sharing my dragon spark without preparation made a dent in your invincible hero's armour,' Mar said, making her eyes roll as he trivialised his injuries.

When he turned around, lifting her chin to look into her eyes, she felt his possessive streak was tempered with loving tenderness. 'How do you feel?

I know we'll need to talk about what I did. You were adamant you didn't want to use the circlet or have the bonding ritual, but I had no choice. You can be mad at me, curse my name or vow never to see me again, but you need to know I would do it again because I'm a selfish bastard who can't live without you.'

The look in Mar's eyes was a mix of stubbornness and hope, prompting Ina to sigh and kiss his grizzled cheek. 'The circlet, yes, well. I was so scared it would turn me into a crazed monster once I claimed it, but strangely enough, I feel calmer instead.'

'Calmer?' Mar asked, tilting his head while curiosity filled his voice, followed by mischief in his eyes. 'So, how much in trouble I am for pushing this calming trinket onto your head? Oh, and this might be related, but your eyes have changed. They are marked with chaos.'

'You're not in trouble, you bloody nuisance. Although, I hope I still have my orein to ride when I return home, as I'm guessing Skarbnik was not keen to part with his treasure.'

'We may have had an interesting discussion, but he conceded to the substance of my argument. Now, don't avoid the question. What do you mean by calmer?'

Ina reached up and stroked his beard, touching the silver strands that had appeared overnight. Since she'd awoken, every sensation was amplified, most noticeably touch, as if the magic of life were stroking over her skin like a friendly cat. She felt simultaneously connected and balanced.

'I don't know how to describe it. I feel... complete,' she said with an apologetic smile.

Mar's lips quirked at this answer. 'You are definitely complete, even if I'm unsure what was missing,' he said. He played with her hair before adding, 'Did you check your connection with Ren? I would love to know if I still have to share you, or if I'm solely responsible for my complete woman. Just be gentle. You don't want to shock him into falling face-first in the mud.'

Ina blinked, having completely forgotten the other in the excitement. Following Mar's advice, already feeling her friend's emotions, she focused on the silver strand. The witch tried to be gentle, but the joy and love that flooded her senses caused her to sob with relief. Ina basked in Ren's steadfast friendship, but when she focused more, under the burst of emotion, there was an underlying worry that made her frown before she closed the connection, turning towards Mar.

'I'm so sorry, my love. Let me heal you again because I feel we must go.'

'What's wrong?'

'I'm not sure, but Ren was trying to hide something from me. I.... That is new; whatever is troubling him is bad enough that he wants to shelter me from it. I can't stop thinking about Veles's warning. We need to go to Osterad. I know you can't fly, but Rurik walked to a nearby village for supplies. We can try to get horses there,' Ina said, and the determination in her voice made it clear she was firmly set on departure.

Mar reached for her hand, and she saw the tension in his shoulders. 'Gear up, my spitfire. If you say we must fly, then we must, and I will get us to Osterad much quicker than any horse.' He must have seen the guilt that flashed over her features, because he stopped and gently stroked her cheek.

'Don't worry. I'm a big, bad dragon, and Osterad is only a day or so away when flying.'

As soon as they were in the air, Ina could feel Mar struggling, though the stubborn dragon refused to admit it. She suggested, several times, that they stop and rest, but Mar just smirked and said he would rest once they arrived at the capital.

Nothing could convince him otherwise, so grumbling under her breath, Ina placed her hand between his shoulder blades and poured all her energy into trying to heal his wound. While the witch lacked the skills to make a proper repair, she could use her magic to encourage the damaged tissue to speed its natural healing and ease his exhaustion. His pain drained her emotionally, but if he could withstand it, so would she. Mar didn't say anything, but Ina could feel the relief and extra effort he gave till, in the red glow of sunset, they saw the gates of Osterad.

Mar landed heavily on the grass field next to the gates, his legs collapsing, leaving him gasping out a laugh as he looked at his passenger. 'Another dignified landing for the Dragon of Liath.' He laughed again, transforming before the witch could dismount, leaving her sprawled in his arms and very flustered.

'You wicked man.' Ina lightly kissed his cheek as she stood up.

'I didn't think we would make it today. Thank you for your help, my love. Once we check up on Ren, I will ask the boon of a hot bath and my pretty lady to assist her exhausted dragon if you have any strength left.'

Ina nodded absentmindedly, her thoughts drifting towards Ren, whose connection radiated shock and distress.

'Ina?' he said, grabbing her arm.

'We must hurry,' she said, and Mar's face lost all cheerfulness.

'Lead the way.' The sharp command and the desperation in her bond had her rushing towards the city gates. The guard, already closing them for the night, barely acknowledged visitors until Mar grabbed him by the shoulders, and then the poor man couldn't stop talking. Thankfully, he revealed the general was stationed within the city despite the army being camped to the east. Mar commandeered the post-horses, and within minutes, they were galloping through the town towards Ren's house.

When they found the townhouse empty and dark, Ina struggled to control her distress, turning to Mar with a desperate plea.

'Could he be at the palace? I know you're tired, but I must see Ren. I have never felt him like this. He's... afraid?' Her warrior just nodded, wheeling his mount and pushing the beast to gallop through the streets.

They didn't find him in the palace, but a passing servant recognised the distraught witch and mentioned a recent commotion involving the palace nature mage and a stranger demanding help from any available healer.

Ina swooned, realising Velka was in trouble and would have fallen if Mar hadn't caught her. The next thing she knew, Ina was seated in front of him on an exhausted horse, racing towards her friend's home. Their arrival was greeted by sheer pandemonium. A carriage, its doors torn from their hinges, stood abandoned in the courtyard as servants ran around it, shouting rushed instructions to each other, oblivious to the new arrivals.

'Where is that bloody witch when we need her?' Daro's roar from the house shocked Ina back to life. Without looking to see if Mar followed, she dashed inside, colliding with the crowd in front of Velka's bedroom.

'Let me pass,' she said, pushing forward until she saw Daro, one arm in a sling, the other hammering against the wall in mindless fury.

'What's going on?' she asked breathlessly, gasping as Daro grabbed her by the shirt, lifting her off the ground and shaking her violently.

'This is your fault, you meddling, thrice-damned witch. Get in there and stop that thing from hurting my wife.' The orc roared in her face, and Ina blinked before turning towards the open door. Velka lay there, her serene face motionless, hands clutching a tummy bloated by pregnancy. Zmij coiled around her, emitting a pale gold light that dispelled every shadow in the room. As soon as her sight landed on the spirit, it raised its head, looking Ina in the eye, and a terrible suspicion formed in the witch's mind.

'Put me down and bring Nerissa here,' she said

'Daro, you heard her. Put Ina down. I will summon the arch healer.' Ren's voice was a calming balm in the storm of fear as his words broke through Daro's panic. He nodded when their eyes met, and she could feel his relief through their bond, making the stones in her regalia flare to life as she struggled to control the maelstrom of emotion. He is safe. Velka was the target of Veles's prediction, and now she had to fix it. *Stupid, reckless wench taking on a god!* she scolded herself, entering the room as soon as Daro released his grip.

Zmij raised his ethereal head, the unblinking stare focused on Ina's every move as she walked forward. With wary respect, the witch bowed to Lada's guardian and approached her friend. When Ina touched Velka's face, her eyes snapped open, and the winged serpent withdrew, shrinking to cover the child within the mage's womb.

'Ina? How?' she mumbled. Hearing her quiet voice, Daro burst into the room.

'My love, I'm sorry. I didn't know what to do. That monstrous snake chased me out of the room as soon as I put you down. What is going on?' The gentleness of his hand stroking his wife's cheek starkly contrasted with the panicked voice.

Velka smiled slightly, resting her cheek on his palm before her pupils widened and, moaning loudly, she grasped her belly. 'Gods, that hurts.'

Ina looked down, eyes widening as a wave of crimson spread out from beneath her cursing friend. Suddenly Velka flinched, bending forward as a spasm tore a sob from her throat.

'Daro, sit behind her. She's going into labour, and she needs you,' Ina commanded, taking Velka's hand. 'It'll be all right, Flower. I won't let him take you. You were right. I shouldn't have tried the potion, but you won't be paying for my stupidity.' She wiped the sweat that beaded on her friend's forehead. Velka turned towards Ina, and the witch could see a glimmer of understanding in her friend's eyes before another contraction wiped away all thought, sending another wave of blood onto the white linen.

'Clear the corridor. Bring the midwife or any woman with some knowledge of childbirth. Make sure Lady Nerissa has free passage through the town.' She heard Mar's voice as he took control of the household. Ina looked at Zmij as it observed them with an unblinking stare.

'You protected her from Veles's call. She is the chosen of Lada. Do your duty, whatever the price, serpent,' she said, and the creature grew, spreading his wings above their heads.

'Ina, what is going on here?' Daro was as pale as his wife, holding her tight, and Ina inhaled deeply.

'I escaped Veles's realm, but the veil demands what it's due. Don't worry, I promise it won't take Velka or your son. Now that I can say goodbye to my friends, I will pay death's price,' Ina said, looking down as her soul-sister gripped her hand with what little strength remained. The baby was coming, but the witch worried Velka was losing too much blood to deliver him. A twinge of anxiety stole her breath as she remembered the dragon spark in her chest, but it hadn't been that long since Mar had shared it, so surely he'd be fine? Looking at Velka and Daro, Ina smiled. For a love this pure, she would happily return to Nawia, and this time she would cross the veil holding her best friend's hand.

Ina took a deep breath and linked her meridians to Velka's. The witch smiled as she remembered doing this for Mar and Ren, but there would be no spell this time. Instead, Ina opened the wellspring of her soul and poured all that she was into her friend's struggling body.

Ina could see the problem in her mind's eye. The placenta was ruptured, the blood escaping at an alarming rate, but she could only slow its progress, hopefully buying them enough time for a healer to work their magic.

The world began spinning as Ina's magic drained from her body, strengthening the mother. *I'm so going to kick Vele's arse when I see him again. He will have his entertainment but regret every moment in my com-*

pany, she thought, each scheme in her mind making her smile darker and more vicious.

Suddenly, calloused hands ripped her away from Velka's side, and through the haze of her dizziness, Ina saw Nerissa looking at her with deep concern in her eyes.

'Mar, take her away. This stupid girl is on the verge of draining herself to death. Foolish girl!'

'No, you don't understand. The veil needs a soul. I should have stayed, but I hoped.... Now it won't rest till someone I love dies. Even if you save Velka, there will be someone else; Mar or Ren. It has to be me. I thought I could escape this, but even a chaos archmage can't cheat death. It has to be me, Aunty.' Ina finished in tears, struggling against Mar's grip.

'No, child, it doesn't have to be you. I'm proud of the woman you became. I love you, my bright, beautiful Ina, and I hope what I do now will go some way to repay you for the future I stole from you. Remember, this was my choice. Mar, take her away before she does something stupid.' Nerissa's scowl softened into a compassionate, loving smile, tearing something deep within Ina's heart, and the witch started losing control of her chaos magic.

'No!'

A wave of crimson magic pulsed out as Ina tore herself from her dragon's grasp, but before she could take a step, Nerissa's smile dropped as she nodded sharply to Mar, and the world went dark.

After following Ina through the city, Mar worried she was becoming too distraught about who Veles would take to Nawia in her stead, so rather than interfere, he took control of the household, willing to support her no matter what happened. Once the servants had clear orders, their panic receded, and soon everyone had work to occupy their minds, with Ren fetching Ina's aunt and a few elderly women preparing the items necessary to deliver the baby. Mar paced, watching as Ina became still, then nearly stumbled as his crazy, wonderful spitfire began giving her life force to Velka. He knew the witch hadn't realised she was dooming them both, but seeing the deathly pallor of the pregnant mage, Mar kept his silence, gritting his teeth as the life drained from his body, happy he was helping Ina save someone she loved.

Mar stood watching the colour fading from Ina's face, feeling their strength fading as she kept Velka alive. By the time Nerissa arrived, he was nearly on his knees, at the end of his endurance. As the arch healer strode towards her patient, Mar held up a hand, preventing her passage, and, before she could berate him, told her why Ina was trying to sacrifice herself for the pregnant mage. Nerissa's face was ashen as he finished his story, and the old healer sighed deeply.

'This debt has to be paid, Marcach. Even magic has limits, and while healers and necromancers can affect the body, only the divine rule over the soul.'

'Then let them take mine. I took the choice from her, so I must shoulder the blame for this mess. I can't live without Ina, so in the end, it doesn't matter if Veles gets my hide.'

'What about the bonding ritual you told me about? If one of you dies, the other will follow. I will handle this. Just promise me you will keep her safe and happy.'

Guilt burned its presence on Mar's face as he stood helpless before the arch healer. With a smirk, Nerissa dismissed his feelings, pragmatic as usual. 'Everybody dies, boy. Stop being so touchy about it. I'm lucky my last battle will save a child I love as my own.'

Nerissa was a tower of strength who would face down monarchs and wilful nieces, but Mar knew her brusque manner hid a generous heart and smiled his gratitude, nearly missing her following words.

'When I give you the sign, knock her out cold, or this could all go very wrong. Ina will understand my reasons in time, but she'll never stand idly by if I offer myself in her stead. You and Sa'Ren are the only ones able to withstand her magic as she begins losing control, so be ready, because I'm sure she won't be happy. Now less of this maudlin talk; let us bring a new life into this world.'

The old healer had been right. When Ina realised Nerissa's intentions, chaos magic escaped her control, threatening everyone's safety. With one precise strike to her temple, Mar knocked the witch unconscious and caught her limp body just as Zmij hissed a warning to the shadows gathering in the room's corners.

Mar looked at the creature, its scales shimmering like molten gold, its magic protecting Velka rather than Ina, and for once, he was grateful he could defend his woman, even if retreat might be the only solution, but that moment wasn't now, as Mar watched, awestruck, while the healers worked at saving mother and baby, Nerissa standing over them, chanting and gesturing, creating a barrier of light and love that held the shadows back from their prey.

The healthy wail of a newborn child made everyone smile, the healers concentrating their efforts on Velka as the midwife swaddled the small boy, but it didn't take long till the mages sighed their relief, and Velka regained the colour to her cheeks.

However, as congratulations were passed around, Mar felt the bitter touch of the veil, its mists gathering building despite Nerissa's efforts, power older than the gods themselves filling the room

'I, Nerissa of Thorn, arch healer of Cornovii, claim blood right to the debt owed by my niece, Inanuan Zoria Thornsen; my soul for hers, a life lived for a destiny to be fulfilled.' Respect and sorrow filled Mar's heart as he bore witness to the healer's sacrifice, the mists gathering up Nerissa's soul, and as he cradled Ina tenderly, the warrior silently bowed and left the room.

As Mar gently laid Ina on the bed in a spare room, refusing to release his hold, Ren joined them, stroking the witch's face as the dragon confessed to his friend.

'I caused this. My stealing Ina from the mists of Nawia led to the death of the one member of her family she truly loved, but I couldn't let her die. Maybe I should have joined her instead and saved her heartbreak,' he whispered, shaking his head slowly as Ren frowned.

'No, I would have made the same decision in your place, but she will need someone to blame, or she will turn all this guilt into self-loathing.'

'It's a burden I shall gladly bear if this made Ina's life easier, but when her anger turns on me, she will need you. Now more than ever. Don't let her withdraw into herself. Tell her it was not her fault.' His focus was on the sounds outside, and he missed when Ina opened her eyes, only looking when she struggled in his embrace.

'Let me go, Marcach.' Her voice was as cold as her eyes when she looked at him, and even Ren flinched at her icy gaze.

'Velka or Nerissa?' she asked, looking at Ren.

'Lady Nerissa. The arch healer offered her life in place of yours, my lady.' Ren lowered his head when she pushed past him, heading towards

Velka's bedroom. The men followed, at a loss, watching as Ina paused at the threshold of her friend's room, staring at the scene before her.

An exhausted but content Velka cuddled her son while servants rushed around, cleaning up the blood. Daro looked at his wife with such besotted love and awe that the rest of the world ceased to exist for them. Nerissa was laid out reverently on a makeshift stretcher, flowers from gods knew where adorning her body. Ina approached her slowly, hesitantly, leaning down to stroke the mother of her heart's face, tears flowing over her cheeks.

'Ina?' Mar asked, stepping forward to embrace her, but without even looking, the witch held up her hand, stopping him. His heart broke when he looked at the side of her face, the harsh planes resembling a statue more than a human being. Not even a hint of chaos or anger escaped her control when she turned her eyes towards him.

'Don't. You have done more than enough this day.' Her words, emotionless and cutting, hurt him more than any wound. She walked to her friend's bed, and Daro instinctively sheltered Velka with his massive body, making Mar curse under his breath.

After casting an embarrassed glance at Mar, Daro moved aside, allowing Ina to kiss her friend's brow tenderly.

'Congratulations, Flower. Your son is beautiful, as I knew he would be.' Her voice was so emotionless that, despite his intention to give her space, Mar turned and followed the witch as she left. His initial worry grew as Ina didn't return to her room, instead heading for the exit and not even grabbing a cloak. Finally, before she left Velka's courtyard, Mar caught her shoulder, spinning the witch around to face him.

'Ina, please at least tell me where you are going.'

'Let me go,' she said, her temper at last slipping its reins, and a blast of chaos propelled him backwards.

'I can't, my love. Not whilst I see you suffering. Please, yell, hit me, or even throw me through another door, but don't leave like this.'

'I'm fine,' she said when he approached her again.

'No, you're not. Just because you've got a tight grip on your magic doesn't mean everything is fine.' The longer she was like this, the more worried he was. Ina never bottled up her emotions. Mar expected sadness, anger, even hatred, but this?

'Ina, talk to me. You are not fine. Do you think I don't know you well enough to know that?' He almost missed seeing the rage twisting her features before it disappeared into the emotionless mask once more as she answered him.

'Oh no, Marcach. I am fine. I'm always fine. People drop like flies around me as I move from catastrophe to catastrophe, but good old Ina is always fine. Even when those I love die to protect me. Here I am. Without a single wound, fine and dandy, so please, just this once, leave me the fuck alone.'

CHAPTER FOURTEEN

Ina wandered the streets of Osterad, a chill breeze cooling the warm tears falling unnoticed in her grief. The world ceased to exist as the raging storm within fought to escape. Her thoughts spiralled out of control, guilt and loss fuelling the chaotic, wild magic building up around her.

She wanted to incinerate the pain from existence, to cauterise the raw wound that was the remnants of her soul, but no matter how far she walked, there was no escape from the knowledge that someone else had paid for her stupidity. No, not someone. Nerissa. The one person who'd refused to abandon the freak, loving her despite her various mistakes, helping her no matter what. Who, when Ina had been exiled, at her lowest ebb, had made sure she washed up on the Leshy's doorstep.

'I failed you, and I failed myself. I am a coward; an ungrateful trickster who counted on someone else bailing them out of trouble,' she whispered, her steps absentmindedly leading her home.

Marika looked up in surprise when Ina entered the house like she'd never left for the southern war, sitting in her favourite chair without a word. Boruta appeared from a dark corner to jump on Ina's lap, purring so loudly that her housekeeper gave him a warning glare before she bent and took Ina's boots.

'Rest. You look like you went to Nawia and back,' she said brusquely, falling back when Ina burst into hysterical laughter, the manic sound turning into breathless, pain-filled sobs. The witch pushed her face into the cat's thick fur, wailing till her eyes ran dry and breathing became difficult. When nothing was left, the witch sat cradling Boruta, her anchor to a simpler, innocent time.

'I will make you some tea,' Marika said while stroking Ina's hair back, wiping away the tears still falling from her eyes. The witch didn't react, not even when her housekeeper retreated to the kitchen and burst through the backdoor, sprinting into the night.

Ina flicked her wrist, her magic dousing the flames in the fireplace, wanting to feel the night's dark embrace with only her furred friend for company, unable to stop the intrusive thoughts mocking her confidence. *What is the point? Why fight the inevitable if all I do is hurt the ones I love?* Ina felt hope draining away with each unanswered question until the mournful sound of a flute intruded upon her grief. Unable to cope with the hint of hope within the tune, the witch clutched her head, covering her ears to block the melody out.

Yet still, she could hear it. The soft refrain evoked a feeling of courage, sacrifice, and soldiering on, despite all adversity. How one instrument could make her feel so much would forever be a mystery, but she knew the soul who breathed life into the tune had experienced each emotion he conveyed with each note. Lost within the magical sound, tears once more blurring her vision, Ina felt a familiar masculine warmth enfolding her in its embrace and startled upright, dislodging a disgruntled feline as she broke away.

'Mar, what are you doing here?' she asked sharply.

'It's my home. I know you are angry, and if you tell me to pack and go, I will, but I didn't want you to be alone. If it would ease your pain, I would carve out my heart for you. Please, my love, let me help you. Let me be here for you.' His soft voice radiated with such sadness, but Ina shook her head.

'No, Mar. It is too little, too late.' At Ina's response, Mar's shoulders dropped in defeat.

'My love, I'm not sorry for what I did, only for the sadness my actions have caused you. I don't regret taking your soul from the veil. I would do it again in the blink of an eye, all because I'm a selfish bastard. I know you blame yourself for what happened, but you're not. Nerissa's death is my fault because I couldn't, and never will, let you go. So place the blame where it belongs, on me, the man who made the decision for you and brought you back, despite knowing the consequences.' The raw emotion in Mar's voice cut through the sorrow in her heart; despite this, she still couldn't accept his argument.

'Yes, you did. You came in and saved the woman you love like some maiden's wet dream, all manly and perfect, and yes, I wanted to hate you for that, but the truth is, this is my fault. I caused this. The fear of my magic and losing the bonds that kept it in check led me to make the wrong choices, ignoring Velka's warnings and using the research of the woman who damaged my bonds. I did what I did because I was a coward who skipped to the easiest solution instead of trying harder. I could have claimed the last piece of the regalia, but all I saw was Sowenna using them to destroy Warenga without questioning why she'd done it. All I could focus on were the bonds, feeling you in my heart, having Ren's quiet presence there, always supporting me despite my fears. I wanted the bond so much that nothing stopped me from getting it back. I don't need to destroy the world to be a villain. There is no redemption for me, and... you should go. I don't deserve you or Ren.'

Mar pulled Ina close again, worrying as his tempestuous witch docilely cooperated. 'Do you hear yourself, Ina? A woman capable of such feelings is no villain. And if you won't hate me, then hate those who forced your hand. You didn't start this, and you didn't extinguish the bond. You are a victim as much as Nerissa. Hate those who started this senseless war and poisoned you.'

It surprised Ina how much Mar's words comforted her, loosening the hard knot crushing her lungs, and she couldn't resist resting her head on his broad chest, listening to the strong heartbeat within. Hesitantly, she examined their bond, feeling the pain and exhaustion Mar was trying to shield from her. 'You are wrong to think highly of me. When I realised it was Nerissa who died, I felt relieved it wasn't Velka. That is the type of person I am.'

'So you're not perfect. You fought a god, clung to a dragon's back for hours, then chased around the city to make sure your friends were alive, and felt relief Velka didn't die. Will it help to know I've seen this before, after the battle? Young men and women, happy to be alive, feeling guilty when their friends died instead? Love, never feel guilty for surviving, instead grieve for those you lost.' The desperation in Mar's words was punctuated with the kisses that stole away the tears once again rolling over her cheeks.

'Live your life, Ina. Continue making Nerissa proud and make those who would harm you pay for their crimes,' he said, stroking her cheek with his thumb. Ina hid her face in his arms, letting his warmth envelop her. When the door opened, and careful footsteps joined them, the witch sighed but didn't raise her head.

'My lady, may I join you?' Without waiting for her answer, Ren came close, kneeling beside them. When his head rested against her leg, Ina stroked his hair.

'You are always welcome here, Ren. Thank you for playing your flute. It never fails to touch my heart in a way words never could,' she said, turning towards him with a sad smile ghosting across her lips. *Did I hurt this beautiful soul with my pain?* she wondered, her fingers tracing the side of his enigmatic face. 'I'm sorry for hurting you. I know it's difficult being my friend and even harder to be bonded with me, but I want you to know... if Velka is the sister of my heart, then you are its brother. I love you.' She sniffed, looking in disbelief at the tear that landed on her hand. Mar's arms tightened around her, but he remained quiet. Still, she felt his hand stroking her shoulders, comforting her.

'I don't know what to do, my lady. I can feel your sadness and know how much you loved your aunt. Please tell me how can I help you.'

'Be happy. Love your dragoness, marry her, have children, and do whatever makes you happy, but never sacrifice your life for mine. I can't live with anyone else dying for me. Promise me.' Her chaos flowed from Ina's fingers, gliding over his skin, giving him a demonic visage as she commanded him. 'Promise me, Sa'Ren Gerel. Promise me before I place a geas upon you.'

The power in her voice widened his pupils, and the quiet warrior looked at Mar. 'What is she talking about?'

'Ina died. In order to save her, I split the dragon spark and followed her to Nawia. We didn't realise—no, *I* didn't realise—the price for her return would be Nerissa's life. My life is hers now. We live or die together.'

Ren's hand squeezed her knee, and Ina hissed quietly at the pain, looking at his suddenly pale face. 'You died?' he whispered, lowering his eyes, but Ina saw the flash of anguish within them. However, when he looked back, whatever emotion he felt was hidden beneath the cold visage of the Ghost.

'I cannot promise this, my lady, because I would gladly sacrifice my life for those I love, especially the woman who taught me I deserved that love. If you place me under a geas, then know this: I will fight it with every fibre of my being and never forgive you for denying me that choice.' Ren looked at the tendrils of chaos, feeling the light sting of their magic. 'Ina, fate brought us together, creating a bond of friendship that awoke my heart. We each have our choices—Mar, Nerissa and me—so please don't take that away. I choose to guard you from the darkness of the world and the soul. Do not destroy our friendship by enthralling me.'

Mar gently cupped her face, turning her towards him. 'Please, my love, let it go. With your past, it's difficult to accept that people love you, but they do. Even the soldiers in the barracks use your name as their lucky charm. Deep down, you know Ren is right, and you would do the same for him.'

'You are both idiots,' Ina muttered under her breath, and Mar smiled, gesturing Ren to stay where he was.

'Stay with Ina, please. I will arrange food and a bath. It was a long day, and the future may look better with a full stomach,' he said, heading to the kitchen.

Mar collided with Marika, Ina's one-armed housekeeper, who stopped him in his tracks.

'Thank you for finding me,' he said, looking at the shapeshifter in gratitude. 'I have to ask your assistance once more tonight; something to eat and a bath, please. I know it's late—' He stopped when she raised her hand.

'Food is in the kitchen, so make sure she eats it, she looks like a half-starved beggar, and the bath will be ready by the time you've finished. Your words are right. Many love her, but she doesn't love herself right now. You must help her, dragon,' she said, leaving Mar rubbing his neck before he returned to Ina with a sheepish smile.

'Why do I always have a feeling she's scolding me? It seems I am to feed you so you don't fade away, and once you have eaten your fill, a bath shall be ready and waiting.'

For the first time that evening, Ina truly smiled. The relationship between Mar and Marika was always entertaining to watch, and while the pair would never be as thick as thieves, they both seemed to respect each other immensely.

'That's because she is scolding you, and I can't say I blame her. Even now, you've made a mess, despite so many times being asked to remove your boots when you arrive. Still, at least she trained you to clean your weapons in your little shed. I believe she is the best investment I've made for this household.'

As she finished, Ren stood up, placing a kiss on the back of her hand. 'On that note, I should make my escape before she turns her harridan's tongue in my direction. Please get some rest, my lady. I hope you can tell me what exactly happened during your absence once you've slept.' Ina nodded as he released her hand, the quiet warrior turning to Mar as he readied to leave. 'You must seek an audience with the king and show your face at the barracks. I know it's not the best time, but it can't be postponed.'

'I will go as soon as you arrive to keep Ina company,' Mar said as the men clasped forearms, nodding brusquely to each other.

Ina refrained from rolling her eyes as Ren left, turning to her lover, and strengthening her shields to hide her emotions in an attempt to stop him from worrying about her state of mind.

'You don't need to guard me, my love. I will gladly welcome Ren's company, but I don't want to see you or him shadowing my every step. I will be fine. I just need time to come to terms with losing... with what happened. And when I'm ready, I will ask for your help to find Mirena because I will know no peace till she is brought to justice.'

Her dragon looked down, his possessive stare capturing her gaze. Something shifted in his eyes before he bent down, gathering a handful of hair and inhaling deeply as he pressed it to his face. 'I'm too afraid of losing you again so soon after our last adventure. Forgive this overprotective dragon and allow it for a day or two. Ren is the only man I trust with your safety. I'm the lord marshal, probably the worst this country has ever had, but I need to see to my duties, and he needs time with you. I had the luxury of being able to search for you while Ren was burdened with my responsibilities. This solution will be good for all of us.'

Ina reached up and stroked his beard. 'If you put it that way, how can I say no?'

Mar captured her hand, gently kissing her fingertips. 'Thank you, my love,' he said, swaying a little, his weary look making Ina frown.

'Come, we need to eat. I forced you to fly too much today. You must be exhausted,' she said.

Mar didn't resist as she led the way to the kitchen, but she saw him shrug and straighten his back, acting to hide the previous display of weakness. 'I could eat,' he said, his nonchalant tone hiding his embarrassment. Marika was nowhere to be seen, but three plates piled high with cold cuts and still-warm pancakes waited for them at the table. Ina observed Mar inhaling the lion's share as she daintily nibbled a pancake. *We are both acting to protect one another*, she thought. Despite appearing relaxed after their conversation, Ina was still overwhelmed with a grief and guilt even the sweet, delicious food couldn't dispel.

The bath relieved their aching muscles, and Ina did her best to massage Mar's shoulder, feeling him flinch each time she touched the lightning scar. *If Nerissa was here, she could fix him in no time*, she thought, stealthily erasing the unwanted tears before her dragon noticed. After almost falling asleep in hot water, Ina dragged Mar to the bedroom, where he instantly passed out, leaving the witch to stare sightlessly at the ceiling, lost in thought.

With only a hint of the moon's glow illuminating the room, Ina allowed the dam holding back her tears to break, letting them flow freely as she reminisced about her aunt and their relationship. They were too similar in temperament to have a peaceful relationship, but Ina had to admit, in many ways, Nerissa was more a mother to her than Nessa ever was.

A silent jostle on the mattress presaged the arrival of a deadly hunter as Boruta pushed against Ina's cheek, demanding attention whilst sharing the warmth of his compassion, then curling up, letting the witch press her face to his fur. The scent of forest called to her senses, drying the tears, and Ina sighed deeply when the heaviness in her chest eased. The Leshy always seemed to know when his presence would help, and, surrounded by love, Ina closed her eyes, letting the dragon's heartbeat and cat's purr lull her to sleep.

As Ina woke, the sound of raised male voices left her sighing, opening her eyes to the unblinking stare of a very annoyed cat, clearly upset his pillow had the audacity to move. The witch stroked his soft fur, letting reality set in. So many things had happened yesterday that she wasn't sure what was real. She'd returned from Nawia, flew for hours on a dragon's back, tried to heal Velka during her labour, and then her great-aunt had passed away. It all felt like one long, nightmarish fever dream, and now the men in her life were doing their best to prove life could still fall apart without her assistance.

'You'd think, just once, they'd give me one day to feel sorry for myself.' Ina's tut sounded more like a curse than a comment as she sat up, rubbing her cat's ears affectionately, but instead of his usual demands for cuddles, Boruta jumped off the bed, heading for the exit, miaowing in protest when she didn't follow. 'Right, I thought so,' she said, reaching for a large green shawl. Wrapped in its thick fabric, Ina felt shielded from the world, and that protection helped her walk downstairs.

Mar and Ren were already there, bending over a map and passionately discussing something.

'No, that won't do. Kion's walls won't last long under any sustained attacks. Suppose we're lucky, and they only have battering rams and ladders. In that case, the city might hold out long enough for us to send skirmishers, have them disrupt the empire's camp, destroy their supplies and cause enough havoc to get the main force there so we can crush them against the very walls they're attacking.'

Ren shook his head. 'The empire is too experienced to leave a flank unprotected. If we use communication crystals, we can draw upon Liath's forces and hit them hard with a force large enough to push them back behind the walls of Dancik. It will take longer and likely lead to more civilian casualties, but the army would be stronger for it.'

'You know their tactics. First, they land the vanguard to secure a beachhead and a source of supplies for their main armada. For us to have a fighting chance of defeating them, we need to push forward and ensure the larger ships have nowhere to land.' Mar rubbed the bridge of his nose. Ina could see how tense he was. Still, when they finally noticed her, his deep scowl melted into a warm, inviting smile.

'I hope you had a good night, my love,' he said, approaching her. With Ina still standing on the stairs, she was almost his height, and reaching out, she trailed her fingers through his wild mane, sweeping it back from his face.

'Mostly. I found my dragon's snoring strangely comforting.' Despite her sadness, she needed to tease him a little to erase this deep frown crease from between his eyebrow. 'Care to tell me what you're arguing about?'

'Military strategy, my spitfire. Many things happened whilst we were on our latest adventure. In short, Dancik was taken by the Iron Empire, and I'm trying to catch up with the state of our forces.'

'That's why I asked Mar to go to the barracks. I'm afraid we won't be able to repeat the tricks we used in the south, my lady. I briefed the king on your arrival, emphasising your need for rest. Still, the matter is urgent, and Rewan will hold a special council meeting tomorrow,' Ren said, approaching them, then reached out and trailed his fingers over her forehead, barely touching her. 'Is that what I think it is? The final piece of the chaos regalia? Why are you wearing it, my lady?'

'Because I didn't give her a choice.' Mar's grumpy answer forced a smile from her lips before Ina reached out, following Ren's fingers.

'I forgot about it. It is strange that something I was afraid of became a part of me so quickly. However, walking around with what amounts to a crown won't be the best idea when seeing the king.' Within moments, Ina had a piece of chalk and was drawing something on the floor, whispering a few words to activate the simple illusion spell used by university students to enhance their features. She hid the diadem from view.

Ren allowed his concern to show, even as he smiled. 'But what about your magic, my lady? Does it not bother you any more than usual?'

His question left Ina feeling cared for, her answer more honest and open than the two men expected. 'No. If anything, it feels calmer and not so bound up with my emotions. I suspect last night would have been much different without it. With Nerissa... passing as she did, I doubt even my bonds with you both would have prevented a catastrophe. Which, sadly, reminds me. I must arrange to transport my aunt's body to the temple, arrange her funeral, and visit Velka. The happiest day of her life, and I didn't even congratulate her properly. We need to find Rurik, the necromancer who brought Velka here. He might know more about the Iron Empire. Oh, and I have to talk to Jorge and Arun—'

'Ina, stop. How about you spend the day at home and rest? You are tired and have to recover from yesterday's events. Please, just for one day,' Mar pleaded, making her smile bitterly.

'Just like you're going to rest? If I stay home, I'll only think about my misdeeds and how my actions killed the woman who was more my mother than the one who gave birth to me. I'm not trying to be obstructive. I can't stop and rest because I feel my heart is crumbling to pieces with nothing to focus on.' Ina's breath quickened when she fought her grief. Ren stepped forward, reaching for her hand.

'Then allow me to accompany you, my lady. We will visit whoever you choose while Mar is at the camp, but if I see you struggling, I will bring you back home.'

'You are both so overbearing. Fine, have it your way. I could never refuse your company, especially if you promise to stop Daro from breaking my neck,' she said, turning her gaze to Mar. 'And you promise me you'll be back home before nightfall. I don't want to sleep alone.'

Mar leaned forward, kissing the top of her head. 'You were cuddling the cat more than me, but I'll be back as soon as possible. And for once, be a good girl and listen to Ren.' At the odd choice of words, the witch frowned, looking at the dragon.

'I told you I don't need protection.'

'No, but you need to eat, rest and smile, at least occasionally, and Ren is here to remind you. Don't think I didn't notice that you barely ate anything yesterday. I was just too tired to argue.'

Ina sighed, seeing Ren looking at her with disapproval. 'I'll get dressed before you both make me feel like an unruly toddler. I was simply not in the mood to eat.'

When she turned to go back upstairs, Mar grabbed the hem of her dress, stopping her, and within moments, Ina landed in his arms.

'My intention was not to scold you, but to remind you there are peo-ple who love you and care that you look after yourself, especially now. I promised Nerissa I would do it, and I intend to keep this promise in every aspect of your life.'

Ina rolled her eyes when she escaped his clutches. 'That will certainly be an interesting experience for both of us. Now, please let me go. I have things to do,' she said, running up the stairs, but before disappearing, she looked down at Ren.

'Did Zjawa come back?' The desperate hope in her voice made the quiet warrior answer quickly.

'Yes, my lady. Your loyal, cantankerous mount awaits your pleasure.'

CHAPTER FIFTEEN

Mar left while Ina was getting ready. She heard the men discussing military strategy and felt their anxiety through their bonds. They each worried that the preparations for war would be insufficient, wanting to immerse themselves in planning whilst concern for her made them feel guilty and inadequate.

Mar hadn't left Ina's side all night, his body pressed against hers, arm possessively preventing escape, even at one point losing control of his transformation, a wave of scales covering his body as he muttered in his sleep, 'Don't leave me. You are my life,' and only the touch of her hand stroking his cheek calmed the restless dragon. Their short time in Nawia, followed by Nerissa's death, had traumatised them both, and her heart ached to soothe him, but her own world was a pit of self-loathing and guilt. Mar's touch was the only thing that stopped her from dissolving into the shadows, so she let him hold her close even when the heat from his skin turned their bed into a furnace.

Ina looked in the mirror. The face looked the same, but somehow different. The cheeky glint of mischief in her eyes had disappeared. Their grey-green colour, now flecked with crimson and gold, revealed the influence of chaos and the dragon spark. She removed the illusion spell from the circlet, and the intricate pattern of gold encrusted with peridots and the central stone shone on her forehead, pulsing in harmony with the ring, the necklace and the beat of her heart. *I can break and remake the world, but couldn't save one beautiful soul. Oh, Aunty, I would give it all up to have you scold me again.*

Ina pondered over the implications of wearing all three of Sowenna's jewels. It wasn't as if she could take them off anyway, as each formed a part of her soul, a soul that had grown and felt as if it pressed against her skin, ready to burst out at the slightest provocation. The strangest part, however, was the lack of fear. The witch had never felt so complete, so in control, but was that due to their influence or the golden sun now residing in her chest? Could she have prevented all those deaths at Liath if she'd just accepted the diadem from Skarbnik and freed Marzanna without nearly losing her humanity?

Thoughts of blame and guilt spiralled through her mind as Ina drew upon her magic in its most basic form. Crimson fire surrounded her hand, and as she studied the raw chaos, the witch noticed golden flames interspersed amongst the red. *You should have left me in the afterlife, my love.*

Mar had said he would burn the world to ash for her, but did he realise how close they'd come to it happening? The moment she'd learned about Nerissa's sacrifice, grief and rage had torn through her body, only to be diverted, tamed and harnessed by the magical stones. Even then, if Mar hadn't knocked her out, she would have fought back the veil from its victim.

Initially, she'd wanted to rip Mar apart, to remove him from her life for taking another choice away from her. *The old me certainly would have, and that crazy lizard knew it, but still risked losing the woman he cherished to save my life.* Ina scowled at her thoughts. *I keep making the wrong choices. Is that what the gods planned for me? To have me live long enough to become the wraith overburdened by too many sacrifices?*

'My lady, are you all right?' Ren's voice, as calm as ever, interrupted her dark musing. Ina hastily reconstructed the illusion spell. The fewer who knew about her latest acquisition, the better. As for her friends, she would tell them as soon as she felt ready.

She came downstairs, noticing Mar's absence, as Ren held out a hand to assist her. Without a second thought, Ina ran down, embracing him. Ren smelled like home. His herbal scent, mixed with the crispness of fresh linen, teased her enhanced senses, bringing back happy memories. Ren reciprocated her hug, stroking her back gently.

'I'm happy to see you too, my lady. After yesterday's events, I took the liberty to inform the palace that whilst you had returned, you were not resuming your duties and did not wish to be disturbed. I can see you haven't slept well, so you can rest for the day and tell me what I can do to help you.' Ren's words made Ina bite her lip as she held back her emotions, but it didn't stop him from feeling them through their bond, his hands pausing as he contemplated the feelings. 'It's good to feel your presence again. It felt like a light was gone from my life when your soul disappeared.'

Ina sighed and raised her head, looking into eyes full of compassion.

'I'm sorry, my friend. You guarding a foolish woman who followed her selfish instincts and ruined everything. I failed you, failed everyone, so I can't sit down and rest. I have to see Velka and ensure she and the baby are well. I messed up so much, Ren. I could have killed you all because I was too afraid to face the power of my magic alone,' she said, pulling away, but Ren's arms held her tight.

'You haven't failed anyone; not me, Mar or Velka. You can't control everything in this world, so you do the best you can. My lady... Ina, those who love you would readily sacrifice themselves for you because they know you would do the same for them. Nerissa made her choice, knowing she was saving two lives. Whether it was Velka and her child or you and Mar, she saved two souls for hers. The dragon bond means just this: if you die, the dragon will follow. Nerissa saved the people she loved. Please don't let your grief diminish the beauty of her actions.'

Ina felt moisture pool in her eyes again. 'How do you always know what to say, and how come you know so much about the dragon bond?' she asked, wiping her tears.

'Ayni asked if I would join with her.'

'Please tell me you agreed. Ayni is lovely, beautiful, and makes the most perfect armour. Ren, you must say yes.' Ina rambled with only one thought in her head. She wouldn't have to see him wither and die if he joined with the dragoness. Ren would be safe with the woman he loves, and she could be his friend for as long as they chose.

Ren burst out laughing. 'My lady, you are wonderfully bizarre. I know Ayni is not your favourite person. You two are too alike to have a harmonious relationship, but I'm happy I have your enthusiastic consent. I said yes. I will marry her as per Cornovii's custom and take the dragon spark once our situation settles.'

Ina blinked rapidly, absorbing his words, her silence bringing a frown to his face. 'What is the matter, my lady? I—'

Ina placed a hand on his mouth before he could utter another word. 'I wasn't expecting a wedding, but for you, I will be her flower girl or shut up and stand in a dark corner, whatever she desires. I'm happy for you both. You're right, we are very much alike, both short-tempered and stubborn, but she makes you happy, and her gift means I won't have to say goodbye to you. I can never repay her for this,' she said, feeling Ren's smile under her hand as she pulled away.

'Let's go see Velka. I have to make sure she is well, and you can prove how much you're willing to sacrifice for me by thwarting an angry orc because, after last night, I'm sure he sees me as the root of all evil.'

Ren nodded, and a few moments later, they were trotting through the busy streets of Osterad. After talking with him, the constant biting grief inside her subsided, and Ina let the orein choose their pace. When she had first walked into the stables, Zjawa looked at her, then sniffed every inch of her body before head-butting her to the floor and neighing her indignation. Ren stepped in to intervene, but Ina stopped him and approached the unusual mare, embracing her neck.

'I'm sorry. I know you've been worried, and I smell slightly different now. Thank you for choosing to stay.' She stroked the soft, grey coat, whispering soothing words while the orein nibbled her hair. Ultimately, her mount stepped away from the witch's caress, making her laugh. 'Am I too clingy?'

The neigh carried mocking tones, and the witch saddled her easily, happy Skarbnik hadn't recalled her friend after Mar's encounter.

Velka's house welcomed them with an abundance of flowers and frenetic activity. She could hear Daro shouting orders while the poor servants ran around like headless chickens, trying to satisfy his demands. Ina looked at Ren, barely restraining her laughter.

'Time to beard the angry father in his den. Protect me, my warrior,' she said, directing Zjawa to the yard. The servants didn't stop to greet her, recognising their mistress's friend. Ina promptly walked upstairs, straight to the bedroom, knocking and entering after hearing a whispered commotion behind closed doors. The scene she was confronted with left her speechless.

Velka, as beautiful as Lada herself, looked down in joy as she nursed her child whilst an embattled Daro, bleeding from various cuts, fought back branches and twigs sprouting from the floor. As another stream of cursing issued from the orc's mouth, Ina couldn't restrain her laughter, surprising both parents into looking in her direction.

'I came to apologise and congratulate the new parents, not to prune the furniture. What's going on?' she asked and moved closer to the bed, Velka looking up with a slightly harried expression.

'Daro is attempting to make a cradle because everybody in his tribe makes one for their newborn. Not that he knows how to build one or has any carpenter skills, but it must be done this way. Could you turn him into a frog or something?'

'I want to do something for my son. What's wrong with this? I almost lost him because you two couldn't help messing with the gods. What is so difficult to understand?' Daro said, not even sparing them a glance as a willow switch slipped his grasp, smacking him in the face.

'Well, that explains it. I thought you'd lost control of your magic, Flower.' With a smirk, Ina turned to the lurking Ren. 'I think our newest Papa Bear needs a break from his heroic deed. Could you take Daro for a drink before those stubborn twigs trigger his berserker fury?' The witch grinned as the quiet warrior nodded, rolling up his sleeves with a determined expression.

'I'm not going anywhere. Velka might need me, and I'm not leaving my son!'

Ina sighed and looked the enraged orc directly in the eyes. 'I understand your worry, but you stink, and Velka needs a rest. Hearing your curses and grunts all morning must have been exhausting. With me here, nothing will happen to her.'

Daro wanted to argue, but Ren intervened. 'Come. Give your wife some rest. We'll find a carpenter to help us finish this task.' Ren took Daro by the elbow, leading the grumbling orc outside. Ina waited until the men left the room before turning towards Velka.

'Oh, Flower, let me offer my congratulations. How are you and the babe doing? Does he have a name?' she asked, sitting on the edge of the bed. *I hope she'll forgive me for endangering their lives*, Ina thought, biting her lip when Velka looked up, her gaze lingering on Ina's face.

'So you died. I told you it was dangerous, but you ignored my advice and died. I could have lost you because you were too stubborn to listen, just like we were in university, mixing weird concoctions to see what would happen, but this time, you really did it… and you couldn't even stay dead. Ina, you are a bloody menace provoking the god of death.' She sniffed, pushing her bundle of joy into Ina's hands and wiping her eyes, which turned into a fountain of tears.

'That last part wasn't my fault. Mar burst into Nawia and dragged me out, kicking and screaming. I'm sorry. I thought my potion was right, and it was just a tad too strong for my heart.'

'You and your dragon deserve each other, but why piss off Veles? I know your relationship with the gods is strange, to say at least, but out of all of them, the god of death?'

Velka, scolding her like this, felt as if Nerissa's spirit was standing over her friend's shoulder, nodding in agreement, and Ina couldn't help but savour the feeling. The bundle in her hands moved, and Ina looked down at the scrunched-up face of the newborn child. Something in his expression captured Ina's heart, his mixed heritage plain to see, with skin a fetching soft ochre and eyes the rich blue of his mother, which seemed to glow with a golden light. Velka was still talking, but Ina gaped at the baby, his soul so full of magic it glowed.

'He's shining,' Ina said in wonder.

'Yes, I know, Striga. Don't change the subject.'

'Velka. I know I messed up, and you are absolutely right, but I'm here alive and kicking with the dragon spark and full regalia, and it's still not as important as your son glowing.' Ina opened the wraps and looked at the wiggling child. Magic danced around him, and her own chaos responded, gently touching his skin. The little boy blessed by the goddess of life chirped under her touch, and Ina smiled softly. 'He is beautiful. You and that pigheaded husband of yours created a miracle.'

She heard Velka's soft laugh before the doting mother took the child back. 'Yes, well, this little miracle is Larian, and he's hungry again, so while I feed him, you can tell me what exactly happened and how you ended up with the last piece of the chaos regalia.'

Ina sighed, propping herself on the bed and placing her hand on Velka's thigh, feeling the irrational need to feel the life in her friend's body. Soft warmth calmed her inner worry, and Ina told her the story, starting with an apology for using the sleeping herbs.

'I'm not sure if I can forgive you for drugging me. One moment we were having tea, the next, I woke up in a jouncing carriage with Rurik pushing the horses to get us to Osterad. Oh, and let's not forget the whole new level of weirdness when contractions started in an inn, and Zmij appeared, scaring everyone away. The rest you know.' Velka smiled, placing the child beside her, and Ina frowned slightly.

'Not that it matters right now, but where is Rurik?' she asked, the frown deepening when Velka shrugged.

'I don't know. Daro told me he disappeared as soon as my feet cleared the carriage door, but my husband was so wrapped up in my condition he didn't see which way Rurik went,' said Velka, making Ina worry at her lip.

'He got you here reasonably safely when he could've abandoned you on the road, so that earns him a little leeway. Besides, I have bigger problems than chasing a manipulative necromancer around town. One of Kaian's or Gruff's informants will find him easily enough. I will send them a message later,' she said, distracted by the sound of the men returning. When the doors opened, she saw the wooden monstrosity that was supposed to be a cradle, the proud father placing it carefully on the floor.

'That... is my cue to head out, so I will leave you to enjoy family time,' she said, chuckling as she stood up. When Ina passed Daro, she briefly put her hand on his massive chest, and when the surprised orc looked at her, she smiled.

'Look after them, captain, especially now with war looming. I will handle this, but you are staying in Osterad,' she said, and his chest reverberated in a low growl.

'I'm a warrior, Ina. You can't prevent me from protecting my country. First, I missed the southern battle, and now you want me to stay home? Anyway, it's not your decision. Only the king and Mar may command me.'

Ina looked into his eyes, their warm brown irises filled with anger, and smiled. 'Maybe, but ask yourself who will they listen? We may not see eye to eye, but Velka loves you, and I love her. I'm not losing anyone else. She needs you here, so you will stay here, and if danger reaches the gates of Osterad, you will take her and my household to Liath,' she said, knowing she wasn't earning a friend but protecting the infant she'd guarded with her life from the mamuna, and the mother who'd bonded with her in love and friendship, both—now targets of the god of the underworld—were more important than frail orc's ego. Ina knew she couldn't allow anyone else to be taken from her.

Before the stunned orc could answer, she passed by him and left the room, chased by Velka's words. 'Ina, I'm not running away, and I'm not staying behind when you head to war. Someone has to keep an eye on you.'

Ina knew Ren watched her when they rode through Osterad to the healers' temple, but he remained quiet, letting the witch collect her thoughts. She knew she handled it poorly, but words failed her every time she faced the possibility of losing another loved one. Ina's careless statement wounded Daro's pride when a discreet conversation with Mar or Rewan would have avoided the issue altogether.

Ren took her hand as they walked into the shade of the temple entrance, its cool, pleasant air washing over them before leaving her to talk to the undertaker. The place was almost empty. A healer clad in white muslin led her to a small room near the back where Nerissa's body lay, covered by a thin shroud.

The indomitable woman, feared by nobles and mages alike, looked so fragile without the force of her personality shining out. Ina placed her hand on Nerissa's cheek, mourning the loss of the mother of her heart. The crushing weight of guilt pressed down on the witch, burying her beneath its cloying pressure. The pain she thought was chained deep within her soul broke free, shattering the facade of her control, and a piercing scream tore from her lips as the reality of their last goodbye broke through her denial.

Ina fell to her knees, sobbing uncontrollably, unable to close the floodgates. Chaos roared unrestrained, her mind collapsing into nothingness, unleashing destruction on the world.

Lost in thought, Ren stood in the temple foyer, still debating whether to follow Ina to see her aunt, his concern for her emotional state warring with giving her the privacy to say goodbye. At the sound of screaming, a rare curse slipped past his lips, and the normally calm warrior set off at a run, pushing through the panicked healers as he headed towards Ina.

Ren wasn't even surprised when he rounded the last corner, the whirlwind of primordial magic not slowing him down, the pain of its touch a passing discomfort as he crashed through it and the flimsy door to Nerissa's stateroom. Another curse slipped his control as he took in the scene before his eyes. Ina, a tiny figure curled next to the catafalque, holding her aunt's hand, surrounded by chaos, the magic a wild torrent destroying everything it touched, but miraculously avoiding Nerissa. Without a thought, the warrior continued through the vortex, relying on the bond to protect him, ignoring the pain it caused. As soon as he was close enough, Ren reached for the witch, locking her in a tight embrace.

Ina grabbed him with unexpected strength and wept, her face buried in his chest, and Ren felt helpless. He stroked her back, whispering soothing words, but nothing reached the resilient woman in this broken state. Her tears refused to abate, and the magic became more and more violent, disintegrating their surroundings without pause. *If this continues, she'll bury us alive*, he thought, looking at the cracks in the walls and ceiling, but he didn't relinquish his hold.

A bitter smile appeared on his lips when he closed his eyes. He'd found home, love and happiness, and would now lose it all, buried alive in the temple's tomb, but he could not leave her alone. Ina's sacrifice had brought him back to life, but it was her love and friendship that allowed him to live, to find Ayni and his place in this world. Now she was suffering, and the bond burned fiercely with her grief. *You returned me to life, and it is yours to take. I only wish I could tell Ayni how much I love her.*

When he thought all was lost, a monstrous, snarling figure tore through the veil of magic, heading towards them with unyielding strength. Ren saw Mar walking through the maelstrom of chaos like it was nothing, and when his friend reached out, Ren wordlessly passed him the witch. The dragon took one look at her face and, with deafening force, roared in challenge, forcing Ren to clap his hands to his ears, stunned by its ferocity, but even as Ren stood to defend Ina, the magic subsided, and her eyes snapped open, fury burning in their depths.

'No, my love. Nerissa wanted you to live on in spite of the gods' meddling. The woman I love would never give up, would never let chaos consume her, so cry as much as you want, but don't you dare give up!'

Ren heard the force in Mar's command as he watched his friend stroking Ina's hair, her sobs quietening against his chest. He breathed with relief when Ina looked up, still angry but in complete control of her senses. When she turned towards him, Ren moved closer.

'I'm so sorry, my lady. I shouldn't have left you alone,' he said, reaching for her, stopping when Mar shook his head, pressing Ina's body to his chest. Ren saw his friend struggling, his body still more dragon than man, but Ina reached out to stroke his cheek, tears still glistening in her eyes.

'I lost her, Ren. She will never scold me again, and I'll never feel her touch. The finality of this hurts so much,' she said, leaving him at a loss for words, looking to Mar for direction. His friend nodded slightly towards the doors.

'Calm the healers, please. I will take Ina home. Join us later to play for her... and don't blame yourself, we both failed, but she is so strong I keep forgetting that under all these thorns and brass is a woman who feels so deeply.'

Ren nodded as Ina embraced the dragon's neck, still crying a little, her face pressed to his chest once more. 'I will see you later, my lady. If you need to use the bond... me, if you need anything, please tell me because your tears are breaking my heart.'

He barely heard her answer, but it etched itself deep into his heart. 'Mirena, the empire, they will pay for what they forced me to do. They will pay for her death even if I have to burn them all to ash,' she said, hiccuping her words. Her voice was weak from crying, but the iron will behind it was clear. Ren bowed, hand pressed to his chest, witnessing her oath. He looked at Mar and saw him gently kissing Ina's forehead.

'They will pay. I'll make sure of it. Let me take you home, my love. Ren will handle the temple and the funeral. You are so hard on yourself, my beautiful chaos. I chose your life above the laws of the veil, and I will do whatever it takes to mend your broken heart.'

CHAPTER SIXTEEN

Mar was exhausted. There was no denying that fact. The slight tremor in his muscles mocked his sense of invulnerability, and maybe that was why he'd missed Ina's trauma. When he'd left her with Ren to report to the king, he'd known something was wrong, but Ina had an inner resilience that radiated from her, even in the most challenging of situations, and when her usual sharp humour returned, both he and Ren assumed she was coping. Still, he knew how much she loved Nerissa, and he should have known better. If he hadn't been so focused on ensuring she forgave him for her aunt's death, he wouldn't have missed that she was unusually calm and had accepted Nerissa's passing too quickly.

I should have stayed home, cradling her in my arms till she punched, kicked, or seared my arse in frustration. I should have waited till her grief turned to anger, sealing the rift in her heart, but I had to choose the army like a fool.

Mar looked at the sleeping witch. It had been two days since he'd carried her home from the temple. The dragon couldn't stop seeing the haunted look on Ren's face as he held Ina close, the maelstrom of chaos tearing the walls apart around them, and Mar doubted he would ever forget it. Ren resigned to his fate, true to his word, guarding her to the end. Ina had been too far gone for Ren's soothing words. She hadn't even reached for their bond or try to control her magic. As the tremors increased, the dragon clenched his fists. If Ina hadn't responded to his call, would he have been able to stop her to save the city? Unable to follow that thought, Mar glanced away, ashamed at the possibilities.

When they'd returned home, Ina's fury was prodigious, her magic crushing him against the wall as she screamed in his face, telling him he should have let her die, that her life wasn't worth the life of Nerissa or that of anyone. Ina's words cut deeper than her magic as she told him his actions had doomed the world, her lack of good judgement bound to end in destruction. She hadn't been rational, but Mar had seen it before on the battlefield, when, as the last sword fell, soldiers, shocked at having survived, turned their eyes to the hands that had killed and wanted nothing more than to excise those hateful instruments. So the dragon let her rage. He took every lash of her magic, every barbed word, without complaint, knowing she needed this. When Ina dropped to the floor and cried, Mar held her tight. He couldn't help her grieve, but would ensure the witch knew she was not alone in her nightmare.

Since then, Ina mainly slept, but he couldn't. Mar watched the witch like a hawk, ready to react to any stirring of her power. Ren came and went, playing his flute for her and soothing her nightmares. Boruta refused to leave the bed, piercing him with his unblinking stare each time Mar tried to push him away to lie next to his woman.

Marika helped her to the bathroom when she woke, but that was it. Ina left food untouched, staring glassy-eyed at nothing, and Mar realised he preferred her sleeping. At least then, he could pretend she was just tired because those lifeless eyes told him Ina's spirit was far from his reach.

Ren organised the funeral. Nerissa's body was cremated as custom dictated, and the ashes were taken to the magical university to lie in state with other notable mages from the past. He told Ina about it, and she seemed to listen, but she didn't react, and for the first time, Mar thought that maybe the old duke, her grandfather, was right about putting the geas on her. His little spitfire, so fierce in her actions, loved too deeply.

'Mar?' Ina's voice broke through his musings, and the tired dragon lifted her hand to his cheek.

'I'm here, my love.'

'Please help me up. What time is it?' Her forced smile broke his heart, but without showing his feelings, he swiftly moved her to his lap, wrapping the blanket around her.

'It's evening. How do you feel?'

'Tired, aching, but much calmer. Did I... hurt anyone? How is Ren?'

'He will come later. You didn't hurt anyone, and Rewan already paid for the temple repairs. Let me ask Marika to prepare the bath for you. Food and hot water should help with your aches and tiredness.'

'Of course, as you wish,' she said meekly, and Mar winced in reaction. Her compliant demeanour was uncharacteristic, but he didn't know how to break her from this state. He waited till the bath was ready and then carried her over, thinking of a way to coax her fierce spirit back to life. The tub was full of steaming water, and he instinctively dropped her into it, splashing water everywhere.

'Mar, what the fuck!' It was the first animated reaction he got from her, and the dragon held back his grin. It worked, but did he have the willpower to do what was necessary? To break her out of this condition and allow her spirit to break free? Mar clenched his teeth. He had to do it, and now was not the time to second-guess his instincts.

'It is about time for you to stop wallowing in self-pity and pull your head from that perky arse of yours. I should be with an army preparing for war, not sitting here making sure you don't destroy the city,' he said, clenching his fists so hard his nails cut the skin. *Am I even right in thinking this will help you, my love, or will my cruel words hurt you further?*

Something shifted in her face, and when Ina raised her eyes to him, they were no longer lifeless beads but crimson and full of rage and life. Mar adjusted his stance, bracing himself for the outcome.

'You fucking asshole. I just lost my aunt, and you're telling me to suck it up because you have your toy soldiers to play with?' Her magic threw him against the wall, breaking a small shelf as he collided, but Mar had never felt so happy. 'Why the fuck are you smiling? Why?'

She stood in the bath, her linen robe transparent and dripping, pelting him with soap, but the bond glowed with vigour, and Mar grinned, swatting away another bar of soap as it flew at his head. Her limited energy didn't last long, and Ina finally sagged and sat in the tub. The bathroom was swamped, but Ina was calm, looking at him in accusation.

'You did that on purpose, didn't you? You are such an asshole, Mar. I could have injured you. Now wipe that bloody smug grin off your face. You didn't win a pot of gold,' she said, and Mar dropped to his knees beside her. Her voice had returned to its usual sharpness, and she looked at him with annoyance and calculation. His spitfire was back.

'I won more than that. I have you back. It was well worth a black eye from a few bars of soap. I thought I had lost you to grief. You, our bond, it all felt so dead inside. I should have stayed with you, but I thought you'd be all right with Ren, and the army needed me....' He was still talking when she grabbed his beard and pulled him closer.

'Serves me right for loving a dragon. I just need time, you impatient arse. I loved Nerissa and lost her without expressing how much or how grateful I was to her for watching over me all those years. Life was easier with the geas, but I'm still here, battered and bruised but not broken. Oh, and you're telling Marika about the mess,' she said, kissing him gently. There was a deep sadness in her heart, but his spirited Ina was still here, which was good enough for him.

'Allow me the pleasure of caring for you, my lady love. A warm, sooth-ing, slightly shallow bath.' Mar couldn't help the teasing comment as he gathered her damp, tangled hair. 'Followed by some honey-rich comfort food and a cuddle by the fire.' He took his time washing Ina's hair, turning it into more of a massage, her body melting under his firm, slow caresses, and for the first time since the bond was broken, Mar relaxed.

Marika grumbled when she saw the damage Ina's fury had caused in the bathroom, but when the dragon apologised, the housekeeper shook her head. 'At least you did one thing right. Go; food is downstairs.'

Mar helped Ina don a simple grey house dress, wrapping a shawl over her shoulders. Then, taking her hands, he pulled the witch closer and pressed his forehead to hers, his heart racing. 'I'm sorry I hurt you. I didn't know how else to reach you,' he said as tremors ran through his body.

'No, you didn't, but I was lost in a fog of grief and needed something to drag me out of it.'

He looked into her eyes, and his guilt eased, replaced by amusement. 'And that's why you are better off with an oafish dragon. Your gentle Ghost would never resort to such brutal measures.' Ina's soft chuckle filled him with a joy that only increased as she tucked into the meal with a ravenous appetite.

When the edge of her hunger was blunted, Ina turned to Mar, pointing her knife in his direction. 'You need to resume your duties with the army while I see the king. I need to find Mirena, and I'm betting Kaian knows exactly where that bitch is hiding,' she said, wielding the utensil with murderous intent.

'No, I will not leave you alone until you feel more yourself,' he said, firm in his convictions. After studying his expression, the witch raised one eyebrow and prepared to disagree, but Mar jumped in before she could speak. 'When I felt the surge of your magic without you reaching for the bond, I lost control. I transformed in the middle of the camp, flying to you without another thought. Most of the damage caused at the temple was from me forcing my body inside, not your magic. I refuse to repeat this embarrassing experience, so please humour your poor, exhausted dragon and let me stay by your side.'

He saw her taking a deep breath, but then her lips stretched into a tender smile. Ina moved closer, placing her head on his shoulder, and he kissed her still-wet hair.

'I'm a pain in the dragon's arse, right?'

'Ina, I wouldn't trade you for the world. All I ask is a small mercy. We will go to the king and the camp, but we'll do it together. That's all I ask,' he said, sitting up. The quiet whicker from the orein and a loud rustling outside caught his attention. A glance at Boruta and Marika, each alert and poised, told him he wasn't the only predator who found the sound suspicious. Mar stood up slowly and approached the door, only slightly surprised at finding a weapon in his hand.

'Mar, what...?' Ina said, but went quiet as soon as he placed a finger to his lips.

'Someone is sneaking around outside,' he whispered, positioning himself next to the door before yanking it open. A hooded figure stumbled inside while the other muttered an ineligible curse, but Mar didn't waste a moment. Firmly grasping their throat, he pulled them closer while calling out into the darkness of the night.

'Come into the light, or I will crush your companion's windpipe,' he said, looking outside when he heard Ina's exclamation.

'Rurik? I thought you ran away.'

Mar tilted his head. He had heard this name before. Was this the necromancer who travelled to Marzanna's temple with Ina? The mere thought of what happened there had his fingers digging into the hapless man's throat, turning his panicked face a satisfying shade of puce.

'Let him go, Mar.' Ina's voice was quiet, but he heard the command in her tone and released his grip, turning to face the door and brandish his knife

'Hey, Striga. You wanna chain your guard dog so I can come in?'

The insulting words made Mar's hackles rise, but Ina chuckled and, stepping forward, called out into the darkness.

'Janik, you old goat, are you so desperate to visit Nawia you'd call me striga in front of my dragon?'

Mar couldn't resist growling as the witch held out her hand to greet the redheaded warrior that walked to the door.

'I'm not afraid of dragons, but I do fear you, Lady of the Crimson Veil.' Janik grinned as he, much to the dragon's surprise, bowed respectfully in front of Ina.'I come to beg your forgiveness and offer my assistance. I should never have taken that contract, and I'm sorry you were hurt because of it. I know it's no defence, but I only wanted my company to survive.'

'I have no right to judge a man for trying to make the best of the difficult situation, but I was hurt you didn't warn me.' With a glance and quick smile at Mar, Ina stepped back from the door. 'Come inside. There's food on the table and a small beer in the cellar. Now tell me what brought you to my house in the middle of the night.'

Both men looked at each other, and Mar tensed when their hesitation tested his patience.

'Speak,' he said, stepping in front of Ina.

'The Iron Empire is on the move. They are already laying siege to Kion.'

Janiks's words fell like boulders in Mar's heart. The curses that flew from his lips in response shocked everyone, and he noticed the scales covering his arms, reminding him to control his temper before someone got hurt.

'How do you know this?' he demanded. 'No such information has reached the capital, or I'd already have heard.'

The redheaded giant smirked. 'They slaughtered anyone trying to escape. It took me a week to get to you traipsing through the Leshy's domain.' Janik looked at Ina, who sat quietly, listening to their exchange. 'I came here because I thought if anyone could do something about those bastards, it's my striga.' He stepped forward, but Mar was already blocking his way.

'She's not yours, and she's not here to fix every problem this kingdom has. I will face this threat, not her,' he said, but Janik still looked at Ina, increasing the dragon's displeasure.

'Mar, let him be. Besides, he's right. I can do something about it,' she said, touching his shoulder.

'That's not all. The Iron Emperor keeps distributing notices all over the North,' Rurik said, passing Ina a scrap piece of parchment.

The benevolent Sovereign of the Iron Empire offers freedom to all those oppressed by the foul rule of Rewan, tyrant of Cornovii. As a gesture of goodwill, rise up and free the prisoner known as the Lady of the Red Veil and deliver her to the welcoming arms of your saviours.

'How many?' Ina asked, but none of the men seemed to understand her question.

'How many... what, my love?' Mar was the first to ask.

'How many cities were taken? How many were lost?' she said, looking at Janik.

'The last I saw was Dancik and the surrounding villages. Kion was still holding them off when I left. The Iron Empire is not rushing to take over the big cities, almost like they're waiting for something,' Janik said, and Mar wanted to choke him, seeing Ina's expression change as if his lover had made an important decision.

'I need you to go back to the North, and offer your services to the emperor guards. Join them if you can. I need someone I can trust when I come to visit them,' she said, and before he knew it, Ina rushed forward and approached Janik. 'Can I trust you this time?' she asked, and the giant embraced her, lifting the witch off the floor.

'Kitten, you were my company's lucky charm. I will do whatever you need for me to be your friend again, but can I at least visit the *Drunken Wizard*, or do you need me to go straight back?' he said, and Ina smiled, tugging his beard. That was too much for Mar. Not only had she decided without even consulting him, but now she trusted the man who once betrayed her. Mar tore Janik's arms from Ina and pulled her away.

'Ina, this is not your burden to carry alone, so please don't make plans without talking to the king.' Mar pressed her to his side, the other men looking away, fidgeting uncomfortably when scales flowed over his skin. Ina sighed and stroked his cheek.

'You're right. We need to inform Rewan, you need to prepare the army, and I need to buy us time so you can kick the empire back where it belongs. It's late now, and we all are tired. I don't have a spare room, but you can sleep by the fire if you wish,' she said to the visitors, and Mar grumbled unhappily. The dragon hated having men he didn't trust sleeping under his roof. It went against his every instinct. Still, now was not the time to contradict his woman.

'Fine. Make sure you respect the laws of hospitality,' he said, scooping Ina into his arms and turning to walk upstairs.

'I can walk,' she said, and he could hear the amusement in her voice while she tried to wriggle from his grasp.

'I don't care. You are mine, and if I wish to carry you upstairs, I will.' Mar couldn't keep the anger from his voice, cursing his lack of control when Ina noticed, but gods be damned, why did she need to throw herself into another dangerous trip when she hadn't recovered from the last one. 'A few days, a few fucking days? Is it too much to ask?' he grumbled, aiming his disgruntled feelings at the meddling bastards and their immortal games, but Ina heard him and snuggled into his embrace, sneaking a kiss to the exposed part of his chest.

'No, my love, it's not. You will have your days, and I'll do what you tell me during this time, but we both know what must happen. When you threw me into the bath, you were right. The army needs you, while I'm needed in the court. We'll talk to Rewan, and if there's any other way, I promise I won't put myself in danger, but if not, I will do what needs doing.'

He didn't answer, but something deep inside him roared and thrashed, thinking about his lady shouldering the kingdom's burden again. He stood there, tense, watching as she slipped from his arms, locking the door to their bedroom. Ina approached him, loosening the ribbons of her dress, letting the grey fabric slide down her curvy figure. He sucked in his breath, looking at her breasts, gently swaying as she moved.

'Don't try to distract me. We need to talk,' he said through clenched teeth, feeling his erection tightening his breeches.

'We will, tomorrow,' she said, tracing her hand along his shaft. Mar's breath hitched as he placed a hand over hers, stopping it.

'There are strangers in the house,' he tried again, his resistance crumbling.

'I know. I want them to hear. I want them to know I'm yours and that you can do anything you want to me. All my love, all my power, is yours, Marcach. I want you to claim me again, but not before I show you how much I love you.'

Her offer left him stunned, and before he knew it, Ina had pushed him back onto the bed. He lay there as she kissed him, her lips teasing his mouth, tongue slipping out to taste his flesh while her fingers moved over his clothes, the sting of her magic burning them away. The bemused dragon struggled to think past the pleasure of his Spitfire's lips as she moved down over his body, divesting him of his clothes, trailing over the tender skin with her delicious kisses. When the tip of her tongue stroked up to the tip of his cock, Mar struggled to resist the urge to take control, gritting his teeth as Ina's chuckle sent shivers through his body, her mouth enveloping his length. Ina's head dipped forward, sliding along his manhood, making him groan and push his hips forward. His gasp when his lover took advantage of the movement, pressing a fingertip to his rear, turned into a throaty growl of pleasure as she caressed the tight muscle lightly.

He was taken aback by how good it felt, and, looking down, he couldn't help expressing his desire at the wicked expression on his lover's face as she pressed, pushing her finger inside, exclaiming at the intensity of the feeling. Mar's world flipped around, the suddenly sprouting claws tearing at the bed as he nearly came. The sound of Ina's pleasure nearly undid him, her satisfaction at his helplessness even as she knelt submissively, forcing a roar from his throat as he struggled not to explode in her mouth.

With a predatory growl, he reached out, grasping a handful of her hair and pulled her up. His cock slid out of Ina's mouth with a lurid pop, his powerful arms taking control of her body and forcing her onto her stomach. With a dark, wicked laugh, Mar trailed the sharp edge of his claws along the witch's back, her whimper part of fear and all lust, his body following as he positioned himself between her thighs.

Rearing up, the dragon whispered, voice filled with luscious menace. 'You wanted them to hear, my spitfire, and so they shall. You are mine, and everyone will know it.' As he pushed his cock inside her, Mar leant down, biting her shoulder and thrusting forward, and when Ina arched her back, screaming her pleasure, he slid easily into her tight entrance. Once again, he fought a losing battle with desire, her hips rocking back, driving him insane. Mar groaned, and just like Ina had before, he teased the tight muscle of her rear, her answering cries intensifying till her climax washed over her, the contractions of her pleasure driving away thoughts of control, the deafening roar of his orgasm shaking the windows.

Unsure of how it happened, Mar found himself beside Ina, her body cradled tenderly in his arms. 'My love, you are a marvel, and I will always be at your mercy.'

'Mercy?' she murmured, yawning into his chest.

'Yes, because even on your knees, you have more power over me than kings or gods ever will. I love you, my beautiful chaos,' he said, kissing her cheek, feeling her embracing him tighter.

'I love you, too. And next time, I'll tie you to the bed because you clearly can't just lie down and take it.' Her answer, mumbled between yawns, made him gasp.

'What?'

'You heard. Now sleep.' She was already drifting away while feeling rejuvenated by their reunion. Mar shook with laughter. His little woman had set her mind on their next encounter, and he couldn't wait to see how long her ties would last.

CHAPTER SEVENTEEN

Ina woke up sprawled over Mar's chest, her hand idly tracing the soft golden fur adorning his body, and the witch couldn't help but smile. She noticed there seemed to be more of it, and with the dragon's ability to manipulate their physique, it was clear he did it because he knew she loved it. He was perfect. Her own bundle of overprotective love, brain and muscles. A bundle that had scared the numbness out of her. Ina felt guilty each time her memory returned to the day she lost her senses to grief after seeing Nerissa's body. Without Mar, she would have buried herself, Ren, and gods knew how many others under a pile of rubble. Her laconic Ren couldn't handle her at her worst, but Mar... he did precisely what was needed, even if he almost got burnt to a crisp for his trouble.

Ina looked at the sleeping man by her side. He pulled her closer when she tried moving, while his hand lazily stroked her side.

'No escape,' he muttered, and she rolled her eyes but could not deny his words had merit. The slow, soothing gesture had the opposite effect, leaving Ina wide awake and close to kissing the living daylights out of him. 'No escape, Mar. Never again, especially since I know you can find me even behind the veil,' she muttered, snuggling closer, wishing they could stay like this for the rest of the day. Still, they had things to do. The clattering of dishes and several raised voices told her their guests were already awake and, judging by the sound, were fighting with her housekeeper.

'Just let me help you, woman!' Janik's voice and the loud bang that followed proved the Norse mercenary had met his match. Much to her displeasure, they also woke up Mar, who instinctively flipped her onto her back, covering her with his massive body while his hand sprouted a full set of vicious talons.

He was barely awake, looking around for the enemy, and she couldn't resist pulling his beard to steal a kiss.

'It's all right. I think Janik tried to impress Marika, and she handed him his bollocks on a silver platter. Do we even have a silver platter? '

Mar's lips spread in a big smile, and his low chuckle shook her body. 'Impress Marika? Poor bastard, even I can't stand my ground against that woman.'

Her housekeeper was indeed a force to be reckoned with. After Ina saved the feline shifter from slavery, Marika had become her servant. Initially, Ina objected, but the girl had made up her mind and refused to leave. Since the woman lost her arm in the palace battle, saving several scullery maids in the process, the witch felt it was only fair to let her stay for as long as the stubborn shifter wanted, especially since she kept the house clean, looked after her cat, and made this house a home. Losing her arm hadn't slowed Marika down, but gave her an impressive determination. The house had to be pristine, and to achieve it, men—resident or visiting—were ordered about with efficiency and violence, and no one dared to enter before leaving their dirty weapons in the shed.

'I think we should go down and rescue Janik before Rurik has to reanimate his corpse,' she said, looking with disbelief at her tangled hair in the mirror. 'Where is Ren when you need him?' she moaned, causing Mar to give her his full attention instantly.

'Why Ren? What is wrong?' he asked sharply, hands trailing over her body, worry etched on his features.

'Because, my love, while you are superior in many things, the way he brushes and braids my hair makes me look like a respectable woman, and I need to look like one today. Do you think we should ask him to train you? Just imagine being the man who can fulfil my every need,' she teased, reaching for the brush. Her attempt to dispel the tension was in vain as something in his eyes darkened, and Mar reached for his clothes without further comment. When she finished, her hair vaguely resembled the crown braid, and she pushed herself into a court dress with a little effort. Grey and elegant, with a few golden ornaments, it fit the occasion. Still, she had to ask Mar to lace her corset, and her dragon didn't stay silent for long.

'You're still determined to get involved in this latest threat, then? I thought so, but before committing to something reckless, I'd like you to visit the barracks with me. I wasn't the only one worried when you disappeared last spring. Ren informed me the men you kept safe in the battle wanted to join the search for you. It seems they believe the gods sent you to defend Cornovii and are very protective of their Lady of the Crimson Veil. It would do wonders for morale if they saw you safe and in control of your powers.'

Ina turned to Mar when he finished. 'I would be honoured to visit the army, my lord.'

'That's what I'm worried about, so no kisses for impudent young soldiers. I mean it, Spitfire, do not repeat your antics from last time.'

Ina laughed and pulled Mar down the stairs, pausing at the sight of Janik's rapidly blackening eye and Marika holding a sturdy stick. A handful of logs were scattered on the floor while her housekeeper eyed the red-haired giant with distrust. Janik was the first to notice the witch and raised his hands defensively.

'I was only trying to help her. It was too much to carry, especially with one hand, but she hit me with a tree. I did nothing wrong, I swear. Freya's tits, Ina, did you hire a hellion?'

'*Her* has a name, and you're the prick who ripped the logs out of my grip. Now I have wood all over my floor on top of the mess from your pillow fort in the dayroom. Get your massive arse out of my kitchen and let me work, or I'll colour your other eye.'

Janik withdrew to the couch, mumbling something in his native language, but Ina noticed he couldn't keep his eyes off Marika's back, and something akin to a tender smile appeared on his face. *Trust the Norseman to find a log to the face romantic*, she thought before turning away.

'Rurik, after breakfast, we will go to the king. I hope you'll keep your word and not make me chase you. Rewan can make a judgement on your actions,' Ina said, and the necromancer nodded slowly, keeping his eyes on her face.

'I will, but Ina... I can still help.'

'I know, but it's not my decision to make,' she said, turning to Mar, whose sceptical expression made the witch roll her eyes. 'Trust me,' she whispered when he caught her gaze.

Before breakfast, Ina sent Marika to the palace with a request for an audience with the king, deciding for once to follow royal protocol. It gave the witch no end of entertainment when Janik offered to accompany the housekeeper for, as he said, looking very gallant, safety on the city's dangerous streets. When his proposal earned him an eye roll followed by a huff of annoyance, the mercenary seized on the lack of a no as tacit acceptance and trailed after Marika with a smile as wide as his face. When the king's reply returned before the housekeeper and her attendant, Ina worried at her bottom lip as she hurried to answer the summons.

The palace felt different from her previous visits, and it took the witch several moments to realise it was the lack of disdainful stares. In the past, when she was a failed mage, Ina had been scorned for the nepotism that had gained her the position at court. Then, thanks to her magic saving the king, fear replaced contempt. Today, instead of hateful stares, she received respectful bows with quiet greetings, and the witch didn't know if she liked it.

As soon as she entered the king's office, Rewan stood from his chair and approached her. His demeanour had also changed, and her friend appeared vulnerable, as if the burden of the crown he so gracefully carried finally weighed him down. She missed the cheekiness and boyish charm he usually displayed in her presence, and, unexpectedly, Ina tilted her head, opening her arms to invite him for a hug.

'Will you relax? This is not how you used to welcome your royal witch,' she said, teasing the many times he hugged her, but this time, Rewan only took her hand in his and gave her a court bow.

'Welcome, my lady. I'm glad you brought the lord marshal, and who might your other guest be?' he asked, making her frown at his unexpected formality.

'Rewan, for fuck's sake...' she began, unwilling to accept the change in his attitude before shrugging in exasperation. 'Fine! Your Majesty, let me introduce you to Rurik, a death master necromancer and bastard son of Mirena of Thorn,' she said, feeling something was amiss in this situation.

Rewan paled, and she saw him stagger a little before he supported himself over the desk. 'This day is full of surprises. Thank you for bringing my half-brother home. I have many questions for you, Master Rurik, but let us wait for the others to arrive.'

'Half-brother?' Ina's mouth gaped before realisation dawned in her eyes. 'Oh, the scandal... how could I not remember that? And what's this about others? Rewan, what the fuck is going on here? Why do I feel you treat me like a coiled viper?' Ina stepped forward, darting her eyes between the king and the necromancer. Her magic flared when she remembered the clues, cursing the whole pantheon, that she missed the obvious. Mar's hands on her shoulders stopped her pacing, calming both her agitation and magic. The next thing she knew, the door opened, revealing Ren, followed by Jorge, Arun, Gruff and several army officers. Finally, it hit her.

'You called a war council, Your Majesty? All I asked for was a private audience,' she said, noticing Kaian, who was the last to enter the room.

'I'm afraid we don't have time for private audiences, my lady, and matters concerning you affect the entire country. Please, everyone, be seated and answer my questions as truthfully as possible.' The king gestured to the gathering, and they moved to a seat at the table.

CHAPTER EIGHTEEN

Ina clenched her fists, trying to slow her breathing. *What is bothering him, and why is this brat giving me the cold shoulder?* Nothing was going as she had planned. All she wanted was a quiet chat with Rewan, to introduce him to Rurik and let him know her plans before she headed up north. Instead, she was sitting here, stiff as a rod between Mar and the necromancer, waiting to be questioned. *Well, I will not sit here playing by your rules,* she thought, but Mar's hand held her down as Ina tried standing to challenge the monarch. The scowl the witch gave her lover would have frozen fire, but Mar just shook his head.

One by one, Rewan asked the military commanders to detail the situation, and she learned it was direr than she expected. They already knew about Kion. The city was holding on by a bare thread, the other villages and towns had already been taken, and those who opposed the new ruler were slaughtered savagely by order of the Iron Empire's commander.

'Those who observed him say he is a tall man in golden-plated armour with a face to rival Radowit and a benevolent smile to match, who treats everyone with kindness, allowing his enemies to surrender and serve the empire. However, if surrender is not forthcoming, his smile grows as he happily permits his army to murder every living soul before them, be it a man, woman, or child. He is a beast, but his sister is even worse.' The captain from the northern province shook his head in disgust, and Ina looked at the man with a new interest.

'Sister? I thought the empire didn't allow their women to fight?'

'You are right, my lady, unless the woman is a powerful mage. Our spies inform us that her magic brought their fleet to Cornovii, that she is the emperor's lover and operates with impunity. I saw the hurricane she created to threaten Dancik. They are a proud city, but they know when they are outmatched. To make matters worse, one of the Water Horse clan was instrumental in persuading the merchants to capitulate without a fight.'

Ina saw Kaian pale and rub his neck as if the tension was too oppressive for his muscles. When it was her turn, she detailed the battle with the goddess, the betrayal of her aunt and the bond she temporarily lost, but instead of telling the truth and revealing she possessed the full regalia, Ina only mentioned Rurik and Velka's help with the potion that reestablished her bonds.

When Rewan moved on to Rurik, the witch cursed under her breath. She could try to save the necromancer's life during a private audience, but the people gathered here would surely demand his head for what he had done, and rightly so. However, something inside her protested such a punishment, especially when he was so willing to help fight off the advancing Empire.

She listened to his monotone voice as he detailed his grand plan and involvement in Cornovii's recent misfortunes and realised he was prepared to die after offering his final confession. Mar turned towards him, his eyes glowing gold, skin forming the scales on its surface, with only the witch standing between them.

'You did this to her. You hurt my Ina and made me watch while she suffered. I will kill you, and for the first time in my life, I will enjoy every moment of the pain I bring,' said Mar, rising from his chair, the icy menace in his voice silencing the room.

'That's only fair I pay for my mistakes. I don't deserve your mercy or forgiveness. Just... take care of her. Please,' Rurik said, bowing his head, stunning the witch with his reaction. The quiet sound of a drawn sword drew her sight to Ren, who, without a word, moved towards the necromancer.

'No!' Ina and the king cried out in unison, and a flare of chaos pushed everyone away from the mage.

'Why are you defending him, my lady? He hurt you and damaged Cornovii. He is responsible for thousands of deaths. I will make it quick if you don't want him to suffer,' Ren said, the terrifying emotionless mask of the Ghost in place, but Ina shook her head, looking around the room.

'You're right; he deserves to die for his deeds. I nearly took his life myself, but his death now solves nothing.' The witch carried an iron will as she looked around the room, her gaze landing, finally, on the king. With power settling around her shoulders, Ina seemed to channel her aunt's spirit as she stood before her sovereign. 'I call upon my right as a judicial mage of Cornovii to pass judgement on Rurik, son of Roda.' No one noticed her glance towards Jorge as she usurped his official rights, but with a smirk and a nod, he gave the witch permission to continue.

'Ina, you are making a mistake.' The warning in the king's voice made it clear he had his own plans for his half-brother. But she couldn't let Rurik die, not like this.

It was impossible not to look at the two men who were a part of her heart. Mar, who stood there, barely controlling the transformation in his fury, and Ren, looking at her with raw, searing anger for denying his revenge. One wrong word and these two men would erupt into terrifying violence. All eyes were on her, and a shiver ran down her spine, releasing wisps of

chaos. A steadying breath in, and Ina straightened, locking eyes with the
king.

'There is a difference between malicious intent and misguided ideals.
Rurik's intention was never to destroy Cornovii, but to end the injustices
caused by greed and the abuse of power.' She shook her head, taking a
deep breath. 'His abhorrent and senseless deeds caused too many innocent
deaths to be forgiven. However, he has knowledge and skills we need. He
has contacts and a spy network in every court of Warenga. I can't allow
his death for this reason alone, but also because when Mirena poisoned
me, he risked everything to save me. Imprison him, use his knowledge. I
won't object, but he will live.' Ina turned to Rewan, who looked at her
with an unreadable expression. 'I never ask you for anything for myself. I
don't want power or riches, but I'm asking now. Give me his life. The rest
I leave in your hands.'

Rurik looked at her with haunted eyes, dropping to his knees before
her. 'Your mercy is painful, my lady. You want me to live knowing what I
have done, to look at the faces of those who suffered because of me and see
nothing but repulsion and hatred? Every day till the end of my miserable
life. Why? Why are you so cruel?' His voice faltered, and Ina smiled sadly.

'Because there is no greed or vengeance in your heart. I could have been
hung from the emperor's wall or released like a wild beast to destroy this
kingdom, my mind shattered after your mother poisoned me, but you told
me you could help, and I believed you. This is your chance for redemption,
to make the better world you craved. I want your knowledge, machina-
tions, and everything you possess to save Cornovii. You will spare no effort,
even if this puts your life in peril, and you can forget your birthright and
all its implications. You will swear a blood oath of loyalty to Rewan, and
you will live because that is what I command. That is your punishment,'

she said, and strands of chaos wrapped around Rurik's wrists like magical shackles branding his skin.

Rewan walked around his desk as her magic disappeared and looked down at his newfound relative. 'I don't know if you were merciful or pitiless in your judgement, Lady Inanuan, but I shall grant your request. However, I insist on hosting my dear brother in the palace in case he loses his way in the future.' With that, Ina collapsed back into her chair, exhausted and drained.

'Once again, you favoured heart over good sense, my lady.' The expression on Ren's face made Ina flinch, his anger and disgust clear for all to see.

'Please forgive me, my friend, but he is needed for the defence of Cornovii,' she said, for once, the more emotionless of the two. Deep down, she felt her decision was right, but looking at Mar's rigid features, she drifted away, half listening to Rurik, who, with a zealot's fervour, detailed the plans and connections he'd forged during long years in the Warenga's kingdoms.

Ina kept looking at Kaian, who stood quietly behind Rewan's chair, with his gaze never leaving the portrait of the former king on the opposite side of the room. Mirena had been a minor noble of the advisor's clan, but it was painfully clear she'd been conspiring with the kingdom's enemies for a long time. This and his elders, who'd attempted to depose Rewan, now placed Kaian in a perilous position. While pondering what the current situation did to the relationship between the master assassin and the king, she heard her name.

'Lady Inanuan, Ina. Focus for a moment, please.' Rewan's frown was foreboding as she gave him an apologetic smile.

'I have listened to everyone's information and opinions, and I must insist everything discussed here not leave this room. With Dancik taken and Kion on the verge of defeat, we face an incredibly dire threat. We have learnt that most of the Water Horse clan are actively collaborating with the enemy. With its reputation beyond repair, I have no choice but to excise the family from the kingdom; its title and rights will cease to exist forthwith. Master Kaian will stay with me as my personal guard, so do not question his right to be present.'

Murmurs arose at this pronouncement, but the king quietened all nobles by simply raising his hand, this revelation helping Ina understand Kaian's solemn demeanour. When the voices died down, Rewan continued.

'Our military understands the Iron Empire tactics, but for those who don't, let me remind you that what is attacking us now is only the vanguard of a much larger army, and for some unknown reason, rumours abound saying the emperor himself is leading the main army. Apart from morale, this news should have no bearing on our plans, which are to destroy the vanguard or force them away from Dancik so we can prevent the emperor's ships from making landfall because if one thing's for sure, if that army lands, we are done for.'

'How do you plan to fight them, Your Majesty? We are losing in the North. Unless the royal witch has another spectacular power display in mind?' asked one officer, and Ina had to place a hand on Mar's shoulder when her dragon turned, shooting him a furious glare.

'I wish I were as powerful as you believe, but even with additional resources, I can't deal with an armada. Magic comes with a price, so how many are you willing to sacrifice, captain, to give me my god-like powers?' For a moment, Ina considered telling them about the regalia, but she was untrained and untested in using the complete set and doubted she could control the amount of power needed to bring the mightiest army of the world to their knees. And then what? Slaughter them all, hold them in my power while Cornovii's soldiers cut their throats? The mere thought of it made her shudder.

'I issued a national drafting order. Everyone able to fight, including mages and artisans, will be incorporated into the army. Lord marshal, you are tasked with organising these people into at least a semblance of an army before we march north,' Rewan said, looking at Mar, and nodded slowly.

'How much time do I have?' he said.

When Rewan looked at her, Ina noticed the strange sadness and guilt in his eyes. 'You have as much time as Lady Inanuan can buy us,' he said, and Ina smiled bitterly, knowing where this was heading. It looked like Rewan had seen the pamphlets distributed by the Empire.

'So, this is why you behaved like an ass towards me earlier? Because you thought I would blame you for requesting my involvement in a reasonably dangerous scheme?' Ina put her hands on her hips, giving the king a challenging stare. 'I came here to tell you I'm headed north. If the emperor desperately wants me, I will ensure he thoroughly enjoys my charming company. I will give you time, but I also have my own scores to settle, so I can't promise not to escalate the situation,' she said, noticing Mar's hand on the table clenched so hard she could see blood dripping from his fist. He didn't protest, though. It was Ren who spoke.

'I'm going with you, my lady. I let you out of my sight once, and it ended in disaster. You have a choice. I will go with you or follow you, but I will go, and you cannot stop me,' he said, and the determination in his quiet voice made her shiver. As a last resort, she looked at her dragon.

'Mar...'

'He is going with you, or you are not going at all.' Her dragon's face held an implacable ferocity that, for once, silenced Ina's desire to argue. She had already made both men deeply unhappy, and after a moment's thought, the witch realised the arrogant, capricious character she intended on becoming would most certainly have a personal retinue.

'Fine, I will be ready the day after tomorrow. Can you send a messenger, Your Majesty? Let those bastards know I'm coming, but as a delicate lady, I can't possibly travel quickly,' she said, and Rewan graced her with a genuine smile for the first time that day.

'Of course, my lady. You must take every precaution, even if this prolongs your journey. Do you need a carriage? Something slow and dripping with gold?' he asked, and Ina could bless his quick wit at the moment.

'Don't go overboard. No one would believe I'd travel in such a monstrosity.'

'Why do we need this charade? Why don't you just make them kneel... my lady.' Hearing the outburst to her right, Ina turned her lead, looking at one of the younger officers. Before she could answer, Jorge spoke for her.

'Didn't you hear the first time? To utter the word of power, she needs carnage. Only chaos created by hundreds of dying souls can conjure that energy. Remember this the next time you kneel on the killing fields between the corpses of those who trusted your leadership,' he said, and you could hear a pin drop in the silence that followed his words.

'We cannot rule out this option, but I hope to avoid so much death. I know we can't avoid bloodshed this time, but it's not a problem solved by one battle. We can deal with the vanguard army; I... I can even try to do it all by myself, but what about the armada? And how can we prevent the Iron Empire from sending more? We all need time to think, but I promise to give them something to remember when I finally step in,' she said, trying to lay her hand on Mar's, but he moved away.

Ina slowly exhaled, turning towards him. He didn't even look at her, which hurt more than she was willing to admit. Still, she'd dragged him through Nawia and back, then denied him his revenge. Instead, she looked at the king.

'I have an idea I'm considering. I may not be able to help with the vanguard, but this may deal with the armada,' she said, and the king sent her a questioning look.

'Ina, what is coming is bigger than anything we've ever seen. Do you think you can do it? And most importantly, how?'

'It's complicated and more of an idea than a plan, but if Jorge can predict when the armada will arrive, and Mar can get the army to Dancik simultaneously? Then we might have a fighting chance.' Ina tried to project a confidence she didn't feel when she felt Mar's hand cover her own. He might be angry, but his love and worry slipped through their bond, making her sigh with relief as she gently leaned against him.

'On that note, I will adjourn the meeting for today. Please report your progress to Master Kaian. Marcach, Sa'Ren, come with me. I need a private word with you both,' the king commanded, dismissing everyone else.

His omission of her name annoyed Ina, but the witch looked into Mar's eyes and smiled, slipping her hand free. 'I will wait here. Do you still want us to go to the barracks later?'

He nodded, leaning down and kissing her cheek. Mar's reluctance to leave her in Rurik's company was written in his tense muscles, but he left with only a single growl aimed at the necromancer. Ina stretched, surreptitiously observing the council as they filed out before she approached the window. Summer was in full bloom, with bees and butterflies busily working in Velka's gardens. She gasped when long, icy fingers wrapped around her wrist, and the witch twisted away from the threatening presence. Ina's shock that Rurik would grab her turned to unease as she saw his rapturous expression.

'What are you doing?' she said, pulling her hand away, but he didn't let go; instead, his euphoric smile widened.

'You have accepted the last piece of Sowenna's Regalia. I thought I sensed them yesterday, but I wasn't sure. Now I can feel their power, and the king listens to your every word. You shouldn't have saved my life. My purpose is fulfilled, and I would gladly pay for the suffering I caused. Ina, I'm not afraid of death, but I will follow your command and live till I am of no further use.'

'Then find a better way to create the world you dreamt of. Use your exceptional mind to support Rewan. Let him be the conscience you need to make changes that will help not just the poor but everyone.' Ina moved away after making her point; this time, Rurik let her go.

'Yes, my exceptional mind.' He sighed, looking at her guiltily. 'Before I can... move forward, I.... There was a reason I spirited you away to the North, and it wasn't simply to avoid my mother's spies. When your bonds were stripped away from you, my hope that you'd claim the last piece of the regalia finally died, but I reached for hope from a different place, your dragon. I heard from my sources that you found the circlet by following the draw of its magic, so in a last-ditch gamble, I....'

Rurik's words crashed into place, finally answering the questions she'd dismissed as superfluous, that now became all too important.

'So you betrayed me, again. You used my fear, the loss of my bonds, and my dragon's love to manipulate us into claiming the final gemstone. What the fuck is wrong with you? Is it a compulsion? Is all this *doing it for the greater good* simply a mask for your need to manipulate people? I trusted you, I looked past your crimes, and I trusted you.' Ina could control the sense of betrayal, of feeling so gullible that she'd been tricked repeatedly, then turned around and forgiven him. Her magic reached for his throat, coiling around it with lethal intent, and Ina struggled with giving in to the temptation of his death, but Rurik didn't defend himself, and it occurred to her he wanted her to do it.

'Fuck!' she screamed, dismissing the chaos. 'Why? Just why, why the fuck are you so fixated on me, and why are you trying to push me to kill you? What is wrong with you?!'

Rurik took a deep gulping breath, shaking his head slightly. 'I didn't plan or instigate my mother's actions. I would never strip you of your protection, but I'm a man who can see an opportunity and use it to my advantage. I knew your dragon would follow you to the ends of the world, and I took a gamble, hoping he would remember the hidden regalia. I can't sleep, Ina. The people I sacrificed for your ascension haunt my dreams. Please, end my suffering now that my goal is completed,' he said, reaching for her, but Ina stepped backwards.

'You are insane. I won't do it. I won't let you manipulate me any more,' she said, flinching to avoid his touch, watching as his shoulders slumped in defeat.

'Then I shall endure, my lady, if that is your wish. I am a broken man who found a reason to live and a purpose worth dying for. I know the secrets of Warenga. My network of spies, my knowledge, is yours to command,' he said, looking at her with fanatical fervour, and Ina swallowed hard. *He is dangerous and insane, but the way he planned all this, his knowledge... Rewan will need all of this not just for the war but also to rule.* Her thoughts were racing as she pondered her next move. Suddenly, the door slammed open, revealing Mar, who looked at the scene before him, his eyes flashing gold.

'Step away from her!' he commanded. A menacing growl reverberated in his throat, making clear his intentions towards anyone causing her discomfort. Somehow, it made her decision easier.

'Serve the king with the same devotion you showed me, and once this war ends, I may grant you your wish,' Ina said firmly as Mar approached her, wrapping his arm around her waist.

'Yes, my lady.' Rurik stood up, bowing his head, but she noticed the smile he was trying to hide and felt a chill running down her spine. *I promised him death, and he was happy? What life must he have for him to crave it so much?*

CHAPTER NINETEEN

When Ina returned home after the king's impromptu war council, she found Janik sitting at her kitchen table, dutifully peeling carrots for her housekeeper. The absurdity of a redheaded barbarian giant being bossed around by a tiny, one-armed shifter stopped her in her tracks and, hanging off Mar's arm, fingers digging into his firm muscles, she laughed so hard tears fell from her eyes.

Everybody looked at her with concern, but Ina waved them off and went upstairs, sitting on the windowsill in her bedroom to watch people go by in the busy street. So much had changed so quickly. Velka had a child, Nerissa was dead, and she was the bearer of Empress Sowenna's legendary regalia, yet someone always had to sit in the kitchen peeling carrots. Boruta jumped on her lap, and Ina absentmindedly stroked his fur.

A flash of green on her hand prompted Ina to share her thoughts with the cat. 'You know, even though I'm the supposed harbinger of chaos, people will always flock to order, to stability,' she muttered, closing her eyes and burrowing her nose into the cat's dense fur. She inhaled deeply, finding the unmistakable scent of pine teasing her senses.

'My love, why are you sniffing the cat? Is everything all right? Did something upset you?' The concern in Mar's soft baritone wrapped her in its warm embrace, but Ina didn't want to open her eyes just yet.

'What? Does a woman need to be upset to enjoy a furry cuddle? Besides, he literally smells divine and has a better coat than any man I know,' she said with a voice full of mischief. Mar's theatrical growl made her chuckle, and she finally looked up at his face.

'Oh, have mercy, woman. I already look like someone laid a shaggy rug on my chest, and you want more?' he said, his eyebrows rising when Ina roared with laughter.

'Always. I always want more of you. I love you so much that it takes my breath away. I'm sorry it took me so long to accept you into my heart,' she said, biting back a curse when Boruta bolted, scratching her thigh when Mar dropped to his knees beside her.

'Fuck, Ina, you're not dying again, are you?' Panic laced his voice as he cupped her face, making the witch roll her eyes.

'No, I just haven't said this to you often enough. I wanted to ensure you hear it at least once before I go north. Can we return to the kitchen, or do you want to keep fretting over my sudden flood of feelings? I must send Janik back to Dancik before he makes Marika pregnant with his longing stare.'

Mar nodded, rising to his feet with the lithe grace of a predator, then with an equally graceful bow, held out his hand, smiling. 'Come, my lady, we can't allow the poor maiden's honour to be sullied by such an uncouth giant. We must see to his exile immediately.'

Her hand disappeared in his as they walked together to the kitchen. However, when they arrived, Marika was nowhere to be seen, and Janik sat there with a thunderous expression.

'What did you do this time?' Ina asked, approaching him, but he only shook his head.

'Nothing, but she told me to stop looking at her like a hungry dog at a bone and drooling on the floor. I'm not bloody drooling, Striga!'

'Are you so sure of that?' She chuckled before placing her hand on his forearm. 'I know I asked before, but I truly need your help. I want you to go north and become my spy inside the Imperial Guard, and I'm willing to pay you enough money to rebuild your company, but I must know I can trust you,' she said, observing his face to detect any hint of subterfuge, but she only saw a deep and regretful sadness.

'I made a mistake but never meant you harm, so keep your money, Striga. I have my honour and will swear a blood oath to you to prove it. All I ask is to be welcome in Osterad when all is done, and maybe you could put in a good word or two for me,' he said, looking out the back door.

Ina smiled, knowing who he wanted to impress, and punched him on the shoulder. 'I will pay you, anyway, you freckled troll. I know what happened to your last troop, and it took guts to show up after I threatened to kill you on sight. I'm sorry you lost your men, even if I can't apologise for what I did. You should have told me you had problems with Sophia instead of selling me out. That was not your best decision.' The witch didn't miss the relief that flashed over Janik's features, but she continued without further comment. 'Get your ginger arse going. I will be following as slowly as possible, but I need you in place long before I arrive. If you do well, I will tell Marika how manly you are and that you have a big dick hanging between your legs.'

'How do you know about his dick?' Mar, quiet so far, took offence at her teasing.

'Because he bragged about it in the *Drunken Wizard*, many, many times, and if I remember correctly, he even whipped it out on the table to compare it with an orc's.' Ina's grin couldn't have been bigger when she noticed a faint blush crawling over Janik's cheeks.

'It was ten years ago! And I was drunk!' he bellowed, and she laughed.

'Yes, but I can't unsee it. What a monster.' Ina was choking on her laughter as Janik stood up with a huff.

'See you in Dancik, Striga.' He marched out, back straight, and fists clenched, leaving her supporting herself on the kitchen table.

'I should be concerned that you have the picture of another man's parts so strongly etched in your mind, but it is so good to see you laughing again. Still, maybe I should show you mine, just for the comparison?' Mar said, and she noticed his lips twitch in restrained laughter.

'When I saw Janik busy with trivial household chores, it helped me realise something. I've lost so much in my life, but I have gained a lot, too. Life goes on, and my grief or tears won't bring anyone back. Nerissa, Mirek, the soldiers—all those people who gave their lives to save my hide—they wouldn't want me to shrivel up, crying in a darkened room. So I will honour their sacrifice by living my best life, helping those who need me.'

Ina saw Mar's eyes flash gold as he enveloped her in his arms, supporting his chin on her head while Ina let chaos wrap around them like a warm blanket, her magic feeling calm and more natural than ever.

'Please tell me you're not going to do it in my kitchen?' Marika's grisly voice ruined the moment, and Ina slipped from Mar's embrace.

'Tempting as it is, no. I wouldn't dare to desecrate your domain in such a manner,' she said, biting her lip when Marika looked at her with confusion. 'Anyway, if you are free, please come with me. I need help packing.'

The morning of her journey north brought a sense of determination and the impetus to face the next challenge. By the time Ren arrived to assist with the journey's preparations, Ina was already dressed and had saddled Zjawa. Mar held her tight when she came to say goodbye, and her heart ached to see him so unsettled and worried, yet he didn't try stopping her, and after a long desperate kiss, Ina set off with her companion.

The weather favoured them and let her ponder over recent events. After the upsetting encounter with Rurik, Mar had delayed their visit to the camp for the following day, and Ina had been looking forward to it. However, the king had other ideas, so the witch's morning had been taken up with another meeting at the palace.

Rewan also surprised her when it became clear it was a private meeting, from which even Mar was excluded. The king approached her as soon as they arrived, asking her lover to wait outside. While waiting for him to collect his thoughts, she noticed the pain her friend was trying to hide and gently touched his shoulder.

'Rewan, I've supported you since saving your sorry arse in the palace battle. Whatever it is, I will help,' she said, hoping her smile would give him courage.

'Ina, I know I ask for much. Please believe me, I'm not abandoning you. I just don't have the time and resources. I... I don't know what to do. The Iron Empire sent a letter before we knew you were safe, and they demanded we surrender you. I said no. I want you to know this; I would always say no.' Hearing the anguish in the king's voice, Ina rolled her eyes.

'Because I'm such a gullible goose, I would think you'd sell your best weapon even if we weren't friends? I think spending too much time in bed with Kaian completely addled your brains,' she said with a smirk. 'I'm going because I know I can help you from within Dancik and because Mirena is there; she and I have unfinished business.'

After that, they talked. Ina saw the hope and mischief return to the king's eyes, and he was smiling with ease when Mar knocked on the door to take her to the army.

Ina was surprised when her dragon didn't ask about her meeting, and as she watched him from the corner of her eye, she realised how distracted he seemed. Their visit to the camp was a short, pleasant experience, albeit tinged with a touch of sadness. The soldiers had gathered around with good-natured greetings and teasing, reminding her of Mirek, the young soldier who died protecting her in the South. Mar observed this, his expression unexpectedly unreadable, before bellowing at his men to gain their undivided attention and informing them of the upcoming war in the North without shying away from explaining the threat to their lives. It surprised Ina when the men roared their eagerness; that these warriors were willing to fight and possibly die to defend their homes, despite the danger.

'My lady. Ina!' Ren's raised voice interrupted her thoughts, and the witch sent him an apologetic smile.

'I'm sorry, I drifted into my thoughts. What's wrong?'

'We need to turn here. You wanted to travel slowly, so that is the best way to go, and they are supposed to have a decent hostelry in a village nearby,' he said, and Ina nodded while taking a deep breath, turning her face towards the sun to enjoy the soft caress of its warm rays, eyes closed in contemplation.

'It feels good to be surrounded by nature here with you. Almost like I'm free from the burden of my magic,' she said, and after a moment, guided her orein to the road Ren indicated. When their mounts fell into step, and the sense of his comforting presence intensified, Ina sighed softly, resuming the leisurely pace.

'My lady, as we are alone, care to tell me what you plan to do?'

'My usual. We will *go and see* what happens?' she tried to tease, but Ren's sombre look told her she would have to reveal her plan and face his objections.

'I'm not sure, to be true. Despite having the complete chaos regalia, I don't feel I have enough power or, rather, enough experience to subdue the Iron Empire's army. Maybe if I had a few years to practise with them, I would know how to manipulate chaos to this extent, but I have little time to learn. I don't know how Sowenna raised the Grey Mountains, as I feel no different except more at peace and in control,' she said, stopping when Ren pulled his reins so hard his horse sat on his rear legs.

'Your illusion is so misleading, I forgot about the regalia. Do you intend to use them?' She looked at his face, stilled in a pained grimace, and turned Zjawa towards him.

'Let's stop and talk here.'

When they'd both dismounted, letting the mount rest in a blooming meadow, Ren approached and reached out, gently trailing his finger along the concealed rim of the golden filigree before stopping on the stone. 'Can you take it off?'

'I think I can, but I haven't tried yet. If it's anything like the necklace and ring, removing it will feel like I'm trying to excise a piece of my soul. Physically it should be possible, but I feel very uneasy even thinking about it,' she said, enjoying his careful inspection.

'Who have you told about the circlet—Velka, the king? Was your magic so powerful in the temple because of the regalia?' Ren's curiosity made her smile, and Ina leaned towards him while she unpacked their travel rations.

'I haven't told anyone about the circlet, so only you and Mar know for certain, and I hid the circlet quickly enough to prevent anyone else from knowing.' Here Ina grimaced, remembering Rurik's elation. 'Rurik realised too, but I doubt that secretive bastard will tell anyone. My magic, well, it doesn't feel stronger, but it's no longer fighting me. I do still slip. I'm not sure I can describe it, except as feeling whole, no longer broken. I'm not Sowenna, and if I'm lucky, I never will be. That's why I hid the circlet, to avoid my name being spoken of with fear, to not be treated as a threat or cast out as too dangerous. I don't want to be an outcast, Ren.

Not again, not when I have people I love and a life worth fighting for.' She didn't intend on sounding pitiful, but Ren's eyes softened, and he moved closer, stroking the small of her back while changing the subject.

'Do you feel comfortable telling me your idea for dealing with the Empire? I know you well enough that I see you mulling one over, and I doubt it's just *go and see*.' The sheepish glance Ina flicked at Ren clearly indicated guilt, making the quiet warrior smile.

'I'm going to tame the sea.'

She looked to the side when a choking sound followed her answer and chuckled, looking at Ren swallowing hard.

'I see my plan is not to your liking, but that is the best way.'

'Please clarify, my lady. Your words make little sense. No one can tame the sea.'

'No one ever tired, but to end this danger, I must try. That's why I asked Jorge for a prediction about the armada. It's also why I'll need the army there. As callous as this may sound, to stop the larger threat, I will need the energy from the battle with the vanguard.' Ina paused when Ren looked at her sharply. The witch couldn't blame him. He knew she always tried to avoid bloodshed. Her admission she needed to use violence could look like chaos madness was stealing her emotions.

'I promise no one will die in vain. I have to use what I know because I don't have time to learn how to use the regalia. I'm trying to save this country. I would have to travel to Arknay to find Sowenna's manuscripts, if they even exist, and learn how to conjure wild magic, or I could experiment, risking more lives. I thought about it, and the chaos of battle is something I know, something I can control, so I will use it and command the sea, creating a tidal wave that will push the armada up Veles's arse and beyond.' She smiled, trying to reassure him about her plans, but deep inside, Ina quaked at the thought of trying to manipulate such primordial power.

Still, how else could she fight the armada? If the Empire's forces were as big as the rumours, what chance did Cornovii have otherwise?

'We are bonded, my lady. I can feel your unease at this plan. What are you hiding, Ina?'

The witch sighed, sitting up. 'I simply don't know if my magic will work on the ocean. In Marzanna's temple, when Velka directed the magic of the land through my body, it nearly destroyed me, but even worse, there was a moment it wanted to remake me. Ren, I was offered godhood by something so vast there. I can't describe it, but it ended with me trying to take Marzanna's power. It was an intoxicating experience, and if the power of the ocean is similar, then who knows what will happen? The sea has never been tamed, and its darkest depths are still untouched, hiding the cradle of life. Even with regalia and the protection of my bonds, I don't know if I can do it. I am afraid, but I have to try. I owe this to the people, to the soldiers. We don't have enough people to stop the Iron Empire. The army, as strong as it is, will barely be able to defeat the vanguard. I cannot bear the slaughter if the armada arrives.'

'You don't owe this country anything, my lady. With Rewan's drafting and Verdante aiding us, we are a force to be reckoned with. You don't have to do this. It will be enough if you support us with your magic rather than take it upon yourself to fight the armada.' Ren moved closer, looking at her with concern, but Ina only shook her head.

'It is bad enough we have to fight the empire here as they are. How many more would die if we let the armada land on our shores and spread like a plague? With you and Mar leading the army, we can win, but I can't let this country be entangled in endless war or partisan skirmishes. We need peace, Ren. We need the battle that will end all wars. I'm tired, my friend, and weary. I need peace and will do whatever it takes to achieve it.'

Ina was still talking when she realised Ren's gaze had drifted somewhere behind her, and his pupils widened before he whispered.

'Ayni? What are you doing here?'

'Really? Do you think we need a bloody chaperone or something?' Ina sighed and turned to face the dragoness, but the field Ren stared so intensely at appeared empty to her, with only wind stirring tall grass in hypnotic circles.

'Ren, what do you see?' she asked carefully, half-turned to keep his figure in view.

'Ayni, and she is magnificent,' he muttered to Ina before he turned his gaze towards the field. 'What are you doing here, Mi'kaira?' he said, standing up, his face lit by the softest of smiles.

'No! Whatever you're seeing, it's not Ayni.' Ina grabbed his hand, holding him firmly despite the warrior's anger. 'Please trust me,' she whispered before turning towards the empty field.

'Show yourself,' she said. The command in her voice was answered by a peel of laughter that flowed over the field.

'I have no quarrel with you, autumn girl, but the man next to you... give him to me, and I will tell you the secrets of the North.' The voice was as seductive as a summer breeze, and Ina felt Ren pull towards its temptation.

'Show yourself in your true form. This man's life is bonded to mine, so release your hold upon him.' The open field, its grass swaying hypnotically in the warm breeze, and the voice's desire for Ren told the witch who she was dealing with. Unfortunately, her friend only saw his lover's seductive smile, and Ina suspected only his steadfast loyalty stopped him from ripping his hand from her grasp.

'Yours? You have no claim on him, autumn's child. It's not your image in his mind. His heart belongs to another.' The pressure dropped, and the popping noise told her the latawica was controlling the surrounding air, using it to throw road dust and debris into her face a moment later. Ina shielded them both from the worst, but this sudden attack irked her immensely. Air demons were nasty creatures, and a scorned latawica could become dangerous even for experienced mages.

'You poor excuse for Perun's farts. Show yourself, or I will rip the magic out of you together with your vicious spirit.' Ina shouted into the small tornado of torn grass and dust that sped across the field while Ren fell into a fighting pose, awakened from his beguilement.

Ina shook her head as she pointed at the oncoming whirlwind. 'You can't fight an air wraith with steel; I'll just whip her arse with magic.'

'But I saw...' He was still confused, so she finished the sentence for him.

'You saw the love that you hold within your heart. They use the thoughts and emotions of your loved one to beguile your mind, and as much as I'm thrilled that you love Ayni, could you be a good little warrior and protect the horses from the dust because our friend here caught me with some anger to work through.' Ren's lips quirked in amusement, but he listened, grabbing two blankets and covering their mount's heads just in time as another whirlwind of dust was thrown in their faces. Ina smiled viciously. The last few weeks had almost broken her, and now blind fate offered her a chance to take out her frustration on this malicious, undying spirit.

'Just you and me, you flatulent windbag.' Ina growled, releasing control of her chaos to create two fire whips. The wilful air buffeted the witch as she focused on nature's chaotic energy, willing it to become visible. As she looked towards the fields, raw magic highlighted the contour of every living being on the field. The figure of a svelte woman with long flowy hair appeared behind the weaving whirlwind, and the witch lashed out in that direction.

They fought ferociously back and forth, crimson fire whipping out and burning through ethereal magic as debris and dust scoured the witch's flesh, neither side giving an inch as they battled, Ina's anger rising as the spirit laughed and danced, evading the fire. Finally, after a sharp rock cut her cheek, Ina shouted.

'Will you stand still so we can finish this like women?!'

The latawica only laughed, flying higher, changing her shape into a giant bird. The sheer size of the creature was impressive. Her sharp beak and claws could rip a cow to shreds, but what sent a shiver down Ina's spine was the image of the birds in the central market of Osterad, and the witch shouted. 'What? A new tactic? Don't you dare shit on me, you overgrown pigeon.'

The demon bird screeched in offence, and even mid-air, Ina could see her feathers puffed up. 'You savage bitch. I'm not fighting some crazy mage. You can keep your man, autumn's child, but his heart belongs to another.'

'And thank fuck for that, because he deserves better than me,' Ina said, inhaling deeply to calm herself down before returning to Ren, who'd observed everything with an amused expression.

'I'm fairly certain I didn't teach you the art of offending your enemy, my lady.'

'No, that's all good, clean forest living and a dollop of Mar's inimitable style. I've become more creative since meeting my dragon,' she said, flashing her mischievous smile as Ren leapt onto his horse, laughing.

'We need to find the inn before you offend any more spirits. I don't want any overgrown birds ruining my cloak. We can continue our discussion in a more relaxed locale, but you'd best be ready to answer a few questions, my lady.'

CHAPTER TWENTY

After several nights in villages and small towns heading in any direction but north, Ina was feeling the strain of sleeping in hostelries whose cleanliness, in her opinion, could be vastly improved by cleaning, with fire and a generous helping of salt, so on their arrival at Oakcross, the witch was in no mood for the closed gates and hostile stares from the guards. When those same guards repeated their questions for the third time, Ina lost her famous temper, likening their inquisitors to the unflattering progeny of several swamp creatures and demons before dragging out the king's warrant and announcing her position of judicial mage. However, the next set of events left her regretting such a revelation.

'My lady mage, thank the gods, you've arrived just in time. We need your help!' shouted a portly man in a blood-splattered robe rushing towards them, trying desperately to hold a crumpled biretta to his head in his haste. It appeared the mayor was coming to greet them, and Ina's surprise was eclipsed by a healthy dose of worry at the state of the gasping man's clothing. The witch glanced at Ren, who had already moved closer, ready to intervene if needed, and with a deep sigh, she straightened her posture, smiling with, she hoped, a dignity befitting the royal witch. Whatever the official saw in her face made him stumbled to a halt and begin shaking.

'Well met, good sir, and who might you be?' she asked from astride her orein, who added to the man's terror by snapping her fanged muzzle in front of his face.

'Thomas Neodyn, mayor of Oakcross, lady witch. We desperately need your help,' he babbled, and Ren pushed his horse forward.

'What is so important, Master Neodyn, that you would bother the royal witch?' Ren's words took her by surprise. They weren't travelling incognito, but she wanted the empire's spies to work for their information, so only using her judicial warrant had felt appropriate earlier. Instead, the entire town would soon know the royal witch had visited them and would flood her with petty petitions.

The mayor bowed even lower. 'Blessed Lada. Now I know you can help us. Please follow me. We must go to the town hall, if it still stands.'

Nothing emphasised his determination more than when the mayor reached for Zjawa's bridle to lead her, and only Ina's sharp command saved his fingers from being bitten off by the angry mare.

'Fine, but find us two comfortable beds for the night. Oh, and an excellent dinner. That is my price for assistance, the best accommodation this town can offer,' she said, and the man eagerly nodded his head. Ina followed Thomas, who, with a spring in his step, led them to the centre of town. An inhuman roar shook the windows of the houses as they rode.

'What monster do you have here? A werewolf, striga, a draugr?' Ina asked, trying to prepare herself. She wanted to tailor the attack rather than blasting a creature with the full power of chaos.

'Nothing of that sort, my lady. Our lads, the ones who escaped from Dancik and came home, they transformed. We were just talking, and suddenly, they all changed. Their bodies twisted, and they lashed out. We locked them in the town hall, but I'm afraid it won't be long till they break down the doors and attack.'

Ina exchanged a glance with Ren, and they quickened the pace, leaving the mayor behind and arriving as the doors of the town hall bent and, with a strange pained tearing, burst open, revealing a view into the realm of nightmare as a pack of men, slavering incoherently and lost in the berserker's madness, exploded outside, sending the crowd screaming and running down the streets.

'My lady, contain them here.' Ren issued the terse command, sliding off his horse, the hiss of his sword leaving its scabbard, cutting through the howls of the crazed men as the warrior charged forward.

For a moment, Ina struggled to tame her magic, to create a barrier that wouldn't instantly destroy all life within, and cursed Ren for giving her such a vital but difficult task. She grinned with sudden inspiration, thrusting her magic into the ground, creating a trench too deep to escape. Still smiling from her ingenuity, the witch leapt forward to join the virtuoso killer as he fought with the agility and precision she'd always envied.

'Come on, you incestuous toads, send Veles my regards!' Ina couldn't help herself as excitement burned through her body, and two berserkers turned, charging clumsily, filled with uncontrollable rage. Without thought, the witch punched forward, her magic pouring out and anchoring itself in their bodies, making Ina nearly vomit as she felt their vile, twisted souls.

A memory from the sewers of Osterad bubbled up through the foulness; this was the same as the damage her former lover had done to the poor soul during the coup.

'That fucking Liander's worse than the clap and twice as virulent.' Her desire to kill him fuelled her anger as Ina yanked on the connection. Both creations roared in pain, but the witch didn't let go, pulling on their magic while avoiding the clawed hands until they stilled, withering until nothing but dried husks remained. Ren had already dealt with the others and was cleaning his sword as his last victim crumpled to the floor, a faint smile on his lips.

Gore and entrails covered the cobblestones, making Ina frown when she noticed it slowly flowing towards her feet, startling a little when Ren sheathed his sword and walked over.

'My lady, the other two?' he asked, pointing at the immobilised creatures, and Ina smiled sadly.

'Chaos claimed their lives, but something I felt in their life force concerns me. I think my aunt has Liander's poison, but she or someone else must have changed it as I don't remember the victims in Osterad being humans who suddenly changed after a delay.' Suddenly her eyes widened, and Ina gasped, terrified by the potential outcome.

'Ren, what if there are more like this in Osterad, and we left the capital defenceless? The army may already be marching north.'

'The army is headed north?' The mayor was walking in their direction, avoiding the biggest blood splatters. 'Is that the reason they sent the royal witch here?'

With the threat to his town ended, Master Neodyn had regained his sense of decorum and looked at Ina with a critical stare, expecting her explanation immediately.

As Ren barked out a laugh, Ina answered. 'The food, baths, and the beds. That is your job right now, good sir, or I swear I will revive those husks and set them free. Mind you, when I'm clean and fed, I may feel gracious enough to answer some of your questions.' Her rumbling stomach and the man's puffed chest overcame any feelings of guilt she felt for pressuring him. 'Oh, and find me a messenger. I need to inform Osterad of your problem.'

She would have to do more than talk to the town council to prepare them for the impending army, but first, she would have to learn more about the men who died today. *And eat and take a bath, and rest before you lose your temper*, whispered the small voice in her head. Sensing her annoyance, Ren moved closer, looking directly at the official.

'Show us the way to the inn and delegate someone to care for your dead,' he ordered, and Ina nodded gratefully for his intervention.

The mayor grumbled under his breath, but quickly led them to a large townhouse on the opposite side of the main square. The woman who came out to greet them was not happy at the situation, eyeing Ren's blood-splattered clothing, but after a few moments of persuasion, they were let in and led to a spacious bedroom, then left alone before Ina could ask about a second room.

The witch wanted to scream in frustration. The woman assumed they were a couple and had given them a single room. One look at Ina's face and Ren headed for the door. 'I will sort it out, my lady. Please have a rest, and I will join you shortly.'

Too tired to object, the witch took off her shoes and fell onto the bed. She could hear an angry voice coming from downstairs before everything settled, or more accurately, she drifted into a deep sleep.

The hand on her face radiated warmth, and Ina reached out, stroking it. 'Mar?' she murmured before opening her eyes.

'No, Ina, just Ren. I wanted to wake you to avoid casualties amongst the servants if they startled you.' Ren's gentle smile was easy to return as she stretched her stiff muscles.

'Did you convince our host to assign us a second bedroom, or will I have to sleep in the stable tonight?' she asked with a lazy yawn.

'Yes, my room is next to yours. Also, dropping some gold on the table encouraged the lady of the house to be more hospitable. It looked like the mayor wanted to exploit a merchant's widow. Paying for our stay ensured she was happy to host us,' he said. Soon after, they heard knocking, and servants entered to fill the bath with hot water. 'Take your time, my lady. I will wait downstairs.'

'I miss being able to ask you to stay and braid my hair,' she said, seeing Ren shake his head in response.

'I can still braid your hair. Some things will never change. Call me when you're dressed and ready,' he said, bending and kissing her forehead before leaving the room.

With a deep sigh, the witch stripped as soon as the servants left the room. Finding out someone still used her transmutation serum was disturbing, and she didn't wish to be alone. Ina missed Mar. Ren's presence calmed her down, but the witch wished she could lose herself in the muscular embrace of her dragon. The temptation was so strong she almost reached for the bond before chastising herself. *Mar has enough on his plate without worrying about my longing and anxiety.* Knowing that boneheaded dragon, he would drop everything to fly here because his woman needed him. Somehow this thought made her smile, dispelling the worst concerns, and Ina washed quickly before heading downstairs.

Thomas Neodyn was already there when Ina arrived in the dining room, and the guarded look he gave her didn't bode well for their conversation. Ren gestured her in, his hair slick from what she assumed were his own ablutions.

The mayor was the first to break their silence. 'My lady, you mentioned earlier that you'd be willing to talk?' His question, whilst polite, still irked her, but in the spirit of cooperation, she smiled and sat at the table, nodding as she helped herself to some food before speaking.

'Yes, Master Neodyn.' With years of working at court, it was easy to don the persona of a judicial mage, turning those three simple words into a nuanced sentence that was both an agreement and a question. It was a calculated gamble. Being halfway to Osterad, the major could either be a man desperate to be closer to court life or resentful of aristocratic influence, but judging by the eagerness he displayed in response, Ina was betting the former and got straight to her questions. 'I need to learn more about those men. You said they came from Dancik. As humans or monsters? What exactly happened in the town hall?'

She saw the mayor shift in his chair, becoming increasingly uncomfortable. 'Before we start, my lady, you asked for a messenger. We have the courier station in town, and I can send your message as soon as you are ready. As for your question, I—well, *we*, the council. I mean, Kion is on the brink of defeat. We are the next fortified town south, so—'

'So, you sent those men to talk to the Empire, hoping to negotiate the same terms as Dancik,' Ren finished for the stuttering official, his voice emotionless.

Ina rubbed her temples to relieve the growing tension. The situation must be dire if a town halfway to Osterad was ready to surrender without a fight.

'You will not surrender, offer assistance, or even exchange letters with the empire. You will gird your loins and stand tall. When the king arrives with the army that will save this country, you will welcome them with open arms and support those brave men and women with all your heart. Now, let us return to my questions. Your envoys came back unchanged, yes?'

Ina did not miss the flinching of the mayor's shoulders as she issued her commands, disdain for his cowardice dripping from her voice or Ren's hand as it toyed with a dagger she swore hadn't been there a moment before.

'Yes, they were perfectly normal, just a little despondent, but we assumed it was from an unsuccessful meeting. It was our local mage who got suspicious and tried a spell to check their condition.'

'And where is he now?' Ina asked, hoping the mage could give her some answers.

'Dead, my lady. As soon as the spell was started, all hell broke loose. They ripped him apart with their bare hands, despite him burning them with wildfire. He killed one, but they were all over him.' Thomas trembled, but Ina didn't have the time to indulge his distress. Instead, she moved her attention to Ren.

'So the change was triggered by magic. We need to warn Osterad and Mar. The army must know what they're dealing with. If the empire creates more of them, it could pose a serious problem.' When her friend nodded grimly, Ina turned her stern look to Thomas.

'That's how the empire treats their subjects. Did you really think submitting to them would save your hide? Go, Master Neodyn. Tell the messenger to present themselves to me and forget this idiocy of trying to get into the Empire's good graces.'

She saw the man shudder, avoiding her eyes before he whispered, 'But my lady, the stories...?'

'Stories. Fucking stories, he says. If you've ever listened to a bard, you'll know whose stories should make you shiver under your blankets.' Ina didn't bother restraining the magic that seeped from the corner of her eyes, enjoying the widening of the mayor's pupils and his hasty bow as he left, his crumpled biretta falling to the floor, forgotten.

'What are you thinking, my lady?' Ren's calm voice made her sigh.

'That I have a bloody headache! I made one mistake in my youth, and it keeps returning to haunt me. How Mirena did this is beyond me. I thought I was skilled in alchemy, but this? That bitch is a genius, but then we found that out when she poisoned me.' Ina couldn't help cursing as she angrily dug her fingers into the tense muscles of her neck.

Ren moved to her side, and soon she felt his hand on her nape, kneading her tense muscles before moving to the shoulders. 'You shouldn't,' she protested weakly, but had to admit the pain in her temples eased under his touch.

'No, I very much should, if for no other reason than to preserve my sanity. You are difficult when you are in pain, my lady,' he said, continuing his ministrations until the messenger arrived.

In a much better mood, Ina wrote letters to Mar and Jorge detailing her findings, and before long, she escaped to her bedroom. Ren's massage helped with the headache, but the witch tossed and turned in bed, too disturbed by recent events to sleep. This newest iteration of her formula had surprised her, but there was no mistaking the same twisted signature as the abominations in Osterad. The thought that her soldiers would have to fight monsters who knew no pain or fear, tearing apart friend and foe alike in a blind rage, was frightening.

My soldiers... She couldn't help the chuckle that escaped her lips. Ever since events in the South, she couldn't stop thinking of them as hers. The before-the-battle feast had been her unmaking. The faces, usually so distant as to appear blurred, had gained clarity and, with that, recognition, names, and family stories, along with a place in her heart. Now she was asking them to die for her, their Lady of the Crimson Veil, the damned saviour of Cornovii. Initially, Ina had planned on joining Mar's army and attacking as chaos incarnate, decimating those who opposed her.

If only she were confident about using her magic or had any idea how the regalia worked. At the moment, it was all she could do not to kill everyone around her accidentally, and that was not a helpful talent in battle. If she started actively taking lives, it could turn the tide, and if she lost control, Cornovii would shatter under the power of chaos. The very idea of killing people repulsed her. Ina had no qualms about defending herself, even using the chaos of those dying around her caused little remorse, but being the one who caused it went against her every belief.

Protect life for as long as it strives for existence. Her father's words. A man Ina had no memory of, but whose soul shone brightly in the memory of those who knew him. The many stories of his brave work during the plague in the South had resurfaced in her mind after her grandfather's death—another gift from the mind mage's hateful geas. He'd saved many before sacrificing himself for his wife, and now Ina was going to do the same.

When she heard about the Empire's tactic of sending a vanguard to secure a beachhead before transporting their main force, the witch knew where to focus her magic, devising the outline of a terrifying plan that would kill thousands. Ina would entrust Mar and Ren to lead the attack so she could harvest the chaos of the battlefield in order to risk everything on one enormous task, harness the ocean's power, and send the armada back where they came from.

She briefly considered assassinating the emperor, but a horrified Jorge had thrown schemata after schemata in her face, shouting as he asked why she even bothered to pretend to believe in his predictions. Apparently, assassinating the emperor would create a martyr giving birth to the crusade that spawned generation after generation of oppression and death. Ina had quietly apologised and meekly listened from that point. His predictions were precise in their ambiguity. The only outcome of Jorge's predictions that didn't end in defeat was when they fought the armada and the vanguard in a coordinated attack. The North honoured the death on the battlefield and only that way would they consider themselves truly defeated. Unfortunately, thanks to her involvement, that augury was as clear as mud.

Mages didn't use magic on the sea. Even Sowenna had been wary of the ocean, but with a variation of Velka's sigil from the temple, Ina thought she might be able to commune with its power, and if she adapted that heinous spell Rurik had used on the elvish sacrifices, tying it to her soul instead, then communing might change to commanding. The small voice in her head tried to reason with her, telling her how unlikely it was she would survive such a union, helpfully supplying the memory of the screaming corpses crumbling into dust. But the witch refused to listen. Finally, when her headache returned, Ina gave up and reached for Mar's bond.

The golden strands within her soul wrapped her in a soft, loving cocoon, and Ina closed her eyes, breathing slowly. She could feel her dragon's concern radiating through the bond and something else. Deep-seated exhaustion. *My lord marshal. He must have spent several sleepless nights organising the army*, she thought, masking her feelings.

Ina let only the love and reassurance slip through, touching her chest when a familiar warm feeling spread outward, filling her with Mar's affection. The dragon would never have allowed her to go if he knew how dangerous her plan was. It felt wrong to deceive him, to deceive them both, but what choice did she have?

Once more, the memory of the elves chained at Marzanna's temple intruded. The shudder from the witch was quickly suppressed as she accepted the possibility, knowing that at least Mar would survive her enthrallment if she bound herself to the sea. *That is not hopeless. I have a chance, and that's all that matters. After all, I broke through Marzanna's curse and detached myself from the power of southern lands.*

It was a blessing in disguise that both Mar and Ren knew next to nothing about high arcana and trusted her judgement completely. If hiding the truth was the way to protect them, so be it. She would shoulder the burden of responsibility and their wrath when they finally discovered that the sea couldn't be tamed, and the cradle of life had destroyed many mages who'd tried to access its ever-changing power.

The strong pulse of Mar's affection slowly evened out her breathing, and when the soft notes of a flute entwined with the chirping of crickets and the haunting call of night birds penetrated the night, Ina dreamed about the forest.

From deep within in the shadows, a bearded figure approached the bed, placing a calloused hand on the sleeping witch's cheek. The man leaned forward, cutting his forearm with razor-sharp nails, and shimmering drops of green blood fell onto the peridot lying exposed at her throat. His offering momentarily glistened before silently disappearing into the slowly pulsing gemstone.

The figure turned his face to the moon's light, chanting something in an ancient language, and Ina shifted on the bed, groaning as her body arched at the influx of power from his spell, but the man didn't stop. Green light fused with the crimson hue of Ina's magic, filling the room with the scent of pine and moss. When the chanting finished, the figure leaned forward, gently kissing the witch's forehead before melting back into the shadows.

Morning came too early, the bright summer sun merciless, forcing Ina's eyes open and miraculously dispelling last night's worry. The witch touched her chest, frowning slightly, but before she could dwell on the unexpected buoyancy she felt deep inside, a soft knocking on the doors disrupted her musing.

'Enter.'

Ren, dressed for travel, appeared on the threshold. 'Are you ready, my lady? We have quite the distance to cover today.' He smiled, ducking when Ina threw a pillow.

'Have mercy. It's barely sunrise. Besides, no woman should be forced to travel before breakfast. Or at least not this one.' She couldn't stop yawning. The night had seemed peaceful, but her vivid dreams had left her tired, as if she chased fireflies and danced on soft moss all night. Ren, however, had no heart, and instead of giving in to her demands, he walked straight to the window and yanked the curtains open.

What had been a slight gap, letting in a sliver of sunlight, was now the full force of Swaróg's power, and the witch released a stream of curses.

'Do you have a death wish? What is wrong with you today?'

Ren was openly laughing when Ina launched all the objects within reach at his head. 'Nothing is wrong, my lady. It's time to go, and I prefer to arrive at Kion during the day so that some night-blind archer doesn't take us for enemies up to no good.'

His words quieted Ina's objections. Kion, the city under siege, was her gateway to the Iron Empire. The witch sighed. 'Just give me a few moments to get ready. If I'm to face the enemy, I need to present myself as the high-ranking mage they expect. Gods, this is a royal pain in the arse,' she said, reaching into her bag to pull out a crimson dress, noticing Ren's lips twitch while he tried to hide his amusement at her exasperated complaints.

'One word, Ren. One word, and I will throw something sharp at your smirking face,' she said in sport, and her friend raised his hands in surrender.

'I'll wait for you downstairs with breakfast. Maybe some sweet porridge will change this sour mood of yours. Still, you look better in the dress, almost like a real high-born lady,' he said, closing the doors before another missile flew in his direction.

'Real, my arse. I'll give him real,' Ina grumbled, but she couldn't help but smile. Ren's mirth and an otherwise pleasant morning made the looming threat palatable, at least for now.

CHAPTER TWENTY ONE

I na swayed in the saddle, dressed from top to toe in red, feeling like one of Svaróg's sacrificial virgins. Although her virginity was long gone, and not having the temperament to enter lifelong servitude guarding the sacred fire, the witch still felt like a lamb heading to slaughter. Hopefully, she was more wolf in sheep's clothing than a helpless victim. *All I need to do is play haughty mage until the time is right*, she thought, trying to boost her courage.

Ren had initially set a blistering pace, and after a few hours, even with Zjawa's smooth gait, her back was aching, souring her further with every step. Ina suffered in silence until, in a foul temper, she reminded him he must slow down if he wanted them to arrive at Kion with her at least resembling a noblewoman.

The smaller villages they passed were filled with terrified peasants peering from behind closed curtains. Those brave enough to work the fields fled at first sight of their mounts, arms filled with unripened grain, harvested early to avoid losing their crop to the invading army.

Ina congratulated herself on choosing a red dress when they were surrounded by a horde of small children too young to work or be frightened of strangers and ran beside them, chanting, 'The crimson witch is coming! The crimson witch is coming! All shall kneel for the crimson witch!' falling to their knees and laughing before repeating their antics. Unfortunately, only the smallest and most innocent were friendly. From the desperate looks the adults gave her, Ina deduced they all knew the contents of the empire's pamphlets, and only the fear of retribution stopped them from throwing rocks and mud at her.

'Do you think they blame me for the war or Water Horse clan's demise?' she asked when Ren turned towards her.

'Neither, I think. They're more likely to blame the king. Since Rewan ascended to the throne, the country has been pulled from one conflict to another. Even if he is blameless, people will draw their own conclusions. I think they're simply frightened. The peasantry are always the ones who suffer most in war.'

Ina looked at the fields and people she had pledged to defend, who now averted their eyes at the mere presence of the crimson witch. She didn't mind the hostility directed towards her. Years of living in exile had taught her to have a tough hide, but knowing how much Rewan had sacrificed for his country, the thought that the blame was laid on him angered her.

'The sooner we get to Kion, the better,' she said, harsher than she'd intended, kicking Zjawa to trot, disregarding her previous complaints. Her orein jumped forth, so happy to be going faster that she ignored her rider's temper. Soon enough, the hostile village was left behind, and the landscape began changing. Small hillocks interspersed with a myriad of ponds and streams became more prevalent until the banks of the River Vilia came into view. The wide watercourse, the principal transportation route from Osterad to the northern borders, was unusually quiet. In fact, the entire area seemed empty, and Ina grew more worried as their destination neared.

'My lady, Kion should be on the other side of this hill. Can you tell me what your plan is for when we get there?' Ren asked, leading his horse to the shade of a small copse so they could catch their breath and make themselves presentable.

Ina answered as nonchalantly as she could manage. 'It depends. I intend to ride there openly, surrounded by my magic to announce my presence and prevent any accidents from nervous soldiers, then make a big enough scene that I'm taken to see the commander of the siege or the emperor; either will do. I also hope my appearance will cause enough of a disturbance that the siege will be interrupted. If they're stupid enough to attack me, well, I will need your presence to anchor my soul so things don't get out of hand as I persuade them to change their minds.'

It was clear from Ren's expression that he knew she didn't really have a plan, his smile surprisingly mischievous. 'So essentially, we'll *go and see?* I have no objections; until we face the enemy, there is no way to know their reaction, but what do you want me to do? We haven't discussed my role in all of this. Who do you want me to be, my lady? The General of Cornovii, your guardian, your... lover?'

When Ina's eyebrows nearly disappeared into her hairline, Ren chuckled, his hands raised defensively. 'No, I'm not inviting myself to your bed, but we would be separated if they thought I was a servant or colleague. I'm here to guard you, not to be sent to different quarters, leaving you vulnerable when you're asleep.'

'Then let's keep it simple and tell them the truth. You are my guardian, guaranteeing I can use my magic without shattering the world. If they try to separate us, I will show them how dangerous an unhinged mage can be without her anchor. It might even be fun,' she said, and Ren looked thrilled by the possibility.

'You and Mar. Like two peas in a pod,' she said, shrugging when Ren frowned. 'What? It's clear you don't want to act as my lover, yet you still proposed it, and let me guess, your reason was to keep me safe no matter what?' she said, trying to impersonate Mar, making Ren burst out laughing.

'You're right. I would do anything to keep you safe, sister of my heart. Anything except betray Ayni's trust. I am well versed in court games, and if the situation needs it, I could manage the longing look of a besotted dragon in public and sleep on the floor in your bedroom.'

'The floor? Ren, you are just impossible. And Mar isn't besotted. He simply loves me in his own rough, overbearing way,' Ina said, leading the orein back to the road.

'You're right. He's not just besotted. Mar worships the ground you walk on. Maybe it's because he became a dragon, but you are the centre of his universe. When you disappeared, he dropped everything; the kingdom, the army he loves so much. Nothing mattered. What I saw in his eyes made me believe he could watch the world burn as long as you were safe. Which makes me happy, because you deserve to be loved like this.' The genuine affection in Ren's voice brought a blush to her cheeks, and Ina set her eyes on the road.

'He's a much better person than me, but I love him, Ren, from the depths of my chaos-riddled heart.'

They rode in silence now that they were close to their destination, and even before they crested the hill, soldiers appeared from nowhere, surrounding them in a ring of steel.

'Halt, stranger. State your name and business on empire soil.'

Ina looked at the man who issued the order. He was dressed the same as his compatriots. Practical chain mail with metal plates covered his shoulders and torso, with only a different insignia on his helmet to suggest his rank. Where the rest of the soldiers carried spears and short swords, this one was armed with a plain but well-maintained broadsword. This man carried himself with the confidence of a seasoned warrior, his stance casual but ready. Ina straightened her back and looked at Ren, who nodded slightly.

With forced nonchalance, Ina studied her nails, relaxing the tight control over her magic, allowing its crimson energy to coil around her body as Ren stood in his stirrups and spoke.

'This is Lady Inanuan of Thorn, Royal Witch of Cornovii, and Lady of the Crimson Veil, answering your emperor's plea for discourse.' His voice was calm and composed, suggesting the emperor was lesser than the woman sitting before them. Ina looked away from her fingers to smile at the soldier and gave the man a little more encouragement.

'Take me to your leader, or should I find my own way?' she said, her smile becoming hard-edged as she focused on her chaos, and the crimson energy burst into flame. Much to her displeasure, the soldiers didn't retreat, only lowering their spears to threaten the horses.

'So the crimson witch deigns to grace us with her presence. Come, my lady, no need to display your power. I'm sure the commander would want to meet such a distinguished guest.' He reached towards Zjawa's reins, but her orein took offence, snapping her fanged muzzle beside the man's hand. This finally made him step back, and he eyed the malicious spirit.

'Foolish boy, do you want to lose your fighting hand? Meet my mountain spirit, Zjawa, the blessing of Skarbnik. Now, will you show me the way, or will we stand here posturing in front of your soldiers?' Ina played the part of the arrogant witch from the bard's tales with mounting pleasure. She rode forward with hesitation, her magic ready to defend her mount, but the man shrugged and gestured her to follow, his face set in a disdainful expression as he guided them onwards. The road wound through the impressive encampment. As far as Ina could see, there were soldiers, each a typical northern warrior with sharp faces framed with manes of blond or red hair, often accompanied by an impressive beard, giving her unyielding, hostile glares.

Ina had to admit she hadn't expected so many of them. Suddenly, Mar's army felt small in comparison, making her heart tremble. What if she led them all to a senseless slaughter? She gulped and looked at Ren, whose face held the ice mask of the Ghost, and when she opened their connection, Ina felt the worry radiating from the depth of her friend's soul. *If this is only a part of the vanguard, how big is the armada? The fuckers are toying with us like a cat with a mouse. They could defeat Kion easily, so why wait?* Ina's thoughts were racing. Now the lack of reaction to her magic display made sense. This welcoming committee had expected her to come, and the warriors must have known what she could do.

'I told you this display was unnecessary, woman. Control yourself.' The sharp voice of her guide broke through her thoughts, and Ina looked at him before noticing the red hue of chaos that had slipped past her control, now coating her like a shield.

'You will speak to my lady respectfully, or I will have your head.' Ren's voice was deceptively calm, but both men measured the other with hands resting on their weapons.

'I will speak to her as I please. Soon your *lady* will be one of many women in the emperor's bed. Some even are treated well if they learn their place.' The guard must have no preservation instincts, and Ina's blood froze when she saw Ren's face turn serene, knowing he was ready to strike the deadly blow.

'Sa'Ren, this one deserves punishment from my hand,' she said calmly, noticing their argument had attracted a lot of attention. Ina was almost sure they wouldn't dare to raise a hand against her. After all, the emperor wanted to see her in one piece. Ren, however, could be seen as a troublesome accessory attached to the package.

'Your emperor wants me for a reason, and you're about to learn what that reason is,' she said with a flick of her wrist, stabbing out with a spear of chaos. The guard's eyes widened, and he swung his sword, but nothing could stop the wave of primordial power that hit him in the middle of the chest, sending him to his knees.

Ina savoured his life energy—strong, masculine, and so deliciously vital—as she siphoned it slowly from his body, the peridot on her chest blazing with power in response. This man may not be afraid of her crimson fire, but how would he face feeling his soul being consumed as he watched, helpless as a babe? The witch refused to look away from the warrior's terrified gaze as he finally understood that the woman before him was more monstrous than any creature or malicious spirit he would ever face.

'My lady?' Ren's gentle touch and the concern in his eyes were enough to snap her out of the euphoria. She didn't even need to reach for the bond. The chaos regalia and a friend's touch brought her back to reality with a snap.

'It's all right ,Sa'Ren. I won't take his life. It is fouler than sewage, and I'm not that desperate,' she said theatrically, wiping imaginary dirt from her hands.

'Would anyone else care to share their opinion on my place?' Ina asked cheerfully, looking around, but no one spoke as the now grey-haired soldier was carried away by his compatriots. Her satisfied sigh at their silence was interrupted by the appearance of a frowning, broad-shouldered male.

'Lady Inanuan, I would kindly ask you to refrain from punishing my soldiers. Whilst they are loyal and fierce warriors, they lack the wit to understand your position or the power you wield. If you'd care to dismount and join me, I've had some supper delivered to my tent. You and your companion must be tired and hungry after your journey.'

Supper? Just slather yourself with butter, and I'll gobble you up instead. Ina's thoughts shocked her, but the man standing before her was a gorgeous, mouth-watering mountain of muscle with artfully tousled white-blond hair, and captivating deep blue eyes that twinkled with an intelligence and kindness she hadn't expected from the enemy.

'And who you might be?' she asked, trying to recover her composure.

'Torvald von Roche, second commander of the Iron Empire and scion of the von Roche family. Even if the fame of your beauty hadn't reached the Iron Court, the legend of your magic certainly did, and I'm pleased you accepted our invitation, Lady Inanuan. May I ask who your companion is? I have my suspicions, but....'

'My name is Sa'Ren Gerel. I am the bonded guardian of our Lady of the Crimson Veil. I hope you comprehend enough not to question my presence.'

Ina observed this exchange with mixed feelings. Both men looked deceptively calm and polite, but she could sense the tension building under the false civility.

'Of course. I wouldn't dare to question your presence, general. The emperor, however, may have a different opinion. Please follow me. While we eat, I shall have a tent prepared for you, my lady. We will escort you to Dancik in the morning,' he said, and Ina nodded, looking at the quiet walls of Kion, highlighted by the setting sun, her thoughts concerned. *How long has this siege lasted? Are they starving in there?*

Unable to look away from the castle, Ina took a breath to calm her racing heart. 'I would ask you to honour the emperor's offer and withdraw from your siege of Kion. His correspondence clearly showed that he would cease his expansion into Cornovii in exchange for my presence. Well, here I am, so please stand down your army, or I'll have to turn around and return to my king,' she said, following Torvald into his tent.

The interior was pleasantly appointed, filled with soft furs and lighting, and Ina sighed with pleasure, placing her aching body on something soft. Torvald waited until they all were seated before turning to the witch.

'I must offer my apologies, but without the emperor's express orders, I cannot withdraw the imperial army, but I would like to extend my services as your personal escort to Dancik. The emperor prefers to avoid any chance of impropriety with the ladies he chooses.' Ina caught a flicker of compassion in the second commander's eyes as he finished.

'His... women?' she asked without trying to mask her disdain, and the commander sighed dramatically.

'Yes, Lady Inanuan. His women. Every woman or man born with even a hint of magic becomes a possession of the empire. Female mages are a rarity among those born with magical talents, and once they reach maturity, their place is in the court, or more precisely, in the imperial harem.' Torvald looked at her with bitterness. 'My sister Serennah is one such treasures. She has a particular talent for the manipulation of air, and I'm sure you will meet her in Dancik as it was her talent that brought us here without losing a single ship.'

Torvald's wording of his explanation felt like the opportunity she needed. This man was unhappy with his sister's arrangement, and if she played it well, she could have an ally amongst her enemies.

'I'm sorry your sister was exploited because of her birthright. If I will likely meet her at court, is there any message you'd want me to pass along?' With compassion she realised was genuine, Ina lay a hand on the commander's arm, feeling him tense in response. He was motionless, simply looking at her, but Ina still heard the barely audible words.

'Tell Serennah her family is proud of her.'

'I will, and once I meet with the emperor, I can try to win back her freedom,' Ina said, jerking back as Torvald grasped her chin, gesturing for Ren to stay put as the commander tilted her head back.

'Why, witch? Why would you offer this? You are our enemy,' he snarled, but Ina could hear the pain and surprise laced through his harsh words. She didn't struggle, letting Torvald stare at her like he was trying to search the depths of her soul.

'Because it's the right thing to do, and your sister is no man's possession. I can be your enemy or your ally. I leave this decision to you, commander,' she said calmly and could have sworn his hand trembled.

The next moment Ina was thrust to the side as servants entered the tent; their surprise quickly masked as the commander sneered, pushing the tent flap aside and, growling something incomprehensible, stormed outside.

Ina looked at the piles of meat and sighed theatrically. 'Well, better this than nothing, but why no vegetables or fish? We're almost on the coast, for fuck's sake.' The witch kept complaining, stopping only when Ren grabbed her hand, turning her towards him.

'Ina, what was that? Why did you promise him your help?'

'For two reasons. First, helping our violent second commander might prevent the vanguard from causing further harm. Second, his sister, a powerful air mage, is, according to Torvald, trapped in the emperor's harem, and freeing her from that may gain us an ally willing to help stop the armada. Maybe the stories we heard in court about her were just fables to scare the masses. One way or another, the vanguard is bigger, better trained and armed than we expected, and they are not southern peasants I can terrify to submission. We need an ally, and I just promised him his heart's desire.' Ina's answer was pragmatic but held a hint of hope that had been lacking recently, and with that thought uppermost in her mind, she grabbed the nearest item of food, wincing as her teeth failed to sink into a roasted rabbit. 'Eat. This bloody bunny is a tough bugger. Could you sneak into Kion and see what the situation is like there? Tell them the help is coming, as it must be daunting to see the wall of steel under your gates daily.'

She saw Ren chuckle in silent merriment and shake his head. 'Ina, in one breath, you told me you've possibly made the empire's second commander betray his master, complained about your food, and sent me on a dangerous mission. I love you, my lady, but I'm grateful you chose Mar, because keeping up with your stream of thoughts is utterly confusing.'

Ina smiled at him. 'Did you expect something else from the harbinger of chaos?'

'No, my lady, and I will see what I can do for Kion. It's a shame we don't have a giant dragon who could create a brief distraction,' he joked, shaking his head when Ina eagerly offered her services.

After they finished their meal and argued over the distraction, stalling for time until full night descended, Ina went for a walk. Despite Ren's protests, the witch decided to be the diversion. Chaos coated her like her synonymous crimson veil as she walked among the soldiers.

Initially, the bored soldiers tried goading her with insults, taking her lack of reaction as encouragement until one foolishly grabbed her forearm, and the witch turned, lashing out with her fire whips.

'Lady Inanuan, I specifically asked you not to torment my soldiers.' Torvald appeared out of nowhere, approaching her angrily, and Ina shrugged.

'Where is my orein, commander? I hope your soldiers haven't mistreated my spirit.'

'Your what? That horse you arrived on? She's with the other horses, causing havoc. I can take you to her if you stop behaving like you lost your senses by walking among enemy soldiers,' he scolded her, and as soon as Ina dismissed her magic, he grabbed her elbow.

'What is wrong with you, woman? They could hurt you. What were you thinking, parading yourself like this— Wait, where is Sa'Ren? Inanuan, where is your guardian?' Torvald hissed into her ear while leading her away from the soldiers.

'He's doing me a little favour,' she said when they wandered towards the paddock, away from the eavesdropping men. 'You aren't raising the alarm, commander. Does that mean you decided? Your help for your sister's freedom?' she asked softly, choosing words that might reach his heart.

Ina gasped when a fence post splintered as Torvald's fist crashed into it before he turned towards her, grasping her shoulders. 'You are the tempest that will cause my doom, but have it be your way. The gods will curse me as an honourless bastard, but I will help you. Betray me and I—'

'Take your hands off my ward, Norseman,' Ren's voice called out, and the Ghost materialised from the shadows.

'Ren, it's all right. Torvald agreed to help us.' Ina smiled, approaching her friend, gasping when Ren grabbed her by her waist, placing her behind him.

'Did he agree before or after he told you how he slaughtered the delegation from Kion, or about the younger men he gave to his soldiers as playthings? Or even that he sent those from Oakcross home, twisted by foul magic.' Ren's voice lowered to a quiet snarl while he sheltered Ina with his body.

'Is this true?' she asked, looking at Torvald's eyes, but there was no remorse.

'It is war, Inanuan. Now go back to your tent before I decide your outspoken guardian's life is too inconvenient.'

CHAPTER TWENTY TWO

Ina tossed and turned in the bed for most of the night. Ren's discovery crushed her hopes of using the commander, his duplicity leaving the witch embarrassed for believing him corruptible. In the end, the quiet warrior sat beside her as she worried that while their plan was unchanged, executing it would now be more challenging. In the morning, her red eyes and inhuman glare made even the bravest enemy soldier flinch when she looked at them.

'My lady, I'm pleased to see you out of bed. I hope nothing has changed since last night. Are you still willing to meet the emperor?' Torvald appeared by her side when she stepped away from the tent. Ina looked at his friendly, open face and outstretched hand, and a vicious grimace curled her lips.

'You're still keeping up the pretence of civility? After what I learned? You can skip the pleasantries and be a regular arsehole. It will be a relief for us all.' She saw the hand curl in a fist before it dropped limply to his side, the commander shaking his head with a deep sigh.

'War is horrific, Ina. What do you think the emperor would do if his commander denied him? I would do anything for my family. I thought you, of all people, would understand that we do what we must in order to protect what we love.' Torvald's words cut the witch to the core, and as the commander leapt onto his waiting horse, Ina turned away, her grief too raw to share with the enemy. Feeling the burden of carrying the regalia, the heart-sore witch reached up to touch the unseen diadem, and her thoughts turned to those she loved. *How far would I go to protect Velka, Mar, or Ren?*

'Lady Inanuan, it's time to go.' Torvald smiled gently, looking at her with sympathy, ignoring her harsh words. Ina climbed onto the orein, letting Zjawa playfully nibble her leg. Her mind reached for Mar. The connection pulsed with soft golden light, pushing back the dark thoughts. His steadfast love made her smile, and for a moment, Ina closed her eyes, imagining his muscular arms around her and the slow, strong beat of a dragon's heart.

When she eased back from the bond, the feeling of being held didn't fade, and Ina couldn't dismiss the smile lingering on her lips, even as, from the corner of her eye, she caught Torvald's look of anguish and longing. The fleeting expression made the commander look much older than she'd initially thought, but it disappeared as he dug his spurs into the horse's flank and rode off.

After leaving the camp, Ina and Ren were placed in the middle of a small column of mean-looking warriors, the commander leading them towards the coast.

They travelled for half a day before Torvald ordered a rest. The field he chose was a beautiful summer meadow next to a slow, meandering river. With practised ease, the soldiers set up camp with sentries staring menacingly into the distance, leaving Ina and Ren to look after themselves. Ina sighed deeply, sliding off Zjawa's back, and walked towards the riverbank to wash the road's dust off her face. The witch gave the river an annoyed glance when she realised how far down it was, but after struggling with her skirts, Ren walked into the shallow water and gently wiped the grime off her face. Ina fell back onto the soft grass, enjoying the moment until a dark shadow blocked the sun.

'General Sa'Ren, please leave us for a moment.' The deep baritone of the commander's voice was polite but so stern that it left no room for contradiction.

'Whatever you want to say to my lady, you can say before me. She may be cooperating now, but I don't trust you.' Ren was calm. He didn't even look at her, giving all his attention to the commander.

'I respect your dedication, Master Sa'Ren. However, if I wanted to hurt her, I would have done so in the camp, and even the Ghost could not stand the combined power of my men, at least not for long. So I'm asking you, politely, not to force my hand into violence.'

Ina rubbed the bridge of her nose as both men slowly shifted into fighting stances. 'Please, Ren, give us a moment. You know I can handle one man without difficulty,' she said, trying to sweeten her words with a smile. She could see he didn't like it, but Ren moved to their horses without question.

'What do you want?' she asked shortly, uncomfortable with Torvald's long, assessing gaze sliding over her body.

'Who did you think about?' he asked, moving closer. 'When we were about to leave, who were you thinking about?'

His words confused her. *He sent Ren away to ask this? Why would it matter if he heard?* In fact, her guardian could have answered Torvald himself, but with his avid interest, it seemed the answer meant a lot to the commander. 'My thoughts are none of your business,' she said, satisfied by the flash of anger at her response.

'Your smile could send a thousand ships to war. Who holds your heart that you smile like that? Tell me, Inanuan. I can protect you, from the war, from the emperor. What must I do to make you mine?' The desperate commander crowded closer, leaning over so far that Ina felt threatened for the first time since meeting him. Scrambling to her feet, she noticed Ren running in their direction just as her foot slipped on the muddy riverbank.

'Tell me!' Torvald's face was right above her, and he grasped her waist, dragging her around.

'My dragon. I was thinking about my dragon. He holds my heart, and I will never be yours,' she answered breathlessly, shocked into forgetting her magic by his swift move, but even more by the burning need she saw in his expression. *He wants me to love him, but why?* she thought when he bent down, whispering in her ear.

'The fate of you and the empire is tied together. You belong here now, and I'm pleased to see you are so much more than I expected.' Torvald grinned, releasing her before he pushed her in Ren's direction. 'As you can see, Master Sa'Ren, nothing bad will happen to your ward when she is in my care.'

The way he said it made her blood boil, and whips of chaos sprang forth, scorching the ground before him. 'You bloody son of a bitch. I'm not the property of you or your damn emperor. The last man who tried to touch me against my will died with my knife in his head, so fair warning, do that again, and I will burn your arse in front of your soldiers,' she sneered, and the bastard had the gall to turn around, giving her a dazzling smile.

'Oh, I believe you, my lady, but if you do, Kion will fall, and the army will march further into your beloved country. Are you ready to sacrifice the innocent for a fit of petty anger?' Torvald said, turning towards the soldiers and shouting the order to break camp.

'I will kill him, fry him in a hellfire of chaos, and give the charred carcass to Mar as a snack. What the fuck is going on here, Ren? I feel like I'm dealing with two people. And why does he look at me like I hold the keys to his salvation? What is wrong with him?' She turned towards her friend, confused by the interaction. Ren shook his head slowly before looking after the departing commander.

'I don't know, but I agree. There is something strange about the commander. This whole situation feels wrong.'

'Well, remind me to never complain about Mar's attitude again. My dragon may have been an arsehole when I met him, but at least he was honest. I don't know what to think. And those threats? Like he can singlehandedly decide the fate of the war. Men and their bloody egos!'

Ina was shaking in anger, and adjusting the straps on Zjawa took several moments with her numb, trembling fingers. Worst of all, she was afraid that, despite his subordinate position, his threat against Kion had been genuine. *Could he truly kill those people because I refuse his advances?* That thought, and the ruthlessness behind it, terrified her the most. Torvald had found a threat she couldn't combat since if she killed him, the empire would still have willing soldiers to carry out the heinous act. The very idea of exchanging pleasantries with her enemies made her curse in frustration, but ever the pragmatist, Ina let the moment pass, straightening her spine and donning a lady's mask of disinterest.

The second part of their journey was much shorter, and well before evening, their short cavalcade arrived at the gates of Dancik. Torvald must have sent a messenger ahead while they were resting, or the emperor had an augural mage who'd predicted their arrival because soldiers dressed in black tabards came to welcome them as soon as the city came into view.

'Lady Thorn, the emperor welcomes you to his humble outpost. With your permission, commander, we would like to take Lady Inanuan to the palace so she can refresh herself before meeting His Imperial Majesty.' Ina noticed Torvald nodded absentmindedly, and soldiers surrounded her, leaving her to follow them; however, as soon as Ren moved forward, they turned towards him, hands on sword hilts.

The leader of the guards turned to Ren, his contempt clear. 'Only Lady Inanuan. You are free to leave, General Gerel.'

Despite promising herself to behave, Ina snapped. Chaos coated her in a swirling red veil, crumbling the cobblestones of the road, and those nearest gasped in terror when tendrils of magic reached for their bodies. 'Sa'Ren will go where I go. Lower your swords or face the consequences of your shortsighted decision. I swear to Veles I will annihilate anyone who seeks to separate us forcibly.' Her voice, infused with anger and chaos, forced them to retreat further, its otherworldly tone widening even Torvald's eyes, even as he reached forward with terrified fascination. His gasp of pain as the magic burned on contact made Ina smile, as did his confusion at seeing Ren unharmed beside her.

It was Torvald who broke the stalemate, his voice direct, despite his eyes looking distractedly at the damage to his fingers. 'I would suggest you listen to Lady Inanuan's request and allow the general to accompany her.' Finally, looking up and staring into Ina's eyes, the commander continued, this time to her. 'I can do much more for you, Inanuan...' he said before her new escort cut him mid-sentence.

'Of course, commander. My lady, please follow us.'

Ina stared at Torvald for a moment. The maelstrom of chaos subsided as she tried to comprehend what was happening. The man she'd met in Kion claimed to be the second commander, yet his orders were unquestioned. Who was the first commander? And why did Torvald seem so fascinated by her if she was supposed to belong to the emperor?

'My lady?' The insistence in the guard's voice broke through her musing, and she turned Zjawa to follow him, escorted by a new group of soldiers. The streets were deserted, which was uncommon for this bustling merchant city, but the witch didn't complain. She took the time to contemplate the local architecture and her situation, enjoying the silence until they arrived at the governor's palace.

Despite its size, the building was built similarly to the rest of the city, and while opulence was frowned upon in the northern region, Dancik itself took pride in flaunting its wealth, with the governor's palace dripping with gold and satin being the primary example. Ina was led to the spacious room overlooking the garden with a massive bed and comfortable chairs, all tastefully gathered together for a guest's pleasure. As soon as she crossed the threshold, countless handmaidens rushed in, carrying water and washing accessories, followed by a stern matron.

The woman approached her, giving the witch and her outfit a measuring glare before clapping her hands. 'Bring me the green gown with the gold trim and rune belt. We need to wash you before you meet with His Imperial Majesty. He threw a banquet to celebrate your arrival, so you must be worth something, girl. You look too old to be one of his usual silly geese from the harem. Don't just stand there, birdbrain. Undress, he will punish us if we don't make you presentable.' She tugged the straps of Ina's dress, and the witch stepped away with a frown. Ren instantly stepped between them, ready to rebuff the woman, but she only huffed in annoyance.

'Don't be ridiculous, girl. It is just a bath and a dress. Or do you want the servants to suffer because you're too modest to bathe in front of them? Life is hard enough without your stubbornness.' The matron's curt and disrespectful words showed the care she held for her staff, and Ina sighed, defeated.

'Fine, but I want something modest. The last time I let someone dress me, it ended with me looking like a whore with frostbite,' she said, punching Ren's shoulder when his lips twitched, restraining laughter at her mention of the outfit from Liath's battle.

The older woman nodded, and this time Ina let the maids undress and help her into the bath. Ren refused to leave but sat on the windowsill; his attention turned towards the sunset as it turned the sky as red as blood. Ina cursed several times when the maids scrubbed and shampooed for an interminable period, then dried her so thoroughly Ina was certain a layer of skin had been removed.

By the time she was dressed, the witch was dizzy and close to biting someone, so when Ren stopped the servants and took over detangling her hair, Ina nearly sobbed in relief. With no one buzzing around her, silence settled between the witch and her guardian, neither willing to discuss the upcoming evening until, finally, Ren laid a hand on Ina's shoulder.

'My lady...' he said, and the witch covered his hand with hers.

'It will be all right. Whatever happens, we are together. Remember, we must persevere until Mar arrives. I need to be civil to the emperor, so please don't step in to defend me, whatever this arsehole tries to do. I will handle everything.' Ina was worried, not for herself, because this journey showed her she was an asset, if not for the emperor, then for Torvald. Ren was the obstacle they had to remove to get to her, and Ina was sure her enemies would take any opportunity to get rid of him.

'Ina, I am your guardian. Why am I here if not to protect you?' His voice was quiet, but she could see his eyes darken in the mirror.

'To find Mirena and bring her to me. I can't search for her while I'm locked in this gilded cage playing stupid, and I doubt she'll be brazen enough to flaunt her presence. If we're lucky, Janik may be here. Find everything you can about any weaknesses. The air mage who brought them here, Serennah, find out what you can about her. She might be our biggest threat if she was strong enough to propel the vanguard so far.' Ina turned on her chair and looked at him while smiling bitterly. 'I need you to be my eyes and ears when I draw everyone's attention to myself,' she said, and Ren hesitantly nodded.

A knock on the door reminded Ina of the upcoming ball, Ren's nimble fingers finishing the last braid, creating an intricate crown on her head as a maid answered the door, whispering to her erstwhile visitor. Once Ren stepped away, the remaining servants swarmed around her, applying make-up and jewellery to her already elaborate dress, its heavy fabric reminding her of velvet but softer, shimmering under the light. The mossy, rich green highlighted the colour of her eyes while its gold-trimmed, high wing-tip collar framed her face, giving it more of a heart shape. Her only objection was with the sheer panel below the collar that showcased her cleavage, enhancing the soft mounds of her breasts.

After the maid returned from her whispered conversation at the door, she curtsied and spoke. 'My lady, you are expected.' The glance she aimed at Ren hinted at an emotion Ina could not identify. His sword was clearly visible on his hip, earning several disapproving glares, but Ina didn't care, smiling softly when his fingertips brushed against hers, giving the witch a boost to her confidence. She took a deep breath, turned to the door and followed the maid as gracefully as she could while Ren trailed behind her at a short, respectful distance. They were led through a maze of corridors with soldiers standing guard on each crossing, and when Ina felt utterly lost, the servant bowed deeply and knocked on a set of heavy wooden doors.

'Lady Inanuan of Thorn, Royal Witch of Cornovii.' A deep voice boomed out on the other side before the doors creaked ominously and opened, revealing an opulent ballroom. The witch glanced to the side, noticing Ren's reassuring nod, and stepped forward. It felt as tense as Rewan's coronation ball. All eyes were on her, and Ina deliberately slowed, passing countless nobles and officers, focusing on the walls' gold and blue maritime decor. At the end of the seemingly endless walk sat the man responsible for this whole charade: the emperor; his gaudy, tasteless throne, lifted high above those assembled on an ugly wooden platform.

Murmurs of discontent grew the longer she dallied, which was precisely what she wanted. It was time to make a first impression that would shock the room and set the stage for the future, showing them she would not be intimidated. As she stood before her enemy, Ina frowned, noticing the man wore a polished leather mask with stylised features painted into a look of arrogance, his eyes the only visible part of his face. Next to him stood Torvald, looking at her with a proud smile, and on the other side sat a small man with a narrow face dressed in official robes.

'Well, I'm here.' She opened her arms wide, refusing to curtsy, hearing the indignation behind her grow. To her surprise, the emperor gestured to the official, who instantly bent, listening to the whispered instructions before turning to her and speaking.

'His Imperial Majesty welcomes you to his interim court. Your antics in the presence of his endless beneficence could be none other than that of the infamous crimson witch. His Majesty asks, however, that you consider the suffering of Kion's subjects before compounding your disrespect.'

Ina bit back a curse at the threat to the besieged town as the emperor gestured his mouthpiece close again. *Is he mute? Disfigured?* Her stream of thought split into two, one part analysing the current situation and the other thinking up insults for the silent sovereign.

'I will keep that in mind. Care to tell me why I was called here, uh... sire?' she said, feeling the intrusive thoughts of another mage attacking her mental defences. The official straightened up, a malicious smile blossoming on his lips.

'His Imperial Majesty simply wants you to be his guest for the time being, hoping you will take a liking to his court. However, the invitation was for you only. General Gerel will return to Osterad and inform your king that he escorted you safely. We will take care of your security from this point, my lady.'

'No,' Ina said, letting tendrils of chaos slide over her skin. 'Sa'Ren Gerel is the only one able to be near me when I use chaos, and he is not here to protect me but to protect you,' she said while her magic unfolded, wrapping around her figure. Everyone close collectively gasped, scrambling to pull away from her, but before she could continue her demonstration, a slow clapping started from within the crowd.

'Bravo, my niece. As always, you've exceeded my expectations, but your bonded man can't help you this time, can he? I took care of it.' Ina watched in disbelief how her aunt approached the platform, curtsying deeply before the emperor. 'Sa'Ren was one of two men bonded to my niece. However, the poison I made severed the bond, and he can no longer serve as her protector. I came to you to correct my niece's omission in this matter.'

Ina stood there shaking, speechless upon seeing her enemy. It took all her strength not to strip this old bitch's meat off her bones. Despite her fury, Ina noticed Mirena looked ravishing. Her face looked younger, her hair glossy and draped over her shoulder like a maiden. This only fanned her anger's flames. *Nerissa is dead, and here you are feasting, you fucking bitch!* The voice in her head screamed bloody murder, and Ina slowly averted her gaze, but her flaring nostrils and laboured breathing showed how dearly it cost.

'I see you've settled in nicely, Aunty. Maybe it's time to follow your advice from the temple and let chaos reign. You stripped me of my bond, so let me show you how easy it is to access my power. You took Nerissa from me, and I will feast on your power for this, and when I'm finished, not even the veil will claim the remnants of your soul.' Ina stepped closer. Menace saturated her voice when her magic reached for Mirena.

'Lady Inanuan!' Torvald's voice broke through the red haze. 'The emperor was unaware of this, and for endangering His Imperial Majesty, Lady Mirena will be confined to her quarters, her fate to be decided later.' He gestured for the guards to approach Mirena, and they snatched her from Ina's proximity as soon as she turned to look at the commander. Torvald was still looking at her even as the emperor whispered into his ear.

'No man other than His Majesty may step foot in the imperial harem, but as we have no formal quarters here, an exception shall be made for your guardian if General Gerel can prove his ability to protect you. He can leave now and go to Osterad unharmed and inviolate, or stay with you after the trial of combat. However, if he loses, he will die.' Torvald looked at Ren, his lips stretched in a lazy smile, making Ina's eyes widen when she felt movement behind her as the quiet warrior stepped forward, his hand resting on his sword.

'Do your worst.'

CHAPTER TWENTY THREE

I na watched in disbelief as servants ushered everybody to a balcony that surrounded the room and cleared a large space in the middle of the ballroom with such efficiency that memories of the healer's hall, her Aunt Nerissa commanding the room as her staff worked, flashed through her mind, the scene bringing a tear to the witch's eye. *How did we get manipulated so easily into the emperor's scheme? Bloody Mirena and her big mouth distracted me into missing their ploy.*

Ina tried to walk through life without holding too many grudges, but if she kept one, it was legendary. The witch never was the most rational person. Since Nerissa's death, she needed a target for her anger and guilt, and Mirena's betrayal had provided the perfect quarry. It had nearly led to her forgiving Rurik, placing the blame for his misdeeds squarely on his mother's shoulders, despite all evidence to the contrary. But this? If Ren lost his life because of that woman's schemes, Ina was determined to ensure there wouldn't be a stone left of this building standing; damn the armada to Nawia.

'Ren, return to Osterad. This is too risky; they seem too eager. Our plan... has changed. I will handle this alone,' she said, turning towards him, but Ghost looked at someone behind her.

'I will be fine, my lady. I promised Mar and myself I wouldn't leave your side, but perhaps I should be offended that you've lost faith in my skills. Maybe this is the best opportunity to prove them to you.' He took her hand at the fingertips while Ina placed the other on his sleek raven hair.

'I hope you're right, Sa'Ren. I would hate to see Inanuan sad because you lost your head. With that in mind, I will give you some advice. Kill without hesitation, or you'll face the wrath of a merciless emperor.' The oppressive presence behind her could only belong to Torvald, who placed a hand on Ina's shoulder, the gentle pressure making her look up. 'Come, my lady, respect your warrior's choice. Sa'Ren wishes to remain by your side, and His Majesty wishes you to join him during his trials.'

Ina clenched her fists, seeing Ren's eyes darken before she shrugged off an unwanted touch. Torvald's behaviour confused her, but with no choice, she allowed him to lead her to the emperor. With a signal from the commander, the servants opened the doors, and eight men in black armour marched inside.

'Eight?! You're fucking kidding me!' Ina turned towards Torvald, rising from her chair, but he grabbed her hand, forcing her to sit back down.

'Did you expect something else? Your general is famous even in the Iron Empire. He will die, or he will kill them. One way or the other, our emperor will have his entertainment,' he said without taking his eyes off the makeshift arena. 'If you disturb them now, the duel will be forfeit, and you will lose your friend and Cornovii. Let Yanwo's Ghost of Death's Footfalls compete. I want to see if he is worthy of being your guardian.'

'Compete, Torvald? Are you so desperate to see him dead that you tricked him into this farce?' Ina felt something was very wrong with this situation as she watched her friend about to fight for his life, helpless to intervene. Torvald shook his head, eyes widening when the warriors burst into life, running in every direction, their swords and axes torn from scabbards as they crossed each other's path in an interloping pattern, working together to confuse Ren as they attacked, but as swords sliced through the air, it wasn't the lone warrior who became confounded.

Blood sprayed out, making Ina gasp, but the witch couldn't see Ren within the melee of bodies, the Ghost living up to his name as a blond head crashed to the floor, her friend appearing from behind the collapsing body, sword still sheathed as he tossed aside his opponent's weapon before disappearing once more.

In her surprise, the witch turned towards Torvald, only to watch horrified as the transfixed commander licked stray blood spatter from his lips with relish, but when the influx of chaos from the man's violent death forced Ina to gasp, Torvald's gaze affixed itself to her face.

'Oh, there it is, my beautiful chaos. That rush of power, your general killing anything that keeps him from your side, feeding the inferno burning inside your soul, the beacon that calls to greatness, lighting the fire in men's hearts. You are as glorious as you were foretold, my lady.' Torvald's voice was husky with desire, pulling the witch closer as he caressed the back of her hand. The man who held her captive was a step closer to death when the chaos inside rose in response to her distress, but he was distracted by a nightmarish scream and turned back to the fighting to see another northern warrior fall to the floor, cradling his spilt guts and crying.

The crowd's response caught the witch's attention, their moans of pleasure and not horror with bodies undulating in time with the clash of steel and flesh forcing Ina to turn away towards the emperor and the sight of his body slumped in apparent disinterest in a fight he instigated.

The flood of magic from the fighting was steady despite the slowly dying warrior. Biting her lip, Ina controlled its flow, using the regalia to direct and store it, her eyes closed.

'Don't avert your eyes, my dear; he is doing this for you. Gods, this man is worshipping his queen with his sword. I've never seen such exquisite technique. It's almost a shame to watch him die.' Torvald's excited whisper made her gag. Suddenly, she felt a sharp pain through their bond and watched Ren stagger, blood blossoming on his shirt. Three attackers remained, circling her friend like wolves with a wounded stag, and as their movements slowed, Ina felt oppressive magic pressing on her shoulders. Someone was trying to manipulate the result, and the witch lost the last of her tempers. It was an ambush aimed at eliminating Ren, but they'd underestimated her. Nothing was worth his death, and the consequences? She would deal with them later.

Ina studied the faces of the rabid crowd. One person stood in the shade, his lips moving, hands drawing obscure sigils. Without a second thought, she jerked from Torvald's grasp, her viper whip lashing towards the man, dragging him down.

'Do you have no honour?!' she shouted towards the emperor. The body of an unknown mage crashed to the ballroom floor before him, his bones shattered by the force of her anger, stilling the fight, but the only thing Ina could see were the crimson drops falling from Ren's hand.

'You think to trick the archmage of chaos? Let me show you the consequences that befall those wishing for Sa'Ren's death!' she roared, and the air in the room grew heavy, her power latching onto the life force of every living thing before Ina smirked with disdain. 'You want to bring magic into this? Fine. Fill this gem and tell me if any of you bastards want to stand against me.'

The peridot on her chest burst into life as she siphoned their life force. Her gaze slid over the faces of her victims while they suffered in silence, broken only by occasional muffled cries of pain and choked pleas, but no one dared to move against the raging witch. She had barely tapped into her magic, letting their lives fuel her, the stench of fear fouling the air. Only two people looked her in the eye; Torvald, clutching his chest while looking at her with a fascinated, calculating expression and Ren, who walked towards her, holding his injured flank.

'Ina, no. This is my battle,' he said, placing a hand on her cheek. 'For Mar, he needs more time,' he added in a barely audible whisper only she could hear. When she dismissed her magic, Torvald straightened up, gesturing towards the body on the floor.

'Take the mage to the cells for interrogation so that we may continue the trials, and you, my lady, will refrain from using your magic. If not for this fool's provocation, you would be charged with attacking the emperor. So please humour me, as my patience is at its limit.' Torvald's voice snapped her around, the commander positioning himself between Ren and Ina with a deep frown.

'What about my patience?' she said, letting raw chaos lick his skin, amused as he flinched but didn't pull away, even as her magic left scaling marks on his forearm. Torvald looked up from their confrontation with a wry smile as the emperor finally deigned to speak.

'Your patience is bound to the innocent lives in Kion and the future of Cornovii. It was a marvellous display, but my army awaits their sovereign's command, and the mind mage listening for that command will commence the attack if we lose contact. This emperor knows what you can do, crimson witch, but your ever-helpful aunt told him how you care for your people.'

The laugh that issued from the leather mask was chilling in its inhumanity. 'Did you think we hadn't anticipated your outburst? We know what you are capable of, Inanuan of Thorn, and we are ready. Step out of line, and Kion will cease to exist. You may obliterate this court, but even your magic is not that fast. One thought and our army will raze the city to the ground and fall upon Cornovii in an orgy of death and violence the like this world has never seen. The commander vouched for you, Lady Inanuan, but his admiration for your power may have clouded his judgment. You have a choice, my lady. You can be treated as a guest or as a captive. What you decide will determine the outcome. If you've finished shaming your guardian, perhaps we can finish the trial.'

Ina was shaking. *Mind mages. It's always fucking mind mages and Mirena. Gods, I hate her so much!*

Her rage blazed through her control over magic, but seeing Ren's pleading eyes and Mar's golden thread vibrating with concern helped rein in her anger. She nodded slightly, letting Torvald escort her back to the chair. He seemed to be very content stroking the small of her back, but Ina barely registered the commander's calming words whispered into her ear. It didn't matter. Nothing mattered except Ren and her vengeance.

The rest of the fight was a blur. Without the mage spells slowing him down, Ren cut through the remaining fighters like a scythe through wheat, forgoing his usual lithe grace to end them brutally, and when the last body hit the floor, Ina rushed towards him, embracing his uninjured side before turning towards her enemies.

'Are we done now? Where is the infirmary?' she asked, without even trying to conceal her hostility.

'Yes, we are done. Your general may stay with you. The servants will help him to the infirmary, and the commander will brief you on your new life here. Remember, Inanuan, you came here to be a hostage to gain our forbearance. Any further outbursts and your beloved countrymen will feel my wrath.' With that, the emperor fell silent, his body collapsing into itself with the last word, reminding Ina of Rurik's revenants after they completed their tasks, but the image soon disappeared as the witch felt Ren lean more heavily against her.

'Ren? Can you walk?' Ina asked, holding him upright.

'My lady, I have had worse. Let me go patch up my wound, and I'll be with you in no time,' he said, gently wiping the tears that flowed from her eyes, the blood coating his fingers mixing on her cheeks, leaving rusty marks on her face, and Ren sighed deeply. 'Don't cry, my lady. It is as it is, and I will be with you soon.'

Ina nodded but didn't let go, only turning her eyes towards Torvald, who stood there silently observing their interaction.

'I'm taking Ren to my room. Send the healer there and ensure they know failure will ensure their spirit will never cross the gates of Nawia. I may be your hostage, but this man holds a piece of my soul. You asked me by the river what you can do to make me smile. Now you know. Get me the best healer.' She turned, supporting Ren, but Torvald blocked her path.

'We need to talk.'

'Later,' she said. They stared at each other in a silent battle of wills until the commander smirked.

'As you wish, my lady. I will grant your request, but I hope to see your promised smile once your friend is safe.' His last words were barely a whisper, but Ina wasn't listening, already halfway across the ballroom. Her thoughts were entirely focused on Ren and the pain she could sense through their bond.

CHAPTER TWENTY FOUR

Torvald was true to his word. Soon after they arrived at her quarters, the healer appeared. A slim girl with nimble fingers sutured the wound, muttering healing spells and leaving a generous amount of a herbal paste when she left. Ren let Ina fuss around him with a gentle smile, but when she propped his pillow for the hundredth time, he grabbed her hand, pressing it to his bare chest.

'My lady, it's still beating. I'm feeling better, and the pain is almost gone. You should go outside and enjoy the sunny weather. From what I saw, the gardens here are beautiful, so why don't you take a stroll?'

'I can't leave you. What if you need something? I just can't...' The witch shook her head because even his steady heartbeat could not erase the guilt she felt for dragging him into this situation.

'Ina, please, you're driving me insane with this constant pacing.' The sheer desperation in Ren's voice made her raise her head.

'That bad?'

'Yes. You're worse than Mar when he's worried, so please, for my sake, my lady, enjoy the garden.'

As if by magic, they heard knocking at the door, and without waiting for permission, Torvald walked in, pausing at the sight of Ina's hand on Ren's chest. 'I... I hope my healer fulfilled your expectations. I came to talk to you... alone.'

'Fine. I wanted someone to show me the way to the gardens. It might as well be you,' Ina said, standing up and smoothing her skirt one last time, looking at Ren, but her friend appeared calm and didn't object when Torvald reached for Ina's hand.

She flinched, moving away from the commander's touch, gesturing for him to lead the way. The witch could not pinpoint the feeling, but how he behaved around her was peculiar, almost desperate. Ina couldn't help but find comparisons to Tar'eth and Rurik, shuddering at the thought, then glancing up, hoping Torvald hadn't noticed. It also meant any plans for playing along with his clumsy seduction were useless; she couldn't go through that again.

'It's getting late, and the garden is full of stones and twisted roots. Why don't you take my hand, my lady? We wouldn't want to see you injured from an accident.' Torvald's voice was gentle and concerned, contrasting with the blood-crazed man who'd savoured Ren's fight.

'It will be fine. What do you want to talk about, commander?' she asked when they stopped by a decorative boulder. Roses wrapped around it, blossoming sweetly, their scent infusing the evening with tranquillity. Ina looked at them momentarily, stroking the delicate petals that reminded her of Velka when a hand slipped past, plucking the blossoming flower and putting it in her hair.

'No, please don't. Keep those gestures for a woman who will appreciate them. If you didn't notice, there is already a man I call my own. Tell me what you want. There is no need to court me.' She saw his face darken when she removed the flower, letting it fall to the floor.

'I will court you if I choose, Inanuan. Tomorrow, you will attend a breakfast meeting with Serennah. I hope you two will get along. My sister could use the company of an equal. As for the rest, you are here to answer every call and never contradict our master. Never, Ina. His voice is law, and even you must obey. I called half of my troops from Kion as a gesture of goodwill, but there are still enough to burn the city down if the emperor wishes, so do not enrage him.'

Ina shook her head and moved away. 'Goodwill? Why are you acting like you're doing me a favour? We are not friends, Torvald, not even temporary allies, and I don't believe your sister is forced to be here, so you can drop the act. What do you really want from me? There is something you're not telling me, but if it's reasonable, I can help you if you give me Mirena,' she said, hoping to strike a bargain, but he smiled, reaching out for her, and with no other choice, Ina pushed through the rose bush to get away, hissing when a thorn cut into her palm.

Instantly, Torvald was there, pressing his lips to Ina's torn flesh. His move surprised her, and it took precious moments to struggle out of his grasp. Something ferocious flashed in his features, and only the crimson mist appearing prevented him from stepping closer.

'I want you, Ina. You were promised to me, but that idiot Roda sent you into exile. When you disappeared, I thought the seer was wrong, but I had to try, and thanks to Mirena, you are finally here, so I cannot give her to you. Not yet, anyway.'

Ina stilled, listening, and Torvald assumed it was an invitation to move closer. 'Oh, you didn't know about it, but Mirena knew. She told my father when your power emerged. After years of neglect, the North belonged more to the Iron Empire than Cornovii, and it was common knowledge what we sought, but my father wanted to wait. Inanuan, you belong to me. I was the first to lay eyes on you, to know your potential. Not your dragon, not the general, me. I admit I made a mistake. I should have snatched you away before Roda forced you to call the sacred boar, but I was called home and....' Torvald licked his lips, stroking her cheek.

'I shouldn't have waited. I should have returned once my father's killers were dead, but the news of your exile and disappearance came too late, and I was fighting for my life.' The commander turned abruptly, pacing as he ranted, but Ina couldn't look away, couldn't speak. 'It was years till I heard the stories of your return, only to find you'd bonded with not one but two men, the general and that... beast. Ahh, but Mirena, she put an end to that farce, and now, my beautiful chaos, you will finally belong to me.'

With his long impassioned speech ending, Torvald stalked forward, pushing closer despite her magic burning his flesh, pupils dilating at the intensity of his emotions.

'When you came to the camp, you were so fierce and bold; you were magnificent, exceeding my every expectation. Smile for me, Inanuan. Smile as you promised. After all, I let your general live,' he said, and Ina felt her heart almost stop in her chest.

'Who the fuck are you, Torvald, really?' she asked, horrified, looking at the mountain of a man towering over her.

'I am the man you belong to now, my crimson witch. I am the man who waited ten years to be united with his destined mate. Your king ceded his rights when he sent you here, and now you are mine. Love me, Inanuan, and I will be yours to command,' he said with a satisfied smile ghosting on his lips.

'So you are what? The emperor? His puppet master? The power behind the throne? Who is the fool in the mummer's mask?' Her voice was calm, but the witch was trembling inside. She didn't need a truthseeker to recognise the truth in his words. Mirena had sold her for revenge, one broken child betraying another, starting this path of destruction. Torvald didn't appear insane, simply convinced he was right, demanding her love as if anything else were impossible to imagine. *He keeps saying we were destined. I need more information.* Her thoughts were a chaotic mess as her questions were answered.

'Ah yes, the emperor. You're quite perceptive to spot that. Yes, he is my puppet. I exaggerated a little when I said my father's killers all died. That pathetic soul was a mind mage who bore enough resemblance to my youthful self that once I broke him, he replaced me as I faded into the shadows, connected to my mind, forced to listen to my thoughts and speak as I will. The irony of him sitting on the throne he coveted, unable to do anything, appealed to my sense of justice.'

No longer afraid as her thoughts raced, Ina didn't realise her magic had dissipated, and Torvald used the distraction to reach out, stroking his fingers through her hair, leaning in and inhaling its scent. 'You smell like apples, delicious apples. I know this is all new to you, so I will give you time. I am a patient and generous man who wants to see you happy. Keep the general for the time being. In exchange, you will tell no one my little secret and treat me the same as before, just without your little tantrums.'

'Why?' She knew she shouldn't ask or show any signs that his words bothered her, but Ina could not stop herself. 'Why are you trying to be nice? You have the Royal Witch of Cornovii as a hostage. Wasn't this your goal?'

'Oh, Inanuan, haven't you heard a word I said? I wanted you, I have you in my court, but I want you to look at me the way you look at your guardian, and one day you will.' He laid a hand on her cheek, and Ina did her best not to flinch under his touch or blast him with chaos as he muttered into her ear. 'You were mine before you were born. That's your fate, Ina. Accept it, because I gladly embrace it.' Unable to bear it a moment longer, she hit him in the chest, pushing him away.

'Even if you weren't my enemy, I could never love you. There is only one man for me, so if I'm the only reason you're here, let me go because I will never belong to you,' she said, but the man in front of her only smirked.

'Oh, I know about your dragon. You don't need him. I can bond with you, but I will let you decide. I can let him live or kill him for you, my beautiful Ina. Mirena assured me you will need a powerful man now since the bond is gone, but I don't want to make you sad. Still, I must ensure nothing will hold you back when you finally come to me, so you have until the armada arrives for your decision.'

'You're going to resume your attack, then?' Ina knew the answer, but she needed to hear it from him. Still, Torvald surprised her.

'It all depends on you, Inanuan. I have been financing Mirena's revenge for long enough, letting her son weaken this continent and enticing quarrels between kingdoms. I could have Cornovii's riches, trade routes and mages for the glory of the Empire. I could have it all, but I think I could let it go for you, for your love, so think about what you value the most and how much you'd give to save your precious countrymen. Start with the smile, Inanuan, and let me kiss your hand goodnight.' When she did not react, he tapped his temple. 'Or should I change my mind?'

Ina's smile was instant, if a little false, and the witch raised her hand, hiding the rage inside. She saw the calculation in his expression, the smug triumph almost eclipsing the tenderness that framed his eyes. Instead of kissing her hand, Torvald cupped her face, studying her face as if looking for confirmation. *Gods, give me strength to not burn him to a cinder before everything is ready*, she thought, enduring his touch.

'I will teach you to love me, Inanuan. Go and rest. You must be tired after such a difficult day. Don't forget about breakfast with my sister.'

'How could I forget? After all, she's the mage who brought you here,' she said.

'Yes, she did. She's the head of the mages in the harem. You will like each other, I'm sure. She can't wait to meet you,' he said and bent gently, kissing Ina's forehead before leaving her in the garden's heart.

Ina was gasping, unable to control her breathing. She'd held on till she was sure the emperor had disappeared, then pummelled the rock with all her fury, tearing her knuckles open on the hard stone and thorny roses.

'What the fuck is wrong with these men? Why me? Have they all lost their senses? What in the living fuck should I do now?'

Ina had come here with a simple plan, but each step she took, decision she made, seemed to be anticipated and countered without effort, and it would all go away if she fell in love with this warmonger? Did she have the right to refuse, knowing her sacrifice might spare the lives of Mar's soldiers and civilians suffering in this conflict or trust he would adhere to a single promise?

'Why me? Why is it always an impossible choice? Mar, where are you when I need you so much?' She sniffled, close to crying. Suddenly, she felt someone's hand on her shoulder, and Ina turned rapidly, hoping her enemy hadn't stolen up on her. Lada stood there with a sad smile, and Ina felt her anger transfer to the goddess of love.

'Did you have something to do with this? I'm not even beautiful. Whatever charm you put on me, take it back. First Tar'eth, now Torvald, it is beyond ridiculous.' The desperation in the witch's voice became despair as Lada shook her head.

'It is not my doing, dear child. Your magic attracts those who crave power; it is chaos, the bright energy of life that fills your soul, that draws them in, but your heart is what makes you irresistible. As for sacrifices, you are the harbinger of chaos. Your choices force this world to change. '

'Great! And what should I do now?' Ina sighed, rubbing the bridge of her nose as Lada's comforting presence faded with the evening breeze.

'Follow your heart, autumn child. Always follow your heart.' She heard the quiet words before the goddess disappeared completely.

The baffled witch turned to leave the garden. *If I choose Torvald's peace, Mar will never accept it; in the end, he will die trying to rescue me. If I follow my original plan, soldiers will die to fuel my spell, but would giving up my love truly guarantee peace, or will Torvald resume his conquest once he's finished playing with his new toy?* Ina felt overwhelmed by the weight of her decision. Her thoughts drifted towards the king. Rewan sold his happiness for the future of his country, but she was just a witch; a usurper wearing an empress's regalia too weak to give up the man she loved.

CHAPTER TWENTY FIVE

I t was too early to deal with a gaggle of jealous, petty women, and Ina wanted to express just how unhappy she was with that fact. Torvald had failed to inform her that the breakfast with his sister was, in fact, just a chance for Serennah to sit back and judge her as her sycophants spent the time insulting and belittling her. The witch knew it would take all her strength and forbearance to hold her temper, but she underestimated her tiredness, and her temper flared with each word the seething women threw in her face.

Last night's sleeplessness wasn't helping. She'd returned to her room and sobbed on Ren's lap. Her friend patiently stroked her hair while Ina lay there, detailing her encounter. Ren had listened to her tearful explanation of the impossible choice Torvald had placed before her, and his face showed nothing but concern. Blood seeped through the warrior's bandages as he pulled the witch up, cuddling her in his arms, trying to console her, but all Ina could hear were his words echoing in her ears.

My lady, there is nothing to think about, no choice to make. You belong to Mar, to Cornovii. Even if you sell yourself for peace, who can guarantee it will last, or even work? Mar will never let you go; he would rather die fighting than let another man lay claim to you and... if you choose peace with the emperor, I won't be able to follow you. I can't leave Ayni. I love her, Ina. I will always be your friend, but I can't leave her or force her to go where she will be caged to other man's will. Don't leave, my lady, my beautiful soul. I'm so sorry I can't make it better for you. His words continued until she fell asleep in his arms.

The witch chuckled slightly, provoking surprised stares, wondering if she should tease Mar about Ren. It didn't matter that she was fully dressed and exhausted by her outburst or that he was injured and unable to do much, even if they were willing. She'd spent the night in Ren's embrace, and it felt like a perfect goodbye for the love that had never taken root in their hearts.

A delicate cough broke through Ina's reverie, and the witch looked around. Serennah was a female version of Torvald with the same platinum blond hair, tall posture and overbearing manner, just without the muscles. The intrusive thought made Ina chuckle again, the contemptuous look she received failing to dispel the ridiculous image. It had been hours now, being interrogated under the guise of polite conversation, feeling at least two mages prodding her consciousness, their failure to breach her defences contributing to the smirk creeping onto her lips, all overseen by this arrogant, disdainful—and so far silent—woman.

'Are we boring you, Lady Inanuan?' Serennah's composure finally cracked, her voice radiating menace, and Ina smirked in triumph.

'Yes. I also find your attempt to invade my mind equally pathetic and insulting. Better that you tried and failed, I suppose. I'm sure my dear aunty told you about my grandfather. If that man was unable to break my mind, you couldn't even dream of managing,' she said, provoking the flock of women into muttering unhappily. 'Oh, did I offend you, my ladies? Or maybe Mirena forgot to mention such a minor detail. Let's bring her here so she can tell you herself.'

'Mirena will remain safe until you accept my brother's affection. Then you can do whatever you wish with her, Inanuan.'

Serennah dropping her manners caused Ina's eyebrow to rise. 'And if I don't accept his affection?' The witch's mood soured even more at the obvious pleasure in Serennah's eyes.

'That you even think to deny him amuses me. He will claim you one way or the other. So ask yourself, how will you go, willing or unwilling?'

Ina burst out laughing. The cockiness of the elemental mage was astonishing, and the witch decided she'd had enough. The chaos shimmered around her as she stood up.

'You know what happens to those who dare to touch me? They burn. Every person who has tried forcing me against my will is dust on the wind of hubris. I can't believe I considered freeing you from the emperor's clutches. Find me when you're ready to bring me my aunt.'

Ina rushed back to her room, promising to avoid Torvald and his sister as much as possible. How she'd thought she, a notoriously short-tempered witch, could hold her tongue was beyond her, and she was no closer to cornering Mirena for retribution. Wherever that woman was hiding, it was clear the witch was being kept too busy to look for her. Her initial idea of sending Ren to search had to be postponed because as much as she wanted to find her aunt, she couldn't risk his wound opening again. *I need to find another way before they take her out of Dancik*, Ina thought, looking at Ren. She needed to move around freely while he recovered, and much to her annoyance, Ina realised the only way was to let Torvald believe she was warming up to him.

Two weeks later

The day slowly bled into evening, and the pale moon rose above the horizon. It was the perfect atmosphere for reminiscence. The garden felt like a mystical forest, the hint of mist teasing the edges of her vision, the hooting of night birds, the chirping of crickets filling the air, and the tantalising perfume of night-scented stock easing her mind. Ina walked away from the gravelled path, easing through gaps in the foliage. In the darkest corner, next to a tall pine tree, was her refuge, and the witch escaped there when everything became overwhelming, and it felt that way too often lately.

Two weeks had passed since the unpleasantness with Serennah, and the day hadn't improved afterwards, either. She'd spent the day confined to her room, seething when informed by a sneering guard that the emperor was displeased with such vulgar manners, but Ina hoped it meant an escape from Torvald and his obsessive desires. Unfortunately, later that afternoon, the room filled with servants, and she was again dressed for a meeting with the puppet emperor. Ina's vague hopes of escaping her tormentor's attention had collapsed when, after the introductions, the masked puppet had announced her engagement to his most trusted commander, stating the union would create a remarkable alliance between the Iron Empire and Cornovii.

Ina had rolled her eyes so hard they threatened to pop out of the sockets, but nodded politely. Each minor act of submission gave her more freedom. Ina spent her time walking miles through the corridors of the governor's palace, trying to find Mirena. When Ren recovered sufficiently to search, she batted her eyelashes until Torvald hosted a ball in her honour. The room was filled to the brim with uncomfortable nobles. The commander courted her relentlessly, allowing Ren to search the palace, which unfortunately had still ended in failure. However, as several corridors had been severely guarded, the witch still had hopes Mirena resided in the place.

The last straw had been his order for her to attend a salon. The seemingly innocuous invitation had lulled Ina and Ren into a false sense of security, which soon disappeared when the witch's maids arrived carrying armfuls of diaphanous silks, whispering to each other about the infamous salon of the night, where no vice was taboo. It had taken Ina several minutes to convince Ren not to attack Torvald and stay in the room.

The orgy itself—salon was just too ridiculous a name—reminded the witch of her nights in Roda's court. She'd done her best to hide the disappointment that debauchery was the same the world over; a sea of sweaty, gasping bodies writhing around in desperation. Ina had smirked at the thought, using the smile to pretend she wasn't disgusted by Torvald's hand on her thigh, his expression as excited as it had been during Ren's battle.

'I see your longing, Inanuan. I can fulfil your every need. Why restrict yourself, my beautiful chaos, when I'm here craving your touch?'

Torvald must have thought that she would yield to his caress in a room filled with aphrodisiacs and passion, but she'd remembered a party that Velka had persuaded her to visit, asking her alchemist best friend to provide a little something extra. That something had turned out to be the infamous Rusalka's Tears, which Ina had gleefully added to the punch. After a truly memorable night, her only regret had been making contraceptive tinctures for the next three days when the revellers decimated the healer's entire supply.

Still, many women must have fallen for this broad masculine body, handsome face and brilliant mind because, as much as she hated the man, he was an incredible strategist. Torvald had planned Cornovii's downfall for years, weakening the indolent king, strengthening ties with the northern province, and exploiting Sophia and Mirena's anguish to advance his plans.

The day after the *salon*, something changed, worrying Ina and increasing her anxiety. Torvald disappeared, taking many of his officers, and Serennah had become unavailable, leaving the witch to her own devices for the past three days.

Strolling to her bedroom, Ina noticed the red mane of Janik discussing something passionately with a soldier guarding the corridor and, pretending indifference, she pointed her chin slightly towards a side door. Ina didn't have to wait long till she heard scraping at the wood, and with a swift jerk, she opened it, letting the mercenary in, followed by frowning Ren.

'Striga, get your boots. We need to run,' he said, and Ina frowned, seeing the edge of panic in his eyes. 'Shift your rear end, girl. The commander will be here soon, and he is royally pissed.'

'Care to tell me what happened first? This is the first time I've seen you in, what, a month? You know I can't just run.'

'Your dragon turned up at Kion and wiped out Torvald's forces, good and proper. I heard from a healer that half the besieging army was decimated before Torvald even knew. Cornovii's army is now on the march towards Dancik, and if nothing changes, they will be here tomorrow. There will be a battle, and a bloody one. The emperor has enough soldiers to hold his position here, and the port is ready for the armada's arrival. He also called in reinforcements from Elaran, and what's left of Water Horse clan is marching here as we speak.'

Ina felt the tension fall from her shoulders. This was it, the culmination of their plans, possibly the end of everything. Her dragon was coming, and the armada was on its way. Despite her involvement, Jorge's augury was coming to pass, whatever that presaged for her future. Headed to the door, the witch stopped, looking at the two men.

'Ren, go with Janik. Join Mar and update him on the situation here. Tell him... Tell him I'm ready, and my heart will always belong to him.' It was hard to suppress the sob that tried to escape, but Ren immediately saw through her artifice.

'No, Ina. I know that tone of voice. Torvald is a dangerous man obsessed with you. I refuse to leave you at his mercy.' The stubborn set to his shoulders nearly broke her resolve, but Ina shook her head, staring the quiet warrior down.

'Ren, you will go voluntarily, or I will knock you out, and Janik can carry you like a sack of turnips. I'm sorry, my friend, but if you stay here, that bastard will use you against me. I cannot watch any more of my family die, so please.' Even Janik winced at the pleading tone in her voice, but the witch ignored the mercenary, placing her hand on Ren's arm. 'You heard Janik. The Elaran army is coming, likely intending to attack Mar from the rear. Someone has to be there to defend the position, and Mar can't be in both places at once. Tell him the emperor is just a puppet, that he must target Torvald in the battle.'

'Striga, for the love of Perun, why not come with us? Your dragon could use those talents of yours. I've seen the enemy army. Even with two dragons, it will be a tough battle. You must make them kneel.' Janik stepped towards her, but Ina raised her hand, stopping him.

'I still have to find Mirena and stop the armada. That was the plan from the very beginning.' She exhaled with relief when Ren nodded in agreement, despite his anger.

'You made the right choice, my lady. I know your plan makes sense, but it feels like I'm abandoning you. If something happens...' Ren grabbed her by her shoulders, pressing Ina to his chest so hard she could feel his racing heartbeat.

'If something happens, you will live happily with Ayni and support Mar through his grief. Despite sharing his spark with me, he must stay alive after I'm gone. Please ask Ayni to help him if there is a way,' she said, stroking Ren's face, seeing his eyes widen in shock when he realised the meaning behind her words. Ina couldn't help but flash her mischievous smile. 'I plan to stay alive and kicking, but just in case, I want you to help him.'

When he nodded, Ina raised her head and kissed his cheek. 'See you soon, my friend. Guard my dragon for me,' she said, nodding to Janik, and the mercenary, clearly uncomfortable, nodded.

'I will escort him from the palace and come back to you. You will need my help if you want to get around the palace. You won't be left alone, Striga.'

Ina nodded, slipping out and returning to her room. She sat at the dressing table and looked at her reflection in the mirror. A serious face stared at her, eyes lacking the naivety of youth. Ina placed a hand on her cheek, pretending it was Mar, but her soft fingers could not replace his calloused hands. *Am I ready for this? Does it matter? I can't fail. I won't fail.* She repeated this thought to chase the fear gnawing at her courage. Ina remained like this until the door slammed against the wall, almost falling off its hinges.

'Inanuan, your time is up.'

Ina rose slowly, looking at Torvald bursting into the room, his breastplate covered with blood, a shallow cut across his cheek still open. Not much was left of the attentive suitor, determined to court her. Torvald's face twisted in a predatory grimace as he crossed the room, grasping her shoulders in desperation. He looked at her face for a long moment, searching for something before his lips fell upon hers, crushing them painfully in a long, possessive kiss. His teeth grazed her lower lip, and the metallic taste of her blood, pulsating with magic, tingled on her tongue. This seemed to sober him up, and he pushed her away, pacing like a caged animal.

'I wish I had never heard of you, of the prophecy. I wish you were different so that I could hate you. Whatever spell you put on me will be your downfall. Your time is up, Inanuan. Choose me, and we will leave these shores, or choose him, and I will drown this country in blood.' Torvald pushed her towards the bed when she didn't answer, her legs hitting the frame painfully. One more push and Ina lay flat on her back as he pressed against her, covering her neck with kisses while his hand fought with the leather straps of his breastplate. Ina didn't resist. Instead, she closed her eyes, imagining a dragon soaring through the sky. He had to lead his men to the last battle, and she had to find Mirena so Nerissa's soul could rest in peace. Her soul had a blood debt, and the witch was determined to pay it.

Mar had crossed the veil for her. Nerissa had died to protect her. Velka had risked everything to help her. Rewan had renounced his love to serve his people, the citizens of Cornovii, who believed their crimson witch could save them. Torvald's hands grasping her breast was nothing compared to their sacrifice.

'Tell me where Mirena is. Bring her to me, and you can have me,' she said, forcing her body to soften in his hands.

'No, I'm done playing games with you. Mirena is your weakness, and that makes her still useful,' he said, panting between kisses.

The faces of her friends flashed through her mind as Ina fought the need to kill him. To strip the meat off his bones and burn his spirit with crimson fire, hearing him scream in agony. *I want you to suffer. I want you to feel the pain you brought to this land—you and this bitch. I will make sure your soul never finds its way behind the veil*, her mind howled in anguish. When a loud crash told her Torvald had removed his breastplate, Ina understood he wasn't going to give her Mirena, and, crushed by the weight of a man who wished to take everything she loved from her, something inside shattered. In the silence broken only by his frantic efforts to open her bodice, Ina heard her mocking voice crow.

'How was Kion?' Torvald's hands stilled, and he reared back with a sneer.

'Kion is irrelevant. It never mattered other than keeping you on a leash. Your dragon defeated the small forces I left there, but do not delude yourself, Inanuan. It was only an inconvenience. My army eagerly awaits him in the fields near Dancik, and the entire armada will be here soon.'

'So that's why you're rushing? To taste what is his before my dragon rips it away from you. Where is the noble lord who promised me a choice? You may offer polished words, but deep down, you're nothing but a petty tyrant who can't get hard unless he violates a woman,' Ina mocked, looking at the buttons he'd ripped off her blouse.

She'd expected the hit, but the pain was shocking, leaving her ears ringing and, the witch realised, as the blood flowed freely over her face, a torn cheek.

'Inanuan,' Torvald gasped. His face paled, and for a moment, he looked at his own actions. 'Why, of all the women, did it have to be you? See what you made me do? You could have been happy with me. I could have given you the world,' he said, looking at Ina's smirk when she pointed at her dishevelled clothes.

'I'm sure you've repeated this many times in your head, each time you beat an unwilling woman. You repulse me, Torvald. I will never be yours. Cornovii will never be yours. Now it's the turn of the crimson witch to offer a choice. Take your army and leave these shores, or you won't live to see another sunset,' the witch said calmly, her anger subsiding with each word that belittled her attacker.

Torvald moved away, his eyes narrowed to slits as he looked around. 'Is that so? Where is your guardian, little witch? He will pay for your insults with his blood. How will it feel when I bring you his head, knowing it was all thanks to your hateful tongue?'

'Ren is gone, and you will never catch the Ghost of Yanwo. You failed again, and it feels wonderful; fulfilling, even. I doubted you could please a woman, but seeing your face, I stand corrected. You pleased me, emperor; you pleased me immensely.' Ina stretched sensually, trailing her hands over her thighs, looking at the rage blossoming on his face. Anger, she needed his anger. She needed him reckless, to make mistakes, and to focus on her and her alone. Even if he hit her again, anything that gave Mar an advantage was worth it.

'Did you know the day you revealed yourself, I slept with Ren?' She chuckled when he swung at her, his hand somehow stopping next to her cheek. 'I see you're learning, emperor. A few more lessons, and I will tame you. You're like a rabid dog who needs a mistress to correct him, and I will make sure to correct all your mistakes.'

Torvald was panting, the veins on his neck engorged ropes as he tried to contain his rage, but Ina smiled, easily controlling his emotions.

'I will find your Ghost and then fuck you next to his still-warm corpse. I will break you, Inanuan. I wanted you to love me, but now I know you don't need a lover. You need a master,' he said, and his fist hit the mattress above her head before he stepped away.

'Well, good luck with that. Chaos knows no master, you dumb fuck.'

The emperor tilted his head, and Ina saw something flash in his eyes before a lazy smile spread to his lips. Her heart skipped a beat when he shouted, 'Shield the room! Nobody may enter until my return!'

Suddenly, light burst from under the rich tapestries. Hidden sigils, precisely crafted on the walls and ceiling, even on the floor, sprang to life as a soft female voice chanted in a clear, mocking tone. Ina felt something change. Her body—no, the magic that was such a part of her soul—was missing. Now, completely confused, she studied the sigils, and while she couldn't understand the writing, the configuration seemed eerily familiar.

'What the...' she muttered, her head twisting back sharply when Torvald stepped forward, grabbing a handful of her hair and forcing her to look at him.

'When Mirena told me you would never abandon the dragon, I took some precautions. How do you like it, my beautiful chaos? Your velvet prison is so heavily laid with nullifying spells that even your magic can't break it. That's how we deal with rogue mages in the Empire.' He bent, kissing her roughly.

Torvald pushed Ina away and walked to the exit, pausing just before he left. 'I would ask you to wait for me if you had a choice, but... you'll have to learn patience. I need to hunt your Ghost to fulfil my promise. Then your dragon shall die by my hand.' The slamming door ending his triumphant speech.

CHAPTER TWENTY SIX

*O*sterad, a week after Ina's departure

The sword fell to the ground beside the panting soldier, but Lord Marshal Marcach only raised his eyebrow. 'Pick it up. Never release your weapon before drawing your last breath,' he said, staggering forward when a blast of solidified air hit him between the shoulder blades. The mage responsible joined the fallen soldier, using his magic as a distraction and wrapping his arm around to help him stand.

'My partner is at his limit, lord marshal. Please remember, not everyone has the stamina of a dragon.' The protective tone in the mage's voice was music to Mar's ears. Their hard work at integrating the different races was finally paying off, and watching an arrogant high-born mage rush to the defence of his partner—a rough, former labourer—made him want to roar in triumph.

'Rest, both of you. You worked well today, but make sure you're ready to march tomorrow.' Mar waved them off. He looked at the training field, the area slowly emptying as that day's session ended. 'Ren, I wish you were here. I would so use your help right now,' he muttered, thinking about his second in command. The efficiency his friend displayed in all matters of administration never ceased to amaze him and overshadowed any quartermaster he'd ever worked with.

Distracted, the dragon wiped down his sword, missing the arrival of a messenger, until the young man coughed loudly to get his attention. 'My lord, His Majesty requests your presence,' the man said when Mar raised his head.

'Now?'

'Yes, my lord, now, if you please.'

Without another word, the dragon nodded, heading to the stables. Woron stood there, his black coat gleaming like a polished mirror. Seeing his master, the majestic warhorse of Liath spun around and, with a powerful kick of his rear legs, sent the stable door crashing off its hinges. Mar just rolled his eyes when the stallion trotted towards him, happily neighing before head-butting his chest.

'You growing restless, or just missing Zjawa?' Mar smiled, patting the long, muscular neck of his horse. Woron and Zjawa had formed a strange love-hate relationship that never ceased to amuse him. They would nip each other at every opportunity, but gods pity any who tried to hurt one of them. The image of a fiery redhead flashed across his vision. Yes, he understood that feeling. With a soft sigh, he saddled his mount. Leaping up, Mar clicked his tongue, letting Woron choose the pace to the palace.

He purposefully tried not to think about Ina, busying himself with work till exhaustion took over, falling onto the bed, too tired to dream. With nothing to distract him on the ride, gnawing worry returned, overwhelming thought, and Mar placed a hand on his heart, desperately searching for their connection, exhaling slowly when he felt the golden light of his soul extending into the distance, the connection stronger than ever. *Ren is with her, and she will listen to him, not argue the toss as she does with me.* He chuckled at the thought, gathering curious glances from casual passersby. The idea of Ren guarding his love was comforting. Not that Ina couldn't look after herself, but their friend could also advise her on the more adventurous of her ideas.

'Attention! Lord Marshal Marcach approaches!' The strident announcement by the palace guard interrupted his thoughts. Mar nodded slightly, returning the salute.

With a nod to the waiting stable hand, Mar dismounted, tossing Woron's reins to the eager teen, heading into the palace and gathering his wits in preparation for meeting the king. As expected, the monarch was in his office surrounded by paperwork, so the dragon stopped, waiting for the king to notice him. With a deep sigh, Rewan pushed aside his work and gestured for Mar to sit down.

'Are we ready, lord marshal?' The formality of the title told Mar the king was worried, the dark circles around his eyes confirming that impression.

'As ready as we can be. The army will march tomorrow. With Jorge's predictions and Ina's plans, that should get us to Dancik in time for the armada's arrival.'

'Will you have enough time to break the siege at Kion?' Rewan asked.

'I would prefer not to bleed the army before Dancik. I was going to send a small force to harry them and keep them preoccupied. Why do you ask, Your Majesty?'

'Call me Rewan when we're alone.' The monarch's lips tightened at Mar's attempt to put distance between them.

'Fine, Rewan. Why do you ask?'

'Kaian's network discovered there's barely enough soldiers stationed to prevent Kion's citizens from escaping. Whatever Ina did made the empire recall its forces. It would be wise not to leave enemies behind our backs if we can prevent it.'

Mar sat there calculating how much delay a battle at Kion would cause and how he could minimise losses. 'It would be the safer option. If, as you say, it is a small force. It would be better to remove the threat. We will march tonight.' He rose from his seat, noticing the king joining him.

'Thank you, Marcach. I will be ready before sunset,' Rewan said, rubbing his neck, trying to ease the stiff muscles.

'What? No, it's too dangerous. I will handle this myself.' Mar's voice was more of a groan, and he couldn't restrain the sigh when Rewan came and placed a hand on his shoulder.

'It's not your decision, my friend. Even if everything falls apart around me, I am still the king. I will live or die with my country. Marcach, I trust your skills, but I must be there. If there is ever to be peace in Cornovii, I must be seen facing my enemies.' His words were a rueful reminder of his reputation.

Leaving the office with fresh purpose, Mar worried about Rewan's choice but could not shake the quiet admiration for the man, mature beyond his years, who dedicated his life to Cornovii. Then he recalled Rewan's words. Something Ina did had created an opportunity to free Kion. Although he didn't welcome the idea of engaging prematurely in a battle, Rewan was right. It was an opportunity not to be wasted.

Mar headed towards the stables when the sound of panting made him turn. A messenger toting a heavy bag stood behind him, trying to catch his breath.

'Lord Marcach... a letter, for you. From Oakcross,' she said, reaching out to deliver a single sheet of parchment.

Mar tilted his head but took the sheet, opening it slowly. His curiosity over the mysterious missive was soon replaced with joy mixed with another worry. He could recognise his spitfire's handwriting anywhere.

Hi love,

We are good, albeit Ren had to fend off a latawica's advances on the way. Oakcross is safe for now, but I had to knock a few heads and, well... fight

monsters again. It looks like Mirena gave my serum to the Empire, and they
are doing fuck knows what with it. Be careful and protect your perky arse.
Gods, I miss you so much. We need to try one of my dreams when I come back.
You will like it, so don't worry; I have everything in hand.

Ina

Mar couldn't help but laugh. As chaotic as her thoughts, Ina's letter reassured him, even her warning making him smile, remembering the dangers they'd overcome together. Still, this news was good; his spitfire had exposed one of the Empire's weapons, and now they could prepare for this new threat in advance. Mar carefully folded the parchment, stretching as he approached Woron. 'It's time to go to war, my friend, and the sooner we win it, the sooner we can cuddle our women,' he said, patting his black coat, and the stallion snorted in apparent agreement, eagerly bolting through the gate as soon as Mar jumped into the saddle.

The army's departure didn't go exactly as planned. Mar knew the entire military leaving in such a rushed manner would cause a stir, but he did not expect an impromptu parade, the citizens of Osterad gathering with flowers and torches, paying homage to the brave men and women riding to war. Still, he had to admit the send-off boosted the morale of the worried soldiers.

The king, with Kaian leading his guards, cut a fine figure in his dwarven armour at the head of his army, followed by the officers and archmages. Verdante light cavalry and Cornovii cuirassiers strutted along next, trying to out-peacock their rivals. The *oohs* and *ahhs* from the crowd turned to gasps as the next troop passed by, Ren's pride and joy, his ghost rangers, shapeshifters clad in leather and fur, walking with predatory grace and a hyper-awareness of their surroundings. The thunder of thousands of boots shook the ground as row after row of infantrymen marched past to the beat of kobold war drums. At the rear came wagons loaded with supplies and carrying healers, alchemists, and those who supported the army. Humans, kobolds, mages, shapeshifters, and dwarves, united in defence of a country that welcomed all.

If you only could see this, my love. Despite heading towards war, Mar's proud smile could light the night sky. Together with Ren, they had created an army that incorporated the best of Cornovii with unwavering loyalty to the king and his ideals. Mar felt justified in his pride, as even his father, the battle-worn Lord of Liath, would praise his son, seeing the disciplined rows of soldiers under his command.

> *For the king and our lady,*
> *Here firmly we stand.*
> *She shields us with her heart,*
> *And her gentle hand.*

> *Battle clad in crimson light,*
> *We ne'er shall surrender.*
> *Let her dragon guide our swords,*
> *With his roar so tender.*

> *For her tears and kiss of hope,*
> *We will gladly die.*
> *Knowing that behind the veil,*
> *We'll bask in her light.*

Mar looked at the infantry, where Cornovii's soldiers had started the marching song, quickly picked up by the rest of the troops, when his eyes widened with disbelief. *Oh, my sweet spitfire, what have you done with your one kiss?* he thought, his memories drifting to the battle of Alsia—or rather the feast before the battle—where Ina had, with typical exuberance, gifted two soldiers a kiss for luck.

They all remembered how she raged when the young man died protecting her, showing that her soldiers were more than pawns in some noble's game of war. The remaining scarred veteran turned to Mar as he passed, bowing in respect, his voice loudest as he led his own troop, each man adorned with a crimson heart in memory of that day. These men were Ina's, and now, with one song, an entire army had claimed Their Lady of the Crimson Veil.

Mar cantered to the front of the column, positioning himself close to the king and Kaian.

'Do you think I should cede my crown to the Lady of the Crimson Veil once this is finished? It seems my army has already chosen who they've given their hearts to.' Rewan words would be dangerous if not for the amusement that rang through them.

'At least they acknowledged you, Your Majesty, while I will forever be known as her dragon.' Mar's answer brought laughter, relieving the tension on the king's shoulders.

'Do you think she can handle this? An entire armada?' Rewan asked quietly. His royal persona slipped for a split second, letting Mar notice how worried he was.

'I don't know, but if anyone can, it's Ina. It isn't like there's a choice. This war will engulf the North whether we want it or not. The only question is, on whose terms? I know Ina will do everything in her power to help. My only worry is the cost she'll end up paying,' Mar said, shaking his head to displace the foreboding thoughts. 'Oh, and one more thing. She sent a letter from Oakcross. It looks like the empire has access to Mirena's serum. We will face more than people during the battle.'

'I am to blame for this. Liander, Princess Sophia's pet mage, could not adapt Lady Ina's potion successfully, so I arranged a meeting between him and my mother. She helped him adapt the formula for a sample of the original potion, but she had only a small quantity of it, and without my skills, she won't be able to make more.' Rurik's soft voice came from the side. Mar turned his head to look at the hooded rider. He still couldn't understand why Rewan wanted his treacherous half-brother along, but he knew better than to question a king's decisions.

'Are you sure?' Mar asked, and the necromancer nodded slowly.

'The serum needs chaos magic or a certain level of necromancy to produce a less potent form. Mirena has neither, and once she uses the last batch, that will be it. I will help you deal with them, lord marshal.'

'Why? Why are you suddenly so willing to go against your mother?' Mar couldn't help himself. He hadn't talked to Rurik since Ina had left him in Rewan's custody, and this sudden change from villain to the most devoted helper disturbed him.

'Because my goal was never to see the kingdom fall. All I ever wanted was for Ina to ascend to her rightful place. You made it happen, Marcach, and more; you gave her a reason to resist the call of madness. You heard the soldiers. They are willing to die for her because they know she cares for every single one of them. That is the archmage of chaos I serve. She spared my life when I begged for death, ordering me to live and serve, and so I will. I will go against the gods themselves if I must. As for my mother... she has her reasons, but she cares only for vengeance, and her hatred destroys the innocent.'

The fanatical devotion in Rurik's voice made him shudder. Mar turned towards the king. 'And... you're comfortable with this, Your Majesty?'

'Mar, my world stopped being black and white long ago. I should have killed Rurik in the name of justice, but Ina spared him for her own reasons.

It may be foolish of me to trust a chaos mage, but she's never failed me, and since he's been here, he blackmailed—or rather, negotiated—a treaty with Arknay and Warenna, ensuring we wouldn't be attacked from behind. With war looming, I have no choice but to trust her judgement again.' Rewan's words weren't bitter. He stated the facts, but Mar felt a wave of building anger and, with a shallow bow, left to walk alongside the marching troops.

If you only knew how much your trust cost her, he thought, trying to ignore his resentment at the king's words. The bond gave him insight into her fears and sorrows, turning his blood into ice each time she mentioned that one day, he might need to end her life to stop her from becoming a world breaker.

Suddenly, the soldier's song sounded grubby to his ears. The Lady of the Crimson Veil they worshipped would give anything to save their lives, including her own, but he would never be ready to give up his love, the world be damned. The marshal smirked at his thoughts. His soldiers were right about one thing. Mar was not the hero they deserved; in the bard's tales, he would always be known as her dragon.

It took them two days to arrive at Oakcross. The town looked peaceful, but the citizens had already gathered in the town square to welcome the king. Mar left the duty of entertaining his subjects to the monarch while he oversaw the camp, ensuring no detail was missed, especially regarding security.

When he finished his inspection, the marshal headed to his tent, throwing his cloak on the floor, dismissing the breastplate of his dragon armour with an errant thought before he bent over the water basin to wash. Ina's emotions were a quiet but constant presence in his core, and Mar took it as a good sign, but it didn't stop him from reaching out to brush along the golden thread. *Keep her safe, my friend*. His thoughts drifted towards

Ren. The only man he could trust with her safety, yet after the incident in the temple, Mar wasn't sure even Ren's affection could keep his troubled woman from her breaking point.

Kaian's voice cut through his troubled thoughts. 'This is where you're hiding. Rewan wanted to see you, Marcach, but I explained you might be busy with the army. Our Ina is a true troublemaker. Poor mayor almost cried on Rewan's shoes about his mistreatment.'

Mar turned, still dripping with water, and sighed. 'So what did Ina do this time? Let me guess. Saved their hide, then told them exactly what she thought about them in her usual charming manner?' he said, studying the master assassin, who nodded, placing a bottle of mead on the table.

'Exactly, but let's not forget the damage to the town square where she and Ren fought the newly transformed citizens. Drink, Mar, it may be our last chance for this pleasure.' Kaian pushed the bottle in his direction, and Mar grasped it before it tipped, spilling the liquid. Something was wrong, but the dragon could not pinpoint what set him on edge.

'What are you doing here instead of guarding Rewan?' he asked cautiously. Something dark flashed across Kaian's face before the assassin regained his composure.

'I came here to ask a favour,' he said, and when Mar remained quiet, Kaian smiled bitterly.

'I need to go to Elaran. Rurik's spies and Gruff's runners agree that what's left of the Water Horse clan is now at the disposal of the Iron Empire, and its army intends to support the invaders. I have to sort it out... once and for all, whatever it takes. I need you to look after Rewan in my absence, not only as a military commander but as a friend.' Kaian approached him, placing a hand on the dragon's shoulder. 'He needs friends now, Mar. He's worried sick about Ina, about Cornovii. With me gone, he won't have anyone he can open up to, and if I don't come back... you must help him, please?'

'I can't split the army now, and going alone makes no sense. Why not postpone your mission, and we will see to it when the time comes?' Despite his best efforts, Mar couldn't imagine how this plan would work.

'I'm not going alone. I'm taking Rurik with me. He had much to offer, and if my words won't convince them, his magic will. Please humour me and promise you will look after him.'

It sounded like insanity, but Mar saw the determination in Kaian's eyes and suddenly felt grateful for the firm stone walls of Liath. The betrayals of Castle Thorn and Elaran made him realise that after this war ended, the dukedom of Liath might be the only one still standing. Mar took a long sip from the bottle and pushed it back to Kaian.

'Fine, but don't trust Rurik. Whatever his intentions are now, what he did in the past is unforgivable,' he said, pleased by the understanding he saw in Kaian's eyes.

'I don't intend to trust him, Marcach. I plan to use him to secure our backs from betrayal. Besides, let's not forget I was the scion of the Water Horse clan, and there will be some who might listen to my words.'

The bitter smile didn't reach the assassin's eyes when he gulped the mead down and rose from the seat. 'I will see you in Dancik, my friend. Hopefully, with good news. If not, remember your promise and look after my beloved.' Kaian left the tent as quietly as he'd entered, leaving Mar alone to his thoughts. Tomorrow they would march towards Kion for the first test of Cornovii's strength, and Mar felt woefully unprepared.

If you know the enemy and know yourself, you need not fear the result of a hundred battles. Ren's words, though the humble warrior attributed them to a legendary Yanwo general. Mar couldn't stop thinking about the quote and, with sudden inspiration, dived into his despatch satchel. Ina would confront the armada, but he was entrusted with fighting the vanguard and fuelling her spells, preferably with the deaths of the enemy and not his own men. With a tired grunt, the dragon unfurled the first scroll. It would be a long night, but it was worth giving up his sleep if he could find anything to help him win.

CHAPTER TWENTY SEVEN

Despite mage assistance, the marching column moved too slowly for Mar's liking. Kaian had disappeared with Rurik to Elaran, leaving Mar both the pleasure of informing Rewan and running the army without someone to keep the aristocrats too busy to help with their unsolicited advice.

Sleep became a distant memory, and even working himself to exhaustion failed to help as Mar could feel Ina's turmoil, the moments of hope, anger, pride and fear; it was like flying through the mountains with his eyes closed. The moment Ina broke down was the dragon's undoing. Falling from Woron's saddle, he pushed aside astonished nobles, their protesting voices silenced by Mar's officers, and, fighting to remain human in front of the army, tore through heavy brush into the forest before finally giving in to primal impulse. Each tear Ina shed was transformed into fire, her sadness into fury, as tooth and claw destroyed everything the fire hadn't.

A slightly sheepish lord marshal returned several hours later, surprised to see a well-organised camp set up, its inhabitants subdued, each one saluting silently as he passed.

If the army thought Mar was driven before, now he was a man possessed. The tension that vibrated through his muscles affected his bond with Ina, suppressing his ability to sense her through it. Whenever that happened, he would use Ren's techniques to calm down until he felt her emotions again. Still, her distress drove him wild with frustration each time it happened until it became a vicious cycle. So, with an iron will, Mar restrained himself from touching their connection, trying not to drive himself to distraction with worry.

As the army moved closer to Kion, they began encountering enemy patrols with greater frequency, and Mar took great pleasure in utilising Ren's Ghost Rangers, the shapeshifters effortlessly running down the patrols to prevent them from raising the alarm. Mar had taken to joining them, the brief battles taking the edge from his increasing need to fly after Ina. Rewan couldn't hide his disapproval of the dragon's actions, but not once had the Empire's warriors surrendered, choosing to fight to the death, and Mar was more than happy to grant it, though seeing the blanched faces of even the veterans gave the dragon pause.

'My lord, we are about to come in sight of Kion. Our scouts have all returned, one or two minor injuries, but all report the same thing.' The shifter standing at Mar's side had appeared silently, not even startling Woron, and as the dragon raised an eyebrow at the manner of her arrival, she just smirked.

'How many, Zarai?' The extraordinary woman had become Ren's protégé after an incident at the slave markets, where she had demolished half the building searching for her sister. It had been fortuitous that Ren was passing as he watched her evade the entire city guard, only to fall prey to a falling wall. Once rescued from the rubble, the fierce woman had managed to bloody his friend before being subdued and, after a long conversation behind closed doors with the king, had been recruited into the army.

'One, maybe two thousand? The numbers were difficult to assess accurately as the camp was built for many more. I took a chance and had a wander inside. Apparently, their commander was the one who took

Lady Inanuan to Dancik.' Mar was surprised by this tidbit; a commander abandoning an active siege to escort a prisoner was unheard of. He smiled, wondering what Ina had done to cause that.

'What else did you learn?'

'Soldiers said since then, unit after unit has left for Dancik without explanation. Things got real quiet after that, the men whispering that he was bewitched and that our lady wasn't treated like a prisoner. They said... he liked her.' Zarai hesitated, but Mar gestured for her to continue. 'They said the emperor never refused him anything, and that she is his woman now. Is this true, my lord? Will she be safe?'

Mar smiled with a confidence he didn't feel and leaned down, patting his soldier's shoulder. 'Ina can look after herself. Besides, you doubt Sa'Ren can defend her?' he said, noticing a flash of outrage in the woman's eyes.

'No, of course not, the general... he is intense with his sword,' she said, lowering her head, and Mar burst out laughing.

'Intense indeed. Gather the officers, Zarai, and tell them to join me here, then send more patrols to secure the perimeter. Let's see what the Iron Empire has to offer.'

When his scout disappeared, Mar nudged Woron into walking to the top of the hill and looked at the shallow valley below, a plan forming in his head. They would attack at night, using the superior eyesight of the shifters and the mage's pyrotechnics to create a little confusion. The dragon would join them, striking from above, preventing them from discovering the direction of the attack, and maybe if he bathed his rage in their blood, it would slake it enough that he could touch the bond. 'Ina is mine, my woman, not some arrogant bastard invader's,' Mar sneered, turning back when the sound of hooves told him his officers had arrived.

It took less than an hour to assemble the army, the eager officers directing their units into place with an efficiency that made the marshal proud, the shifters protecting the mages as they wove illusions that would create further confusion for the enemy.

Mar was impatient for nightfall. Everyone was in place, hidden by illusion or the terrain. The battle mages, fire spells constructed, were primed and ready to cause mayhem. The cuirassiers were foaming at the bit to charge through the camp, preventing the fires from being doused. The marshal had archers ready on the flanks, their orders to target any organised resistance, while the Verdante cavalry would charge forward and break any formations that managed to assemble.

With a satisfied nod, Mar dismounted, leaving Woron in the care of the stable hands and transformed, the night sky blossoming into vivid, colourful light, illuminating the battlefield. Mar was ready to propel himself into the air, signalling the mages to begin the attack, when Zarai's quiet voice caught his attention.

'My lord, a patrol of wolves spotted a small group of horsemen heading this way at breakneck speed. The avaricious dogs said one of them had so much gold stuck to his armour that it could pay for Osterad's finest whores for a year. I think that commander's come just in time to get his arse crisped.' Zarai couldn't keep the eagerness from her voice as she recalled their earlier conversation.

'Good, let him come, and make sure he doesn't meet any resistance getting to his men. I want to see him in action.' His voice still sounded like rumbling thunder in the small clearing, despite trying to reduce its volume. Mar shook his head when Zarai darted between the trees. His unexpected guest was a bonus; if it was their commander, this was Mar's opportunity to test his mettle.

As the dragon leapt into the sky, grinning with anticipation, the mages activated their arcana, their spells bursting into life. The sky split open over the enemy camp, flaming rocks flashing into existence before raining down in an orgy of death and destruction. Mar's deafening roar signalled the charge as he twisted and turned, easily avoiding the magical boulders, the cuirassier's thunderous hoofbeats shaking the earth as they descended on the confused enemy.

The reactions of enemy soldiers made him growl with respect. Instead of the panic he'd hoped for, the visibly frightened soldiers escaped their tents, weapons in hand and organised quickly, ignoring the burning camp and forming into small phalanxes, ripping away undamaged tents, creating open areas in which to fight, safe from the fire.

Thankfully, this manoeuvre left a number of units easy prey for the cavalry, and within minutes, several phalanxes were smashed, the men cut down before forming a protective shield wall.

As Mar circled the battlefield, assessing the operation, a hail of arrows tore into the outlying enemy units, those focused on the cavalry charge, their attention, costing dozens of lives, but as each group was broken, the survivors fought a tactical retreat, merging into the remaining phalanxes.

The archers continued to rain death upon the enemy, and the cavalry split into small squadrons, harrying the fleeing soldiers and drawing attention to themselves.

As one of the larger phalanxes seemed on the verge of breaking, a small mounted unit flowed into their midst, their shining leader roaring out his command.

'Hold!' sounded the clear voice from below, and their response was instantaneous.

The commander. With that thought, a surge of anger and possessiveness burned through Mar. *That is the bastard laying claim to my woman!*

When the dragon's roar shook the night sky, its shadow almost eclipsing the moon, the enemy turned as one, assessing this new threat. Some cowered in fear, but with vicious barked orders, they stood, steadying their shields. At the sound of explosions, the dragon turned, catching sight of a dozen hooded figures hurling something in the path of the small cavalry squadrons.

As soon as the missiles hit the ground, they exploded with blinding light, spraying the surroundings with metal shards and fire. Mar cursed, assessing this unknown weapon, its effects a serious threat to his army. It didn't look like a typical mage spell, more like one of Ina's failed alchemy experiments, and that worried him.

Determined to save his soldiers, the dragon tucked in his wings and dived, snapping his wings out at the last moment, swooping past the hooded men, claws raking through flesh like a scythe through wheat. His intervention was well-timed as the cuirassiers split away, leaving the field free for the Verdante cavalry, their horses already at full speed. With a crash that shook the battlefield, lances smashed through shields, breaking the Empire's defensive line.

The vanguard army fought with brutal efficiency, moving in unison, their axes and swords raised with tireless stamina, bringing down the horses until the kobolds appeared from the shadows, black armour an effective camouflage in the darkness, the screams of dying soldiers announcing their presence. The commander tried to regroup, pointing towards the town, his men responding immediately and retreating as their brethren tried to hold off the attackers.

Mar had realised Kion still stood, not from an effective defence, but purely due to the Empire's scheme to capture Ina, and now it seemed this commander wanted to use its walls for his own protection. With no one between them and the town, this well-organised army would easily take it, and nothing could stop them... except one fully grown, raging dragon.

Once again, Mar tucked in his wings, plummeting towards the town gates. Not bothering to slow his descent, the dragon turned just enough to use his momentum to smash into the soldiers rushing at Kion's portcullis; the impact shaking the ground as Mar roared his challenge to the enemy warriors. Everyone stuttered to a halt as fear washed through the gathered armies, but the vanguard soldiers recovered quickly, forming ranks and advancing on this terrifying new threat.

Impressed and frustrated by his enemy's discipline, the dragon readied himself for his last resort. It went against his warrior spirit, but Mar knew this had to end. Breathing in deeply, he concentrated on his neck muscles and exhaled, vaporising his saliva, the mixture igniting as it burst forth, and he used the flames to create a wall of fire before the attacking force.

'Kion is mine!' he roared, looking over the flames for any challenges to his claim, his eyes finding those of the commander, whose blood-splattered face stared back, smirking. Understanding flashed through Mar's mind. Oh, the city attack was a decoy. *Ruthless but efficient. I wouldn't sacrifice my men to save my hide, though.* As soon as this thought flashed in his mind, the dragon watched as a small knot of men formed around their leader and broke free from the fighting. Mar considered going after him, but Jorge's augury insisted they meet at the battle for Dancik. *No, I will face that ruthless bastard again and enjoy destroying everything he holds dear before watching his blood drain into the ocean.*

The Verdante cavalry, pockets of cuirassiers intermingled in their ranks, wheeled along the edge of the battle, hemming in the Empire's rearguard and cutting down anyone in reach of their lethal sabres, opening gaps for the kobolds to force wider until, inch by inch, the enemy was cut down, no single man asking for quarter, each dying where they stood. Mar gave his men a moment to savour their victory before pushing through the dying flames, raising his head to the heavens, roaring in triumph and smiling as his men held their weapons up, joining him in thunderous celebration.

'Make way for the king!' The herald's voice captured everyone's attention as Rewan rode forward, surrounded by his guard, until he stopped his horse next to Mar's immense body.

'Your strategy exceeded my expectations, Lord Marcach. Tell me what the king has to do to get his town back?' Rewan asked with evident amusement, and a snicker of laughter spread over the battlefield.

'My liege, Kion was always yours. Please forgive my slip of the tongue in the heat of battle.' Mar nodded towards the town gates, blinking when he noticed white fabric rolling down from the ramparts. 'I think the mayor ripped the bed sheets from his mistress's bed to indicate their desire to surrender.' The amusement in his voice made the king grin. 'Your Majesty, perhaps the sight of their sovereign might allay their fears of becoming dragon food?'

Rewan nodded, his lips still twitching in an attempt to restrain his mirth. 'I'm sure it will, especially after seeing a fire-breathing dragon claiming their town. That was an interesting choice, Marcach, and spectacular to watch. Now, I will do my duty as you did yours. How much time do we have until you march again?' Rewan's pragmatic question made Mar look around.

'If the grateful citizens of Kion agree to look after the wounded soldiers, I would like to march at dawn. We have enough healers and supplies to leave some behind, and the injured will be better off recovering here rather than dragged to another battlefield.'

Rewan turned his horse towards the gates, gesturing to his herald to announce his arrival before he looked back at the dragon. 'Leave it to me, lord marshal. Your soldiers will have the best care this town can provide,' he said before he rode towards the gates.

The marshal looked at the battlefield and the expectant stares of the warriors and mages, transforming back to address them. 'Gather the wounded, bring them to Kion—enemies too, if any are still alive. Let them know we are not savages. Those uninjured, gather any discarded weapons and bring them to the quartermaster.' Turning to a mage he recognised from training, his robes muddy and torn, pride shining in his eyes as he supported his injured partner, Mar gave him a nod of acknowledgement and pointed at a crater to the east. 'There were some weapons the empire were throwing at our cavalry. Find some trusted mages to gather what they can find and ask the alchemists to examine them. Once you are done, have your rest. We march for Dancik at dawn.' The last words were shouted to the heavens, and as everyone moved away to follow his orders, they cheered, ready to defeat the invaders, once and for all.

Mar felt the surge of pride for his soldiers, warriors all—human, kobold, mage; it didn't matter—they were his, and they'd fought with heart. The marshal couldn't help the pang of guilt he felt for using his flames to kill, but knew in war there was only honour in victory and pushed back his feelings, happy his tactic had saved the town. Mar dared to reach out, seeking consolation in Ina's presence. He'd not dared reaching for their bond these last nights, but she was still there, and the touch of the golden threads soothed him instantly.

'She's with Ren and unhurt. Maybe she has a reason to withhold her touch just like I had mine,' Mar muttered to himself, walking around the enemy's camp.

The place was well organised, even burned and trampled in the battle. He could see the tents were neatly placed, the mounts were corralled near the spring, and even the waste was stored far away, ensuring the troops avoided illness from poor camp conditions. Mar suspected the only reason they had been so easily defeated was the element of surprise and the fact the emperor or the golden-haired commander had left such a small garrison here.

Finally, right before dawn, the frenetic activity of the clean-up calmed down; the injured were safe in Kion, the dead buried in mass graves after their remains were turned to ash by dragonfire to honour their sacrifice and prevent disease. King Rewan had returned in the early hours, staggering slightly from whatever celebration had been held in the town. Mar, however, worked without pause, unable to stop as one thought ran through his mind. *Why did the commander return without reinforcements? Then leave so soon afterwards? Was it all some elaborate test?* That was the only explanation Mar could imagine, and the idea of a man ruthless enough to sacrifice his soldiers to gauge his reaction didn't sit well.

For the next three days of marching, Mar ordered frequent rests and slowed the pace of the troops, making the gruelling journey barely an inconvenience. Even the king was surprised, asking his marshal to report to him in his tent. After mentioning Jorge's augury and the weapons discovered during the previous battle, Mar explained he wanted the army as rested as possible. The king didn't look convinced, but Rewan didn't question his judgment. Only the veterans complained with good-natured raillery that they would be lucky to return home before winter.

Without letting it faze him, the determined marshal returned the jokes, using the opportunity to reassure the soldiers whilst focusing on planning the upcoming battle. Each day brought more encounters with enemy patrols, the shifters making quick work of the humans they confronted until the morning of the third day, when a sudden commotion drew his attention. Mar was sitting by the river bank with paper and charcoal, sketching out various troop placements, his scouts now providing the first sightings of the enemy army. There were so many unknowns in this upcoming confrontation, including the round objects found on the battlefield, which, the alchemists had informed him, were a mixture of substances locked in a fragile shell that were supposed to burn when exposed to the open air.

If the Vanguard had a large stockpile of them, it would change the battle beyond recognition.

The commotion made him avert his eyes from the paper when it came. When Ren appeared on the path, Mar's eyes widened in shock and disbelief. His friend's face was grim, his clothes torn and bloody, and without thought, the dragon was on his feet, reaching out to grasp his friend's shoulders.

'Ina? What went wrong?' he asked, desperately searching the quiet warrior's face for emotion, for anything.

'She was fine when I left her. Mar, we need to talk.'

'Fine? Why did you leave her alone in this viper's den? Ren, for fuck's sake, you were supposed to be her guardian.' Mar barely controlled himself, scowling when Ren firmly pushed him away.

'I am her guardian, but I also became a liability to her, a weakness she could not afford, not after what you did in Kion. Now calm down. We need to talk.'

When his friend's words finally penetrated the dragon's distress, Mar took a deep breath before lowering his gaze. 'Talk. What do you mean, liability? And what does it have to do with Kion?'

Ren visibly struggled, as if he didn't know where to start, the dragon pinning him in place with his gaze. 'First, you must know the remaining Water Horse clan rebels are on the way to Dancik with their private army. They will probably attack our camp as soon as the battle starts, or at least I would do that. You have to—' he started but stopped when Mar raised his hand.

'That is already being addressed, or I hope it is. Kaian and Rurik went to Elaran to deal with this issue. It appears some are still loyal to him. Get to the point, Ren. Why are you a liability?' Mar saw his friend grind his teeth in frustration, but that was all he could read from his face.

'You heard about the commander? The man who led the Iron Army Vanguard and delivered us to the emperor? He is the emperor, hiding behind the anonymity of loyal servant to a puppet he controls by mind magic. I believe you even encountered the ruthless bastard in your last battle. Tall, with golden hair and wearing enough precious metals to draw every eye to his position? He has been courting Ina for the last three weeks. Not that our girl gave him a chance, and for once, I'm glad for her sharp tongue.' Ren smirked, turning towards the river before his lips twisted in a bitter grimace. 'He made her an offer. If Ina agrees to go with him... to be with him, he will withdraw from Cornovii as soon as the armada arrives.'

'Did she agree?' Mar felt hollow. The void in his core opened, threatening to swallow his humanity when his heart hung by a thread. He prayed to the gods for mercy, but deep down, he knew. He would burn the world down to keep her while she would sacrifice them to let it thrive. 'Ren, did she... agree?' His voice was barely a whisper of fleeing hope.

'No, she didn't. I've never seen her cry so much, and I hope I never will again. I knew she loved you. That day when she had to choose between you and her very nature, she chose you, knowing she could stop the war but couldn't break something inside her. That's when I became the liability. He is obsessed with her. I heard whispers about a prophecy, and Torvald seemed convinced Ina was promised to him even before her exile. I don't know why. He tried to spoil her with gifts and entertainment. Anything the lady of the court would like, but Ina was, well, Ina.'

Ren smiled momentarily, and Mar felt the boulder that crushed his chest disappear. 'I should have killed him when he appeared in Kion.'

'You should have, but when Janik told her Torvald was returning, Ina sent me away, even threatening to compel me if I didn't. *Tell him my heart will always belong to him.* That was the message I was supposed to tell you. I wanted you to know I didn't leave her because of her threats. Torvald would use me to force Ina's hand, and while I'm not afraid of his torture, do you think Ina would idly sit by as he carved me up?'

'And Janik?' Mar knew Ren was right, but he hated the thought of Ina alone.

'He helped me escape the city and then told me he was returning to her. He's just another guard, so no one should suspect him. She's not alone, and that is what she wanted.'

'Let Ayni know you're back—she should be in the healer's camp—then meet me at Rewan's tent. We must plan this battle, and I need your expertise. Be ready to tell me all you know about the commander. After all, he's the man I'm going to kill.'

CHAPTER TWENTY EIGHT

After almost a day imprisoned in her room, Ina was pacing in frustration. Her attempt at charming the guards at her door had been an exercise in embarrassment, their flat, emotionless stares not once turning in her direction as she tried persuading them to release her, the shields thrust in her face when she tried walking out had been a particularly low point, and the tricks Ren had taught her hadn't even shaken the solid barriers in her path. When the replacement shift was just as implacable, the witch, horrifyingly, had stomped her foot like a child, slammed the door, and was now almost too embarrassed to look outside.

Ina tried to access the regalia, delving deeply for the reserve of chaos, hoping the sheer power of it could break through the nullifying field Serennah had created in the room. Nothing happened. No matter how hard she tried, for the first time, the witch didn't feel the spark of chaos in her soul, and the force of the nullifying field felt more and more oppressive. She had already tried to wipe the sigil away with no effect other than burning her fingers, and the drawing held even when her fingers bled. Now standing in the room, impotent without her magic, Ina's temper flared, and she grabbed a small statue, throwing it at the wall while the door to her prison opened, revealing the emperor's sister.

Her outburst brought little relief, and Serennah took great pleasure in using the fit of temper to gloat. Since the breakfast meeting, Ina had done her best to avoid the emperor's sister, knowing the Iron princess didn't like to be second best. Ina's appearance pushed the talented elemental mage behind the archmage of chaos, and if not for her brother's attention, the witch was sure she would be in the oubliette, especially after she blatantly threatened Torvald.

'I see chaos mages can't help being destructive, even without magic.' Serennah entered the room accompanied by a muscular guard, and through the briefly opened door, Ina saw two other fully armed soldiers stationed outside.

'Did you come here to deliver Mirena?' Ina said, feigning disinterest.

'You still won't give up on that. She is safe, and you... what a pleasure to see the all-powerful crimson witch imprisoned like a stray cat thrashing in her cage.' Serennah looked around, smiling, her gaze falling on the sigils. 'Do you like my work? It took a lot of research to get it all set up for you; shame it blocks all magic, but now you're ready for my brother's affections.'

Ina exhaled slowly. 'His affections? Oh, you mean when he has to force himself on me to get what he wants? He would not imprison me here if he wanted my affection. No, Serennah, your brother won't get anything from me except maybe a dagger in the eye. That's the best he deserves,' Ina said with a smirk, the thought of a dagger teasing an idea into being. *Could I threaten this bitch to force the guards to release me? Once I have my magic back, the rest will be child's play, but I'll need a weapon first.*

'Oh, he'll be disappointed to hear that. He truly believes you're his fated mate, the prophesied one, even more so since seeing your face. Make no mistake, if you think that gives you any power over him, the emperor's word is law, even when he wants something as ridiculous as bedding a filthy witch.' Serennah paused beside the table, pouring a generous measure of wine. 'Get used to this feeling. You will never be free to leave him, and I will hold you in confinement till the end of your days. Just give up and allow him the illusion of your love. Life will be much easier afterwards, and I won't have to listen to his petulant complaints.'

Ina rolled her eyes and moved towards her enemy, eyes scanning for anything to use as a weapon, spotting the porcelain shards next to the wall. Too far away to grab before Serennah's guard could react, she needed more time to find another weapon, and encouraging her tormentor to keep talking about her brother would provide that.

'What prophecy? And why would Torvald ever think I could love or be fated for him? He might be the emperor, and handsome, but he is my enemy. Besides, I already love my dragon,' she said, moving even closer to Serennah.

'Ah, the prophecy. The imperial obsession that's driven the men in my family to waste their lives and resources to fulfil. I kept forgetting it was the grand secret of the empire known only by the royal family, but as you will be my sister-in-law soon, I see no reason not to tell you. Three centuries ago, we had a seer born from imperial blood, a babbling idiot in truth, but every once in a while, her voice would change, and she would offer a prophecy. Her predictions came true every single time. However, as she aged, all she mumbled about was the red terror in the South, the world breaker with roots as strong as the forest. Nothing made sense until the day she died. As the breath left her body, she uttered one last prophesy, and you know what she said? *The blade of the Iron Sword will be tempered in the heart of chaos. Love borne of a woman marked by gods will decide your fate.*'

Serennah gasped theatrically before she laughed, raising her glass in a toast to the witch. 'Since then, the prophecy has been used by at least one man each generation to justify their fight for the throne till my father, who had no interest in finding his fated bride, his rule unchallenged. It was then that Swiatowid's high priest interfered, telling Father the empire would fall if the heart of chaos wasn't found and made empress. One consequence of this interference is the imperial harem, claiming all female mages for the emperor's exclusive use. Years it took him to give up his obsession, countless wars, and forced marriages bleeding our resources dry, and then along comes Mirena with tales of a child of chaos. Thankfully, the emperor was too old to care, dismissing her words as conjecture and ignoring the woman, but Torvald couldn't stop thinking about it. His obsession killed our father—or rather, our brother killed him. Torvald returned the favour, placing that puppet on the throne so he would still have the freedom to play war hero. He paid for Mirena's scheme, further draining our coffers, and came for you, so when I say he will have you, he will, and no one can stop him. No one except me.' Serennah put the glass down and reached into her dress, removing an ornamental dagger, and Ina felt her senses tingle with impending danger.

'He is a fool, Inanuan. All men are, but I will give him the heart of chaos. He can keep it in a glass jar, never knowing how you had this little accident. All he will learn is that you tried to escape, and I did my best to contain you,' she said before turning to her guard. 'Hold her.'

The witch noticed the hint of movement before they lunged to attack. *The bloody bitch wants to carve out my heart.* Ina's blood ran cold when she jerked, barely avoiding the guard's grasp. Her attackers wouldn't stand a chance if she only had her sword or the dragon's armour. Without them, Ina focused on staying upright, evading her assailants.

Falling back from the deadly weaving dagger, Ina looked for her chance, for the opening to tackle a taller woman and her guard to the ground. Suddenly, her heel clipped the stone fireplace, leaving the witch off balance, clutching for something to steady herself, her wildly waving hand grabbing a familiar shape as her training kicked in, and she twisted, moving to the side.

Pure instinct made Ina raise the object to fend off the next attack, the cold hard iron screeching against Serennah's blade, the sight of the poker bringing a disbelieving smile to the witch's lips. The situation was dire, but she couldn't resist laughing as memories of her first foray into duelling came back to haunt her. Armed with a heavy, albeit blunt, weapon, Ina felt better and parried another blow before spotting an opening and lunging, hitting the nameless guard in the temple with all her strength. With a loud crack, the man crumpled, and Ina rolled to the side before settling into the fencing stance Ren had taught her.

Something predatory flashed in Serennah's eyes at the sight of blood pooling on the floor, and she dealt blow after blow while Ina fended her off with the fire poker. Soon it was clear they were at an impasse, neither woman able to break through the defence of the other, and the witch started losing her patience. She wasn't sure what time it was, but she had to deal with Mirena before heading towards the port, as Jorge predicted the armada's arrival would be in a few hours on the dawn tide.

'Guards!' Serennah's voice startled her, and for a moment, the witch hesitated, which cost her a deep gash on the forearm when she reacted too late to avoid the tip of the dagger. It was then she realised there was a commotion outside, her fight not the only conflict. With her hand losing purchase and Serennah leaping forward to exploit her advantage, Ina tossed the poker to her other hand in a risky move Ren had forbidden her to use, and with all her force, the witch smashed it against Serennah's head.

The princess's eyes widened when the poker's hook broke through her temple, blood spraying across the room with the force of the blow. Ina gasped, pulling back, ivory fragments tearing out of the wound when she released the poker, Serennah's body following the slow fall of the iron weapon, folding like a rag doll, just as the door behind her burst open.

'You knight has arrived, Striga— Oh. You did her well.' Janik's voice trailed in awe. She turned to see the bloodied Norseman studying the scene in front with a dreamy expression before he grinned at her like a madman. 'I would pay to see how you did it, but we have no time now. Ren is out of the city, and those idiots delayed my rescue. This is our best chance to escape.' Janik seemed to be very pleased with himself. Ina approached his giant body and tiptoed, kissing his cheek.

'Thank you for the rescue, but I'm not done here. I need to find Mirena.'

She saw him frown, shaking his head and looking at her with disapproval. 'We have no time for this. Half the palace guards will be here in a moment. We need to go.'

The witch stalked into the corridor, the wave of chaos rushing through her body as she left the confines of the spell, flowing through her like the finest wine. 'Let them come,' she whispered, inhaling deeply. Her magic was back, filling her with warm reassurance. 'Let them come, Janik. I'm ready.' With a feral smirk, Ina twisted her wrist, lighting the corridor with crimson fire.

The first soldier who crossed her path fell, clutching his chest as she took his life. Two others faltered at the sight of the witch standing over the withered corpse.

'Where is Mirena?' Ina asked as the darkness of night slowly transformed into the grey light of dawn. Time was running out, but she didn't want to leave the palace before confronting the woman behind Nerissa's death. 'Where is Mirena?' she asked again, seeing the fear in the men's eyes.

'Better tell her before she loses her patience.' Janik's voice broke through the soldiers' stupor, and one of them pointed a shaking finger at the corridor to the right.

'The east wing, at the end. She is guarded.' His voice trembled as badly as his finger, and Ina felt a hint of pity when she looked at his boyish face.

'Shut up! The emperor will skin you alive,' hissed his older partner.

'Your emperor will die today, just as I promised, and so will you if you try to stop me. You have one chance to flee before I take the essence of your soul,' she said calmly, almost hoping for their defiance. Her whole life, she'd been afraid of the pull of chaos, but with the regalia, something had shifted. The darkness was still there, but now she accepted its presence as part of her soul, the powerful gems aiding her control over this unpredictable force. For the first time, she wasn't afraid, but curious about what she could do.

When they moved to the side, letting her pass, part of her sighed with disappointment while the other rejoiced she didn't have to kill again. Janik nudged her shoulder, and he grinned once they left the soldiers behind.

'For a moment, I thought you were going to do it. Take their lives, just because you could,' he said, grinning at her while toying with his massive axe.

'I was going to do it. Today... everything will end, and I refuse to hold myself back.'

His eyes widened, but after an initial stumble, he walked beside her. 'We all die one day. I'm with you, Striga, for whatever you plan.'

Ina just nodded, rushing to the east wing, laughing as court members fled for their lives at the sight of the crimson witch. Those who turned against her, Ina sent to Veles without a hint of remorse. She stopped in front of a door guarded by two massive Norsemen. *This has to be it*, she thought when they charged in her direction, meeting the blade of Janik's axe. The fight was brief, and Ina observed it for a moment before, with a single burst of her power, she ripped the carpenter's creation off its hinges, crushing the spines of the sentries.

'Good Morrow, Aunty.' She smirked when Mirena tried to shield herself from flying debris. 'See? I listened to your advice and let the chaos reign.' She held up her hands coated in a crimson fire before approaching the older woman.

Mirena recovered from the initial shock quicker than Ina had expected and stood proudly before her niece, chin held up in a last act of resistance. 'I see you found a way to reverse it. I should have driven you insane like your fool grandfather or killed you, but I always had a soft spot for you, Inanuan.'

'Oh, but you did kill me, Aunty. You bloody did it, but as you can see, it didn't stick. I crossed the veil and became the personal guest of Veles, but you underestimated my dragon's determination and your son's scheming. Mar brought me back, while Rurik's plan forced me to accept the regalia. And here I am, your judge, jury and executioner, because you won't leave this place alive,' Ina said, laughing through the tears, noticing with pleasure Mirena's face turned a few shades paler. 'I can make it quick, or I can make you suffer. It is all in your hands now. Help me understand. Was it worth it? To doom your own son just to see the kingdom fall? Did Rurik mean nothing to you?'

'You mean Roda's bastard? Each time I looked at his face, it reminded me of that sick fuck who promised to love me, only to brutalise me when I refused to lie with him, then pass me around when I was no longer a virgin. Rurik was a tool; useful, I admit, especially with those ideas of helping people by putting a righteous, overpowered mage in charge of justice. So how did you kill him?' The glee in Mirena's voice made Ina shudder in shocked revulsion.

'You are such a bitch. If you'd killed the king or any of the degenerates who forced themselves on an innocent girl, I would stand back and applaud, but the entire country? Your own son? Those people did nothing to you. I thought I could understand you, but no. Perpetuating the violence inflicted on you by manipulating Rurik into wreaking havoc all over Cornovii? You went too far and took someone I love in your revenge. I didn't kill Rurik. As you said, he was just a tool, a weapon in your hand, and as much as he caused those deaths, you were the hand who wielded the sword.' Ina saw her aunt's sight drift to the side right before her hand moved, the witch casually scattering a stack of books with her magic, revealing a hidden dagger.

'You've become predictable, Aunty. A poisoned blade? Am I right? Is it oleander again?'

'So you didn't kill Rurik but want to kill me? I was good to you when you were a child. I defended you from that prick of a grandfather and cured your swamp fever. Why does he deserve forgiveness, but I do not?'

Her aunt withdrew, trying to hide in the shadows, but with the snap of her fingers, Ina flooded the area with a crimson light. 'I didn't forgive him, Mirena. His life is his punishment because, contrary to you, he has a conscience, and it is eating him alive, robbing him of dreams, hope, and rest. He is suffering, but maybe one day I will give him the release of death when his knowledge and deeds grant him redemption.' Ina paused, taking a deep breath when tears pooled in her eyes. It was the worst moment to show her weakness, but ignoring the emotions she held deep inside made her feel like she was rubbing a festering wound.

'You will perish because Nerissa died to fix what you'd broken. Daro was almost killed, and Velka and her child were put in harm's way because of you. If you'd only harmed me, I could've forgiven it, but you raised your hand to those I love, and for this, you will die,' she said bitterly, letting the wisps of chaos trail off her body, filling the room with quivering tendrils.

'I didn't kill Nerissa! Ina, wait, we can talk. I have information about the emperor. If you think Rurik knows it all, he doesn't. I can help you defeat the Iron Empire.' Sheer blind panic crept into the older woman's voice when the first strands of crimson touched her skirt.

'You are wrong, Aunty. When you killed me, the veil took my soul. When I returned, the power that kept this world in balance demanded a soul back, and Nerissa sacrificed herself so I might live. You killed the only person who cared for an unruly child of chaos when even my mother could barely love me. I want to be just, but you must bear the blame; you must because I can't be responsible for everything. I can't! So you die because I can't live with myself if Nerissa's death remains unpunished.'

Ina cried. Her heart crumbled into pieces when, once again, she relived the moment she saw Nerissa's body. She almost missed when her aunt lunged towards the dagger in the last attempt to save her life. The blade flew past her face, and the witch snapped her fingers. A weave of chaos tendrils caught Mirena, wrapping around her wrists and ankles, immobilising her mid-air, and the witch wiped her tears.

'It's too late for bargaining, Mirena. You warped my trust, extracting the information that left me vulnerable to my enemies. I suspect the nullifying sigils that trapped my magic in Torvald's velvet cage were also your idea.' Ina pulled her magic tighter, lifting Mirena like those men and women crucified by the drows on the battlefield of Liath. The small voice inside her whispered of the wrongness of what she was about to do, but Ina was lost in her vengeance.

'I saved your life!' Mirena screamed when her joints creaked in the tightening restraints.

Ina stood motionless. There was something inevitable in finally dealing with the one who'd entangled her in the web of lies and intrigue. The witch felt a strange calmness when she looked at Mirena's face, twisted with fear and fury.

'For the fallen of the Osterad, the slaughtered citizens of Liath, for the starving in the South, for my soldiers, for Mirek who gave his life to protect mine, for Daro, for Velka and her child, for Nerissa, I Inanuan of Thorn, Judicial Mage of Cornovii, condemn you to death.' A tempest of chaos burst forth, hitting Mirena's midriff, tearing through the core of her magic, and Ina closed her eyes. The dying woman's screams filled the room as the witch ripped it from her body. She didn't rush as she took it, ensuring the woman she hated felt every second of her demise. The healer's magic slowly flowed into her body, and the screams turned into gasps and moans, Mirena hanging slack from her shackles.

Ina stood there watching how, with each drop that revitalised her body, Mirena's skin became wrinkled, her body hollowing out, stripped from the source of life. Ina walked slowly forward when her aunt whispered, barely audible, and raised her head to look into Mirena's eyes to capture the moment her soul departed behind the veil.

'You are a monster.' Mirena's lips moved soundlessly.

Ina smiled bitterly, playing with the whitening strand of her aunt's hair. 'I am the monster you created,' she said, watching Mirena's eyes turn milky white, the veil finally claiming her. The last breath passed her aunt's lips, and the emotionless witch turned from the desiccated corpse, lowering it gently to the ground before dismissing her magic and walking away, seeing Janik standing at the door, tugging at his beard. He flinched when she approached, but Ina didn't hold it against him.

'Help me get to the cliff overlooking the port,' she said, and the red-haired giant nodded, moving aside to let her pass. Ina looked at the room for the last time. Her enemy was dead, but her trial had just begun.

'Why there?' Janik asked when they walked through the corridors.

'Because I need to see the battlefield and port simultaneously. It's the only place I can do it safely. Once we're there, I need you to go back and rally citizens and anyone who still supports Cornovii to fight for their freedom. Once the battle starts, close the gates and defend them until Mar arrives,' she said, smirking while in the corner of her eye, she saw courtiers running away to avoid meeting with the Scarlet Witch. 'Oh, and set my orein free. Let her go back to Liath.'

'Ina, what are you planning?' Janik stopped dead in his tracks at her last words.

'You will see, my friend, and trust me; you will never pay for beer again if you tell them you were the one who witnessed the crimson witch taming the sea.' Ina tried to sound cheerful, but deep down, foreboding and doubts spread their dark wings. *What if my power isn't enough?* she thought before shaking her head and elbowing Janik's side.

'Look, I even have the proper attire. A crimson witch in a crimson dress. The bards will earn their wages for months warbling about it. I can hear it now. *The crimson witch in a crimson dress, turning skies red with her caress.*'

She laughed, composing more silly rhymes, but her companion was strangely sombre.

'Just don't kill yourself, Striga. The world is a better place when you're around,' he said, and with a sigh, she draped her hand over his arm as he led her through the palace.

CHAPTER TWENTY NINE

Mar pressed tired heels into Woron's sides, urging him past the marching army. Since Ren had returned from Dancik, the marshal had been restless, and only his willpower had kept him from rushing the soldiers. *Tomorrow I will hold you in my arms again*, he repeated in his head, imagining the moment. His unique woman liked him rough on the edges, and he promised to sweep her off her feet, even covered with grime and gore from the battle. She might even like it. Mar looked at the sky. The sun was setting, making it necessary to order the soldiers to march faster, especially if he wanted to set the camp before nightfall and give himself time to prepare his troops for battle.

While Ren spent most of his time at the back of the marching column, conveniently next to Ayni's wagon, Mar focused on assessing the area. Dancik was an ancient town settled on the river estuary surrounded by salt marshes. The whole terrain was a mix of mud flats, marshland, and dunes that quickly turned into a deceptively undulating grassland, a complete nightmare for a conventional battle. However, thanks to the deep natural harbour created by the granite cliff thrusting into the estuary, the indomitable stone protecting the area from storms, people had taken advantage and settled in the area.

As the economy grew, the population followed, and, as a result, they'd shaped the landscape to suit them, building up the ground to make farming possible, which, to Mar's eye, made it perfect for fighting a battle. It was lucky that the builders of Dancik had only foreseen the need to defend themselves from the sea; the defensive walls meant only to hold back wild animals and monsters, meaning it would be suicide for the emperor to fight a siege.

Mar wondered where Ina would stand to use her magic against the armada. He knew she would want to avoid civilian casualties, so Mar concentrated on the cliffs above the city, focusing on a small path that led to the beacon fire over the harbour wall, a smile teasing his lips. That is where she would stand, visible to the city, the sea, and the battle. He could already hear her groans at the bard's songs describing it. The smile fell as worry about Ina's epic task finally hit home, and he turned to his officers.

Everything was so much easier with Ren next to him. It was his friend who, after carefully studying the area, had suggested a deceptively low hill that commanded a view of the potential battlefield but would be easily protected by the uneven ground, making it ideal for infantrymen to defend. He planned to use the dunes to hide their numbers and give the mages a higher position to cast over the battlefield.

Mar sent sentinels to scout the surrounding area, knowing his shifters could slide between the enemies almost unseen. However, only Zarai returned with a report of thousands of soldiers behind entrenched earthworks and deadly traps. What was even more concerning were the ballistae, obviously from the vanguard ships, set up throughout the defences.

'How big are they?' Mar asked when the woman mentioned them.

'Big enough to spear the sea viper. I suspect they have you and lady Ayni in mind, my lord,' she said, and Mar poured himself a cup of mead. Sea vipers were rarely seen, but being the size of the dragon, they could easily sink a ship if a neglectful captain allowed them to come too close. The ship ballistae were far-ranged, slim, and deadly weapons, and it looked like his demonstration in Kion had allowed his enemy to devise the method to hurt his kind.

'Anything else?' he asked, putting his cup down and looking at the tired shifter.

'They have several carts of those alchemic balls we saw in Kion, and... they need to be destroyed, sire. Their army is three times our size. We can even up the odds if I can destroy them in their camp. Will our lady be joining us?' He could hear a slight tremor in her voice and raised his head to look at his best sentinel.

'That would be suicide, Zarai. You saw the explosions. Even with your speed and agility, you won't be able to outrun it. As for Inanuan, she has a different battle to wage. Her task is to repel the armada.' Zarai's idea would remove a significant advantage from the enemy and help a great deal, but Mar struggled to accept the consequences of this proposition.

'My lord, if it helps us win, I will do it.'

'Why Zarai?' His feline shifter seemed determined, but as much as Mar admired her conviction, he struggled to justify her sacrifice.

'Because of our lady. She helped my people. Now we can walk in the daylight, and no one hunts us, not even in Osterad. And my sister. Lady Ina and you, my lord, saved her and made her feel useful even when she lost her arm. You respect her... us. That matters,' Zarai said with a smile while Mar's mouth fell open, only now seeing the resemblance between his sentinel and Ina's housekeeper.

'That is even more reason to keep you alive. Marika would make my life a nightmare if she knew I let you do it. I appreciate your spirit, Zarai, but my answer is no.'

'Please reconsider, my lord. One life for many,' the woman argued, going quiet when Mar approached her.

'No, Zarai. If anything, Ina and Marika's example has shown me the value of people's lives. It will be carnage tomorrow, and I will spare no blood or suffering to expel the invaders from our country, but not like that. If you could do it with a chance of survival, I would take your offer in the blink of an eye, but I won't send my soldiers on a suicide mission.'

'Then I will find a way, my lord,' she said with a bow, slipping out of his tent.

Mar ran a hand through his hair, hissing when it stuck in a knot. Ina was restless, and so was he. He could feel it even if she tried to shield herself from him, and the idea that his spitfire didn't want him sensing her made his heart hammer in his chest. He bent over the map once again, studying the position of his troops, when the flap of his tent opened, and Rewan, flanked by Ren, walked in.

'Everything ready, Marcach? I would like to know your plan before our Ina makes us change it,' Rewan tried to jest, but his tense shoulders and rigid posture betrayed the forced merriment in his voice.

'As ready as we can be, and we already had to change the plans. They dragged the ship ballistae to their defences. It looks like they're set to target dragons. Ren, please make sure Ayni knows this and keeps herself on the ground,' Mar said, and when Ren nodded, he continued. 'We'll send our light cavalry first to harry the defences under the cover of the archers. With their speed and manoeuvrability, they can identify any traps and hopefully avoid most of them. I have combined the pikemen with the kobolds, creating two companies that will advance as columns splitting the field into three for cavalry charges and light infantry support. The rest depends on our enemy's response and how well both sides perform. All I can promise at this moment is that Ina will have plenty of power for her spell.'

Rewan frowned slightly. 'Where do you want me, lord marshal? How can I help you win this battle?' he asked, and Mar sighed slightly, scratching his beard. 'Do not engage, sire. I'm sorry, but you are our weakest link and an obvious target. Your skills will be needed if we win the battle. I will leave a company of veterans with you for protection. There is one other thing. I want a mind mage to listen to mine and Ren's thoughts. If things go wrong, I want you to withdraw to Osterad and save whatever is left of the country.'

'So I'm going to be a figurehead again? Fine, Marcach, but I won't abandon my soldiers.'

'You have no field experience, my lord, and if we fail, there won't be much to abandon. You have a responsibility to the rest of the country, Your Majesty. I'm just trying to prepare for every situation,' Mar said, sending the king an apologetic smile.

'Very well. Any news of Ina or Kaian?' Rewan asked, but Mar could only shake his head.

'No, and that worries me, but as we're in no position to help them, we need to trust those we love will do their part. No news could be good news, and neither our scouts nor we have encountered the Elaran army, so I assume that's thanks to Kaian's efforts.' Mar drummed a distracted beat on the table as his thoughts spiraled into doubt and worry, the king reaching over and clapping him on the shoulder in reassurance.

'We'll leave you to your plans, lord marshal,' the king said with false cheer. 'Come, Sa'Ren, we need to talk about our position, and Marcach? Take a rest. We need you on top form tomorrow.'

Mar blinked at this sudden departure and turned to Ren, who looked at him with shame laced with compassion. 'What? Why did he leave? We haven't finished.'

'Look at your hands. Rewan was right, have a rest. We need a commander on the field, not a raging dragon. I'm sorry, Mar. I'm sorry I left her. Maybe it was a mistake. She is unsettled, and I... never mind. I will be with Ayni if you need me,' he said, and following his words, Mar looked down. His hands, now scaled claws, gripped the table so tightly that the sturdy surface had splintered under the pressure. With a deep sigh, the lord marshal threw himself on a travel cot, closing his eyes and forcing himself to relax his muscles. He wasn't tired. They'd marched here in beautiful weather and at a leisurely pace, but his muscles ached from constant tension. *One way or another, this will end tomorrow*, he thought, closing his eyes, hoping the oblivion of sleep would allow him a few hours of relief.

Mar woke up covered in sweat with a racing heart and a blazing bond that seared his soul. His spitfire was using her chaos and not in a good way. He jerked up, touching his chest to find the source of the problem. *She's fighting*, flashed through his mind, and instantly, he was on his feet heading towards the tent exit when a shadow stepped in his way, stopping him.

'I know what you feel, but you can't go to her now. The army needs a leader.' Ren's quiet voice smacked him like a whip.

'Maybe you can abandon her, but I can't. Move, Ren!'

'No. We cannot do anything, so trust her. I—*we* trained her well. Ina will find the way. Mar, she needs you to lead an army, not to rescue her.' Ren put a hand on his shoulder, and Mar had to fight the urge to rip it off.

'Fuck! I know you're right. I just can't... Fuck! Signal the alert. If I can't get to her, at least I can distract our enemies.' He growled, his eyes turning into molten gold, as his clothes tore away to reveal the wave of polished grey scales covering his body, forming the dragon armour of Liath. A menacing growl reverberated in the small space when Mar snarled before he looked at Ren.

'They will die, Ren. Just like we promised at Marzanna's temple, we will walk on a mountain of corpses today,' he said. When Ren raised his eyebrow, Mar finished with a manic laugh. 'I have no mercy left. If Ina gets hurt... I can't take it anymore. She's fighting again, and I'm here, desperate and helpless, and if I can't protect her, I will burn the world with my vengeance.'

He walked out of the tent. Dawn's soft touch gave the sky a rose blush as trumpets sounded and a sergeant-at-arms shouted orders to the sleepy soldiers.

'Shift your arses, you lazy cunts. We have a war to win!'

His roar was answered with laughter and much more vigorous activity. He let his officers supervise their units and jumped on Woron, heading towards the edge of the camp. On the other side of the floodplains, between the ocean shore and a fork of the river, stood Dancik, proud of its merchant and maritime architecture. Still, Mar wasn't looking at the city, but the army gathering before it. Thousands of soldiers were moving like ants on a giant nest, making him sigh. Under a rapidly rising sun, he could see Zarai had been correct in her calculation, and the enemy's forces could easily overpower his much smaller army. Still, he had the advantage of his heavy cavalry: mages, archers, and his spitfire—whatever she managed with her immense power.

'You're more energetic this morning, marshal.' King Rewan's cheerful voice made Mar turn from his evaluation of the enemy, his return smile more feral than glad.

'More like bloodlust, my liege,' Mar said, turning to a herald. 'Signal the march. We need to position ourselves on the field before exchanging pleasantries.'

As soon as the teen trumpeted the signal, a wall of steel marched forward, splitting and reforming, taking up their posts, Mar and the king at the forefront, leading a small contingent of warriors to a position in plain sight of the empire's forces. It was clear the enemy saw him as a flurry of activity revealed two riders heading in their direction.

Mar gestured towards the king. 'Care to join me, sire? We'll make sure to mark the face of the man I'm going to kill today.' Leaving Ren with the army, he directed Woron towards the men. They stopped in the middle of the field, and when the taller man removed his helmet, Mar recognised the face. The commander, or rather, the Iron Emperor in disguise, here to greet him.

'We meet again, dragon. As you can see, this time, we prepared a proper welcome.' Torvald smiled, pointing to the wooden towers armed with powerful ballistae.

Mar tried to look disinterested. 'If you came to beg for mercy, this is a poor start. I see you have learned nothing from our skirmish at Kion,' he said, but the other man only smirked.

'Kion? That little shithole unworthy of being called a town? Why do you think I left it with a single brigade? Once my empress was by my side, all I needed was the threat to her precious countrymen to bring Inanuan to heel, so compliant with the right motivation.'

Mar knew he shouldn't react, but this remark made him shift in the saddle before he controlled his anger, but it was Rewan who spoke first.

'If she were truly to heel, as you say, she would be standing by your side, resplendent in her magic, and we would already be dust on the wind. How little you know of our Lady of the Crimson Veil. Her absence speaks volumes.'

Mar smirked, hearing Rewan's words, but better still was the grimace the commander failed to restrain.

'I preferred not to risk her talents here after Mirena helped her escape the bonds of such lesser men. You gave up your claim when you sent her to me. Now she's safe in her room, awaiting my return. When I finish here, I will ensure she knows the reality of her situation. If I remember right, this man... Rurik wanted to make her an empress. Now she will become one. I won't make your mistake. You let her choose the dragon just because you prefer your boys. Maybe I will let you live to hail your new empress. My empress, the Crimson Lady of the Iron Throne.'

Mar's hand drifted towards the sword before he stopped himself, roaring with laughter. This tirade told him Ina never shared her thoughts with this man, not even briefly let him close enough to realise she would sooner incinerate the court than become empress.

'I wouldn't count on it,' Mar said. His sudden relaxed attitude made the emperor frown, especially when Mar nonchalantly added, 'Do you want to fight, or are we standing here like fishwives in the market, bickering over a woman no one can control? Or maybe you reconsidered surrendering?'

'You are a cocky bastard. It will bring me great pleasure to remove your head and deliver it to my Ina,' the commander said, jerking the reins of his horse, forcing it to turn, fighting his control. 'Give me your worst, dragon. I have craved this fight for long enough.'

Mar sat there, a menacing smile curling his lips upwards as he caressed the bond within his soul, feeling Ina unharmed and determined, which meant she'd escaped whatever padded cage the emperor had locked her in and was already causing havoc.

'Marcach, the seawall.' A barely audible voice from the side reminded him of the king. Mar focused on the stone construction protecting the port from the raging storm, sucking in a breath when he noticed the flaming hair and red dress swirling in the wind, heading up the stairs towards the top of the cliff.

'We need to keep them busy,' he said, turning his horse and letting Woron return to the waiting army at a gallop. Mar turned, cantering along the rows. Pride and calm washed through him. The army he'd carefully prepared was ready for the challenge.

'For Cornovii, for the king and our lady! Charge!'

Trumpets answered his call, and with that sound, a young Verdante officer led his squadron to the battlefield. The powerful horses built up their speed, moving together in perfect unison, from a walk to a trot, then a canter. When a volley of arrows leapt into the sky, thrumming their song of death, the cavalry was already turning, their coordination as perfect as a murmuration of starlings as they avoided the deadly missiles. *If they survive this, I have a perfect name for them*, Mar thought, gesturing towards the mages as the archers pulled back their bows again, targeting the rapidly approaching cavalry.

Magical fog rolled down the hill, muffling sound and hiding the lancer's advance but not stopping the release of the arrows. Even changing direction, anticipating this, the cavalry couldn't avoid all the missiles, the screams of men and horses cutting through the thunderous hoofbeats, even as the spearhead crashed into the empire's first line of defence, lances thrusting forward as horses leapt over men and fortifications, warriors and horses dying as the momentum of the squadron forced a gap for the cavalry to exploit, before they wheeled away, killing and maiming as they retreated, only to break apart as explosions tore apart their unity, the men splitting up to avoid the blossoming death, and resulting craters.

The scent of freshly torn earth and grass mixed with the horrifying stench of death, but Mar whispered a silent prayer of thanks as survivors escaped the carnage returning to resupply or seek the healers, his ploy a success as his own archers were now in range of the enemy lines. Rows of archers strengthened by battle mages sent a hail of arrows across the battlefield, only to split or burst into flames, the magic attached to them activating and decimating the waiting infantry.

The smell of burning meat and death made him curse. He should have let Zarai sabotage the alchemic weapon. The fog and fumes from the explosions made it challenging to see. Still, after a quick command, his mages changed their chant, dissipating the fog slowly as Ren signalled the kobold infantry and their human pikemen into position, and Mar had to look twice as the ordinarily slow, methodical movement of the columns became a fast jog, the kobolds, supporting their human counterparts as they ran. The dragon nearly cursed as they would reach the enemy before he wanted them to, but it seemed his friend had anticipated this and was already signalling the heavy cavalry.

In response to the speed of the kobolds, the empire soldiers were reforming, archers, running to the flanks and setting up, wagons of explosives moved for soldiers to gather their deadly cargo in anticipation and men with massive shields and axes blocking the advancing infantry, but their formation began falling apart as the armoured horses of Mar's cavalry, charged into their flank, smashed through the lightly armed soldiers protecting the archers and slaughtered them.

The cacophony of battle, screams of pain and the sharp sound of clashing blades, rang louder as the kobolds advanced, their casualties lower as only one troop of archers now targeted them, the power of their legs driving them onwards into several explosions, the death toll massive as their impetus drove them on. A quick-thinking officer yelled something, and the survivors split away, now too close to the shield wall for the enemy to use explosives, the humans thrusting their pikes forward as selfless kobolds dragged away the heavy shields, dying by the dozen for their bravery.

Now was the time, as Mar felt power flood his chest. He knew Ina was drawing on the chaos of death and destruction he'd caused and lifted his arm, pressing his heels to Woron's sides to lead the last wave of warriors, the mage-augmented infantry, trained and working in concert. He inhaled slowly. *I hope that's what you need, my love; bloody mayhem.* Countless empire warriors lay dead or injured on the bloodstained earth, but a thousand more took their place, his army still valiantly fighting on, but outnumbered by the enemy, they would soon be forced to retreat, fighting on the backfoot bleeding the enemy for every step lost.

Mar looked at the clifftop. Somewhere there, his fiery spitfire fought her own battle, the overwhelming magic tugging at the strings of the bond, stabbing his chest painfully. Down here, it was all up to him. Suddenly, two explosions shattered the rear of the enemy's forces, rocking the ground and toppling fighting soldiers from both sides as an invisible force thrust them to the ground. Woron reared when the blast of air reached him. Mar could only watch the devastation, countless dead and two massive smoking craters where the enemy's explosives had been. *Zarai! You stupid, stupid girl. Thank you, my brave soul. Thank you*, he thought.

With over half the enemy's army gone, Cornovii's chances would have rapidly improved if not for the widening smudge of darkness on the horizon, the arrival of the armada spelling defeat for the remains of Mar's brave army. *If you're going to do anything about it, my love, do it now, because once they land, there will be no hope for Cornovii*, he thought for a moment before his mind drifted to Zarai, grieving for the little shifter woman who had outdone herself, paying the ultimate price to give him a chance at winning.

He couldn't do anything about the sea of ships. Even if he tried to burn one, the ballistae would shoot him down in no time. The peace that washed over him felt unreal. Mar kicked Woron, galloping to the centre of the battle, seeing Ren ploughing through the enemies like a dark reaper. The massive man with the mane of blond hair turned in his direction, hearing the dragon roar.

'Commander! Come here, boy. It's time to die!'

CHAPTER THIRTY

Ina didn't know how many in the Iron Court knew about her imprisonment, but courtiers fled as soon as they saw the power of chaos surrounding her like an otherworldly halo. Not that she paid much attention to them, anyway. Janik, grinning like a madman, led the way as if strolling along on a tour of the palace, his massive, intimidating presence not once receiving a second glance once Ina came into sight, and the witch wrinkled her nose at the stench of fear that filled the corridors.

Unfortunately, to her annoyance, two men clad in plate armour blocked the way when they reached a guard post. Ina did not have time to dally, not if she wanted to be at the clifftop on time for the augured arrival of the armada. The sun was high in the sky, much higher than she would like, signalling she must hurry to fulfil her part of the plan.

'Move,' she commanded, but the men didn't budge, eyeing Janik, who twirled his axe with a smirk.

'You are going nowhere, witch. Do you think bringing that traitor will help you? Tell your lover to lower his weapon, and we may even deliver you to the emperor unscathed,' said the taller of the two, while his companion sported a scornful smile. Ina simply sighed deeply. If stupidity could fly, those two would soar through the sky like eagles. Using her power to hurt people went against the very grain of her nature, but today, scruples be damned, she would descend to a hell of her own making.

'Your choice,' she whispered, chaos dancing around her. To take their lives was as easy as plucking flowers and not without pleasure. As soon as she called for it, two crimson wisps caressed their cheeks and, eyes widening in shock, the men crumpled to the floor, dead.

This time, Ina didn't release the chaos of their deaths into the world, its seductive power making her shiver in pleasure, clear evidence that whilst her mind was lucid, her body still enjoyed the allure of power. That worried her as their plans called for so many deaths, and she would gather all that chaos to ensure her country would survive the invasion.

'You're playing dirty today, Striga. I would have given them a clean death,' Janik said, looking down at her, but he lowered his head when she met his gaze. 'But who am I talking to? You will do as you please, as always.'

'I have no time for pandering to fools. Take me to the cliff,' she said, refusing to accept his judgement.

He nodded, still avoiding her eyes, and this hurt more than she wanted to admit. Janik had known her when she'd been nothing more than the failed offspring of the grand House of Thorn, yet now he shrank back rather than meet her eyes. *I'm the hero who lived long enough to become a villain, even to a friend.* The bitter thought crossed her mind, but Ina shrugged it off, knowing deep down she was on the path of no return. Janik led her through the streets of Dancik, carefully manoeuvring to avoid Iron Empire patrols, Ina's magic swiftly and quietly dealing with those who crossed their path. Their walk seemed endless, and Ina became increasingly unsettled, hoping she would have enough time for the ritual before Mar started the battle.

Finally, they reached the city wall. Janik led her to a squat tower that straddled the ramparts, guarding access from the sea, and after despatching its guards, Ina was finally free of the empire's influence. She stepped on the stone path leading to the cliff, turning towards the Norseman.

'Thank you, Janik. I can handle this now. Look after Marika, tell her she can keep my house. After all, she's lived there longer than I did,' she said, stretching to kiss his shaggy cheek softly. 'Don't let any minstrels spew shit about me in the *Drunken Wizard*.' Ina couldn't help the tear that escaped, turning away to hide it, leaving him with a stunned expression.

'Striga, don't you dare fucking die! Your dragon will have my head on a stick if you do!' his voice roared behind her, but Ina didn't look back. The wind whipped the dress around her legs as she marched the cliff path, only briefly glancing towards the battlefield. *I hope you will forgive me one day for dooming us both*, she thought, seeing the sea of people on the other side of the wall. Mar was somewhere there, holding up his side of the bargain, unaware that her spell would consume her mind.

He must have seen her because, for a moment, Ina felt warmth and reassurance pulsating through their bond before it disappeared, while she did her best to hide her fear behind the mirrored wall of her thoughts. The witch continued climbing, her shaking hand gripping the rails when the fear of heights took over, but the witch needed a commanding view, so she pushed forth with an unyielding expression. Her eyes were fixed on the sails of armada ships preparing to enter Dancik Bay, some already heading towards the port, thousands of them, each containing soldiers, weapons and supplies to overwhelm Cornovii. White sails covered in runes extended over flat decks. While the vanguard ships were built for speed and agility, those were made purely to transport a massive army, and even from so far away, Ina saw they were filled to the brim.

Suddenly protectiveness surged through the witch, staggering her. *I will cut off the hand that reaches for what's mine.* The anger helped her, hardening her resolve. She was the Royal Witch of Cornovii, and this was her land to protect.

The clifftop was barren, with a low crumbling wall around a blackened area and a massive structure of firewood inside. The granite was polished by time and weather, dotted here and there with moss and sparse grass, trying to survive in harsh, salty conditions.

'At least it's not a barren desert with bleached bones, yet.' She chuckled at the darkness of her joke, remembering the place from her nightmares, but her bleak merriment was cut short when a wave of chaos jolted her body. The battle had started, and as soon as she allowed it, the life of the lost drifted towards her, filling the witch with godlike power.

'Behold the monster who came to shatter the world. You all will witness it in awe and despair.' She whispered the words she remembered from the Saga of Last Empress. They seemed to fit the situation. With each wave of primaeval power filling her core, her peridot stones shone brighter, capturing and repurposing the chaos according to her will, and Ina laid her hands on the ground. Her circlet directed her magic while she shaped the world around her. The granite stones crumbled, forming a smooth surface. Soon, guided by her thought, lines appeared, recreating Velka's sigil from Marzanna's temple. The sigil, meant to bind the power of the land, now changed to tame the boundless chaos of the sea. Now she only needed an offering, a blood sacrifice, to activate it, just as Rurik had when he'd set the curse in the temple. Nobody could tame the ocean because no mage was reckless enough to dare connect their life force with death through the constant renewal of raw chaos.

'Well, let's do it and see what will happen.' She laughed, imagining Mar's expression if she'd told him that was her grand plan.

A loud explosion reverberated in the air, sending a blast of magic that filled the surrounding space with a maelstrom of chaos. Brought to her knees by the sheer amount of energy that hit her body, Ina raised her face, watching the darkening of the sky, where rapidly gathering heavy clouds reflected the crimson hue of her magic. The witch sucked her breath. The sheer amount of power was difficult to control, even with the regalia.

She closed the lines of the sigil, and for a moment, Ina let her body tremble with pleasure, the rejuvenating bliss reverberating in her bones, the horrific sounds of the battlefield teasing her senses. *So many are dying today to save countless innocents*, she thought, pulling a small dagger from her belt.

Ina barely felt any pain when she cut her forearms. Her mind drifted to those she loved when a long line opened in her flesh, letting the blood dribble, filling the lines of the spell. Her eyes were fixed on the armada. Thousands upon thousands of trained soldiers were brought here to enslave her people, and the image of Velka in chains hardened her resolve. 'No one will hurt you, Flower, for as long as I live,' she muttered, her heart pouring more blood into the carved sigils.

The witch smirked, directing her power into the magic in her blood. There was no other way. She had to tie herself to the sea and make herself a who that would forever guard those waters. The secret she'd kept hidden even from Mar, the doom she feared almost as much as losing him. *Was this how gods were born, from a reckless mage stupid enough to tie themselves to the elements?*

She'd found it mentioned inside a dusty volume in the forbidden section of the university library. A taboo amongst the mages that even Sowenna feared to break. A spell to mix blood magic with a massive amount of pure chaos that created an entity linked to their power. Forever the ruler and the slave of the force they called upon. *Is that how you came to be, Leshy? If this happens to me, Mar will live. Even if we are forever apart, he will be alive.* This thought brought her solace, as did the knowledge she could watch over the family of her heart; Velka, her child, Mar, Ren, and even Ayni.

'I can hear them now, calling me impetuous, impulsive, but Mar, Ren, you will still be proud!' She laughed, raising her arms and thrusting blood-soaked fingers to the heavens. The regalia pulsed, stabilising her power, helping mould its form as she chanted. The low melodic voice of the witch entwined with the howling of the wind and thunder of crashing waves when she called upon the sea.

Ina twisted her wrists, using her ring to direct the magic and recreate the sigils above the bloody diagram. Lowering her arms, the witch pressed the second spell into the first, binding them together with the chaos from the battle, its uncontrollable power reined in by her necklace, the unyielding energy brushing temptingly, sensuously over her mind and soul.

Sweat beaded her forehead as blood continued flowing into the sigils, its loss now causing her heart to beat faster as it tried to keep her upright. Her circlet shone like a fey lantern, but despite her efforts, the power of the sea refused to be constrained. Despair broke through her focus, and the witch snarled. She needed more time. She needed to open herself to the inhuman power and give herself to fate. Ina exhaled and destroyed the mirrored protection of her mind, stretching her consciousness over the raging waters and thrusting it deep into the heart of the ocean.

'I am yours to take, but you shall bend to my will,' she said, gasping when the power of the ocean engulfed her, binding her soul. The torment of connecting with something so wild and unique that it eluded her comprehension was immense, and, screaming her defiance and pain to the world, she grasped the immensity of the force transforming her soul and commanded its essence, moulding it to her will, binding it as she herself was bound.

'I've got you now, you bastard. You are mine to command. Yield to your mistress. I gave you my soul, freedom, and love, so yield to me. Please.' The last word was a hissed plea as Ina felt her soul tearing under the pressure.

As if in answer to her words, something inside Ina unfurled, letting the witch catch her breath. The untamed chaos of the sea lit up in her mind; its patterns, once confusing and frightening, were now comforting and familiar. The enemy ships crossed the bay entrance, heading towards the port, but their fate was sealed. She felt pure ecstasy when she raised her hand over the waves, building them up. The cliff peak was barely visible within the kaleidoscopic colours of her power growing to a crescendo. One on another, she raised the waves higher, water pilling up, crashing against the might of the granite cliffs beneath her, laughing in joy at its sheer destructive potential.

She could drown the city if she released it onto the land, but that was not what she'd planned. Ina looked with satisfaction at the floundering ships before reaching into the depths of her magic, purging it all in one powerful push to send a massive tidal wave in their direction.

The mighty wall of water smashed through the forefront of the armada as though it were kindling, scattering men, equipment and broken hulls against the rocks and each other, its force spreading out as it escaped the confines of the estuary, picking up ships as it pushed outward, their crews desperately trying to ride out this horrifying phenomenon, many still colliding and sinking unable to navigate its fierceness.

Ina screamed again, this time in satisfaction as the remaining ships were flung back towards the Iron Empire, unable to escape her vengeful power, but, as the vessels receded, so too did her memories, the vast untameable ocean taking its payment for her hubris, leaving behind pure emotion and singular purpose: destroy and create, change the world, fill it with life and magic. Scour away the old for a beautiful new existence. Each crashing wave felt like the caress of a lover calling her to surrender to the beauty of creation. Ina stepped towards the edge, reaching out her hands again when a tearing pain blossomed in her chest. Golden and silver strands held her captive, anchored to the essence of her being even as godlike power tore it to pieces to escape its cage.

'No, my child, it's not your time nor your fate.' A large figure stepped from the shadows, fireflies dancing between his antlers as he embraced her tightly. 'Come back to me, Inanuan, my herald, my autumn child. Come back to who you truly are,' he said, kissing her forehead. Green energy danced around him when he winced in pain, fighting the power raging through her soul, coaxing the forest magic he'd placed within her to grow. Ina's body went rigid as he faded, but memories flooded her mind, disrupting the connection with the sea.

The witch felt her body again, even as it collapsed beneath her, bereft of magic and weak from blood loss. Something inside her screamed at the absence of such all-consuming power, craving the touch of the ocean, and the witch stumbled closer, pushed by its unyielding demand. The view that greeted her was a landscape of nightmares.

Before her lay not a damaged estuary filled with broken hulls, men, and equipment, no. Lost within the primordial chaos of the ocean's power, Ina hadn't just raised the sea, but also the land, creating islands and fantastical reefs, a kaleidoscope of strange, fantastical shapes and colours, and, as she looked closer, vegetation that defied explanation.

'Mar is going to lose his mind this time.'

The witch smiled, trailing her hand through the air, gasping in surprise as the ocean responded, white foaming waves repeating her gesture. The connection was still there, pulling to her senses even if her mind remained hers, but searching within herself, Ina could find only remnants of her chaos magic.

She could create so much more; new lands, new life. Ina's breath stilled, her heart slowing, its pulse echoed by the weak glow of the regalia. *Will this ever end? I did it. I am the chaos archmage and now the Wraith of the*

Sea. Will it call me again? Will I slowly lose my soul to the ocean? Thoughts tumbled through the witch's mind, and she laughed, tears falling unnoticed from her eyes as the sky above bled into crimson light.

Her mind was free, but not her magic. Godlike power gathered in her chest, building slowly, inexorably, scouring away her musings, as the chaos she had lost was replaced by the killings continuing on the battlefield, taking control of her now that her defences were destroyed and dragging her focus to the armies locked in combat below.

Relief washed over her as she watched her chaos erode the cliff, sending tumbling rocks into the sea.

'This is the way to end it. It will die with me when I leave my body joining with the sea.' She sighed, even now feeling the need to transform, to reshape the world into a new, primal, ever-changing land. *Veles was right. The true power of chaos is not destruction, but everlasting creation*, she thought, exhaustion overwhelming her.

Ina had known the price of her magic from the start and the risk of connecting with the ocean. The witch hoped she would fade away, her soul merging with the sea to guard these shores, watching those she loved thriving in peace from afar. Now, if she lived, the hunger for change would make her a threat to their very existence. Ina looked at her forearms, wiping away the crusted blood until it bled again, while shuffling closer to the edge.

If only she had one chance to explain it to her dragon. *He will be so pissed, the grumpy oaf, but at least he won't have to watch it.* She smiled when her thoughts drifted to him, feeling the bond's comforting presence. *I love you so much. You helped me become a better person. You loved me when I was at my worst, and I... I'm so sorry, Mar. I wish I could see you for the last time.*

'Inanuan! Don't you fucking dare die on me again!'

Through heavy eyelids, Ina saw the blurred silhouette of a plummeting dragon.

'I don't want to, but I have to. Shut up and let me do the right thing,' she muttered while warmth spread through her chest. *At least I won't die alone.* Ina reached out to Mar, suddenly feeling weightless when the ground beneath her disappeared, and for the second time in her life, she was falling into nothingness. *What an epic end*, she thought, smirking at the dark humour before sweet oblivion took her away.

CHAPTER THIRTY ONE

(in the same time, in the midst of the battle)

Mar's world narrowed down to the one man he'd promised to kill, the man who, thanks to Ren's arrival, now had a name. Stood before him wasn't the commander; this was the Iron Emperor Torvald, the seed of Ina's torment and Mar's misfortune, the invisible enemy behind Mirena's and Rurik's manipulation, whose greed had caused so much suffering in Cornovii, pushing his spitfire from one trial to another.

Mar had never wanted to kill someone so much in his life, and rage boiled in his heart whilst he rode Woron through the fighting to get to the man he hated. Torvald fought like an ensnared wolf, fending off his enemies with a massive Zweihander. The dragon in him purred its pleasure at meeting a worthy adversary because, even hating the man, Mar couldn't help but admire his combat skills. Torvald looked at him, understanding flashing over his grimacing face, and Mar leapt from Woron's back, sword cleaving through the chest of a soldier unfortunate enough to be in the dragon's way. Only one of them would leave this battle alive, and Mar knew he would see his woman again. Whatever it took.

'Are you ready to die?' Mar asked, tracing his opponent's movements, parrying Torvald's lazy swing of his sword.

'Are you? Because I will not die today, and not by your hand, lizard,' he said when the clashing of the swords brought them together.

Mar couldn't help but laugh, lowering his blade and sliding the emperor's weapon past his shoulder, pushing forward to headbutt his opponent, forcing him to stumble back. 'Half your army is gone, and the puppet you used to hide your identity will meet his demise at the end of some unknown soldier's blade. You are done, Torvald. Your schemes will end with at my hand,' Mar said, attacking swiftly, his sword a blur, looking for gaps in his enemy's defence.

Torvald gasped, falling steadily backwards under the strength of Mar's attack, but just as he tried to disarm the emperor, sudden pain tearing through his forearms distracted him, spoiling the strike and leaving an opening Torvald was quick to exploit.

'Half my vanguard may be gone, but my armada is arriving as we speak. All I need is to persevere a little longer; that shouldn't be too hard. Are you tired already, old man?' Despite gasping through his own exhaustion, Torvald smirked, pushing through the slight opening in the dragon's defence and thrusting his blade, its sharp edge slicing through the scales over Mar's ribs.

It was becoming difficult for Mar to concentrate on the duel as his bond with Ina burned through his chest like a swordsmith's glowing blade, turning the world before him crimson as he saw her magic rise from the battlefield. Seeing the sheer magnitude of power Ina was channelling was terrifying, and within their connection, he could feel his lover changing, no longer his irreverent spitfire but more a being of spirit, like the Leshy, or Marzanna.

The dragon parried and attacked by instinct as he assessed the conflict. His soldiers fought tooth and nail, their efforts worthy of a legendary saga, but the empire's forces held them off even now. Ren rallied the infantry, smiting the enemy like a warhammer, crowding them against the deep waters of the river, but even this was seemingly not enough to break the Norsemen.

The clarion call of a lone trumpet signalled the king's presence, catching Mar by surprise and making him grind his teeth in frustration. Rewan joining the battle disrupted every strategy the dragon had in place, jeopardising the country's future. With his mind discarding plan after plan on how to secure the king's safety, Mar nearly lost his head as Torvald caught the dragon's blade, twisting his wrists to use the marshal's momentum to make him stumble, then turned and struck out, his sword cutting a long gash in his shoulder. It took precious moments for the dragon to recover, but he parried the next strike, pushing the emperor several feet back, confusion clouding his thoughts, when, eyes widened in shock and anger, the emperor screamed.

'Your king has no honour! You have no honour, dragon. You desecrated the gloried dead for your army. Damn you to Veles. If you like corpses so much, let me help you join them,' he spat.

Torvald's words left Mar confused until several revenants leapt upon an empire soldier, tearing at his body and dragging him down with the sheer weight of numbers. He almost smiled as the emperor renewed his attack, fury burning in his eyes, and the weight of the dragon's injuries seemed to fall away when the war cry of the Troll Nation echoed over the battlefield.

Mar stepped to the side with an almost lazy feint, and as his gaze fell upon Cornovii's king, he couldn't help but laugh. The monarch sat on a pure white steed, his armour shining like some hero from a bard's tale, the white-haired Kaian by his side and Rurik, his half-brother, gesticulating wildly as he directed his undead army, the three of them surrounded by an honour guard of trolls, goblins and wiły.

'You've lost, and I'm done toying with you,' Mar said, trying to ignore the strength of the pull in the depths of his soul. He braced himself against the influence of Ina's magic, dealing blow after blow, seeing his enemy's eyes widen in shock, staring over his shoulder.

They fought sword to sword, barely aware of the battlefield growing quieter with each passing moment. Mar raised his sword to deal the final blow when Torvald tripped, losing his grip on his weapon as he stumbled. Mar looked at Torvald's face, his pupils dilated, reflecting the crimson glow the dragon finally noticed, and against his better judgement, turned to look behind him.

Is that a wave? No, that's impossible. The marshal couldn't believe the sight before him, this wall of water rising higher than the city walls, nearly reaching the clifftop, held in place by the god-like power Ina wielded. *She did it; my spitfire tamed the sea.* Mar was awestruck, but as he focused on their bond, Ina's consciousness was barely there, replaced by something so primal that he staggered, whipping his head back. A sharp pain in his side shocked him back to reality as the emperor screamed in his ear.

'You may have the heart of chaos, but for her sins against me, I will ensure it withers to nothing from the grief of losing you.' Torvald's pale face was next to his as he slowly forced the dagger deeper through Mar's unyielding scales.

Mar roared, his fist, now more claw than hand, smashed into the emperor's face, launching him across the battlefield, limp and broken. The wound in the dragon's side burned as thick golden-hued blood spilt to the ground, making Mar stagger through his transformation even as a crescendo of magic raged through his soul, instinct making him turn to see Ren lost in the same euphoric agony. The moment stretched, his soul tearing before, with the burst of magic, the roaring wall of water crashed back into the sea.

Torvald screamed, his eyes fixed on the rampaging tidal wave. Mar knew not even the armada could withstand the force of the sea and Ina's magic. When the emperor's eyes drifted to the dragon's, a grimace of pure malice distorted his face, and Mar knew he was looking at a man who'd lost it all. Torvald reached for his sword, but Mar didn't wait for the next attack. Something deep inside him shifted, the battle rage washing away, replaced by worry. The link was as strong as ever, but his spitfire was no longer there, her touch so alien that only his love tethered her to this world.

I need to get to her before... Unable to finish that thought, he turned towards the attacking emperor, feeling nothing but pity for this lost and broken fool. *There is no honour in war, just survivors and death.* Dragon fire engulfed Torvald, turning the Iron Emperor to ash in moments, and Mar turned away, his giant wings already lifting him into the sky, heading to the eye of raging chaos.

Ren saluted the dragon as he flew past, the quiet warrior leading a reinvigorated infantry against a failing enemy. The small teams of mages and soldiers working together in unison filled Mar's heart with pride, for which he would always be grateful to his friend. His inspired idea, the sword and shield, had come close to overturning the overwhelming odds stacked against them and had undoubtedly saved lives in this cauldron of death.

Muscles straining, Mar fought against unnatural winds to reach Ina, marvelling as the brave cuirassiers rushed into heavy fighting to rescue the struggling Verdante cavalry, cutting down anyone in their path and corralling the beleaguered soldiers as Rurik's revenants rushed in, tearing apart anyone wearing the enemy insignia.

The king seemed in control of the situation. With Ren leading the attack, and Rurik, supported by several mages, piloting the revenants, Rewan directed the foreign allies, sending drow swordsmen and elven archers to the periphery of the battle, attacking the empire soldiers attempting to flank the infantry.

The scales of the battle had tipped in their favour, and Mar roared his approval as he bade them farewell, fighting to reach his witch.

The sight before him was terrifying. Where he expected to see wrecked ships and bodies were fantastical islands filled with strange vegetation and animals, all under a blood-red sky, chaos raging in the heavens, making flying near impossible. With the armada gone, Ina should have dismissed her magic, but with it still out of control, the dragon knew he had to get to his lover's side before she lost herself completely.

I need to stop the fight. It's too much chaos for Ina to control. Mar opened his muzzle, raining fire on the enemy, dodging an arrow from the forgotten ballistae as it flew past his shoulder. With a banking turn, he crashed onto the ballistae tower before the enemy could reload and roared.

'Your emperor is dead, and the crimson witch destroyed your armada. You have nothing left to fight for. Surrender, or die knowing you will fight for Cornovii as an undead revenant forever.' It was a bluff, something Mar would never do, but Torvald's reaction told him the Norsemen would choose anything over becoming mindless thralls to a necromancer's will. They were not afraid of death, but might lower their weapons if it meant escaping the shame of eternal bondage.

When a powerful tremor shook the ground, knocking down hundreds, Mar blasted another stream of fire into the sky, highlighting the crimson storm of roiling chaos. 'Drop your weapons, you fools!'

The tower next to him was hit by a magic wave, collapsing onto the people below. Soon more followed, and without waiting for their acquiescence, Mar unfurled his wings, launching himself against the tempest to reach the clifftop before Ina's power turned them all into dust. The wound in his side tore, spraying golden-red blood each time he beat his wings, but Mar ignored it, willing his body to get to his spitfire.

Strands of magic thicker than his arm brushed against Mar as he flew, scouring his scales like hot sand but leaving him mostly unharmed, his bond with Ina still protecting him, the incandescent light of its power guiding the dragon through the violent winds. Finally, he spotted her kneeling at the edge of the cliff, and he bellowed her name, only to watch as she collapsed, her body falling closer to the crumbling precipice.

The pain in his side was nothing compared to the sight of his fiery spitfire, deathly pale, struggling up and scrubbing at the bloodied flesh of her arms. He felt the bond blazing with love and sadness, the maelstrom of chaos around her pulsing in unison with her heartbeat. *I will lock her in a bloody padded box and chain her to my back! What is she doing?* His mind raced when she shuffled towards the edge, and he realised what she was about to do. Desperation and anger clawed his heart when he roared.

'Inanuan! Don't you fucking dare die on me again!'

His impossible woman raised her head, her surprise evident when she saw his outstretched wings, the shock turning to happiness as she smiled in welcome. Ina stretched her hand towards him, and to his horror, he saw the torn and bloody wounds on her arms. Mar fought harder to reach his lover, the realisation that the crimson diagram before her was filled not with chaos but her lifeblood stopped the breath in his chest. His woman was dying, bleeding to death to fulfil a promise.

Mar dived, desperate to save Ina, but as he stretched out his claws, the world fell away, his spitfire gasping, a contented smile gracing her lips as she disappeared, her body falling before his eyes into the waves below. The dragon's curses turned the air blue as he harangued his lover, refusing to accept her sacrifice, and he tucked in his wings to follow Ina to her fate.

'*Stop! I will bring her to you!*' The mental command was followed by an aquamarine shape that plummeted from the sky, the slender figure diving into the waves with a grace of an arrow aimed into the heart of the ocean. Mar nearly forgot her words as the waves loomed large below him, unfurling his wings at the last moment and flying back to the damaged cliff. '*Men, always thinking with their dicks when any woman knows those wounds will attract every monster for miles.*' Ayni's mental voice, acerbic as usual, left him feeling like a child, and he belatedly remembered his injuries. Ignoring all but the stab wound, he twisted his long neck around, releasing an intense stream of fire over the damage, screaming in defiant pain as the injury was cauterised.

I can't leave her there... Mar couldn't keep the image of the falling witch from his mind, but Ayni had long since disappeared beneath the waves. He could see her flashing form between the submerged, jagged rocks with an agility he would never have. His heart was pounding, urging him to join her in the search, but she was right. The last thing he wanted was monsters where his woman had fallen. Instead, he focused on scanning the waves, ready to strike at the sight of any predator.

Nothing happened for a long, agonising moment, but as the ocean erupted, Ayni emerged, resplendent, holding Ina's limp body in her claws. A few bloodied scratches marred her aquamarine scales, but Mar focused more on Ina's pale face and the flickering light of her life slowly fading in his chest.

'Healer, we need a healer!' he roared, his wings beating furiously again, stretching his claws out to take Ayni's precious cargo.

'*Mar, stop and think! Trying to take her while airborne will only delay things. I'll fly to the camp, now move.*' The marshal felt adrift, unable to think clearly, but the dragoness's mental command centred him, and with a beat of his massive wings, he flew ahead to announce their arrival, praying to all the gods his stubborn woman didn't make him visit Nawia for the second time this year.

CHAPTER THIRTY TWO

A glance over the battlefield told Mar that Ren and the king had taken control of the battle, and for a moment, he felt guilty. Still, most of the Norsemen were subdued, having laid down their weapons after his command. Rurik's revenants granted those who still fought a quick death, Rewan being unwilling to see more of his valiant warrior's lives wasted, but as he overflew the battlefield, the dragon was surprised and deeply moved as the soldiers below bowed, fists over their hearts in salute as he passed, an honour usually reserved for king's and heroes.

'Healer!' he roared, transforming before his feet hit the ground, twisting around to grab Ina from Ayni's outstretched claws, stumbling as his charred stab wound opened up. The poor healer who rushed up was shocked at the curses Mar spat out as he tore a cloth from her hands, jamming it into the bleeding injury, and rushing to rip Ina from Ayni's grasp with a possessive snarl had made the dragoness startle, but the marshal was already gone, running back to the frightened man.

'She can't die; she used blood magic! Help her, use my strength, use any spell you have, but she can't die! Do whatever it takes, or by Perun's beard, this world will burn!' His shouted tirade nearly had the healer in tears, but he withstood his anger to take control.

'Yes, my lord, we... Follow me to our tent.' But Mar was already striding towards the healer's tent, the poor physician trailing behind, wringing his hands in consternation. *I organised this camp, why would I need to follow anyone? If only Nerissa were here, Ina would be safe.* He had to force himself to release his grip when he laid Ina on the nearest bed before several assistants ushered him outside, knowing, compassionate looks in their eyes, but the furthest he allowed their meddling was the tent entrance, where the dragon stopped, pressing a fist to his heart, trying to push strength and love through his bond to his mate.

The next thing he knew, Ren was crashing into him, graceless in his desire to reach Ina's side.

Mar's hand grabbed his friend's collar, wrenching him back and holding him still. 'No, Ren, they are helping her, I... It's bad. There was so much blood, and then she fell from the cliff, smiling, fucking smiling. Shit, it hurts so much, brother. I can't live without her. If not for Ayni, I don't know what...' Ren grabbed him when his knees buckled.

'She won't die. We won't let it happen. Focus on her. She needs your strength and our bond. She won't die,' he said softly, but with such confidence that it gave Mar the strength to open his eyes.

'What was your woman doing airborne in the first place? I told her to stay in camp.' Mar's fists clenched when he tried to distract himself.

'I asked her to oversee the battlefield, above the ballistae range before you say anything, so that's how she knew about Ina,' Ren said before stuttering to silence, both men shuddering when agony tore through their chests, Ina's scream piercing the noise of the camp.

'What the fuck are they doing?!' The little trust he had in the new arch healer vanished, and Mar burst into the tent with Ren on his heels, only to notice the pale faces of everyone and a roiling white light coating the witch's body, pinning her to the bed. They were supposed to heal her, yet his woman thrashed and screamed her lungs out.

'She will need a bloody miracle, so don't give me that look, marshal. She lost too much blood and tied herself to wild magic. Inanuan used an ancient spell to become a wraith, forever united with the ocean. It shouldn't be possible, it was just a legend, but she did it, then the transformation was disrupted by something... someone.' The healer thumped her chest when Ina screamed again, turning towards the witch.

'The first we can fix, blood is easily replaced, wounds stitched, but we can't sever the connection. Inanuan is like a lightning bolt searing anyone who touches her. We tried, but as soon as one of us linked to her, they were thrown across the tent and barely survived.'

When Mar ground his teeth, the healer approached him with an unyielding look on her face. 'Whatever protected her from becoming a wraith left her halfway bound by the spell that precedes mage wars. She is still linked to the wild magic by blood. We can transfer this connection to another chaos mage strong enough to withstand it to complete the process, but only to a chaos mage. Anyone else will be stripped of their magic in moments, and their life will be consumed by the sheer power of the spell. You must return her to the ocean or kill her, marshal. We don't have another chaos mage, and as harsh as it sounds, no one should sacrifice themselves for such a....'

The moment she looked away, Mar knew the healer would rather his lover die, and he barely held his temper as she continued. 'I can keep her under the spell, but when she awakes... She is in pain. The sea is clawing at her soul, demanding her return, and if you keep her on land, Inanuan will become a monster that devours us all,' the arch healer snarled, and the dragon lost control, grabbing the woman by the throat.

'Ina sacrificed everything for your sakes, and you treat her as a monster? Keep her under the spell, sedated if you must. I will find a way.'

Suddenly, Ina's eyes snapped open. Red and full of swirling, maddening chaos seeing beyond this world, making Mar's blood freeze. *She's looking beyond the veil.* He rushed to her side, pushing healers away, cupping her face and turning it in his direction.

'Stay with me my beautiful, brave spitfire. Please, Ina. Come back from wherever you are. I know you can do it. You let no one rule you; not me, the king, or even your chaos. Don't give in to the sea. Stay with me, my love,' he whispered, covering her face with kisses.

'Lord marshal, she can't hear you. She used blood with an ancient curse, which always comes at a high cost,' the diffident healer from earlier said behind his back, and when Mar glanced back, he grimaced. 'I know what you think, sire. She is fighting, and if not for you and General Ren, her soul would already belong to the sea, but death is a mercy when one is in pain like this. Death or returning her to the ocean. We have no other way to fix it other than killing another mage in her place while we transfer her binding spell. If we leave things as they are, this bond will consume her, and Sowenna won't be the only world breaker.'

Mar's lips drew to a snarl. 'So it's her life or yours, yes? Fine, take mine and do what needs to be done to help her.'

'Sire, I can't. You have no magic. Not human magic, anyway.' The healer's voice was the final nail in his coffin. Mar put Ina's hand to his cheek, wracking his mind for ideas. He barely noticed when the tent flaps opened again, and Rurik walked towards the bed. Instinctively, every healer moved aside, avoiding the touch of a death master when he approached the other side of the cot, taking Ina's hand.

'Transfer the connection,' he said calmly, stroking Ina's face tenderly.

'What are you doing?! This will kill you!' shrieked the arch healer, but Rurik didn't even look at her.

'I killed for her. What makes you think I wouldn't die for her?' he asked softly. His voice carried no doubt or hesitation; it was peaceful and contented. Only a slight twitch of his cheek revealed how painful her touch was to him.

'Fine!' the arch healer gestured, and on that sign, the tent filled with the chanting of every gathered mage.

For a moment, nothing happened, then, with a sudden gasping breath, Ina turned, looking at Rurik with pupilless eyes, her inhuman gaze fixed upon him as magic tore through his body, wrenching a torturous sound from his soul. Her skin regained colour as fast as he lost it, the red hue slowly bleeding out of her eyes. Mar heard Ren gasp behind his back, but all he could think of was Ina growing more robust with each passing moment, her presence returning to their bond.

The necromancer's face became gaunt, more like one of his revenants than human, but he smiled when consciousness returned to Ina's eyes, even as she tried to rip her hand from his.

'No, Rurik, you fool... you are not of chaos. You can't survive this,' she whispered when he stopped her, his breathing growing shallow, placing his other hand on hers.

'You promise me death. I served the king as you wished, so please allow me this. My beautiful chaos, you gave my life purpose. If you could tell Velka, I will always love her... or maybe not, she's happy now... but if you have it in your heart, please forgive me,' he whispered. His eyes lost their focus, but he didn't let her hand go despite the witch struggling in his grasp.

'For fuck's sake, no! I don't want another death weighing on my conscience. Rurik, let me go, you bloody bastard!' She was crying, looking around for help to shake off his touch, but the necromancer's face made it clear he was at peace with his choice, and Mar wrapped his fingers around their hands, locking them together. Ina fought him, but stopped when a torturous ecstasy washed over Rurik's face.

'You are the gods' perfect creation,' he whispered, falling limply to the side. Nothing but a dry husk of a man remained when the healer's chant quietened, completing the transfer. Mar saw her tears and felt her sadness tearing him up inside, but he could not deny his joy. His spitfire was safe now, or as safe as any chaos mage could be. Ren gestured to some men outside the tent to remove Rurik's remains.

'Be gentle and respectful. This man died with honour,' Mar said, leaving them to their task while gently stroking Ina's hand. Relief washed over him, and he felt the world spin around him, searing pain blinding him momentarily. A glance at his flank revealed the source. The rag was soaked with his blood, dripping slowly to the ground.

Leaning down, the dragon whispered to his lover. 'I will be back, my love. I need to check on something. Stay with Ren. You, come with me,' he snapped at the nearest healer, trying to hide his pain while excusing himself. As soon as he stood up, a wave of dizziness overcame him, and Mar looked up, wondering why so many people were leaning over him. After blinking several times, the dragon realised what had happened, his mind wandering in delirium as his forgotten wounds reminded him of their presence, Ina's love and worry flowing through their connection.

'I'm not having a second man dying on me today! Marcach, you obstinate lizard. There are enough healers in this bloody camp to help us both,' she scolded him, stroking his face when Ren helped him to a nearby cot. Mar let his dragon armour disappear, only to hear her exasperated whisper. 'You were flying like this? Gods, help me, and you burned yourself too? That's not how you treat wounds, you idiot. Someone heal him so I can kill him properly.'

Despite the pain, he chuckled weakly, happy his stubborn woman's fiery temper had returned, drinking a disgusting tincture the healer put in his hand. If Ina were strong enough to yell, she would survive.

He saw the healers take her aside while the witch protested, pointing towards him. Mar groaned and tried to sit up, but his vision blurred as the pain subsided. His thoughts became fuzzy and disorganised, despite shaking his head to get them straight. Ina was safe; now she was doing something, some magic that soothed their bond, sending him into a happy stupor. He vaguely felt the touch of the needles and spells when healers cut away charred flesh and debris, working on his body.

Instead, he gazed into Ina's green eyes while she approached him, letting him reach for her hand to place it against his cheek. She smelled divine and tasted even better. Dry, crusted blood still covered her forearms, and he trailed his tongue over it, sighing with pleasure at the salty metallic taste of her magic.

'What did you give him? Why is he acting like an overgrown puppy?' Ina's worried voice broke through his meandering thoughts. He grunted, squeezing her tight in case she wanted to take her hand away, but much to his pleasure, she didn't.

'It is just a powerful painkiller. He's a dragon, so we gave him a little extra. I didn't want him injuring any healers when we stitched him up.' He heard the healer's voice, but he didn't care. Ina's face floated in front of him, making him smile.

'I love you. You are a pain in the arse. Why do you keep dying on me? Death may want you, but you are mine. Do you understand Ina? You are mine, and I'm not allowing you to leave me. I've had enough fighting off every twat on both sides of the veil who desires to possess you. You are mine,' he rumbled, his nose trailing along her skin before looking up, expecting her to yell.

'Yes.'

'I will take you to the valley in Liath, and I will fuck you hard in the hot spring, and when you're all soft and satiated, you will admit— Uh, what did you say?' He stuttered to a halt, looking at her suddenly serious eyes, confident Ina had said something incredibly important during his rambling. 'Ina, what did you say?' he said, trying to slow his erratic thoughts.

'I said yes, Marcach of Liath. I am yours, and I always will be yours,' Ina said, and his mind suddenly snapped to focus.

'No! I mean, not like this. Ina, you can't just say it. I must convince you first,' he said, and she rolled her eyes.

'Well, make you up your mind, you hairy oaf. I have a reputation to uphold. I won't be shouting, *"I'm yours"* on every street corner.' She chuckled when he grumbled, twisting her hand from his grasp, and when Mar protested, she turned towards the healers. 'You don't have to be slow or gentle now that he's drugged up to his eyeballs. The sooner he returns to his normal self, the better.'

Mar tried to stand up, watching as Ina supported herself on Ren's arm to walk out of the tent, but when the healer snapped, threatening to restrain him if he didn't stop moving, Mar gave up. A lazy smile blossomed on his face that had nothing to do with a drug-induced haze. Ina was his, and she was a step away from marrying him, and even if he messed it up now, he would fix it by courting her as she deserved. He'd rehearsed it too often not to propose correctly, but when she admitted she was his in front of so many people, he knew she was ready, and he couldn't wait till he knelt before her.

My beautiful, thorny rose, you told the world you're mine. The sense of completeness brought a joy he hadn't known was possible. Ina was his. The war was over. He lay on the pillows, letting the healers finish their work while his mind drifted towards the army, pride and sorrow threatening to overwhelm his senses. With Ina's words, everything in his world fell into place, making him a very content dragon. Mar sighed in satisfaction, closing his eyes and allowing himself the luxury of well-deserved rest.

CHAPTER THIRTY THREE

Ina maintained her strong facade in front of Mar and the healers, but inside, she was heartsore and exhausted, the burden of surviving weighing her down as she stumbled on the uneven ground and fell into Ren's comforting arms.

'My lady, you gave me a fright,' he murmured, supporting his dear friend and brushing a stray lock of hair from her eyes. The gentleness of his voice, contrasting so starkly with the violence of war, loosened the tight knot in the witch's chest, allowing her to relax, the tears flowing freely from her eyes as they embraced.

'I thought I would never see you again, or Mar, certain I would die there. I just wanted to end it all.' She sniffled, hiding her face in the cuddle. 'Did we at least win the battle? How many... How many didn't make it?' she asked, clenching her fists whilst waiting for his answer.

'Many paid the ultimate price, Ina, but we won, and Cornovii is safe now. You and Zarai won this war for us.' Ren's words made the witch frown as he stepped back, still supporting her weakened body.

'Who is Zarai?' she asked, not recognising the name.

'Who *was* Zarai,' Ren corrected her, placing a hand on the small of her back. 'She was a shifter, the best sentinel we had, and she single-handedly wiped out a third of the empire army, exploding their alchemy supplies,' he said, guiding her along.

'Ren, where are you taking me? Mar is still unwell. I just needed a bit of fresh air,' she said when he gently pushed her forward.

'To the battlefield, Ina. To our soldiers who fought and died whispering prayers to the Lady of the Crimson Veil. They fought for king and country, but they believed in you. Grant them a boon and let them see the goddess who reshaped Dancik's shoreline.'

'This is too much. I can barely stand and... I don't know if I can face the death I caused right now.' Ren embraced her again, and she hated the whining tone of her voice, but his touch and the compassion flowing through their bond helped hold back the despair.

'Oh, my sweet lady. I'm sorry, but this can't wait. Despite the healers helping the wounded, many of the injured still cannot leave the battlefield. Please forgive me, Ina, but they need to see you.'

'That was a low blow, Ren; you know me too well.' A short, hollow laugh escaped her. 'It looks like I'm a little wilting flower today, and my knight in shining armour is lying down in a drug-induced stupor. Take me to the wounded and the king. I need to see Rewan, so we can detour through the soldier's tents.'

The quiet warrior nodded gratefully, guiding the exhausted witch through the camp, a faint whisper sweeping before them, followed by the mass exodus from the surrounding tents, men and women of all races and creeds silently bracketing the path and saluting Ina, their fists clenched over hearts, tears in their eyes. 'I know you and Mar love discipline, but is there really a need for the soldiers to salute when we simply walk through the camp?' she asked, but before Ren could answer, the scarred veteran she remembered from the South approached them, kneeling before Ina and saluting.

'My lady, will you honour us with your presence tonight? The soldiers want to celebrate the victory and see the miracle that is their Lady of the Crimson Veil.'

'Miracle?' Ina asked, the man flinching uncomfortably before answering.

'Yes, my lady. War is always the same. We fight, and we die, but this time… Not many expected to survive this battle even if we won, but everyone witnessed your power and knows what you did to the invaders. Your blessing saved us, our lady's miracle.'

With her stinging eyes threatening to betray her again, Ina tried to deny his words. 'It's rather the lord marshal and General Sa'Ren's miracle. They trained you all for this moment,' she said, but the soldier remained kneeling. She could see the muscles of his jaw twitching so hard his scars jumped, and while everyone silently stared on, Ina freed herself from Ren's hold and approached the kneeling man.

He looked at her with such glowing devotion that the witch almost broke down, and she impulsively leaned down and placed a small kiss on his cheek. The brief and light touch was enough to brighten his expression. 'My lady…' he stuttered, pulling away.

'I could never refuse my favourite soldier. I will be there, but please don't be disappointed if I don't stay long. It was a long and challenging day for all of us, and I still haven't fully recovered,' she said, and the soldier nodded before moving away.

Ren approached, hand raised to assist her again, and she could see the pride in his eyes. 'Thank you, Mi'Khaira. That's why I asked you to come. They needed to see their miracle,' he said, leading her to the king's tent.

Ina briefly stopped at the top of the hill, gazing down at the battlefield. Countless bodies lay there, their life forever lost to the veil. Ren allowed her a moment to contemplate the incredible sacrifice of the dead as she stared down at the floodplains before turning away and shaking her head.

'Torvald?'

'Dead. Mar's doing, although I admit I wished he'd fallen to my sword.' The regret in his voice brought a smile to her face as Ren guided her further into the camp. Ina was struck by how ordinary life seemed for the survivors, the atmosphere one of camaraderie, and not loss, with tired soldiers cleaning their equipment while bickering with mages about the recent battle, only quietening once they spotted her, saluting as she passed, their regard weighing heavily on the witch's soul.

In front of a large ornate tent, Ren bowed slightly, pulling back the flap.

'I will wait here, my lady. The king may need to consult you privately. The last weeks were tough for him... For all of us.'

The rest of the evening felt like a blur after she entered. The king looked solemn when he approached, embraced her, and led her into the contrived privacy of his quarters. Their relationship had developed from the witch being a not-so-humble subject to someone who cared deeply for the man burdened with a broken kingdom but still willing to serve it, no matter what. Ina hugged him again, this time leaning into the embrace, gently patting his back when he thanked her for saving them once again.

'Silly man, we did it, Rewan. You did it. I hope it will be enough for lasting peace. I don't think I could ever face another war.' Her words were heartfelt, as was her frown when Rewan sighed deeply.

'It will be enough, at least for now, but we lost so much, Ina.' His words gave her a pause, and for a moment, Ina worried about Kaian, the master assassin not at his lover's side, but before she could ask, Rewan released her and turned and poured some wine.

'Let's drink this before Kaian returns and tells me off for using his personal supply. He should be back any moment... or tomorrow, depending on how long it takes to prepare Dancik for its king's arrival. After all, we only need one man on the throne,' he said, passing her a goblet. While she sipped, Rewan detailed their journey north and the battle at Kion.

Ina also learned how Rurik's magic and a newly raised army of undead had helped to *convince* the remaining rebels from the Water Horse clan to lay down their weapons.

'Your brother, he sacrificed himself to save me. Despite his transgressions, I couldn't... He was...' Ina was lost for words, running her hands through her hair, grimacing at the emotions she couldn't control before huffing in annoyance. 'What is wrong with me? And what does it say about me that I liked him? He did terrible things, but he never did it for personal gain, and I can't stop thinking I'm not so different. Those I killed, who died to fuel my magic. It could easily be my name vilified as the monster who plunged the country into war and despair.' The face of the young soldier and his scarred compatriot filled her mind as guilt took its toll.

'You inspired a genius raised in a living hell who worked to create a better world despite his suffering and horrifying methods. I spoke with him often after you left, initially to ensure he didn't betray us, but the conversations grew into a rapport that had been missing between Sophia and me. Few believe in the gods as strongly as he believed in you. I hope he is at peace now, and maybe it's for the better. He was a tormented, broken soul full of remorse for the suffering he caused. I think he died happy knowing you became the person he dreamed you would be.'

'I am no god, nor should anyone think that of me. No one should have this kind of power or expect others to sacrifice themselves. I thought I'd lived long enough to know how ignorant I was, but there is no harder task than living up to a dead soul's expectations. First Nerissa, now Rurik. I wish I could get my life back,' the witch said, smiling bitterly, stretching out her goblet for a refill.

'I never wanted to be king. I would happily live with Kaian someplace quiet as the scorned younger brother, but here we are, you, the archmage of chaos, and me, the monarch of the most powerful nation of Warenga. So let us raise a toast. For Rurik, a bastard who paved the road to despair and salvation with his good intentions, and for us, the ones left to carry the burden,' he said, raising his cup.

'You are not alone, Rewan,' she said after they drank. 'I will stand by you, whatever comes and... you can confide in me. I know they say the king has no friends, only subjects or enemies, but I am your friend, and I know the weight of a crown you never asked for. At least you can take yours off whilst I'm forever attached to this piece of junk,' she said, removing the illusion from her circlet.

They spoke more, and after finishing the bottle, Ina staggered slightly when leaving his tent. Ren was already there, insisting she rest, but the witch remembered her promise to join the soldiers, and a moment later, she wobbled to the centre of the camp, where the troops celebrated next to a roaring fire.

They surprised her with an absurd nest of army blankets and makeshift pillows arranged in the most prominent spot.

'You did this?' she asked the scarred man she'd kissed before the battle of Alesia.

'Yes, my lady. You said you were tired, and I knew you would come, even if only for a moment. So I asked the others, and they came up with this.' He lowered his gaze when she came closer.

'I never asked your name, did I?' Ina felt a pang of guilt. This soldier of few words had helped her several times now, and she'd been too busy to get to know him.

'No, my lady, but it's not needed. You don't have to know every soldier in the barracks. It's enough that we know you care for us.'

His words made her sigh. 'Your name and rank, soldier,' she said in a stern voice, mimicking Mar.

'Master-at-arms Zbych, my lady,' he said, standing tall, and the witch couldn't help but chuckle when she noticed how his sight darted down when she approached.

'Well, master-at-arms Zbych, thank you for taking such good care of me. You would make an excellent adjutant for the lord marshal. I like how you take the initiative in looking after your compatriots and me,' she said, tiptoeing to peck his cheek again.

While a roar erupted from the gathered crowd, Ren pulled her back with a smile while shaking his head. 'My lady, don't cause this man more trouble. He already has more volunteers for his unit than he can accommodate.'

'They know his value. What's wrong with that?' she said defiantly, allowing Ren to guide her to the strange nest. The soldiers resumed their drunken antics, occasionally broken by a magical display after the mages joined the festivities. Warmth spread through Ina's chest when she observed them, their camaraderie forged in fire and death.

'Little witch, may I join you?' Ina heard Ayni's melodic voice and raised her head, looking at the beautiful dragoness standing over her, her hand entwined with Ren's, who looked at his partner in utter devotion.

'Hop in. There's plenty of space,' Ina said, moving to the side, observing with a hint of envy how gracefully Ayni settled into the tussled blankets to watch the carousing crowd.

'Thank you, Ayni, for giving me a chance. I know you did it for Ren, but thank you for saving my life,' Ina said quietly.

Her words were met with silence, but the witch hadn't expected much, knowing from the moment they'd first met, Ayni considered her a walking disaster.

'I was wrong about you. I rarely am, but I misjudged you, allowing my prejudice to get the better of me. Ren saw the love in your heart, but I couldn't. Thankfully, you proved me wrong, little witch, humbling this old dragon in the process. When I dived into the waves for you, I did it because I wanted to save you, not for Ren, but for me. For the hope you brought into my life. I believed that harbingers of chaos always brought destruction, but the change you bring comes from a loving heart, and the dragon in me bows to this.' Ayni placed a hand on Ina's shoulder and smiled when the witch's mouth fell open, astounded by the sentiment.

'I, uh... Thank you,' she said, blushing heavily. Her reaction made Ayni chuckle before she tilted her head, pointing to Ren.

'Would you mind if I take this one?'

'Oh, Ayni, he's all yours. Please ensure you tire him enough to give me an upper hand in morning training,' she said, finally finding the right words. Ren didn't comment, but looked at them both with open amusement.

'I'm glad you decided on returning to your training, my lady. I apologise in advance if you're unable to converse with Ayni tomorrow. She may be too tired to walk,' he said in his most stoic voice, and Ina burst out laughing, waving them off. She felt Ren's happiness radiating through the bond. *Be happy, my beautiful guardian*, she thought, relaxing in her seat.

'General Gerel loves Lady Ayni very much.' Zbych's voice trailed off, and Ina looked up at her remaining guardian, nodding at his words before she turned her eyes back to the celebrating people, gesturing surreptitiously. Chaos gently swirled over the field, touching the life force of every living being and rejuvenating it without them even noticing her little intervention. The laughter and merriment increased, with someone soon bringing snacks and drinks for her to try. It didn't take long until Ina drifted to sleep, her mind caressing the golden light of Mar's soul, guarded by Zbych, who never left her side.

CHAPTER THIRTY FOUR

At first, the decadent feeling of waking without having to focus on a scheme or a problem made Ina smile. The warm body next to her helped even more as her fingers stole through the luxurious hair on his chest. It was only a little disappointing that Mar was still asleep, but it did mean she could indulge in stroking him to her heart's content.

After his time with the healers, her handsome man looked exhausted but whole, the dark circles under his eyes and the sunken cheeks giving his expression a hard edge that hadn't been there before, and the witch realised how much strain Mar had been under these past months. *I love you so much*, she thought, gently stroking his cheek. Their bond felt deeper than ever, making Ina want to caress it with her fingers. Instead, she focused on the golden strands, sending her consciousness through the connection. His tiredness and still-healing injuries made her wince, but once she examined his body, gratitude to the arch healer and her team left her sighing.

Mischief danced through her mind as Ina gleefully eased a thread of chaos into his body, using her recently discovered skill to renew and recreate the damaged parts of Mar's life force, adding energy to his meridians to speed his recovery. It didn't take long for her meddling to yield results as the bruises around his eyes faded, and the harsh planes of his cheekbones softened into familiar territory. Mar grumbled but didn't wake up, and Ina sighed with contentment. In the past, healing like this would have been impossible, leaving her comatose for days for even attempting it. Now, apart from some transient discomfort, she didn't feel anything; not even a dent in the power at her disposal.

Her desire for mischief grew, her questing hand sliding down over Mar's body, teasing fingernails lightly scoring the skin over quiescent muscles, intending to take advantage of his renewed strength when the tent's flap opened, and a young squire pushed his head through the entrance. Ina put a finger to her lips when he gasped at seeing them together and gestured him inside.

The poor boy turned deep crimson when she stood up, quickly pulling one of Mar's long shirts over her head.

'How did I get here?' she asked, and after a short whispered conversation, it became clear that after waking from his drug-induced nap, Mar had stormed out of the healing tent and searched the camp for her, roaring at anyone who got in the way till he came upon the celebration and, without a word, picked up the slightly drunk witch, pillow nest and all, storming from the party to hundreds of ribald comments.

'What an oaf. It's no surprise he looked like he needed a week in bed.' She rolled her eyes despite the pleasure that blossomed inside her.

It took a combined effort to wake the sleeping dragon, but Ina and the squire eventually managed. After stretching out tired, tight muscles, Mar patted his body before sending her a look full of suspicion. Ina shrugged at his scrutiny, admitting nothing, and it was Mar's turn to roll his eyes before he sighed and requested food, making Ina direct the squire to the quartermaster, knowing his mood would improve after a rich breakfast.

After breakfast, she'd wanted to talk to the mages, but Mar grabbed her hand with an uncertain, pleading look in his eyes.

'I almost lost you again yesterday, so please, just for today, leave the country's problems to someone else. I feel on edge not having you by my side.'

That was how she ended up trailing behind her possessive man, who couldn't take his own advice to leave the problems to others, and, after the fifth request for a decision from harried officers, stormed out of the tent with Ina's hand in his grip to take charge and organise the battle's aftermath. Now he stood beside her, his arm casually resting on her shoulder, looking over the noxious field. The ground was still covered with bodies of the fallen, mostly empire soldiers, but enough of Cornovii's army that Ina could see Mar's hold on his temper fraying.

'They don't deserve to be left like this, enemies or otherwise. They should have a funeral pyre, but there would be no way to do it respectfully with this many dead. I could use my dragonfire, but that would leave the ground barren for years and the city unsustainable.' Mar lapsed into silence, his anguished thoughts clear on his face, wincing when he seemed to remember whom he embraced. 'I'm sorry, my love, it isn't fair of me to burden you with my troubles. This was not how I intended to spend my time with you.'

Ina stroked the warrior's hand gently with her thumb. *He has to think about everything and care for everyone, even the fallen. And those people... Mar is right. They don't deserve this; their bodies picked over and rotting.* She felt a compulsion to honour the dead and take this burden from her dragon's shoulders.

'Follow me, my love,' she said, remembering the first time she'd encountered the drow in Liath.

Mar didn't try hiding the deepening of his frown when Ina led him down between the dead. The bodies were already beginning to bloat, the heat and moisture making the stench challenging to withstand, but the witch was determined to give the soldiers a proper burial. She'd only done it once, in fear and loathing at her magic during a skirmish in Liath. After killing several drows with chaos, she'd purged the magic into the ground, their bodies returning to the earth in what she now knew was the renewing power she possessed. Then it had been an impulse, but it felt right that now the soldier's sacrifice should reinvigorate the damaged landscape.

Smiling at Mar's growing confusion, Ina knelt in the middle of the battlefield.

The witch closed her eyes, opening herself to the elements. Her regalia shimmered with power, the magic eager to be used. Chaos surrounded Ina, a dangerous swirling mass of energy released by the death and decay around them, but she wasn't afraid to touch it anymore. Ina had seen this moment countless times in her dreams, the bleached bones under a scorching, crimson sun, the fertile ground turned into a desert when she stripped it of life and magic, but this time would be different, her fears vanishing when she reached for the sea's power and persevered.

Tears for the fallen saturated the dirt when Ina dug her hands into the desecrated soil, connecting with the land and letting the magic flow through her. She felt her bond with Mar flare to life with a beautiful golden light. The astonished dragon kneeled before her, their hands connecting within the roiling earth.

'My love, please, whatever you are doing, don't cry. These warriors fought for what they believed in, dying with honour.' In his desire to ease Ina's suffering, Mar laid his forehead against hers, laying bare his soul when she released the magic, shuddering as chaos slid over his skin, submitting to her command, willing the earth itself to take her bloody offering.

'Makosz, our forgiving mother, take your sons and daughters into their mother's loving embrace so they may finally rest.' Ina whispered her prayer to Mother Earth, feeling her warm response.

Makosz, revered mother of all, the goddess who never toyed with mortals, ever compassionate, answered Ina's prayer. The chaos that coated the couple's bodies sprang forth, spreading over the battlefield, shimmering and distorting the air. One by one, the fallen warriors disappeared into the ground. A murmuring disturbed the silence surrounding Ina and Mar as the living gathered to witness this miracle. When the last of the departed found their resting place, Ina was filled to the brim with the essence of their being, but this burial wounded the earth that listened to her prayer. *From death comes life.* The voice in her soul demanded a restoration to this imbalance. It was so easy to surrender to something that felt so right. Ina inhaled deeply, smiling as she uttered a last command.

'Heal.'

It was barely a whisper, and the immeasurable power released moved a gentleness belying its strength, repairing and renewing the hope of new growth as the torn earth smoothed and grasses sprang forth, followed by a cornucopia of flowers in a riot of colour, forget-me-nots growing over each grave, returning dignity to the souls sacrificed to war.

'My lady?' Ren's careful voice drew Ina back from her communion with the land's spirit to look around, exhaling slowly. Her gaze met the dragon's golden eyes. Mar embraced her, lifting her up, her attention distracted by the peacock butterflies that fluttered in the summer's breeze. The joyful smile that graced the witch's face shone as Ina stroked Mar's beard before turning to Ren to lay her other hand on his smooth cheek.

'You made it possible,' she said, knowing she'd be willing to suffer more than she had to keep these incredible men in her life. *You did it. You stayed with a broken witch until she found the courage to piece herself together.*

From this day forth, a flowery meadow would replace the desert, bleached bones buried under a carpet of blossoms in her dreams, and despite feeling their concern blazing through the bond, Ina couldn't find the words to express the pure serenity of this moment. She was whole and free from fear. For the first time, she accepted the possibility of a happy ending and dared to plan her future next to the man she loved. Ina raised her face to the sun and laughed while tears of joy flowed from her eyes.

'My love, what's going on? Please talk to me... us.' Mar grasped her hands, turning her around and pressing them to his chest. She could see translucent scales shimmering over the surface of his skin.

'Everything is perfect; you, me, and Ren. I finally feel at peace with who I am. Maybe it took going that far to understand that I am the harbinger of chaos, an archmage and bringer of change. I can't deny it, but I can decide how I want to live, and I will not waste another day brooding over my magic.' She saw Mar's smile blossom as he brought her hand to his lips, kissing her palm softly while Ren tentatively touched her shoulder.

'I'm so happy, my lady. You finally see yourself for who you truly are.' The reverence in his voice brought out her mischievous streak.

'Oh, no. You, out of all men, should not put me on a bloody pedestal. We both know who I truly am, a royal pain in the arse and a nightmare to guard. I didn't change; I just accepted the part of me I hid in the shadows. Now I will live as my conscience decides without fear or second guessing.' She grinned, freeing herself from Mar's embrace.

'Ina, life will change now. The army saw what you did with your magic. Now, not just the army, but an entire city witnessed... whatever you just did. You can't hide in the *Drunken Wizard* any more. You will always be their Lady of the Crimson Veil, who they fought and died for. I'm sorry, my love. I will do my best, but your carefree life in Osterad may no longer be possible.' Mar was reaching for her hands, and deep down, Ina knew he was right, but she shrugged it off.

'Yeah, well, try me. Oh, and Mar...? I will geld whoever tries to sing about my recent achievements. Make sure your soldiers know, or else you will have a lot of choir boys in your ranks,' she said, giving both exasperated men a big grin before Ren shook his head, trying to rein in his amusement.

'My lady, it's too late for that.' His words made her groan, and Ina felt heat crawling up her cheeks.

'What now? I'm the ruler of the ocean or something equally nonsensical?' she asked, but her friend shook his head.

'I dare not say. I will leave this part to Mar. Besides, we must return to the camp. The king wants to ride into Dancik and requested your presence. He also asked if you would be kind to consider presenting yourself as the Lady of the Crimson Veil.'

Ina rolled her eyes and sighed. 'Right, because why the fuck not? More fuel for the bards because the royal witch is no longer a big enough title. Did he also want me to ride a dragon? I'm sure you wouldn't mind, love,' she said with a roguish grin, noticing Mar biting his lip while a wave of pure lust burst through their connection.

CHAPTER THIRTY FIVE

Their visit to Dancik had gone better than expected. Kaian had prepared the city well, the masked puppet quietly despatched by the assassin's unseen killers and Gruff's spy network cleansing the streets of any empire supporters. As soon as the king's delegation had stood under the walls and announced their presence with Ina and Mar flanking Rewan, the city gates had opened, and the mayor, with merchant guild leaders, strutted out, presenting the proverbial keys on the velvet pillow. No one with an iota of common sense had any qualms about giving all maritime power to the king of Cornovii.

Still, if Ina had hoped for leisure time, she was sadly mistaken. Rewan was adamant about solving any issues, insisting on using the King's prerogative. Unfortunately for her, he also decreed she play a leading role, and the witch had to take part in Rewan's rulings as a judicial mage of Cornovii.

On the first day, she had told Rewan, more or less politely, what he could do with such a decree, focused on finding her orein. Thankfully, when the witch arrived, Zjawa was still there, snorting and ripping apart the stall with her clawed feet and vicious teeth. However, the king and his lover had brought mead, appealing to her conscience, before Kaian convinced her to help.

Now tired after a long day of obsequious politicking, Ina wandered to the stables, hoping for a moment of solitude with the mountain spirit. She was immensely grateful her orein stayed with her. She ran towards the approaching creature, wrapping her arms around Zjawa's long neck and cuddling her face to the soft coat of the unusual mount, laughing when the spirit pulled her braid.

'I missed you so much, my sweet. People are so annoying and petty, but mostly annoying,' she said, stroking the delicate muzzle. 'Zjawa, my fierce, beautiful soul, we will go home soon, and I will bring you a whole coup of chickens, I promise,' she rambled, inhaling the orein's musky smell.

'I knew I would find you here. What do I get when we return home?' Mar's voice murmured behind her, but Ina didn't open her eyes, still stroking her orein's back.

'Everything all right with the army?' she asked, knowing while she'd spent the entire day flattening her arse on a decorated chair passing judgment, he'd been equally busy chasing marauders and making sure the remaining Norsemen were put in confinement before they were shipped back to the Iron Empire as a statement that Dancik belonged to Cornovii and always would.

'Yes, my spitfire. However, after turning the farmland and half the flood plains into the most beautiful summer meadow, the soldiers and mages unequivocally announced you as the patron of the army and now are quarrelling about which formation will be carrying your banner of crimson flames. I'm trying not to interfere, especially since your arcane-gifted friends went into battle alongside ordinary soldiers, but they need to calm down. Oh, I had to rescue your scarred friend, Zbych, from his comrade's attention. Stop kissing the poor man. I should be jealous; instead, I pity him. After he survived two battles without a scratch, all the younglings believe your kiss blessed him with luck, and they want to serve in his unit.

Now he doesn't have a moment alone, poor man. He even requested a position as my adjutant for no apparent reason.'

Mar chuckled slightly, laying his hand on hers and bending slightly, whispering in her ear. 'Can I get blessed by the Lady of the Crimson Veil's kiss? I miss your touch, beloved. Do you know how hard it is to command the army when your cock has a mind of its own? Help this poor frustrated dragon,' he teased, nipping her earlobe.

Ina turned to face him, placing a finger on the sharp plane of her neck, where it joined with the shoulder. 'You think you're a poor, neglected man? I had to sit on the city's most uncomfortable chair and listen to quarrels about the shipyard and laundry. Now I ache everywhere. My neck, my breasts, all are so tense,' she said, her finger trailing over the white skin of her neck down her open collar and teasing the deep valley of her cleavage.

'You are killing me, woman.' The whisper turned into a smouldering purr when Mar's lips followed obediently after the questing finger, lightly kissing the soft skin, his breath burning a trail of desire until he paused at the mark of his claiming, her moan of encouragement ignored when he leant back after kissing it.

'And... he stops,' she muttered, confused and disappointed as he took her hand, pulling her out of the stable. Ina let Mar lead, the darkening sky barely registering as they entered the garden. The scent of night stock filled the air, and the witch smiled, looking up at the cloudless sky when they finally stopped near the fountain.

'Beautiful, isn't it? Mar, what the—?' she said, stepping back when the warrior's massive body dropped to one knee before her.

'Hush, woman,' he said, the corner of her lips twitching in a barely restrained smile when she huffed in annoyance. 'Ina, I love you. I fell for you when you opened the door with my body back in the Black Forest. Since then, I've learned to cherish your brilliant mind during the crisis in

Osterad, was humbled by the mercy you showed to those who captured and tortured you in Liath, and will be forever grateful you saw something inside me that helped you choose this flawed warrior over that maddeningly perfect Sa'Ren Gerel. I have never felt so happy as I do with you in my arms. When you disappeared, I learned I couldn't live without you. I will move the mountains and sea, challenge the gods and death itself to be with you. I have no words to express the love in my heart, so I will simply ask. Inanuan Zoria Thornsen, my beautiful spitfire, will you consent to be my wife?'

The witch looked at him, blinking rapidly, startled by his sudden declaration. Finally, his words broke through her surprise, and Ina's lips quirked in a mischievous smile.

'You rehearsed it, didn't you?' she said, before pulling at his hand, urging him to stand up, but Mar didn't budge, looking at her earnestly. This tug of love lasted until an annoyed witch bent to look into Mar's eyes. 'Are you done? You are a hairy oaf, stubborn, infuriating, and the noblest man I know. I didn't have time to prepare a speech, but of course, I will marry you. Now stand up so I can kiss you, or will you kneel here like some bard pining for his damsel in distress?'

Mar rose to his feet with sinuous grace, but the witch caught him rolling his eyes before they came together in a passionate embrace, lips crashing together in mutual desire and need, tongues seeking and dancing together, but Ina didn't care. Her hands slid under his shirt, stroking his chest, trailing along the narrow line of hair, but he grabbed them before they disappeared into his trousers.

'You will?'

'Gods, give me patience with this one. Yes, I will. I will marry you, Marcach of Liath. I love you. My choice was made when I accepted your mark. I would even bear you children if I could. You are my everything, and now I want my dragon. I want you to mark me again,' she said, smiling when a deep growl rumbled in his chest.

'So, my most powerful mage, you want to submit to your dragon?' Mar asked, a predatory smile blossoming on his face.

'Must I submit for you to bite me?' she teased, enjoying their power play.

'Yes, because you are mine. You can command life itself, but you are mine to take,' he said, playing with her hardened nipple while his mouth teased her neck.

Tremors ran through her body, warring with the need to be taken and moulded by the dragon's desire. Mar's golden eyes looked at her with such love and passion that words, hidden deep in her soul, escaped their prison.

'Fuck, you make me feel so... human,' Ina stuttered, her gaze drifting down when a heavy blush crawled up her cheeks. She wanted it. The greater the burden her power became, the more the witch needed to submit to this magnificent beast, who now looked at her in predatory lust, willing to take all that responsibility away. If only for a moment, she wanted to be nothing but Ina, a woman who, without boundaries, gave herself to the man she loved.

'Such dirty words from such a pretty mouth. Maybe I should silence it with my cock.' His voice trailed off when her hand slid lower.

'Whatever you wish, my lord. I am here to please,' she said, her tension melting away when she let him take control.

'Gods, woman, you will be the end of me,' Mar moaned, grasping her arse and lifting her to his hips before pushing through the garden's lush greenery and pressing her against an ancient tree.

He cursed, fumbling with their clothes while she kissed and nipped his skin, her body throbbing with anticipation.

'Look at me, Ina,' he commanded, and her eyes snapped open, feeling his cock sliding through the wetness of her folds.

'Look at me when I take you. You are mine, my spitfire. There is no escape because I find you even behind the veil. You are, and always will be, mine,' he snarled, the intensity of his words burning a blazing trail through their bond as he thrust forward, impaling her on his shaft, and the witch gasped as pleasure flooded her. Mar stilled for a moment, but when he moved, he was perfectly, mercilessly brutal. Animalistic, with a need born of danger and abstinence, the dragon roared his desire, driving his shaft to the hilt, and Ina felt her body pulse around him, sending delicious waves through her spine.

'Tell me you're mine.' He growled as he bit her ear, ripping her blouse with clawed hands, slowly losing the battle with his control, exposing the soft flesh of her neck. Mar thrust harder, his pace becoming chaotic, chest heaving as his release loomed closer.

'I'm yours, Mar. Please, I want it so much,' she pleaded, wanting the last delicious morsel of their reunion.

As soon as those words left her mouth, his head plunged down, teeth sinking into the soft flesh while he climaxed inside her, triggering her release as pain exploded into pleasure.

Ina was barely conscious when he lowered her to the grass. Her thoughts were still lost in euphoria as the witch's eyes languidly opened. Mar's golden eyes looked at her with love and devotion as he trailed his tongue over the bloody mark.

'Well, fuck me sideways. You outdid yourself this time.' Ina grinned, gazing at his sheepish expression.

'Oh, that was just a taste, my spitfire. To show you what you get when you submit to your dragon. We like our virgins raw,' he jested, cuddling her shaking body when she burst into laughter.

CHAPTER THIRTY SIX

The torture device, currently masquerading as a seat, had long since stopped being a prominent complaint for Ina's tired mind. Now she was concocting a scheme to murder every friend she currently spent time with. Since returning from Dancik, her small townhouse had become a nexus of chaos, which had nothing to do with her magic.

First, there was Mar, who, in his infinite wisdom, moved his office to their home, wanting to spend more time with his spitfire. He'd said this, but it had actually turned into a confrontation with Marika, who, through the use of some miraculous sorcery, actually won, kicking the mighty marshal to the shed used for the dragon's armoury. Despite that, with a constant stream of messengers and officers traipsing around, it did not a quiet home make.

Second was the feisty shifter herself, who had claimed the attic as her personal domain, which wouldn't have been so bad if that didn't mean Ina's workshop was now a tiny desk in the parlour. With Marika came Janik, who, like a bad penny, had not only survived the battle but earned himself somewhat of a reputation for his fighting prowess on the streets of Dancik, helping save several families from rampaging soldiers. He was now regaling her housekeeper daily with his exploits, wooing her in his gruff, clumsy manner. Marika looked annoyed, but Ina noticed she was warming to the brutish Norseman, always ensuring he had food and ale in his corner of the kitchen.

The final nail in the coffin had been Zbych, who, thanks to her drunken suggestion after the battle, was now Mar's adjutant, working so diligently he'd earned the marshal's trust, and while Ina appreciated the workload he took from Mar's shoulders, his quiet devotion was slowly driving her mad.

I never thought I would miss the solitude of my cottage in the Black Forest, she thought before shaking her head. As much as she loved her townhouse, she had outgrown it, and now she had to get something bigger before her sanity flew through the window from the constant squabbles and hero worship.

'Inanuan, is everything all right? Why are you frowning? Do you disagree with the new policy?' Rewan's voice broke through her haze, and Ina realised she had drifted away again.

'Which policy Re—Your Majesty?' she asked, sending the king an apologetic smile before turning with disdain to the nobles, trying to show their disapproval. After they'd lowered their gazes, she leant back, the shift in position reminding her of the current torturous meeting, but the smirk she gifted the annoying councillors was unflinching. *I'm getting good at this. Nerissa would be so proud.* The pain of losing her great-aunt was still raw, but something had changed, and recently Ina had been comparing herself to the arch healer, wanting to make her proud. Since sending Mirena to Veles's cauldron, the witch had enjoyed employing her aunt's little mannerisms, savouring the bittersweet reminiscences of the woman who would always be the mother of her heart.

'The trade offer to whatever is left of the Iron Empire? Your rather useful idea to trade our ore for their alchemy knowledge…?' Rewan stopped, a resigned sigh escaping. 'Let me guess; you weren't listening.'

'You know me too well, Your Majesty. Indeed, personal matters weigh heavily on my mind, and of course, I agree with whatever you say, o' wisest of rulers. Just let me know if you want my help persuading our friends.' Ina couldn't help the mischievous grin as she stretched to hopefully ease some blood into at least one buttock, pretending not to see Rewan's exasperation.

It had been a meeting like this in Dancik that the witch had proclaimed herself the archmage of chaos, and it had in no way been a temper tantrum. Ina had expected some political backlash from claiming the position, but the title and experience itself were strangely liberating. Just as Rurik had predicted, she became a person above the law, almost above the king, and though she had made it clear she was fiercely loyal to Rewan, few dared to contradict her words. That was precisely why Ina drifted away from any decision-making, leaving it to those whose opinions could be questioned and challenged rather than a terrifying witch who could destroy anyone with a thought.

'What personal matters? Dare I ask, or should we invite the lord marshal to enlighten us to the complexity of the female mind?' Kaian's voice was filled with amusement, making Ina grimace towards the master assassin.

'Nothing that complex. I just need to find a new house. It's getting crowded in my old one, adding Mar's soldiers, coming and going with messages, the petitioners Jorge sends my way to solve their issues, to students of the Magical University who seem to find getting into my yard and leaving unscathed as a badge of honour. It's becoming unlivable.' She looked at the assassin, whose broad grin made her realise she was airing her domestic life during the royal council meeting, 'As you can't do anything about it, let's move on. The sooner we end this, the better, for both my backside and my temper.'

Rewan bit his lip, surprising Ina with the rare expression of emotion other than exasperation, and the witch wondered what the cunning monarch was up to, worrying when he slowly began smiling. 'I can help with that if you'd like. My mother had a small manor on the west side of the palace, tucked away in the palace grounds. It has been neglected for years, but is large enough to house a small army. The garden is beautiful, lying next to the river with easy access to the palace, close enough to the university and city centre only students would find inconvenient. I dare say, even Master Gruff's establishment would be close enough to stagger home from. If you don't mind dealing with a few repairs, I would be honoured if you accept it, my friend,' he said, and Ina stood up to approach the king's seat.

'You're giving me the queen dowager's manor? And I can change what I want, yes?' she asked, unsure where this all was heading. She knew about the sparse manor hidden behind its overgrown garden, the vegetation so wild it felt like a forest in the middle of the bustling city, but since the late queen had died there after abandoning the court and her drunkard of a husband, no one dared to even peek through the rusty gates.

'You can change as much as your heart desires. My mother would be happy the woman who saved her son will live in her home. You made it possible for me to be king. I see no better place for you than a manor where true power behind the throne should live,' he said, and Ina gasped. Even if his words were true, Rewan admitting this openly and during the council meeting was a mistake.

'Thank you, my king, but you are mistaken. I would never stand as the power behind the throne. I am, and always will be, the shield and sword that protects you and your realm. You are my king and friend, and I will always defend what is dear to me.' The witch smiled as Rewan swallowed his emotions with difficulty. 'Now, before we gallop far from the subject on our high horses, where can I get the keys to my new home? Oh, and don't expect me at the next few meetings. I hope you don't mind.'

'Ina...' the king groaned when she turned to leave. 'The keys are with my chamberlain. Just don't forget about my wedding with the pearl of Verdante. I need you there,' he said, shaking his head when the witch waved him off, heading towards the exit. 'Now, noble council, where were we with our debate?' she heard him say before she closed the door and laughed happily.

It didn't take long to find a messenger and send him to fetch Velka, and with that task organised, Ina dived into the palace underbelly in search of the chamberlain. Several coins lighter, the witch soon confronted an uncomfortable official, demanding access to her prize, and despite putting up a spirited defence, the poor man quickly capitulated, handing over the keys.

With a spring in her step, Ina ran to the gardens, almost crashing into the harried nature mage at the entrance, a panicked look in her eyes.

'You said it's urgent. What is happening—war, plague, flood?' Velka panted the words out, gripping a bundle of cloth to her chest. Ina couldn't help chuckling as she delved into the swaddling, kissing the smiling baby's cheek.

'Hello, little one. Your mom is panicking again. Anyone would think she expects me to be in trouble. Should we tell her before she smacks my rear with a vine?' the witch cooed, stroking the infant's dark hair. 'There is no war, but I have been gifted a new home, and I want you to be with me when I open its doors,' she said, pointing to the wild copse in the distance.

'The dowager manor? How? Oh, Ina, that is wonderful! I heard it's so beautiful. Are you sure you don't want Mar to be with you?' Velka asked, but Ina was already shaking her head.

'My dragon and Ren are in the camp today doing soldiery stuff, and I just can't wait. Anyway, who besides you could I explore the gardens with? And maybe even persuade to use her talents on its untamed greenery. I hate to admit it, but the Black Forest will always feel like home, so if you could help a silly homesick witch?' Ina turned to her friend, fluttering eyelashes over big doe eyes.

Velka nearly snorted as she laughed, grabbing her best friend's hand. 'So what are we waiting for? I've always been curious to see inside.'

They strolled along, happily chatting and enjoying the still-warm autumn sun until the witch opened the gate to the mansion, the path before them somewhat overgrown but still suitable for a large carriage. The whole tableau was peaceful and inviting, like standing on the threshold of Wyraj, waiting to take the first step into paradise. The women admired the vivid colours of the rampant vegetation that seemed to frame the beautiful manor without stealing its charm.

The house itself had seen better days. The two-storey building, with its large windows, two dainty columns guarding the entrance, and balcony above, looked elegant if you ignored the white paint peeling off the walls. The rest was covered in climbing roses, reminding the witch of Castle Thorn.

'Ina, it looks wonderful. It needs work, but this place has so much charm, and I think it suits you. It's as wild as you, but with a beautiful heart. Yes, this manor is exactly like you and will only need a little love to blossom to its full beauty,' Velka said, stretching out one hand while wiggling her fingers.

It took Ina a moment to understand, but in the end, she reluctantly placed the key into Velka's hand, and after a brief struggle, they opened the door. A large open atrium, with a decorated staircase, took their breath away, but the view of the sitting room soon diverted Ina's attention, its walls filled with bookshelves ready to be filled and an enormous fireplace, its mantle decorated with carved heads of mythical beasts. On the other side of the atrium was the dining room, another smaller space, likely used as an office or study.

'Ina, come quick, look at this. Oh, you will love it,' Velka's voice called down from the top of the stairs, surprising the witch, who'd forgotten her friend's presence.

'I will love what?' she asked, rushing upstairs only to halt, gaping in the doorway of the master bedroom. The large—no, *palatial*—room was filled with light, its bay window the perfect spot for cuddling Boruta and reading a book. Specks of dust danced in the air as the witch walked around, touching wooden beams and the wide windowsill before Velka's voice lured her to the bathroom; well, if you could use such a common word for a chamber with what could only be described as a small swimming pool. Ina could feel the spells holding it in place, and hopefully, there would be other enchantments for heating water because, although the pool was empty, the witch already saw herself bathing here with Mar.

'Velka, hold me. I've walked into paradise... Wyraj could never be this perfect,' she moaned, the nature mage laughing at her stunned expression.

'I'm guessing you've found your perfect home. You deserve it, Striga. Of all people, you deserve your little piece of paradise, and I will create a forest where your soul can thrive,' she said, cuddling her child before coming closer and gathering the witch into a loving hug. 'I have to go back, but I will come here tomorrow, and we can plan your forest garden. Give me a chance, and I will make it worthy of the Leshy's child.'

'I'm sure you will. Go before we have a raging orc storming in, thinking I made his wife disappear again.' Ina chuckled slightly, feeling the warmth spread through her chest. This place already felt like home. *I hope Mar likes it*, she thought, inhaling deeply, letting the tranquillity seep into her soul.

Ina returned to the bedroom and sat on the carved bench inside the large bay window, knowing she should go home to organise everything. The house needed substantial renovations, so she would have to wait before moving in. There were other domestic issues to deal with. Despite her resourcefulness, Marika would need someone to look after such an expansive house. There would be many things to sort out, but Ina didn't want to leave, not just yet.

CHAPTER THIRTY SEVEN

A slow clop of heavy hooves made the witch look through the window. A rider on a massive Liath stallion emerged from the trees, and Ina's heart skipped a beat, recognising Mar. Her dragon looked around, scanning the surroundings before he lifted his head, looking straight at her. *He looks dashing with this roguish smile*, she thought when the corner of his mouth lifted, and he wagged his finger, mockingly scolding her.

They met at the main entrance, the crushing hug leaving Ina breathless and smiling. 'I think you like me chasing after you, my spitfire.' Mar's lips still couldn't hide his smile as he tried to chastise her. 'I visited our house, the university, and even the court searching for you, and if not for the sheer luck of meeting Velka, I would think you escaped to the country again. So what's going on here, then?' he asked.

'I was bored during the council meeting, Rewan noticed, and I may have told him I needed a bigger house, so we now have a bigger house,' she said, grinning before she ducked her head, playing with the clasps of his cloak. 'You'll like it here. You'll have a proper armoury, and Zbych can move it to help you with administration and running errands. There's enough space for a small training ground. Mar... I really like it here, but if you prefer something else...' she said, sneaking a look at him, hoping he shared her love for this new house.

'Deep down, you will always be an autumn child, my little witch from the forest,' he said with a smile, caressing her hair. 'Ina, I don't care where I live. I only care that I live with you. If this place makes you happy, I will make it a nest worthy of a dragon's bride.' He hadn't finished before she wrapped her arms around his neck, pulling him down. His lips were warm and dry when she kissed him, and Mar moaned when she parted them with her tongue, toying with them before he deepened the kiss, his rough, calloused hand sliding down her back, pressing her harder to his muscular body.

'Please tell me there's a bed somewhere in the house? A couch—mattress? Anything will do.' His voice, rough with desire, sent a shiver down Ina's spine.

'No, but there's an enormous fireplace in the living room and a very available floor in this bedroom,' she said, her hands drifting towards the hard length pressed against her thigh.

'I won't take you on the dusty floor. I'm not a beast,' Mar grumbled, pressing hard into her grasp.

'Not a beast, you say? How disappointing, or is my magnificent dragon desperate to claim his mate in her true home?' Ina briefly looked outside towards the glade nestled in a small copse of blackthorn, smiling slyly at the sight of the witch's tree.

The yelp that escaped her lips as Mar scooped her into his arms left the witch breathless, the dragon no longer pretending he was no beast as he carried his prize outside. As they neared the grove, Ina couldn't help herself, coaxing soft green moss to carpet the ground with her magic, luminescent mushrooms maturing to add their glow to the beautiful scene, the gentleness with which her man laid down belying the wild look in his eyes.

'Will this do? Just not a word to Velka,' she said, blushing slightly as her body shivered in anticipation.

'Enchanting, sweet witch. You will be the end of me, woman. How... I don't know if I should fuck you now or admire your new magic.' His dark chuckle sounded like a promise as his lips trailed down her neck.

'Why not both?' Ina asked, the words more of a moan as shivers turned into pleasure. 'If I must be an archmage of chaos, I should have some perks with the title.'

'In that case, it's time to reintroduce you to the perks of loving a dragon,' he said, deft hands lifting her foot. Mar's kisses trailed along her leg, eliciting soft gasps and moans before his mouth descended on her sex. Ina arched her body when his hot breath caressed her folds.

'You are such a tease, Mar,' she murmured when he stopped for a moment, and his beard brushed over the sensitive skin. The slow draw of his tongue made Ina forget all rational thought. *Oh gods, he did it again!*

Long and forked, with a dexterity that should be illegal, the dragon's tongue delved into her moist sex, savouring the taste of her excitement, mercilessly teasing his willing victim.

'Will... you... please... fuck me,' Ina panted, feeling her body tense and the intense, desperate sensation build at the base of her spine.

'First, I want to feel your pleasure. Only then will you have your dragon.' She barely heard him as a wave of bliss swept her away and stole all control, Ina's magic turning their bond incandescent with rapture.

'You are amazing, my love. If you only knew how good it feels. You are divine, my beautiful, passionate woman,' Mar muttered, tearing at his trousers while she basked in the afterglow of her release, moaning with pleasure when his thick shaft teased her entrance. Ina jerked her hips, using magic to drag him down, impaling her body on his cock. She saw his eyes widen and translucent scales shimmer over his skin.

'Ina, don't play with fire.' He growled, and she laughed, looking at his golden eyes.

'I'm not playing with fire. I am the fire. I want you, all of you, and I want the flames to consume all thought,' she moaned, rocking under him, gasping when Mar grasped her hips, pushing hard.

'As my lady commands,' he rasped, pushing into her, his strokes forceful and demanding. Ina cried, arching her body as Mar pounded into her mercilessly with bestial fury, each move bringing her closer to a soul-shattering climax. When she stilled, swept away in ecstasy and shouting his name, the eruption pulsing inside showed the witch her dragon joined his lover in bliss even as his roar shook the grove.

Mar leaned down, kissing Ina breathless, still buried deep inside, his eyes dancing with mischief. 'We are keeping this house. I love it already. Gods, Ina, if I knew moss and a copse of trees would make you this wild, I would buy you a fucking forest. I thought you would rip my soul away.' He chuckled, then rolled to the side and pulled her into his warm embrace.

Everything was so right. Her magic no longer threatened her existence, harnessed by her blood and the chaos regalia. She was at peace, knowing the man she loved would always be by her side. There was no war to fight, no desire for vengeance. She could rest, living as she saw fit, limited only by her own choices.

Yes, she was still the royal witch, but it was her choice to stand by the righteous king. It was her choice to teach at Magical University, making sure no other chaos mage, pure or otherwise, would be scorned. She'd chosen to be a judicial mage, upholding justice for those too weak to fight for themselves. Her opponents had been defeated, her enemy's souls screaming in Veles's cauldron, while her friends lived by her side, basking in their happiness.

Maybe it was the magnificent sex or an overload of every emotion, but the witch pressed her face to Mar's chest and cried. A hard sob shook her body while her dragon held her tight, stroking her tussled hair.

'My love, did I hurt you? I'm so sorry.' His voice trailed off, his worry and confusion making her shake her head.

'No, it's not this. I'm just so bloody happy, Mar; so happy that it hurts.' His hands stilled. Mar took a deep breath, and with a heavy sigh, he resumed his gentle stroking.

'Woman, I don't understand you sometimes,' he said, but under her cheek, his rapid heartbeat slowed, and when she calmed down and raised her head, Ina noticed his gaze fixed on the tree behind her. Ina slowly turned around, her eyebrows shooting up when her sight fell on the bark, looking suspiciously like a bearded man's face, with fireflies dancing around it.

'I think the Leshy approves of your choice, my love.' Mar chuckled, and the witch felt the sudden urge to punch the tree.

'And I bet he was watching every moment,' she said, her lips tight in disapproval.

'If so, I hope we gave him an excellent performance because we both know he cherishes you, and my greatest fear is him finding me wanting. The gods chose the perfect herald, so I don't mind entertaining them as long as they're not trying to take you away from me,' he whispered, nuzzling her ear, and Ina snorted.

'Like I would ever let that happen. You're stuck with me, dragon. Even death cannot pry us apart. Now pick the date for our wedding.' She laughed at his surprise, but Mar quickly embraced her before whispering into her ear.

'For me, it can be even tomorrow, but we have eternity to plan.'

'Eternity sounds too long for me. Pick a date and make me a decent woman.' She grinned when he laughed, looking forward to their new life, bright and filled with hope.

Because she was finally, genuinely free.

Two figures walked from the grove, warily watching each other before one of them broke the silence. 'Will you ever tell your scion what she has become, or will you let her wander this world unaware of her purpose?'

The Leshy smiled before replying. 'Even after all this time you haven't learnt, you can never tell her anything. Ina will grow and learn at her own pace, like she always has. Her heart will show her the way, so for now, let the autumn child enjoy her happiness.'

Lada rolled her eyes at her companion's indulgence before nodding silently and disappearing into the shadows. The Forest Lord took one last look at his dearest child before he, too, disappeared.

GLOSSARY

Ayni – water dragon, over 1000 years old partner of Sa'Ren Gerel. Her initial attempt to bond with Marcach failed. Later discovering mutual understanding and respect, she falls in love with Ren, who reciprocates her feelings.

Baba Yaga: (Slavic mythology) The wild old woman, the witch, a mistress of magic, and a mythical creature.

Bi chamd hairtail: I love you (Yanwo dialect) – actually Mongolian (from Google translate, but I love it)

Botchling: A lesser monster. A small creature resembling a highly deformed foetus. A botchling is created from the improper burial of unwanted, stillborn infants, and prey on pregnant women.

Boruta: (Slavic mythology) A forest demon who is often considered an avatar of Leshy.

Chram: (Slavic mythology) The most sacred place; a temple for the Slavic deity associated with specific rituals, prophecies and miracles. Chram could be a building, a forest, a swamp, or any natural setting.

Cornovii: Merchant kingdom between the Black Forest and Grey Mountains. Because of its geographical position, it is the multiracial centre of trading.

Dancik – Large northern port and maritime city. For the last fifty years, its citizens have considered themselves a free city but still under the sovereignty of Cornovii.

Daro: ("dark power") Steppe Orc, the rebellious son of a tribe, drafted into the King's Guards. A known womaniser until he married Velka.

Domowik: In the Slavic religious tradition, domowik is the household spirit of a given kin. They are deified progenitors, the kin's fountainhead ancestors.

Gruff: ("the rock") Rock troll, owner of the *Drunken Wizard* and spymaster of Osterad.

Gamayun: A mythological creature with a bird's body and a beautiful woman's head. They derive from Slavic and Old Russian folklore and are described as mythical beings that can mesmerise humans with their enchanting voices. Their role is to be a messenger of the gods.

Hela: Also called the "Two-Faced Terror", is a goddess of the dead, especially those who drown in the sea.

Imp: A lesser demon. Imps are often shown as small and not very attractive creatures. Their behaviour is described as being wild and uncontrollable. Imps were fond of pranks and misleading people.

Inanuan: ("beautiful destruction"). Also known as Ina or Inanuan Zoria Thornsen. High-born lady of the principal ducal house of Cornovii and the first pure chaos mage born in a generation. Sometimes referred to as Striga by friends and Autumn's Child by older races.

Iron Empire – military lead kingdom north of Cornovii, known for their unyielding warriors, military prowess and ferocity in a fight. The kingdom implements strict patriarchy and, during the last two centuries, declared any magical user is the property of the Emperor.

Jarylo/Jaryło: God of vegetation, fertility, and springtime.

Jorge: ("supreme knowledge"). Arch-mage of pure order. He can foresee the future by applying his order magic to reality in patterns.

Kaian: ("strong warrior"). Scion of the primal ducal house of Cornovii, the House of the Water Horse. Also head of the Assassin Guild. The lover of King Rewan.

Kings's Guards: Also called the Second Son's Company. Unit designed strictly to guard the palace and investigate issues related to high-born nobles or state affairs.

Kobold: Member of the kobold race. Cruel and proficient warriors and metalworkers living in the mines and tunnels in the Grey Mountains. Shorter than humans, often seen in bulky black metal armour. Their race has zealous adherence to oaths, pacts, or customs.

Lada/Łada: (Slavic mythology) Goddess of love, spring and nature's rebirth, patron of weddings and matriarchy, and protector of families and ancestors who've passed away.

Lady Midday/Południca: A mid-class demon who makes herself evident in the middle of hot summer days. She takes the form of whirling dust clouds and carries a scythe, sickle, or shears. She may appear as an old hag, a beautiful woman, or a 12-year-old girl. It is dangerous at midday when she can attack workers, cut their heads off, or send sudden illness.

Latawica – An air demon, luring unsuspecting victims by taking the image of their greatest desires before feasting on their lives.

Leshy: (Slavic mythology) God of wild animals and forests. He protects the animals and birds in the forest and tells them when to migrate. He is a shapeshifter who can appear in many forms and sizes but is usually a tree, wolf, cat, or hairy man. His fickle nature causes him to help one he deems worthy and punish those who mean harm to the forest.

Liander: ("flower of pride"). Half-elf, the strongest psychic mage in the court. Also, he becomes the court mage after Ina's departure.

Liath: Dukedom of Cornovii associated with the House of Liath. It is located on a mountain in the West and defends the Grey Mountains. Liath is known for its military power and dragon-blood origins.

Litha or Kupala night: A midsummer solstice celebration dedicated to love, fertility, and water. Young people jump over the flames of bonfires in a ritual test of bravery and faith. The failure of a couple in love to complete the jump while holding hands signifies their destined separation.

Makosz – the primary deity of the Cornovii pantheon. Makosz has no temples, as she is worshipped in the open fields. She is Mother Earth itself. The most loving and compassionate of gods that never toys with other living being, considering them all her children.

Marcach: ("wind rider"). Also known as Mar or the Scion of Liath. The oldest son of the principal dukedom house of Cornovii. A war veteran and former Captain of the King's Guards, currently holds the title of royal dragon and Lord Marshal of Cornovii.

Marika: ("kitten"). A were-cat from the Grey Mountains clan. Inanuan's housekeeper.

Morena/Morane/Marzanna: (Slavic mythology) Also known as Winter's Death. A personification of the repetitive cycles regulating life on earth, the changing seasons, and a master of both life and death. Morena symbolises death on the battlefield. In folklore, the death of Marzanna symbolises the rebirth of the world.

Morganatic marriage: A marriage where a high-born woman marries a commoner, losing her status.

Meridian: The meridian system is a concept in traditional Chinese medicine adapted for this series. Meridians are paths through which the life energy known as "qi" or chaos flows. In the book, meridians are an energetic highway that distributes life energy/raw chaos along the body.

Nawia: (Slavic mythology) The afterlife. Also used as a name for an underworld over which Veles exercises custody.

Nerissa: Grand-duchess of the House of Thorn. Arch-healer of Cornovii. Inanuan's grand-aunt.

Osterad: The capital of Cornovii. Started as a simple river port, but with time, it grew in riches and became the centre of human magic on the continent.

Orein: A mountain spirit in the shape of a horse, often with a grey or black coat with sharp lynx-like fangs and lynx paws instead of hooves. However, it can curl the paw into a hoof shape and disguise itself as a horse. Mischievous and, by preference, carnivorous. They are called the blessing of the mountain because they often came to aid travellers they found worthy.

Phoenix: Immortal bird. A good omen. Dies in flame to rise from the ashes.

Rewan: ("the cunning one"). Cunning but fair. The current ruler of Cornovii.

Roda: ("the nest"). Womaniser and drunkard. King of Cornovii. Also known under the "Limp Dick Roda" moniker after Ina's outburst.

Sa'Ren Gerel: ("son of a moonlight"). The native name of Ren. He is also known as Ghost for his martial skills and calm demeanour. Ina's best friend and guardian, and the current general of Cornovii's forces.

Senad: The bastard child of a high house, a lesser noble. Second in command of the King's Guard and Marcach's friend. (deceased)

Skarbnik: Mountain spirit/god called the Guardian of the Mountains. Depicted mostly as an old man, but can shapeshift into any given form. Guards minerals and ores from greedy miners and helps lost travellers on their path. Often mischievous and unpredictable. He lives in self-imposed isolation.

Sophia: ("The white gem"). Princess of Cornovii, sister of King Rewan. Renowned for her beauty. After an unsuccessful coup, she was killed by the king's order.

Sowenna, the Last Empress – drow queen, the last known Archmage of Chaos and bearer of Chaos regalia. She was also known as The World Breaker when, after the death of her partner and losing her bonds; she broke the continent of Warenga, raising the Grey Mountains in the flux of chaos and madness. She was killed by her son and buried in the tomb in the Grey Mountains.

Striga/Strzyga: (Slavic mythology) A female creature who feeds on human blood. Their origins are connected to the belief in the duality of souls. A common explanation was that a human born with two souls could become a *strzyga* after death. Such people were easy to recognise, born with two rows of teeth, two hearts, or other similar anomalies. They could die only partially—one of the souls leaves to the outer world, but the second one gets trapped inside the dead body, losing many aspects of humanity. *Strzyga*'s appearance can resemble an average person with a mean character. The longer they live as a *strzyga*, the more they change. They are often presented with bird-like features: claws, eyes, and feathers growing off the back.

Swaróg/Swarożyc: God of fire, blacksmithing, and creation. Depicted as an old but powerful man with white hair and a hammer. Often believed to be the creator of the world.

Truthseeker: A branch of mind magic associated with the order. A psychic mage who can connect with another person's brain to trace patterns of lies and, if needed, dissect memories to look for the truth.

Tomb hags/ Grave hags: Territorial creatures. Their lairs resemble caricatures of human homes and are built near burial sites. They venture out at night to hunt, stalking straggling travellers or mourners too lost in their grief to notice the sun's setting.

University of High Magical Arts/ The Magica Council: School and the highest authority for practising mages, witches,s and warlocks. They have supreme jurisdiction over the magic of Cornovii.

Volkhv: A high-ranking priest of Slavic religion.

Veles: (Slavic mythology) God of earth, waters, livestock, and the underworld. A shepherd and the judge of the dead that rules Nawia. Associated with swamps, oxes and magic.

Velka Powoj: Lesser noble. Gifted nature mage with a strong association with trees and flowers. Ina's best friend.

Vyvern: A large winged lizard, distantly related to the dragon, with a poisonous stinging tail and sharp teeth.

Shifter tribes: Shapeshifters with the ability to change into three forms, human, animal and were-form, that contain both aspects of their soul.

Wyraj: (Slavic mythology) Part of Nawia. The equivalent of heaven.

Wila/Wiła – old race also considered a minor demon of swamps and floodplains, associated with water and wild vegetation. Fearless in a fight but benevolent to those who respect nature.

Yanwo: Far east land, ruled by the Dragon Emperor. Yanwo trades silks, spices, and gems with Cornovii. Polygamy is widely practised there as dragon lords believe in the survival of the fittest, pitting their offspring against each other to strengthen the bloodline. (Yup, I took this from the ottoman empire and the rules of the sultanate).

Zhrets: Low-ranking priests in the pagan religion. A man who performs the sacrifices.

Zmij: (Slavic mythology) A winged serpent with fangs that drip with venom. Ability to breathe fire. He is a ferocious and dangerous creature and a mighty protector of those he finds worthy.

ABOUT AUTHOR

 Olena Nikitin is the pen name of a writing power couple who share a love of fantasy, paranormal romance, rich, vivid worlds and exciting storylines. In their books and out, they love down-to-earth humour, a visceral approach to life, striving to write realistic romances filled with the passion and steam people always dream of experiencing. Meet the two halves of this Truro UK-based dynamic duo!

Olga, a Polish woman, has a wicked sense of humour with a dash of Slavic pessimism. She's been writing since she was a small child, but life led her to work as an emergency physician. While this work means she always has stories to share, it often means she's too busy to actually write. She's proud to be a crazy cat lady, and together with Mark, they have five cats.

Mark, a typical English gentleman, radiates charm, sophistication, and an undeniable sex appeal. At least, he's reasonably certain that's what convinced Olga to fly across the sea into his arms. He's an incredibly intelligent man with a knack for fixing things, including Polish syntax in English writing. If you give him good whiskey, he might even regale you with his Gulf War story of how he got shot.

Olena Nikitin loves hearing from their fans and critics alike and welcomes communication via any platform!

WEBSITE: https://www.olenanikitin.uk

For Newsletter, social links and free books, please check the QR code

ALSO BY

AUTUMN CHAOS – FIRST BOOK FROM SEASON'S WAR SERIES

When fate tips the world towards destruction, the gods step forth to name their champion.

Peasants proverb

Chaos knows no peace or mercy, but even this primordial power is challenged by a woman willing to defy kings, gods and magic itself, fighting for what is right.

When her past returns to haunt her, saddling her with an ill-tempered warrior and death lurking in the sewers of Osterad, Inanuan must face the truth of her birthright and embrace the magic that threatens to destroy her. As she fights for her freedom and to save the kingdom, she must also confront the knowledge that the man she yearns for may never learn to trust her.

What will it take to convince Marcach she is not his enemy, especially when his eyes burn golden each time he looks at her?

Immerse yourself in Season's War series and learn about the kingdom of Cornovii, where passion is mixed with cruelty, and the unwilling hero with world-shattering power has to make impossible choices. Epic Fantasy with mature themes - reader caution advised.

WINTER DRAGON– SECOND BOOK FROM SEASON'S WAR SERIES
"When a Chaos mage fights, only blood and scorched earth remain."
Mage War Chronicles

Some victories are more costly than others, and Ina was the one that paid the price. Determined to rescue her dragon, the newly appointed royal witch embarks on a gruelling journey through the wintery Grey Mountains. The weather is not her only obstacle, as the enemy forces gathered in the kobold mines have only one goal. To capture the Chaos mage and deliver her to the heart of the mountain. With the help of Sa'Ren, Ina arrives at Castle Liath almost unscathed, but her joy is short-lived, as its granite walls hide a shocking revelation. With blossoming love shattered by a possessive dragon's claim and an impossible mission to fulfil, will the mysterious Blessing of the Mountain help or hinder her efforts to protect Cornovii?

Immerse yourself in the second book of Season's War, where passion mix with cruelty and the world-changing power is buried deep in the ancient tomb guarded by the stern Mountain God.

SPRING BLIGHT– THIRD BOOK FROM SEASON'S WAR SERIES
"Chaos and the wicked soul know no rest."
(Old folk proverb)

Ina has no time to enjoy domestic life with Mar. As soon as life settles down after the Winter War, King Rewan calls his Royal Witch to give her a new task. Southern rebellion, crops dying, and an endless stream of assassins attacking the king, leaving a trail that backs to a neighbouring kingdom. To make matters worse, an ancient cult has emerged from the shadows offering sacrifices to Winter's Death.

One fateful letter and Ina is back on the road with an unlikely companion. But what can one Chaos mage do against so many enemies and the power of the Old Gods?

Immerse yourself in the third book of Season's War, where passion mixes with cruelty, and the world-changing power can shackle even goddess to the mortal plain. The book is NOT standalone for the best experience, consider reading in the series order.